THE
AUSTRALIAN
SHORT STORY

UQP AUSTRALIAN AUTHORS

This is a series of carefully edited selections which represent the full range of an individual author's achievement or which present special themes in anthology form.

General Editor: L.T. Hergenhan,
Reader in Australian Literature,
University of Queensland

Also in this series:

In preparation:

THE
AUSTRALIAN
SHORT STORY

A Collection
1890s — 1990s

Edited and introduced by

Laurie Hergenhan

University of Queensland Press

First published 1986 by University of Queensland Press
Box 42, St Lucia, Queensland 4067 Australia
Reprinted 1987, 1989
Second edition published 1992

Typeset by University of Queensland Press
Printed in Australia by The Book Printer, Victoria

Distributed in the USA and Canada by
International Specialized Book Services, Inc.,
5602 N.E. Hassalo Street, Portland, Oregon 97213-3640

Cataloguing in Publication Data
National Library of Australia

From the 1890s to the 1980s.

  Bibliography.

  1. Short Stories, Australian. I. Hergenhan, L.T.
(Laurence Thomas), 1931-   . II. Title. Australian
  short stories. (Series: UQP Australian authors).

A823'.0108

ISBN 0 7022 2348 4

Contents

Contents

Acknowledgments

It is a pleasure to thank the following for their advice: first and foremost Stephen Torre, for use of his PhD thesis on the short story and for discussions; Elizabeth Webby, Michael Wilding, Martin Duwell, Bernard Hickey; and for typing, Sandra Gough. For permission to reproduce the stories in this volume, acknowledgment is made to Allen & Unwin for "Pension Day" from *Going Home* by Archie Weller; to Collins/Angus & Robertson Publishers for "Short-Shift Saturday", from *Short-Shift Saturday* by Gavin Casey, copyright G.C. Casey, 1942; for "Shadow", from *The Unploughed Land: Stories* by Peter Cowan, copyright Peter Cowan, 1958; for "Wedding Cake", from *Surly Girls* by Susan Hampton; for "the Airport, the Pizzeria, the Motel, the Rented Car and the Mysteries of Life", from *Tales of Mystery and Romance* by Frank Moorhouse, copyright Frank Moorhouse, 1977; for "Josie", from *The Rainbow Bird and Other Stories* by Vance Palmer, copyright Vance Palmer Estate, 1957; for "A Double Because It's Snowing", from *Selected Stories* by Hal Porter, copyright Hal Porter, 1962; for "Happiness", from *Happiness: Selected Stories* by Katharine Susannah Prichard, copyright R.P. Throssell, 1967; and for British Commonwealth rights to "And Women Must Weep", from *The Adventures of Cuffy Mahony and Other Stories* by Henry Handel Richardson, copyright Olga Roncoroni, 1979; to Curtis Brown (Aust.) Pty Ltd for "The Persimmon Tree", from *The Persimmon Tree and Other Stories* by Marjorie Barnard; for "Trees Can Speak", from *The Complete Stories of Alan Marshall* by Alan Marshall; for world rights outside the British Commonwealth for "And Women Must Weep" by Henry Handel Richardson; for "The Unicorn", from *The Unicorn and Other Tales* by Dal Stivens; and for "Down at the Dump", from *The Burnt Ones* by Patrick White; to Thelma Forshaw for "The Mateship Syndrome", from *An Affair of Clowns*; to Fremantle Arts Centre Press for "Green Grow the Rushes", from *Wong Chu and the Queen's Letter Box* by T.A.G. Hungerford; for "Winter Nelis", from *The Travelling Entertainer* by Elizabeth Jolley; and for "The

Courts of the Lord", from *Hostages* by Fay Zwicky; to Hale and Iremonger Pty Ltd for "Sex in Australia from the Man's Point of View", from *Pacific Highway* by Michael Wilding; to Laurence Pollinger, London, for "The Triskelion", from *The Salzburg Tales* by Christina Stead; to McPhee Gribble for "Ismini", from *Milk* by Beverley Farmer; for "Lizards", from *Headlocks and Other Stories* by Barry Hill; and for "Land Deal", from *Velvet Waters* and The Educational Magazine, no. 3 1980 by Gerald Murnane; to Penguin Books Australia for "Heart is Where the Home is", from *It's Raining in Mango* by Thea Astley; to Helen Garner for "What We Say"; "The Incense-Burner", from *North Wind* by John Morrison; to Thomas Nelson for "Running Nicely", from *Running Nicely and Other Stories* by Morris Lurie; to the University of Queensland Press for "Ore", from *Contemporary Portraits* by Murray Bail; for "What Do You Know About Friends?" from *Things Could Be Worse* by Lily Brett; for "Crabs", from *The Fat Man in History* by Peter Carey; and for "The Rages of Mrs Torrens", from *The Home Girls* by Olga Masters; and to Judah Waten for "Mother" from *Alien Son*.

Introduction

In the twentieth century, the short story proved itself more flexible and more open to experiment than the novel.[1] Nadine Gordimer and others found this comparatively new form more adaptable to the modern world: "Why is it that while the death of the novel is good for post mortem at least once a year, the short story lives on unmolested? . . . and, like a child suffering from healthy neglect, it survives".[2] The short story has outstripped attempts either to define it satisfactorily or to come to terms with it critically. In 1936, Elizabeth Bowen said: "The short story is a young art: as we know it, it is the child of this century. . . . An art having behind it little tradition is at once impetuous and halting, and is affectable. Its practitioners are still tentative, watching one another. . . . "[3]

The European and also the American influence help to explain why the short story form has proved adaptable in Australia, flourishing here in a "new" culture since the 1890s, when writers achieved a breakthrough in representing experiences which differed from those of the parent society. In the 1980s the short story is generally seen as a thriving literary form, for readers and writers alike.

On the other hand, the fact that the Australian short story could be overshadowed by overseas developments may explain why it has been critically undervalued, at home as well as abroad; notable exceptions are its supposed progenitor and folk figure, Henry Lawson, who is little known outside Australia, and Nobel prize winner Patrick White. Yet there is a line of distinguished short story writers extending from the 1890s to the present. This achievement has also been overshadowed by the local development of the novel and by the tendency to see the short story as an inferior form. Perhaps, too, the novel has lent itself more — except for Lawson and some campfire followers — to those discussions about Australian identity and national values which criticism welcomes, but in which it can get bogged down, leaving the lonely short story writer sprinting on ahead.

Before looking at the development of the Australian short story as I see it, a comment on the rationale of this present selection is appropriate. Beatrice Davis has summed up the occupational hazards of the anthologist: "Injustice must be done, false impressions given. . . . I could from the excellent stories excluded compile one, or even two, other anthologies of equal merit."[4] Frank Moorhouse repeated the last claim in compiling his anthology of the early 1980s alone.[5] I have departed from previous approaches in Australian anthologies by combining more stories of the present of the 1980s and the near-present of the 1970s with stories from the 1890s onwards. Anthologies are never completely up to date, and not simply because of the time lag in publication. The need to represent many authors from the past can make it difficult to choose from the present where reputations have not stabilized. The usual solution is to split up the two areas into such categories as the "classic" (giving either token or no representation to the nineteenth century) and the "modern" or "contemporary".

In choosing "representative" stories, my aim was to concentrate on authors who have made an important contribution to the form of the short story as practised in Australia. The justly publicized formal innovations of the 1970s have overshadowed previous ones. The criteria here must be partly subjective and I have tried to make them clear in my outline of the development of the short story. To make this development apparent to readers I have arranged the stories chronologically according to first publication, so far as I could determine this.

In concentrating on writers who have made a contribution to the form of the short story, I have taken into account that form and subject are inseparable, and that any development in form opens up new subjects or revalues familiar ones. Accordingly, such subjects as national identity, women, migrants, Australians abroad, the bush-city dichotomy, are prominent all through this selection. Indeed it is encouraging to realize that it would be almost impossible to compile a representative selection in which any of these concerns would not be prominent.

One of the problems of anthologists trying to bridge past and present is the difficulty of finding sufficient space to represent authors across a wide spectrum. My criteria have allowed me to

omit some writers often represented for their historical interest,
because they map special social areas or belong to a chronological
outline of good writers. These include Rudd, Dyson, Warung,
James, Schlunke, Davison and Hackston, whom I have omitted
reluctantly, but with the consolation that they have been regularly
anthologized to the relative neglect of contemporary writing.
Similarly, Frank Moorhouse's 1980s anthology, designed to offset
this neglect, has allowed me to feel more comfortable about my
selectiveness at the contemporary end, where I have included
some writers he omits. No attempt has been made to cover the
pre-1890s, for here only Marcus Clarke's stories are notable and
unfortunately he remains an isolated figure.[6]

Some of the stories in this anthology are well known, others less
so. Marjorie Barnard's familiar "The Persimmon Tree" is widely
and justly considered an outstanding story. On the other hand,
Christina Stead's "The Triskelion", so redolent of her special gifts,
has been passed over previously, as has T.A.G. Hungerford's
"Green Grow the Rushes". Some of the contemporary writers —
Olga Masters, Elizabeth Jolley, Beverley Farmer and Barry Hill —
have rarely or never been anthologized before.

Although the first flowering of the short story in Australia in the
1890s coincided with the peaking of the European short story in
Chekhov, the two developments do not seem to be connected.
It was the emergence of a new local forum in the *Bulletin* which
enabled some writers to break through old formulas, though the
Bulletin encouraged the old as well as the new and established its
own formulas. It appears to have been the *Bulletin* — its propriet-
ors, editors and readers as well as its writers — more than overseas
influences, which fostered Lawson and Baynton. However, the
reading of each was not confined to Australian material and the
Bulletin encouraged an interest in overseas writing, for instance in
French naturalism, as well as Australian writing.[7] Not until the
1930s did contemporary overseas influences, always reaching
Australia belatedly, begin substantially to affect Australian
writers.[8] These influences included Anderson, Joyce, Mansfield
and Hemingway. Such influence has been obscured partly because
of the critical fixation on the search for a national tradition, partly
because the opinions of writers themselves were not sought by
critics or widely known. In fact the history of the short story in
Australia remains to be published. Generalizations about it,
including my own, should accordingly be taken cautiously.

The only history to date, a Ph.D. thesis by Stephen Torre covering 1940 to 1980, is so far unpublished.[9] It reveals not only com-
plexities and contradictions which should deter generalizations
but also an unexpected mass of material:

> In his [selective] *Annals of Australian Literature*, Grahame Johnston
> lists 52 collections of short stories published between 1900 and 1939.
> In the period 1940 to 1980 I have listed in the [non-selective] biblio-
> graphy 217 collections. . . . In addition, 163 anthologies and miscellan-
> ies containing Australian short stories of contemporary origin were
> published during the forty year period. Approximate figures for the
> number of collections published in each decade are 35 in the 1940s,
> 25 in the 1950s, 60 in the 1960s and 107 in the 1970s. It is notable that
> the figure for the 1970s almost equals the combined figure for the
> previous thirty years.[10]

One of the appealing theories about the short story has been that
it is distinguished by its concern with "submerged population
groups".[11] The above statistics suggest that in Australia the writers
themselves and their wares have remained "submerged" in comparison with novelists and poets. (Drama, on the other hand, may
offer a parallel.)

The *Bulletin*'s encouragement of indigenous material had its
precursors in newspapers which published sketches about
Australian life.[12] Though Lawson emerged as the *Bulletin*'s "star",
it encouraged a variety of material and he himself wrote various
kinds of stories, as well as developing beyond the *Bulletin*'s scope
and such of its prescriptions as the famous "boil it down". The
Bulletin emphasized brevity, realism, especially of bush experience, and a casual, colloquial tone; it also encouraged Price
Warung's dark, melodramatic but often compelling stories of the
convict system; Louis Becke's stories of romance and adventure in
the Pacific; Steele Rudd's broad comedy of the bush poor. Yet
what many of the *Bulletin* writers had in common was the
dominating site of the bush and some of the values or myths
associated with it and with "true Australianness", incuding male
mateship and egalitarianism, values by no means endorsed by all
writers, especially Lawson and Baynton.

A number of qualities combine to make Lawson an outstanding
writer, although over the years he has not been valued for the
same reasons. Today his themes that appeal most are not his
comic ones of resilient battling through but rather those concern-
ing "loneliness, failure . . . and a compulsive insistence on the
gossamer precariousness of happiness",[13] in other words, themes
reflecting main twentieth-century concerns. The qualities of

Lawson's style that are admired are also modern: his economy and simplicity; his deft use of implication, to evoke what is left unsaid; his feeling for the fragmentary, random quality of life; his sympathy for the outsider, and an air of truthfulness which is not simply a matter of spare but telling documentation but of feeling, of sensitivity and voice. This voice, while exploiting the possibilities of unaffected Australian speech, is a controlled and varied one.[14] Recent critics have stressed, in "producing" the Lawson they prefer, that these foregoing qualities are the result of art, of the aware storyteller not the naif.[15]

Lawson's work, like that of the other early Australian fiction writers, was undervalued for being concerned with the local and particular not the "universal" (the vague, artificial, if not magical European standard for keeping colonials in their place). But in reaching beyond time and place Lawson's power is partly a mythic one: with some help from publishers, critics and patriots, his stories convinced generations of Australians that his characters' bush experiences represented the "real" Australia, showing Australians as they like to think of themselves by crystallizing folk images, such as the battle with the physical environment, which are paralleled by those in Paterson's popular ballads. These images were so influential that later writers up to the 1970s felt that they impeded the development of the short story.

In looking back as early as the 1920s in search of an indigenous literary flowering, Nettie Palmer found that the 1890s had been exaggerated and mythologized so far as the "subtle, delicate art" of the story was concerned: of the many short story writers of that period only Lawson stood out, and next to him, Barbara Baynton.[16] To date general opinion has endorsed Palmer's view, though with growing appreciation of Baynton, who offers a striking contrast to Lawson that is emphasized by the common and harsh bush setting. While Lawson offered the pleasures of recognition or, if he challenged the familiar and probable, did so quietly, Baynton used such departures from the accepted norm as gothic violence to express her subversive views. Some of her lurking ironies are only now being uncovered by feminist critics.[17] The threats to her female protagonists are only partly the environmental ones of Lawson's Mrs Spicer; they also take the form of male violence, intimidatory or fatal. As a result a climactic action is more appropriate in Baynton than in Lawson with his themes of passive failure or powerlessness. Baynton exploded the male chauvinism and other limitations of mateship more angrily than Lawson, as well as recoiling more dramatically from the uncouthness of life in the bush. Baynton's stories are notable for their sustained emotional intensity to which only those of Stead, Barnard and Olga Masters offer parallels. Like Lawson, Baynton is a conscious artist, as in the departure from probability near the end of "The Chosen Vessel" where the "vision" performs a retrospective ideological function.

The 1890s and the 1940s, which saw the beginning of the influential regular story anthology *Coast to Coast*, as well as the new literary quarterlies *Southerly* and *Meanjin*, have been seen, along with the 1970s, as the main periods of growth and change in the Australian short story. Stephen Torre has suggested that the stories of Vance Palmer, Frank Dalby Davison and Gavin Casey linked the old and the new in the 1930s and beyond.[18] In particular Palmer, Casey, Cowan and Stivens brought to bear on the short story modern preoccupations with form. In addition, Cowan and Stivens explicitly turned away from the Lawson influence, anticipating later reactions.

Palmer is probably the most underestimated of Australian short story writers, as a practitioner and an influence. His novels have not yet been successfully revived, for in spite of their innovatory craftsmanship a reticence of feeling has kept readers at a distance. This is not the case with the stories, where the shortness of the form helped to concentrate his psychological understanding and sensitivity of feeling. He wrote four volumes of stories between 1915 and 1955, and his last collection, *Let the Birds Fly* (1955), includes modern stories written between 1934 and 1955.[19] The bridging of past and present may be seen in some of his bush stories, where old values, such as mateship or closeness to the land, are shown as changing or under attack, and where there is more emphasis, as in Casey and Cowan, on the individual's relation to society, with increasing emphasis on town or city. Palmer also extended the scope of the short story through his psychological handling of human relationships, including love (not a strength of Lawson or Baynton); his use of symbolism, as in the dominating image; and perhaps most skilfully in his stories of the fantasy and feeling of childhood and adolescence, including "Josie", "The Foal", and "The Rainbow Bird".

As well as contrasting the worlds and values of the bush (harmony or disharmony with nature) and the town (conformity and materialism), Palmer contrasts the individual's inner and outer life, presenting at his best an uncertainty or conflict, and thus freeing the story from the limits of external realism by assert-

ing the importance of the inner, "secret" life in a way that looks
forward to White, Moorhouse and other writers. The modernity of
Palmer's conception of the form of the story, its poetic potential
and its delicacy of implication, including sexual overtones, is
suggested in his statement in *Coast to Coast* (1944):

> . . . the scope of the short story has been enlarged. We no longer
> demand that it shall have a formal beginning, a middle, and an end;
> that it shall contain a plot as easily extracted as the backbone of a fish.
> . . . Nowadays a short story may be a dream, a dialogue, a study of
> character, a poetic reverie; anything that has a certain unity and the
> movement of life. . . . Because of its length, the short story must move
> on more delicate lines of implication than the novel. It should suggest
> more than it states, lure the reader into co-operating by the use of his
> imagination. Its solidity may rest, not on any array of detail, but on
> the integrity of its style.[20]

This description surprisingly foreshadows the new directions
sought by younger writers in the 1970s, and indeed Palmer's
"Josie", as well as the stories by Cowan, Stivens and Marshall in
this anthology, would not look too out of place in Frank Moorhouse's collection of stories of the 1980s, *The State of the Art* (1983).
Palmer's claim for the liberation of the story was influenced by
modernist writers such as Joyce and Mansfield as well as by
Chekhov.[21] Marshall and Porter continued in their different ways
to widen the scope of the short story by using a child's point of
view, as in "Trees Can Speak" and "At Aunt Sophia's", while
Beverley Farmer uses the same device to revivify the realist
migrant story in "Ismini".

Christina Stead's *The Salzburg Tales* (1934), which shows her
individual and extraordinarily varied talent as storyteller, has
been critically overlooked though it was no doubt read by Australian writers. Her story "The Triskelion", set partly in Australia,
partly in Austria, is a tale of aberrant sex and murder. Its combination of the psychological and the supernatural shows her distinct-
ive qualities of the "scientist" linked with something of the power
of "The Brothers Grimm", a description of herself that she
welcomed.

Of the 1940s writers, Gavin Casey is the closest in temperament
and style to Lawson, but he extended the bush story into the
mining urbanism of Kalgoorlie, as in "Short-Shift Saturday". It
moves between varying settings: men at work; domesticity,
including the bedroom and tensions between the sexes; the urban
pleasures of shopping and of the pub, the male preserve of mateship and violence. These settings are not used simply for environ-

mental realism but to allow a central socio-emotional problem to
be viewed from different angles. It is not the connections of
incident that are important but, as in the modern fragmented
story, the implied connections readers can make for themselves,
as in White's "Down at the Dump", or as foreshadowed in "'Water
Them Geraniums'".

Casey, again like Lawson and also like Cowen and Palmer, deals
with inarticulate characters not simply in the cause of social
realism, though Casey's sympathies for miners and their families
are finely controlled, but also because of the modern awareness of
the expressiveness of implication, as in the fine open ending of
"Short-Shift Saturday".

Peter Cowan, in his long dedication to the art of the short story,
was at an early stage more influenced than any other Australian
short story writer by Hemingway, in his sensitive austerity and
submerged implications as he probes the isolation of his characters from one another, from society and from any supportive sense
of meaning.[22] These are themes found in Lawson, but Cowan's
world is felt to be part of a wider twentieth-century world of
alienation, and can be a piercingly comfortless one. "Shadow"
shows a sure command of modern techniques, such as challenging
time-shifts and resonant symbols (the banging window), which
create a subdued intensity of feeling. Spareness is a hallmark of
the Cowan world and technique.

Barnard's "The Persimmon Tree" shows a rich development of
the modern story of the inner life, where outer events are few and
fragmentary, even indeterminate, and the emphasis falls on a
lyrical patterning of images of sterility and renewal (compare
"Down at the Dump"). We do not need to know what illness the
narrator is recovering from, or what sustains "the other woman".
The unresolved "heartbreak" at the end bursts with an unsenti-
mental but tender force. In the reliance on impressionistic images,
and the accompanying fluidity and fragility of feeling they
convey, Barnard is perhaps the Australian writer closest to
Mansfield, but there were no conscious influences on her practice
of "organic form" whereby her stories "happened . . . as complete
as a bubble".[23]

"The Persimmon Tree" seems to be at the opposite end of the
spectrum from social or socialist realism, which has always been
an important strand in Australian fiction but in a variety of
expressions While these writers relied on effects of social truthfulness and historical concreteness, illuminated by ideology, no
doctrinaire formulas were followed in the better stories. Rather,

as Judah Waten has suggested of himself, these writers aimed to combine social experience, or personal experience which is also inescapably social, into a harmonious or aesthetic whole.[24] Stephen Torre has pointed out that one of the by-products of socialist realism was the establishing of a number of short story outlets: *Australian New Writing* (Sydney) and *Realist Writer* (Melbourne), which later became *Overland*, and the series of anthologies, *The Tracks We Travel*.

Realism is a complex and varying concept though, as Elizabeth Webby comments, it has often been restricted in Australia to cover subject matter rather than method.[25] But if one looks at writers in this anthology who have been seen as belonging to the heterogeneous category of socialist realism – Prichard, Marshall, Waten and Morrison – their variety of both matter and method are apparent. In Prichard's "Happiness", the criticism of the whites' failure to adapt to outback life and their treatment of Aborigines is mainly indirect. It emerges through the skilful use of the point of view of an Aboriginal grandmother, blending past and present in reminiscence, and through an infusion of lyrical symbolism into the realism of setting. The old woman who narrates sits contentedly chanting amidst the offal of the slaughter yard in a way that suggests the influence of Lawrentian "deeper rhythms". In Morrison's "The Incense-Burner", there is complex and understated symbolism in the narrator's discovery that the poverty stricken old man has been burning eucalyptus leaves, as a ritual bond both with the Australian dead sacrificed in World War I and with the homeland from which he has been exiled. This discovery gives resonance to the story of the narrator's own comparatively easy escape from a similar exile and to the picture of the alienated London poor which occupies the foreground. In Judah Waten's "Mother", autobiographical memory and what the author has called "social memory" are intertwined in terms of the changes involved in a family's leaving an old culture for a new. Marshall's "Trees Can Speak" is a lyrical, delicately elusive story, yet it deals with his favourite social theme of victims reaching out towards a sense of the community of struggling human beings.

The type of realism which "pretended that it was not the product of a writer but of life itself was the dominant note of Australian short fiction in the first half of the century, a note which Hal Porter, Patrick White and the contemporary short fiction all in turn rejected".[26] While this may be broadly so, such realism was by no means completely dominating, as we have seen. White's famous attack in the 1960s on "dreary, dun-coloured . . . journalis-

tic realism" was part of a polemical defence of his own work
before its wide acceptance. Some commentators have seen his
criticism as all embracing.

White's frustration is paralleled by an attack on the dominance
of the so-called Lawson tradition of formula bush realism
mounted by "new" short story writers of the 1970s, Frank Moorhouse, Murray Bail and notably Michael Wilding, who is also an
influential critic.[27] This was another attempt to overcome a disadvantaged position, for it represented the frustration of some
younger writers at not being able to get controversial new work
accepted by the main magazines, which favoured conventional
stories. Wilding commented that a problem facing writers in the
1970s was that "Australian" proclamations, including the celebration of rural Australia, had been "the preserve of conservatives,
conservative aesthetically and politically" – including the right
and the left. The emergence of the *Tabloid Story* as an "alternative"
publication vehicle was a positive outcome of such protest. Nevertheless, in the process the dominance of realism in the past and
present was once again polemically exaggerated, if with justifica-
tion, as is apparent from a glance at the work of the "new" writers'
older contemporaries already discussed, Cowan, Barnard and
Stivens, as well as of others such as White, Porter and Elizabeth
Harrower, or of Thea Astley and Thelma Forshaw, whose stylish
and subversive clowning challenged conventions of the short
story form as well as of society.

It seems true, however, that tired conventions such as bush
realism did severely cramp the short story as late as the 1960s and
1970s, though more at the all-important practical level of publication than in critical discussion.[28] In discussion there was some
conservative side-influence from the promotion of a so-called
Lawson-Furphy tradition in the novel but, more importantly, of
the nationalism which was associated with Lawson and with a
limiting realism which was another conservative influence.[29]
In 1967 Douglas Stewart edited an anthology covering work up to
1940 and subtitled "The Lawson Tradition", but in his introduction
Stewart was vague about what this meant in practice, and he may
have been simply looking for a catchy title. A companion volume,
subtitled *The Moderns* and edited by Beatrice Davis, included
stories that she and Stewart saw as having "a new kind of flavour:
more graceful, more subtle, more sophisticated".[30] The young
writers who were only just appearing were, however, not
represented.

Hal Porter, the main writer emerging in the 1950s, moved the short story in a challengingly modern, even modernist, direction towards the "new" self-conscious writing whereby language and the very process of story writing were foregrounded. Porter's brilliance and flamboyance have, however, overshadowed the contribution of Cowan and of Dal Stivens. The latter was a master of the fabulist and fantasy story, as well as the realist story, before they came into fashion in the 1970s, and he was also a writer congenial to younger contemporaries such as Wilding. Porter's stories are a curious combination of the innovatory and the conservative. In a climate of self-effacing realism he was welcomed (by both the older generation, including Stewart, and the "new" writers) for his coruscating style, through which he steps forward indirectly as "producer" of his stories. But while he aimed at what he saw in Mansfield, a combination of stylish "surface texture" and an embodiment of "what the X-ray showed",[31] he is also an adapter of the De Maupassant well-made story with its build-up to a climax. Porter's imagination is in his style not his plots, for while he is traditional in insisting on the importance of first-hand, "real" experience as subject matter,[32] there is an interplay in his stories between observed detail and transforming artifice of style. His master theme of transience (and the superiority of the past) is often conveyed through a shower of "facts" which his style transforms into selective impressions, thus paradoxically confirming the subjectivity of "historical" detail. His neglect abroad may suggest that the particularity of his detail has been misunderstood as mere localism.[33] Michael Wilding was to give a timely warning in the 1970s, when short story writers were welcoming overseas influences, that a standardizing "internationalism" (often West-Europeanism) could be another way of confirming colonial status, not of escaping from it.[34]

A "new wave" enlivened the Australian short story from the later 1960s through the 1970s. It was stimulated by the resurgent radicalism of anti-Vietnam protest, the influence of contemporary American and South American writing, and the finding of new publishing outlets and a younger audience. The patronage of the Literature Board was of vital assistance in the publishing area, as in the setting up of *Tabloid Story*.

The "modernist impetus" in America in the 1960s, as described by Richard Kostelanetz, is applicable to Australian "new" writing:

the narrative is more discontinuous and the chronology even more distorted . . . [the] endings seem less an integral conclusion than a

> reflection on the author's artistic decision to stop. . . . the characters
> are more radically marginal if not irrefutably isolated; and most of the
> stories have extremely limited if not nonexistent moral dimensions.
> . . . the narrators . . . rarely make any discoveries (indeed their inabil-
> ity to understand is often the reader's discovery) . . . the [writers]
> emphasise the technical elements so strongly that the story can even
> become a non-narrative succession of fragmented impressions . . . the
> main interest is often centred less upon the plot or theme than upon
> the processes of composition. . . [35]

All these elements are used by the main "new" writers: Bail,
Carey, Moorhouse and Wilding. They are all authors of individual
talent, and if they are sometimes grouped together for conven-
ience it is because of their common concern for innovation and
experiment. As well as questioning the restrictions of realism,
ideological as well as aesthetic, they also fundamentally question
the limited view of "reality" fostered in Australia by realism and
censorship and by the conservatism which encouraged them.
(Of course in an earlier age realism could be an effective mode of
questioning convention, as in Richardson's "'And Women Must
Weep'".) These younger writers wanted to open up a variety of
"realities" in terms of liberating forms of consciousness and of
liberating new possibilities for the short story form.

A favoured method was a new emphasis on fantasy. Randall
Jarrall comments that "a story may present fantasy as fact, as the
sin or *hubris* that the fact of things punishes, or as a reality
superior to fact".[36] Fantasy as "sin" or as "superior" was not uncom-
mon in previous Australian fiction, but the "new" writers were
innovative in presenting it as an alternative "reality" and, in the
case of Carey and Wilding, suggesting its superiority to realism as
a shock weapon of social criticism. Fantasy can be a way of
questioning the conservative authority of socially determined
reason, for as Elizabeth Bowen suggests: "Fancy has an authority
reason cannot challenge. The pure fantasy writer lives in a free
zone: he has not to reconcile inner and outer images." And as
Nadine Gordimer adds, fantasy can be more successful in the
short story than the novel because "it is necessary for it only to
hold good for the brief illumination of the situation it dominates".

Fantasy enters in different ways into these stories by Bail,
Carey, Moorhouse and Wilding, disrupting our preconception of
both life and the short story. In "Ore" and "Crabs", part of the
interest is in the imperceptible slide from one reality to another,
the second interrogating the first. There is a fine irony in "Ore" in
having all the "happenings" located in the protagonist's head, in an
ambiguously "physical" way. Moorhouse's story is more attached

throughout to recognizable social reality, but this relation is questioned by shifting ironies. Wilding's story is the most freely playful and problematical, yet it covertly mocks sexual censorship, in terms of official and individual attitudes.

Bail has agreed that "'the artist should not hesitate to exceed the norm'. . . . I find it natural to dwell more on situations, propositions, speculations than traditional character analysis, and since they are peopled and anyway come from me seated, quite by chance, in Sydney, they cannot be entirely unrelated to 'reality'".[37] Similarly Moorhouse has commented more recently: "The great need in Australian short story writing is still that it should 'go too far' and resist blandness".[38] All the "new" writing stories represented here and some others, such as those of Olga Masters and Barry Hill, push in different ways in this direction. They have an element of what Moorhouse has called "the gameful", a freewheeling playfulness involving form and the expectations brought to it. Thus these writers implicitly question conventional ways of telling a story and so invite attention to their own fictionalizing processes.

"Sex in Australia from the Man's Point of View" is illustrative of what Wilding has called "the literature of process", of a kind of "spontaneous" writing that is certainly spontaneous seeming, partly in being open in its direction, or apparent lack of it. Moorhouse's story is one of his "dialogues" with a number of issues, rationality and irrationality, gender, notions of freedom and commitment, nationality, and with short story forms. The confessional, realist and autobiographical modes are wittily questioned, and the ironic dialogue between the narrator's would-be "volupté" and his ex-wife's preference for the mysterious calls into question Moorhouse's recent comments about Australia being "a robustly hedonistic society", at least in so far as his own stories are concerned.

The younger writers of the 1970s attempted to break new ground by opening up the short story to changing values in three main areas. First there was an attack on sexual censorship in an attempt at presenting a new honesty and openness in personal relations; second, a questioning of traditional and simplistic values from the point of view of a younger generation disillusioned with the old values and seeking alternative ones; third, a new emphasis on the inner city, partly in a reaction against the domination of the bush environment and values — "the rotten landscape [which] dominate[s] everything", as Murray Bail's narrator comments in "The Drover's Wife".

Other writers from the 1970s and 1980s included in this anthology have extended the reach of the short story in less apparent but important ways. Women writers have always been a force in both the Australian short story and the novel, if not always sufficiently recognized (as with Baynton, Barnard and Stead). Contemporary writers such as Jolley, Masters, Farmer and Zwicky are opening the story up to some of the less chartered areas of women's experience. In "Winter Nelis" and "The Courts of the Lord", glints of wry comedy and a lightness of touch are used not to allay but to sharpen the moments "of wounding, of unhappiness and of pain". Masters' "The Rages of Mrs Torrens" transforms the conventional bush/city story of family hardship, partly through its evocation of intense passion (not usual in the Australian short story) and its extinction.

This points to a way in which the short story is being developed in the 1980s. Whereas the "new" writers overtly and experimentally challenge "tradition" and the status quo, one of the main contributions of other writers is to use traditional materials but in such a way as to transform them, quietly but devastatingly, and seemingly from within. This is in contrast to, say, "The Drover's Wife", where Bail uses a detaching self-conscious view. Thus revaluation is a common concern. Barry Hill's "Lizards", for instance, takes changing family life in the industrial suburbs and transforms such social realist materials and the methods associated with them, achieving a powerful but elusive effect. The story combines politics, at their grass roots, with national identity and feminism. In fact it is one of the most probing stories about Australian politics, which are rarely taken as a main focus. In "Green Grow the Rushes" (1976), veteran writer T.A.G. Hungerford has achieved a striking story through a novel combination of old and new elements, the one helping to revalue the other. The story embraces the old pioneering Australia of the desert and the bush, the encroaching high rise development in the contemporary cities and the virtually untouched theme of Chinese in Australia. This theme involves an Australian's experience of Asia, and moves the story on to the new Perth, Hong Kong and Macao, after World War II.

In the early 1980s diverse collections by both new and established writers have proliferated, helped by the assistance of the Literature Board and often taking advantage of the freer climate established by the "new" writers of the 1970s. Premature attempts to find an Australian tradition in the short story have not surprisingly been limiting, if not distorting. If no one can be sure where the short story in Australia will go from here, this is a tribute to its inherent possibilities and its achievements so far.

February 1984

Postscript 1984-1990

A new edition of this anthology offers an opportunity for including stories from the period since its compilation in 1984. Thus it is not so much a matter of bringing the selection "up-to-date" as of reinforcing the original aim of bringing together stories from the past with recent and contemporary ones, of trying to press as close as possible in a short space to the elusive "what-is-happening-now".

The period 1984-1990, rather than seeing any overwhelming new directions, has seen the development of trends from earlier in the decade and flowing over from the previous one. If there has been no revolution there has been no backsliding but rather, increasing vitality and flexibility as changes are still working themselves out.

The 1980s has been viewed as the time of the flowering of women's writing and also of the increased visibility of the experiences of minorities.[1] The two trends are inter-linked. Emphasis on disadvantaged groups — on women, migrants and Aborigines — raises issues about gender, ethnicity and race which in turn all involve an increased questioning of what is regarded as normative. These groups are, however, disadvantaged in different ways and to different degrees that affect their literary expression.

If the flowering of feminism in the 1970s continued into the 1980s, allowing for increasing diversity within itself that came with increasing confidence, ethnic or "multicultural" writing by migrants (almost exclusively with European affiliations) achieved more attention in the 1980s, both in terms of publications and the critical championing of it as a cause. Indeed some have seen it as being made into something of a band wagon, with the entrepreneurial efforts of some promoters serving counter-productively to marginalise ethnic writings rather than release them into a wider stream of writing.[2] Writing by Aborigines, on the other hand, remains the most disadvantaged of any social group, and developments in the short story lag behind that of other forms, such as poetry, drama, and autobiography. Nevertheless, the first collection of stories by an Aborigine appeared in 1986, Archie Weller's *Going Home*.

A focus on unexplored or under-explored social groups does not necessarily produce "new" kinds of stories, but form and content are indissoluble, and "different" experience can build up different exchanges with readers, and also create new readers, and so can, in Frank Moorhouse's words, "prise or trick fresh meaning from the form."[3] Form responds to the pressure of "content", of social forces, and is not simply the result of authorial creation or aesthetics.

Changes in the short story are linked with changes that cut across social groupings. Early in the 1980s Moorhouse saw "the fashion of the personal [as] a clue to the flux of our times: the rene-gotiation of the terms of personal relationship, the definition of what a woman is supposed to be and a man is supposed to be. Con-sequently this is written about — as a way of coping with it and as a way of recording it — and it produces its own aesthetic. The sub-ject is political in the broad sense".[4] This actually became a contin-uing preoccupation rather than a "fashion", and the "renegotiation" of the personal was increasingly presented in terms of its inseparability from social power structures. This was not new, but with some influence from feminist thinking and the rise of cultural studies, the relation of the "personal" to "society" was reformulated. Indeed Moorhouse's own cycle of stories, his Australian version of the "comedie humaine" is a sensitive guide to such changes. His influential anthology, often short-titled, *The State of the Art* (1983), has as its fore-title, *The Mood of Contempo-rary Australia in Short Stories* and it connects "the art of story-tell-ing in Australia . . . [with] the State of the art of living in Australia." Yet Moorhouse was proposing no simple one-to-one relationship.

What was also being renegotiated in the 1980s — assisted by such changes in production as more women's presses — was a changing readership, as a new generation of readers came along, responding to new trends in writing and at the same time hoping to call them forth. The most striking evidence of this is in antholo-gies. Moorhouse's *The State of the Art*, and its successor, *Trans-gressions* (1986), edited by Don Anderson, achieved wide popularity, as did Kerryn Goldsworthy's *Australian Short Stories* (1983), the first historical anthology along feminist lines. These were followed by a number of anthologies (including this one) of new and varied kinds. These differed from the more conventional collections which had dominated previously, such as the long-lived annual, *Coast to Coast*. This resisted energetic attempts at resusitation. A sign of the times, and one of the sign-posts to the 1990s, was Helen Daniel's *Expressway* (1989), a collection of twenty nine invited stories "based on" Jeffrey Smart's supra-real painting of the Sydney "Cahill Expressway". This, interestingly enough, had been used for the cover of Peter Carey's innovative first collection, *The Fat Man in History* (1974). Daniel's anthology was widely popular, and in its basic concept, its range of stories and its unconventional internal arrangement, it confirmed that many readers were happy with stories that were formally adventurous.

This suggests that the rebellion against the restrictions of realism (rather than realism in itself) by younger writers of the 1960s — notably Bail, Carey, Moorhouse, Wilding and Viidikas — had borne fruit. Nevertheless, both Moorhouse and Anderson found it necessary in their anthologies to "speak out" for the "experimental", for the need of the Australian short story " 'to go too far' and resist blandness." Murray Bail, enlisting Patrick White, as exemplar, also kept fears of conservatism alive.[5] But, while there is no room for complacency, these efforts seem, from 1991, to have been something of a rear-guard action.

In fact, the later 1980s was not a scene of either polarized positions or of conservatism but offered instead a more flexible situation, and a hive of activity. Short story collections flowed from the presses and women writers, who did so much to change the scene, came close to dominating, in terms of production, impact on readers and critical recognition.[6] In creating diversity women authors showed that writers did not have to strain after the experimental to be new and different. In their work, there was a heightened awareness of regional and ethnic dimensions as well as class differences. This enabled gender differences to be seen from varying perspectives. There was less distrust of acknowledging the connection between content ("social concerns") and form — rather, the reverse was true. On the other hand, both Moorhouse and Anderson had paradoxically been at pains in their anthology introductions both to uphold and to undermine the separation of the two. If realism did not exactly make a "come-back", it appears as a protean, vitalizing element, interacting with others; for instance producing "a powerful shock of recognition when details of women's lives and conversations are presented intimately and naturalistically."[7] And if Moorhouse, Carey and Wilding, for instance, have maintained a long term commitment to innovation, they also have remained committed to registering social change.[8]

A few words about the stories added in this edition. Once again a limited selection necessarily excluded many fine stories and I was painfully aware of Randall Jarrall's comment that compiling an anthology is like trying to fit a zoo into a wardrobe. (The *Australian Book Review* and *Australian National Bibliography*, along with the selective recent anthologies listed in the general bibliography of this selection, are useful guides to the wealth of short story writing.) The stories added in this edition were chosen because I found them outstanding and believed that many other readers would too. Also, they embody many of the trends of the period 1984-1991 discussed above.

Gerald Murnane's story "Land Deal" depicts a different kind of discrimination from that practised against minorities other than Aborigines. Its title calls up one of the most burning of current social issues, Aboriginal land-rights, but it treats this in an unexpected way. Using metafiction to pursue the ambiguous "real", the story deals with the primal white take-over, the capture of the very minds and spirits of Aborigines as they seem to themselves to become part of the "unreal" but powerful dream of the white colonizers. Originally published in 1980 but not collected until the appearance of Murnane's first collection of stories, *Velvet Waters* (1990), its inclusion cuts across the chronological sequence I have generally tried to follow throughout this anthology. But while rooted in the 1980s, this story leans into the 1990s in both its art and social concerns. And it is a superb story.

In "Pension Day", a story about and by an Aborigine, Archie Weller uses the form of the selective life-history, recalled by flashback, but it is a life that calls up a different patterning. The language can be different, too, because it is rooted in a specific way of seeing: "The old Aboriginal lies underneath his tree that cannot help him, for it, too, is old and sparse of gentle green leaf. The tree and the men get wet, neither cares though."

Helen Garner's distinguished first collection of stories, *Postcards from Surfers* (1985) was published shortly after the first edition of this anthology was compiled. "What We Say", a quietly ironic story, revolves around language as it depicts two feminists' expectations of males, and of themselves. Thea Astley's "Heart is Where the Home Is", another story about Aborigines, shows the impulse (also seen in the work of Jean Bedford and Kate Grenville), to rewrite early Australian history from a woman's point of view, this time using the oppression of black women and regional history. Lily Brett's "What Do We Know About Friends?" looks beneath the surface lives and relationships of a female group, in this case isolated, ageing migrants in Melbourne. Susan Hampton's "Wedding Cake" uses a blend of sly humour and seriousness, of realism and the reality of fantasy to de-solemnize conventions surrounding marriage. All these added stories by women, except Astley's (where there is no room for it), show a blend of humour, ranging from gentle to sharp, and they all have a political edge. They also provide counter-evidence to the view — perhaps truer of male writers — that "short stories show Australia as a non-spiritual nation, an existentially casual community that does not brood about the meaning of life or the nature of death."[9]

The additional stories have something of their own to contribute to this anthology but at the same time they also extend the dialogues between stories that any such collections set up.

Laurie Hergenhan
March 1991

1. See the introduction to Gillian Whitlock (ed.), *Eight Voices of the Eighties* (St Lucia, UQP, 1989), p. xi. This introduction is a useful survey of the decade.
2. Robert Dessaix, "Nice Work If You Can Get It", *Australian Book Review*, 128 (Feb/March) 1991, 22-28.
3. Frank Moorhouse (ed.), *The Mood of Contemporary Australia in Short Stories: The State of the Art* (Ringwood, Vic., Penguin Books, 1983), 3.
4. Moorhouse, 2.
5. See Glen Thomas, "Patrick White and Murray Bail: Appropriations of 'The Prodigal Son' ", *ALS* 15 (1991): 81-86.
6. These comments are based partly on my experience as co-judge (1988-90), of the Steele Rudd Award, the major short story competition in Australia for published collections.
7. Whitlock, xix.
8. See Gay Raines, "The Short Story Cycles of Frank Moorhouse," *ALS*, 14 (1990): 425-35.
9. Moorhouse, 3.

The Union Buries Its Dead

Henry Lawson

While out boating one Sunday afternoon on a billabong across the river, we saw a young man on horseback driving some horses along the bank. He said it was a fine day, and asked if the water was deep there. The joker of our party said it was deep enough to drown him, and he laughed and rode farther up. We didn't take much notice of him.

Next day a funeral gathered at a corner pub and asked each other in to have a drink while waiting for the hearse. They passed away some of the time dancing jigs to a piano in the bar parlour. They passed away the rest of the time sky-larking and fighting.

The defunct was a young union labourer, about twenty-five, who had been drowned the previous day while trying to swim some horses across a billabong of the Darling.

He was almost a stranger in town, and the fact of his having been a union man accounted for the funeral. The police found some union papers in his swag, and called at the General Labourers' Union Office for information about him. That's how we knew. The secretary had very little information to give. The departed was a "Roman", and the majority of the town were otherwise − but unionism is stronger than creed. Drink, however, is stronger than unionism; and, when the hearse presently arrived, more than two-thirds of the funeral were unable to follow. They were too drunk.

The procession numbered fifteen, fourteen souls following the broken shell of a soul. Perhaps not one of the fourteen possessed a soul any more than the corpse did − but that doesn't matter.

Four or five of the funeral, who were boarders at the pub, borrowed a trap which the landlord used to carry passengers to and from the railway station. They were strangers to us who were on foot, and we to them. We were all strangers to the corpse.

A horseman, who looked like a drover just returned from a big trip, dropped into our dusty wake and followed us a few hundred

yards, dragging his pack-horse behind him, but a friend made wild
and demonstrative signals from a hotel verandah − hooking at the
air in front with his right hand and jobbing his left thumb over his
shoulder in the direction of the bar − so the drover hauled off and
didn't catch up to us any more. He was a stranger to the entire
show.

We walked in twos. There were three twos. It was very hot and
dusty; the heat rushed in fierce dazzling rays across every iron
roof and light-coloured wall that was turned to the sun. One or
two pubs closed respectfully until we got past. They closed their
bar doors and the patrons went in and out through some side or
back entrance for a few minutes. Bushmen seldom grumble at an
inconvenience of this sort, when it is caused by a funeral. They
have too much respect for the dead.

On the way to the cemetery we passed three shearers sitting on
the shady side of a fence. One was drunk − very drunk. The
other two covered their right ears with their hats, out of respect
for the departed − whoever he might have been − and one of
them kicked the drunk and muttered something to him.

He straightened himself up, stared, and reached helplessly for
his hat, which he shoved half off and then on again. Then he made
a great effort to pull himself together − and succeeded. He stood
up, braced his back against the fence, knocked off his hat, and
remorsefully placed his foot on it − to keep it off his head till the
funeral passed.

A tall, sentimental drover, who walked by my side, cynically
quoted Byronic verses suitable to the occasion − to death − and
asked with pathetic humour whether we thought the dead man's
ticket would be recognized "over yonder". It was a GLU ticket, and
the general opinion was that it would be recognized.

Presently my friend said:

"You remember when we were in the boat yesterday, we saw a
man driving some horses along the bank?"

"Yes."

He nodded at the hearse and said:

"Well, that's him."

I thought awhile.

"I didn't take any particular notice of him," I said. "He said something, didn't he?"

"Yes; said it was a fine day. You'd have taken more notice if
you'd known that he was doomed to die in the hour, and that those
were the last words he would say to any man in this world."

"To be sure," said a full voice from the rear. "If ye'd known that,
ye'd have prolonged the conversation."

We plodded on across the railway line and along the hot, dusty road which ran to the cemetery, some of us talking about the accident, and lying about the narrow escapes we had had ourselves. Presently some one said:

"There's the Devil."

I looked up and saw a priest standing in the shade of the tree by the cemetery gate.

The hearse was drawn up and the tail-boards were opened. The funeral extinguished its right ear with its hat as four men lifted the coffin out and laid it over the grave. The priest — a pale, quiet young fellow — stood under the shade of a sapling which grew at the head of the grave. He took off his hat, dropped it carelessly on the ground, and proceeded to business. I noticed that one or two heathens winced slightly when the holy water was sprinkled on the coffin. The drops quickly evaporated, and the little round black spots they left were soon dusted over; but the spots showed, by contrast, the cheapness and shabbiness of the cloth with which the coffin was covered. It seemed black before; now it looked a dusky grey.

Just here man's ignorance and vanity made a farce of the funeral. A big, bull-necked publican, with heavy, blotchy features, and a supremely ignorant expression, picked up the priest's straw hat and held it about two inches over the head of his reverence during the whole of the service. The father, be it remembered, was standing in the shade. A few shoved their hats on and off uneasily, struggling between their disgust for the living and their respect for the dead. The hat had a conical crown and a brim sloping down all round like a sunshade, and the publican held it with his great red claw spread over the crown. To do the priest justice, perhaps he didn't notice the incident. A stage priest or parson in the same position might have said, "Put the hat down, my friend; is not the memory of our departed brother worth more than my complexion?" A wattlebark layman might have expressed himself in stronger language, none the less to the point. But my priest seemed unconscious of what was going on. Besides, the publican was a great and important pillar of the Church. He couldn't, as an ignorant and conceited ass, lose such a good opportunity of asserting his faithfulness and importance to his Church.

The grave looked very narrow under the coffin, and I drew a breath of relief when the box slid easily down. I saw a coffin get stuck once, at Rookwood, and it had to be yanked out with difficulty, and laid on the sods at the feet of the heart-broken relations, who howled dismally while the grave-diggers widened the hole. But they don't cut contracts so fine in the West. Our grave-digger was not altogether bowelless, and, out of respect for that human quality described as "feelin's", he scraped up some light and dusty soil and threw it down to deaden the fall of the clay lumps on the coffin. He also tried to steer the first few shovelfuls gently down against the end of the grave with the back of the shovel turned outwards, but the hard, dry Darling River clods rebounded and knocked all the same. It didn't matter much − nothing does. The fall of lumps of clay on a stranger's coffin doesn't sound any different from the fall of the same things on an ordinary wooden box − at least I didn't notice anything awesome or unusual in the sound; but, perhaps, one of us − the most sensitive − might have been impressed by being reminded of a burial of long ago, when the thump of every sod jolted his heart.

I have left out the wattle − because it wasn't there. I have also neglected to mention the heart-broken old mate, with his grizzled head bowed and great pearly drops streaming down his rugged cheeks. He was absent − he was probably "Out Back". For similar reasons I have omitted reference to the suspicious moisture in the eyes of a bearded bush ruffian named Bill. Bill failed to turn up, and the only moisture was that which was induced by the heat. I have left out the "sad Australian sunset" because the sun was not going down at the time. The burial took place exactly at mid-day.

The dead bushman's name was Jim, apparently; but they found no portraits, nor locks of hair, nor any love letters, nor anything of that kind in his swag − not even a reference to his mother; only some papers relating to union matters. Most of us didn't know the name till we saw it on the coffin; we knew him as "that poor chap that got drowned yesterday".

"So his name's James Tyson," said my drover acquaintance, looking at the plate.

"Why! Didn't you know that before?" I asked.

"No; but I knew he was a union man."

It turned out, afterwards, that JT wasn't his real name − only "the name he went by".

Anyhow he was buried by it, and most of the "Great Australian Dailies" have mentioned in their brevity columns that a young man named James John Tyson was drowned in a billabong of the Darling last Sunday.

We did hear, later on, what his real name was; but if we ever chance to read it in the "Missing Friends Column", we shall not be able to give any information to heart-broken Mother or Sister or Wife, nor to any one who could let him hear something to his advantage − for we have already forgotten the name.

"Water Them Geraniums"

Henry Lawson

I. A Lonely Track

The time Mary and I shifted out into the Bush from Gulgong to
"settle on the land" at Lahey's Creek.

I'd sold the two tip-drays that I used for tank-sinking and dam-
making, and I took the traps out in the waggon on top of a small
load of rations and horse-feed that I was taking to a sheep-station
out that way. Mary drove out in the spring-cart. You remember
we left little Jim with his aunt in Gulgong till we got settled down.
I'd sent James (Mary's brother) out the day before, on horseback,
with two or three cows and some heifers and steers and calves we
had, and I'd told him to clean up a bit, and make the hut as bright
and cheerful as possible before Mary came.

We hadn't much in the way of furniture. There was the four-
poster cedar bedstead that I bought before we were married, and
Mary was rather proud of it: it had "turned" posts and joints that
bolted together. There was a plain hardwood table, that Mary
called her "ironing-table", upside down on top of the load, with the
bedding and blankets between the legs; there were four of those
common black kitchen-chairs − with apples painted on the hard-
board backs − that we used for the parlour; there was a cheap
batten sofa with arms at the ends and turned rails between the
uprights of the arms (we were a little proud of the turned rails);
and there was the camp-oven, and the three-legged pot, and pans
and buckets, stuck about the load and hanging under the tail-
board of the waggon.

There was the little Wilcox and Gibb's sewing-machine − my
present to Mary when we were married (and what a present, looking back to it!). There was a cheap little rocking-chair, and a
looking-glass and some pictures that were presents from Mary's
friends and sister. She had her mantel-shelf ornaments and
crockery and nick-nacks packed away, in the linen and old
clothes, in a big tub made of half a cask, and a box that had been
Jim's cradle. The live stock was a cat in one box, and in another an

old rooster, and three hens that formed cliques, two against one,
turn about, as three of the same sex will do all over the world.
I had my old cattle-dog, and of course a pup on the load – I always
had a pup that I gave away, or sold and didn't get paid for, or had
"touched" (stolen) as soon as it was old enough. James had his three
spidery, sneaking, thieving, cold-blooded kangaroo-dogs with
him. I was taking out three months' provisions in the way of
ration-sugar, tea, flour, and potatoes, etc.

I started early, and Mary caught up to me at Ryan's Crossing on
Sandy Creek, where we boiled the billy and had some dinner.

Mary bustled about the camp and admired the scenery and
talked too much, for her, and was extra cheerful, and kept her face
turned from me as much as possible. I soon saw what was the
matter. She'd been crying to herself coming along the road. I
thought it was all on account of leaving little Jim behind for the
first time. She told me that she couldn't make up her mind till the
last moment to leave him and that, a mile or two along the road,
she'd have turned back for him, only that she knew her sister
would laugh at her. She was always terribly anxious about the
children.

We cheered each other up, and Mary drove with me the rest of
the way to the creek, along the lonely branch track, across native
apple-tree flats. It was a dreary, hopeless track. There was no
horizon, nothing but the rough ashen trunks of the gnarled and
stunted trees in all directions, little or no undergrowth, and the
ground, save for the coarse, brownish tufts of dead grass, as bare
as the road, for it was a dry season: there had been no rain for
months, and I wondered what I should do with the cattle if there
wasn't more grass on the creek.

In this sort of country a stranger might travel for miles without
seeming to have moved, for all the difference there is in the
scenery. The new tracks were "blazed" – that is, slices of bark cut
off from both sides of trees, within sight of each other, in a line,
to mark the track until the horses and wheelmarks made it plain.
A smart Bushman, with a sharp tomahawk, can blaze a track as he
rides. But a Bushman a little used to the country soon picks out
differences amongst the trees, half unconsciously as it were, and
so finds his way about.

Mary and I didn't talk much along this track – we couldn't have
heard each other very well, anyway, for the "clock-clock" of the
waggon and the rattle of the cart over the hard lumpy ground. And
I suppose we both began to feel pretty dismal as the shadows
lengthened. I'd noticed lately that Mary and I had got out of the

habit of talking to each other — noticed it in a vague sort of way that irritated me (as vague things will irritate one) when I thought of it. But then I thought, "It won't last long — I'll make life brighter for her by-and-by."

As we went along — and the track seemed endless — I got brooding, of course, back into the past. And I feel now, when it's too late, that Mary must have been thinking that way too. I thought of my early boyhood, of the hard life of "grubbin'" and "milkin'" and "fencin'" and "ploughin'" and "ring-barkin'", etc., and all for nothing. The few months at the little bark-school, with a teacher who couldn't spell. The cursed ambition or craving that tortured my soul as a boy — ambition or craving for — I didn't know what for! For something better and brighter, anyhow. And I made the life harder by reading at night.

It all passed before me as I followed on in the waggon, behind Mary in the spring-cart. I thought of these old things more than I thought of her. She had tried to help me to better things. And I tried too — I had the energy of half-a-dozen men when I saw a road clear before me, but shied at the first check. Then I brooded, or dreamed of making a home — that one might call a home — for Mary — some day. Ah, well! —

And what was Mary thinking about, along the lonely, changeless miles? I never thought of that. Of her kind, careless, gentleman father, perhaps. Of her girlhood. Of her homes — not the huts and camps she lived in with me. Of our future? — she used to plan a lot, and talk a good deal of our future — but not lately. These things didn't strike me at the time — I was so deep in my own brooding. Did she think now — did she begin to feel now that she had made a great mistake and thrown away her life, but must make the best of it? This might have roused me, had I thought of it. But whenever I thought Mary was getting indifferent towards me, I'd think, "I'll soon win her back. We'll be sweethearts again — when things brighten up a bit."

It's an awful thing to me, now I look back to it, to think how far apart we had grown, what strangers we were to each other. It seems, now, as though we had been sweethearts long years before, and had parted, and had never really met since.

The sun was going down when Mary called out —

"There's our place, Joe!"

She hadn't seen it before, and somehow it came new and with a shock to me, who had been out here several times. Ahead, through the trees to the right, was a dark green clump of she-oaks standing out of the creek, darker for the dead grey grass and blue-

grey bush on the barren ridge in the background. Across the creek
(it was only a deep, narrow gutter – a water-course with a chain
of water-holes after rain), across on the other bank, stood the hut,
on a narrow flat between the spur and the creek, and a little higher
than this side. The land was much better than on our old selection,
and there was good soil along the creek on both sides: I expected a
rush of selectors out here soon. A few acres round the hut was
cleared and fenced in by a light two-rail fence of timber split from
logs and saplings. The man who took up this selection left it
because his wife died here.

It was a small oblong hut built of split slabs, and he had roofed it
with shingles which he split in spare times. There was no verandah, but I built one later on. At the end of the house was a big
slab-and-bark shed, bigger than the hut itself, with a kitchen, a
skillion for tools, harness, and horse-feed, and a spare bedroom
partitioned off with sheets of bark and old chaff-bags. The house
itself was floored roughly, with cracks between the boards; there
were cracks between the slabs all round – though he'd nailed
strips of tin, from old kerosene-tins, over some of them; the
partitioned-off bedroom was lined with old chaff-bags with newspapers pasted over them for wall-paper. There was no ceiling,
calico or otherwise, and we could see the round pine rafters and
battens, and the under ends of the shingles. But ceilings make a
hut hot and harbour insects and reptiles – snakes sometimes.
There was one small glass window in the "dining-room" with three
panes and a sheet of greased paper, and the rest were rough
wooden shutters. There was a pretty good cow-yard and calf-pen,
and – that was about all. There was no dam or tank (I made one
later on); there was a water-cask, with the hoops falling off and the
staves gaping, at the corner of the house, and spouting, made of
lengths of bent tin, ran round under the eaves. Water from a new
shingle roof is wine-red for a year or two, and water from a stringy-
bark roof is like tan-water for years. In dry weather the selector
had got his house water from a cask sunk in the gravel at the
bottom of the deepest water-hole in the creek. And the longer the
drought lasted, the farther he had to go down the creek for his
water, with a cask on a cart, and take his cows to drink, if he had
any. Four, five, six, or seven miles – even ten miles to water is
nothing in some places.

James hadn't found himself called upon to do more than milk old
"Spot" (the grandmother cow of our mob), pen the calf at night,

make a fire in the kitchen, and sweep out the house with a bough. He helped me unharness and water and feed the horses, and then started to get the furniture off the waggon and into the house. James wasn't lazy – so long as one thing didn't last too long; but he was too uncomfortably practical and matter-of-fact for me. Mary and I had some tea in the kitchen. The kitchen was permanently furnished with a table of split slabs, adzed smooth on top, and supported by four stakes driven into the ground, a three-legged stool and a block of wood, and two long stools made of half-round slabs (sapling trunks split in halves) with auger-holes bored in the round side and sticks stuck into them for legs. The floor was of clay; the chimney of slabs and tin; the fireplace was about eight feet wide, lined with clay, and with a blackened pole across, with sooty chains and wire hooks on it for the pots.

Mary didn't seem able to eat. She sat on the three-legged stool near the fire, though it was warm weather, and kept her face turned from me. Mary was still pretty, but not the little dumpling she had been: she was thinner now. She had big dark hazel eyes that shone a little too much when she was pleased or excited. I thought at times that there was something very German about her expression; also something aristocratic about the turn of her nose, which nipped in at the nostrils when she spoke. There was nothing aristocratic about me. Mary was German in figure and walk. I used sometimes to call her "Little Duchy" and "Pigeon Toes". She had a will of her own, as shown sometimes by the obstinate knit in her forehead between the eyes.

Mary sat still by the fire, and presently I saw her chin tremble.

"What is it, Mary?"

She turned her face farther from me. I felt tired, disappointed, and irritated – suffering from a reaction.

"Now, what is it, Mary?" I asked; "I'm sick of this sort of thing. Haven't you got everything you wanted? You've had your own way. What's the matter with you now?"

"You know very well, Joe."

"But I *don't* know," I said. I knew too well.

She said nothing.

"Look here, Mary," I said, putting my hand on her shoulder, "don't go on like that; tell me what's the matter?"

"It's only this," she said suddenly, "I can't stand this life here; it will kill me!"

I had a pannikin of tea in my hand, and I banged it down on the table.

"This is more than a man can stand!" I shouted. "You know very well that it was you that dragged me out here. You run me on to this! Why weren't you content to stay in Gulgong?"

"And what sort of a place was Gulgong, Joe?" asked Mary quietly.

(I thought even then in a flash what sort of a place Gulgong was. A wretched remnant of a town on an abandoned goldfield. One street, each side of the dusty main road; three or four one-storey square brick cottages with hip roofs of galvanized iron that glared in the heat – four rooms and a passage – the police-station, bank-manager and schoolmaster's cottages, etc. Half-a-dozen tumble-down weather-board shanties – the three pubs, the two stores, and the post-office. The town tailing off into weather-board boxes with tin tops, and old bark huts – relics of the digging days – propped up by many rotting poles. The men, when at home, mostly asleep or droning over their pipes or hanging about the verandah posts of the pubs, saying, "'Ullo, Bill!" or "'Ullo, Jim!" – or sometimes drunk. The women, mostly hags, who blackened each other's and girls' characters with their tongues, and criticized the aristocracy's washing hung out on the line: "And the colour of the clothes! Does that woman wash her clothes at all? or only soak 'em and hang 'em out?" – that was Gulgong.)

"Well, why didn't you come to Sydney, as I wanted you to?" I asked Mary.

"You know very well, Joe," said Mary quietly.

(I knew very well, but the knowledge only maddened me. I had had an idea of getting a billet in one of the big wool-stores – I was a fair wool expert – but Mary was afraid of the drink. I could keep well away from it so long as I worked hard in the Bush. I had gone to Sydney twice since I met Mary, once before we were married, and she forgave me when I came back; and once afterwards. I got a billet there then, and was going to send for her in a month. After eight weeks she raised the money somehow and came to Sydney and brought me home. I got pretty low down that time.)

"But, Mary," I said, "it would have been different this time. You would have been with me. I can take a glass now or leave it alone."

"As long as you take a glass there is danger," she said.

"Well, what did you want to advise me to come out here for, if you can't stand it? Why didn't you stay where you were?" I asked.

"Well," she said, "why weren't you more decided?"

I'd sat down, but I jumped to my feet then.

"Good God!" I shouted, "this is more than any man can stand. I'll chuck it all up! I'm damned well sick and tired of the whole thing."

"So am I, Joe," said Mary wearily.

We quarrelled badly then — that first hour in our new home. I know now whose fault it was.

I got my hat and went out and started to walk down the creek. I didn't feel bitter against Mary — I had spoken too cruelly to her to feel that way. Looking back, I could see plainly that if I had taken her advice all through, instead of now and again, things would have been all right with me. I had come away and left her crying in the hut, and James telling her, in a brotherly way, that it was all her fault. The trouble was that I never liked to "give in" or go half-way to make it up — not half-way — it was all the way or nothing with our natures.

"If I don't make a stand now," I'd say, "I'll never be master. I gave up the reins when I got married, and I'll have to get them back again."

What women some men are! But the time came, and not many years after, when I stood by the bed where Mary lay, white and still; and, amongst other things, I kept saying, "I'll give in, Mary — I'll give in," and then I'd laugh. They thought that I was raving mad, and took me from the room. But that time was to come.

As I walked down the creek track in the moonlight the question rang in my ears again, as it had done when I first caught sight of the house that evening —

"Why did I bring her here?"

I was not fit to "go on the land". The place was only fit for some stolid German, or Scotsman, or even Englishman and his wife, who had no ambition but to bullock and make a farm of the place. I had only drifted here through carelessness, brooding, and discontent.

I walked on and on till I was more than half-way to the only neighbours — a wretched selector's family, about four miles down the creek — and I thought I'd go on to the house and see if they had any fresh meat.

A mile or two farther I saw the loom of the bark hut they lived in, on a patchy clearing in the scrub, and heard the voice of the selector's wife — I had seen her several times: she was a gaunt, haggard Bushwoman, and, I suppose, the reason why she hadn't gone mad through hardship and loneliness was that she hadn't either the brains or the memory to go farther than she could see through the trunks of the "apple-trees".

"You, An-nay!" (Annie.)

"Ye-es" (from somewhere in the gloom).

"Didn't I tell yer to water them geraniums!"

"Well, didn't I?"

"Don't tell lies or I'll break yer young back!"

"I did, I tell yer — the water won't soak inter the ashes."

Geraniums were the only flowers I saw grow in the drought out there. I remembered this woman had a few dirty grey-green leaves behind some sticks against the bark wall near the door; and in spite of the sticks the fowls used to get in and scratch beds under the geraniums, and scratch dust over them, and ashes were thrown there — with an idea of helping the flower, I suppose; and greasy dish-water, when fresh water was scarce — till you might as well try to water a dish of fat.

Then the woman's voice again —

"You, Tom-may!" (Tommy.)

Silence, save for an echo on the ridge.

"Y-o-u, T-o-m-*may!*"

"Y-e-e-s!" shrill shriek from across the creek.

"Didn't I tell you to ride up to them new people and see if they want any meat or any think?" in one long screech.

"Well — I karnt find the horse."

"Well-find-it-first-think-in-the-morning and. And-don't-forget-to-tell-Mrs-Wi'son-that-mother'll-be-up-as-soon-as-she-can."

I didn't feel like going to the woman's house that night. I felt — and the thought came like a whip-stroke on my heart — that this was what Mary would come to if I left her here.

I turned and started to walk home, fast. I'd made up my mind. I'd take Mary straight back to Gulgong in the morning — I forgot about the load I had to take to the sheep station. I'd say, "Look here, Girlie" (that's what I used to call her), "we'll leave this wretched life; we'll leave the Bush for ever! We'll go to Sydney, and I'll be a man! and work my way up." And I'd sell waggon, horses, and all, and go.

When I got to the hut it was lighted up. Mary had the only kerosene lamp, a slush lamp, and two tallow candles going. She had got both rooms washed out — to James's disgust, for he had to move the furniture and boxes about. She had a lot of things unpacked on the table; she had laid clean newspapers on the mantel-shelf — a slab on two pegs over the fireplace — and put the little wooden clock in the centre and some of the ornaments on each side, and was tacking a strip of vandyked American oil-cloth round the rough edge of the slab.

"How does that look, Joe? We'll soon get things shipshape."

I kissed her, but she had her mouth full of tacks. I went out in the kitchen, drank a pint of cold tea, and sat down.

Somehow I didn't feel satisfied with the way things had gone.

II. "Past Carin'"

Next morning things looked a lot brighter. Things always look brighter in the morning − more so in the Australian Bush, I should think, than in most other places. It is when the sun goes down on the dark bed of the lonely Bush, and the sunset flashes like a sea of fire and then fades, and then glows out again, like a bank of coals, and then burns away to ashes − it is then that old things come home to one. And strange, new-old things too, that haunt and depress you terribly, and that you can't understand. I often think how, at sunset, the past must come home to new-chum black-sheep, sent out to Australia and drifted into the Bush. I used to think that they couldn't have much brains, or the loneliness would drive them mad.

I'd decided to let James take the team for a trip or two. He could drive alright; he was a better business man, and no doubt would manage better than me − as long as the novelty lasted; and I'd stay at home for a week or so, till Mary got used to the place, or I could get a girl from somewhere to come and stay with her. The first weeks or few months of loneliness are the worst, as a rule, I believed, as they say the first weeks in jail are − I was never there. I know it's so with tramping or hard graft:* the first day or two are twice as hard as any of the rest. But, for my part, I could never get used to loneliness and dulness; the last days used to be the worst with me: then I'd have to make a move, or drink. When you've been too much and too long alone in a lonely place, you begin to do queer things and think queer thoughts − provided you have any imagination at all. You'll sometimes sit of an evening and watch the lonely track, by the hour, for a horseman or a cart or some one that's never likely to come that way − some one, or a stranger, that you can't and don't really expect to see. I think that most men who have been alone in the Bush for any length of time − and married couples too − are more or less mad. With married couples it is generally the husband who is painfully shy and awkward when strangers come. The woman seems to stand the loneliness better, and can hold her own with strangers, as a rule.

* "Graft", work. The term is now applied, in Australia, to all sorts of work, from bullock-driving to writing poetry.

It's only afterwards, and looking back, that you see how queer you got. Shepherds and boundary-riders, who are alone for months, *must* have their periodical spree, at the nearest shanty, else they'd go raving mad. Drink is the only break in the awful monotony, and the yearly or half-yearly spree is the only thing they've got to look forward to: it keeps their minds fixed on something definite ahead.

But Mary kept her head pretty well through the first months of loneliness. *Weeks*, rather, I should say, for it wasn't as bad as it might have been farther up-country: there was generally some one came of a Sunday afternoon — a spring-cart with a couple of women, or maybe a family — or a lanky shy Bush native or two on lanky shy horses. On a quiet Sunday, after I'd brought Jim home, Mary would dress him and herself — just the same as if we were in town — and make me get up on one end and put on a collar and take her and Jim for a walk along the creek. She said she wanted to keep me civilized. She tried to make a gentleman of me for years, but gave it up gradually.

Well. It was the first morning on the creek: I was greasing the waggon-wheels, and James out after the horse, and Mary hanging out clothes, in an old print dress and a big ugly white hood, when I heard her being hailed as "Hi, missus!" from the front slip-rails.

It was a boy on horseback. He was a light-haired, very much freckled boy of fourteen or fifteen, with a small head, but with limbs, especially his bare sun-blotched shanks, that might have belonged to a grown man. He had a good face and frank grey eyes. An old, nearly black cabbage-tree hat rested on the butts of his ears, turning them out at right angles from his head, and rather dirty sprouts they were. He wore a dirty torn Crimean shirt; and a pair of man's moleskin trousers rolled up above the knees, with the wide waistband gathered under a greenhide belt. I noticed, later on, that, even when he wore trousers short enough for him, he always rolled 'em up above the knees when on horseback, for some reason of his own: to suggest leggings, perhaps, for he had them rolled up in all weathers, and he wouldn't have bothered to save them from the sweat of the horse, even if that horse ever sweated.

He was seated astride a three-bushel bag thrown across the ridge-pole of a big grey horse, with a coffin-shaped head, and built astern something after the style of a roughly put up hip-roofed box-bark humpy.* His colour was like old box-bark, too, a dirty bluish-grey; and, one time, when I saw his rump looming out of

"Humpy", a rough hut.

the scrub, I really thought it was some old shepherd's hut that I hadn't noticed there before. When he cantered it was like the humpy starting off on its corner-posts.

"Are you Mrs Wilson?" asked the boy.

"Yes," said Mary.

"Well, mother told me to ride acrost and see if you wanted anythink. We killed lars' night, and I've fetched a piece er cow."

"Piece of *what?*" asked Mary.

He grinned, and handed a sugar-bag across the rail with something heavy in the bottom of it, that nearly jerked Mary's arm out when she took it. It was a piece of beef, that looked as if it had been cut off with a wood-axe, but it was fresh and clean.

"Oh, I'm so glad!" cried Mary. She was always impulsive, save to me sometimes. "I was just wondering where we were going to get any fresh meat. How kind of your mother! Tell her I'm very much obliged to her indeed." And she felt behind her for a poor little purse she had. "And now — how much did your mother say it would be?"

The boy blinked at her, and scratched his head.

"How much will it be?" he repeated, puzzled. "Oh — how much does it weigh I-s'pose-yer-mean. Well, it ain't been weighed at all — we ain't got no scales. A butcher does all that sort of think. We just kills it, and cooks it, and eats it — and goes by guess. What won't keep we salts down in the cask. I reckon it weighs about a ton by the weight of it if yer wanter know. Mother thought that if she sent any more it would go bad before you could scoff it. I can't see — "

"Yes, yes," said Mary, getting confused. "But what I want to know is, how do you manage when you sell it?"

He glared at her, and scratched his head. "Sell it? Why, we only goes halves in a steer with some one, or sells steers to the butcher — or maybe some meat to a party of fencers or surveyors, or tanksinkers, or them sorter people — "

"Yes, yes; but what I want to know is, how much am I to send your mother for this?"

"How much what?"

"Money, of course, you stupid boy," said Mary. "You seem a very stupid boy."

Then he saw what she was driving at. He began to fling his heels convulsively against the sides of his horse, jerking his body backward and forward at the same time, as if to wind up and start some clockwork machinery inside the horse, that made it go, and seemed to need repairing or oiling.

"We ain't that sorter people, missus," he said. "We don't sell meat to new people that come to settle here." Then jerking his thumb contemptuously towards the ridges, "Go over ter Wall's if yer wanter buy meat; they sell meat ter strangers." (Wall was the big squatter over the ridges.)

"Oh!" said Mary, "I'm *so* sorry. Thank your mother for me. She *is* kind."

"Oh, that's nothink. She said to tell yer she'll be up as soon as she can. She'd have come up yisterday evening — she thought yer'd feel lonely comin' new to a place like this — but she couldn't git up."

The machinery inside the old horse showed signs of starting. You almost heard the wooden joints *creak* as he lurched forward, like an old propped-up humpy when the rotting props give way; but at the sound of Mary's voice he settled back on his foundations again. It must have been a very poor selection that couldn't afford a better spare horse than that.

"Reach me that lump er wood, will yer, missus?" said the boy, and he pointed to one of my "spreads" (for the team-chains) that lay inside the fence. "I'll fling it back agin over the fence when I git this ole cow started."

"But wait a minute — I've forgotten your mother's name," said Mary.

He grabbed at his thatch impatiently. "Me mother — oh! — the old woman's name's Mrs Spicer. (Git up, karnt yer!)" He twisted himself round, and brought the stretcher down on one of the horse's "points" (and he had many) with a crack that must have jarred his wrist.

"Do you go to school?" asked Mary. There was a three-days-a-week school over the ridges at Wall's station.

"No!" he jerked out, keeping his legs going. "Me — why I'm going on fur fifteen. The last teacher at Wall's finished me. I'm going to Queensland next month drovin'." (Queensland border was over three hundred miles away.)

"Finished you? How?" asked Mary.

"Me edgercation, of course! How do yer expect me to start this horse when yer keep talkin'?"

He split the "spread" over the horse's point, threw the pieces over the fence, and was off, his elbows and legs flinging wildly, and the old saw-tool lumbering along the road like an old working bullock trying a canter. That horse wasn't a trotter.

And next month he *did* start for Queensland. He was a younger son and a surplus boy on a wretched, poverty-stricken selection;

and as there was "northin' doin'" in the district, his father (in a burst of fatherly kindness, I suppose) made him a present of the old horse and a new pair of Blucher boots, and I gave him an old saddle and a coat, and he started for the Never-Never Country.

And I'll bet he got there. But I'm doubtful if the old horse did.

Mary gave the boy five shillings, and I don't think he had anything more except a clean shirt and an extra pair of white cotton socks.

"Spicer's farm" was a big bark humpy on a patchy clearing in the native apple-tree scrub. The clearing was fenced in by a light "dog-legged" fence (a fence of sapling poles resting on forks and X-shaped uprights) and the dusty ground round the house was almost entirely covered with cattle-dung. There was no attempt at cultivation when I came to live on the creek; but there were old furrow-marks amongst the stumps of another shapeless patch in the scrub near the hut. There was a wretched sapling cow-yard and calf-pen, and a cow-bail with one sheet of bark over it for shelter. There was no dairy to be seen, and I suppose the milk was set in one of the two skillion rooms, or lean-to's behind the hut — the other was "the boys' bedroom". The Spicers kept a few cows and steers, and had thirty or forty sheep. Mrs Spicer used to drive down the creek once a week, in her rickety old spring-cart, to Cobborah, with butter and eggs. The hut was nearly as bare inside as it was out — just a frame of "round-timber" (sapling poles) covered with bark. The furniture was permanent (unless you rooted it up), like in our kitchen: a rough slab table on stakes driven into the ground, and seats made the same way. Mary told me afterwards that the beds in the bag-and-bark partitioned-off room ("mother's bedroom") were simply poles laid side by side on cross-pieces supported by stakes driven into the ground, with straw mattresses and some worn-out bedclothes. Mrs Spicer had an old patchwork quilt, in rags, and the remains of a white one, and Mary said it was pitiful to see how these things would be spread over the beds — to hide them as much as possible — when she went down there. A packing-case, with something like an old print skirt draped round it, and a cracked looking-glass (without a frame) on top, was the dressing-table. There were a couple of gin-cases for a wardrobe. The boys' beds were three-bushel bags stretched between poles fastened to uprights. The floor was the original surface, tramped hard, worn uneven with much sweeping, and with puddles in rainy weather where the roof leaked. Mrs Spicer used to stand old tins, dishes, and buckets under as many of the leaks as she could. The saucepans, kettles, and boilers were old kerosene-tins and billies. They used kerosene-tins, too, cut longways in halves, for setting the milk in. The plates and cups were of tin; there were two or three cups without saucers, and a crockery plate or two – also two mugs, cracked and without handles, one with "For a Good Boy" and the other with "For a Good Girl" on it; but all these were kept on the mantel-shelf for ornament and for company. They were the only ornaments in the house, save a little wooden clock that hadn't gone for years. Mrs Spicer had a superstition that she had "some things packed away from the children".

The pictures were cut from old copies of the *Illustrated Sydney News* and pasted on to the bark. I remember this, because I remember, long ago, the Spencers, who were our neighbours when I was a boy, had the walls of their bedroom covered with illustrations of the American Civil War, cut from illustrated London papers, and I used to "sneak" into "mother's bedroom" with Fred Spencer whenever we got the chance, and gloat over the prints. I gave him a blade of a pocket-knife once, for taking me in there.

I saw very little of Spicer. He was a big, dark, dark-haired and whiskered man. I had an idea that he wasn't a selector at all, only a "dummy" for the squatter of the Cobborah run. You see, selectors were allowed to take up land on runs, or pastoral leases. The squatters kept them off as much as possible, by all manner of dodges and paltry persecution. The squatter would get as much freehold as he could afford, "select" as much land as the law allowed one man to take up, and then employ dummies (dummy selectors) to take up bits of land that he fancied about his run, and hold them for him.

Spicer seemed gloomy and unsociable. He was seldom at home. He was generally supposed to be away shearin', or fencin', or workin' on somebody's station. It turned out that the last six months he was away it was on the evidence of a cask of beef and a hide with the brand cut out, found in his camp on a fencing contract up-country, and which he and his mates couldn't account for satisfactorily, while the squatter could. Then the family lived mostly on bread and honey, or bread and treacle, or bread and dripping, and tea. Every ounce of butter and every egg was needed for the market, to keep them in flour, tea, and sugar. Mary found that out, but couldn't help them much – except by "stuffing" the children with bread and meat or bread and jam whenever they came up to our place – for Mrs Spicer was proud with the pride that lies down in the end and turns its face to the wall and dies.

Once, when Mary asked Annie, the eldest girl at home, if she
was hungry, she denied it — but she looked it. A ragged mite she
had with her explained things. The little fellow said —

"Mother told Annie not to say we was hungry if yer asked; but if
yer give us anythink to eat, we was to take it an' say thenk yer,
Mrs Wilson."

"I wouldn't 'a' told yer a lie; but I thought Jimmy would split on
me, Mrs Wilson," said Annie. "Thenk yer, Mrs Wilson."

She was not a big woman. She was gaunt and flat-chested, and
her face was "burnt to a brick", as they say out there. She had
brown eyes, nearly red, and a little wild-looking at times, and a
sharp face — ground sharp by hardship — the cheeks drawn in.
She had an expression like — well, like a woman who had been
very curious and suspicious at one time, and wanted to know
everybody's business and hear everything, and had lost all her
curiosity, without losing the expression or the quick suspicious
movements of the head. I don't suppose you understand. I can't
explain it any other way. She was not more than forty.

I remember the first morning I saw her. I was going up the creek
to look at the selection for the first time, and called at the hut to
see if she had a bit of fresh mutton, as I had none and was sick of
"corned beef".

"Yes — of — course," she said, in a sharp nasty tone, as if to say
"Is there anything more you want while the shop's open?" I'd met
just the same sort of woman years before while I was carrying
swag between the shearing-sheds in the awful scrubs out west of
the Darling river, so I didn't turn on my heels and walk away.
I waited for her to speak again.

"Come — inside," she said, "and sit down. I see you've got the
waggon outside. I s'pose your name's Wilson, ain't it? You're
thinkin' about takin' on Harry Marshfield's selection up the creek,
so I heard. Wait till I fry you a chop and boil the billy."

Her voice sounded, more than anything else, like a voice coming
out of a phonograph — I heard one in Sydney the other day — and
not like a voice coming out of her. But sometimes when she got
outside her everyday life on this selection she spoke in a sort of —
in a sort of lost groping-in-the-dark kind of voice.

She didn't talk much this time — just spoke in a mechanical way
of the drought, and the hard times, "an' butter 'n' eggs bein' down,
an' her husban' an' eldest son bein' away, an' that makin' it so hard
for her."

I don't know how many children she had. I never got a chance to
count them, for they were nearly all small, and shy as picca-

ninnies, and used to run and hide when anybody came. They
were mostly nearly as black as piccaninnies too. She must have
averaged a baby a year for years – and God only knows how she
got over her confinements! Once, they said, she only had a black
gin with her. She had an elder boy and girl, but she seldom spoke
of them. The girl, "Liza", was "in service in Sydney". I'm afraid I
knew what that meant. The elder son was "away". He had been a
bit of a favourite round there, it seemed.

Some one might ask her, "How's your son Jack, Mrs Spicer?" or,
"Heard of Jack lately? and where is he now?"

"Oh, he's somewheres up country," she'd say in the "groping"
voice, or "He's drovin' in Queenslan'," or "Shearin' on the Darlin'
the last time I heerd from him." "We ain't had a line from him since
– le's see – since Chris'mas 'fore last."

And she'd turn her haggard eyes in a helpless, hopeless sort of
way towards the west – towards "up-country" and "Out-Back".*

The eldest girl at home was nine or ten, with a little old face and
lines across her forehead: she had an older expression than her
mother. Tommy went to Queensland, as I told you. The eldest son
at home, Bill (older than Tommy), was "a bit wild".

I've passed the place in smothering hot mornings in December,
when the droppings about the cow-yard had crumpled to dust that
rose in the warm, sickly, sunrise wind, and seen that woman at
work in the cow-yard, "bailing-up" and leg-roping cows, milking,
or hauling at a rope round the neck of a half-grown calf that was
too strong for her (and she was tough as fencing-wire), or humping
great buckets of sour milk to the pigs or the "poddies" (hand-fed
calves) in the pen. I'd get off the horse and give her a hand sometimes with a young steer, or a cranky old cow that wouldn't "bail-
up" and threatened her with her horns. She'd say –

"Thenk yer, Mr Wilson. Do yer think we're ever goin' to have
any rain?"

I've ridden past the place on bitter black rainy mornings in June
or July, and seen her trudging about the yard – that was ankle-
deep in black liquid filth – with an old pair of Blucher boots on,
and an old coat of her husband's, or maybe a three-bushel bag over
her shoulders. I've seen her climbing on the roof by means of the
water-cask at the corner, and trying to stop a leak by shoving a
piece of tin in under the bark. And when I'd fixed the leak –

"Thenk yer, Mr Wilson. This drop of rain's a blessin'! Come in
and have a dry at the fire and I'll make yer a cup of tea." And, if I

* "Out-Back" is always west of the Bushman, no matter how far out he be.

was in a hurry, "Come in, man alive! Come`in! and dry yerself a
bit till the rain holds up. Yer can't go home like this! Yer'll git yer
death o' cold."

I've even seen her, in the terrible drought, climbing she-oaks and
apple-trees by a makeshift ladder, and awkwardly lopping off
boughs to feed the starving cattle.

"Jist tryin' ter keep the milkers alive till the rain comes."

They said that when the pleuro-pneumonia was in the district
and amongst her cattle she bled and physicked them herself, and
fed those that were down with slices of half-ripe pumpkins (from a
crop that had failed).

"An', one day," she told Mary, "there was a big barren heifer (that
we called Queen Elizabeth) that was down with the ploorer. She'd
been down for four days and hadn't moved, when one mornin' I
dumped some wheaten chaff − we had a few bags that Spicer
brought home − I dumped it in front of her nose, an' − would yer
b'lieve me, Mrs Wilson? − she stumbled onter her feet an' chased
me all the way to the house! I had to pick up me skirts an' run!
Wasn't it redic'lus?"

They had a sense of the ridiculous, most of those poor sun-dried
Bushwomen. I fancy that that helped save them from madness.

"We lost nearly all our milkers," she told Mary. "I remember one
day Tommy came running to the house and screamed: 'Marther!
[mother] there's another milker down with the ploorer!' Jist as if it
was great news. Well, Mrs Wilson, I was dead-beat, an' I giv' in.
I jist sat down to have a good cry, and felt for my han'kerchief − it
was a rag of a han'kerchief, full of holes (all me others was in the
wash). Without seein' what I was doin' I put me finger through one
hole in the han'kerchief an' me thumb through the other, and
poked me fingers into me eyes, instead of wipin' them. Then I had
to laugh."

There's a story that once, when the Bush, or rather grass, fires
were out all along the creek on Spicer's side, Wall's station hands
were up above our place, trying to keep the fire back from the
boundary, and towards evening one of the men happened to think
of the Spicers: they saw smoke down that way. Spicer was away
from home, and they had a small crop of wheat, nearly ripe, on
the selection.

"My God! that poor devil of a woman will be burnt out, if she
ain't already!" shouted young Billy Wall. "Come along, three or
four of you chaps" − (it was shearing-time, and there were plenty
of men on the station).

They raced down the creek to Spicer's, and were just in time to

save the wheat. She had her sleeves tucked up, and was beating
out the burning grass with a bough. She'd been at it for an hour,
and was as black as a gin, they said. She only said when they'd
turned the fire: "Thenk yer! Wait an' I'll make some tea."

After tea the first Sunday she came to see us, Mary asked –

"Don't you feel lonely, Mrs Spicer, when your husband goes
away?"

"Well – no, Mrs Wilson," she said in the groping sort of voice.
"I uster, once. I remember, when we lived on the Cudgeegong
river – we lived in a brick house then – the first time Spicer had
to go away from home I nearly fretted my eyes out. And he was
only goin' shearin' for a month. I muster bin a fool; but then we
were only jist married a little while. He's been away drovin' in
Queenslan' as long as eighteen months at a time since then. But"
(her voice seemed to grope in the dark more than ever) "I don't
mind, – I somehow seem to have got past carin'. Besides –
besides, Spicer was a very different man then to what he is now.
He's got so moody and gloomy at home, he hardly ever speaks."

Mary sat silent for a minute thinking. Then Mrs Spicer roused
herself –

"Oh, I don't know what I'm talkin' about! You mustn't take any
notice of me, Mrs Wilson, – I don't often go on like this. I do
believe I'm gittin' a bit ratty at times. It must be the heat and the
dulness."

But once or twice afterwards she referred to a time "when Spicer
was a different man to what he was now."

I walked home with her a piece along the creek. She said
nothing for a long time, and seemed to be thinking in a puzzled
way. Then she said suddenly –

"What-did-you-bring-her-here-for? She's only a girl."

"I beg pardon, Mrs Spicer?"

"Oh, I don't know what I'm talkin' about! I b'lieve I'm gittin'
ratty. You mustn't take any notice of me, Mr Wilson."

She wasn't much company for Mary; and often, when she had a
child with her, she'd start taking notice of the baby while Mary
was talking, which used to exasperate Mary. But poor Mrs Spicer
couldn't help it, and she seemed to hear all the same.

Her great trouble was that she "couldn't git no reg'lar schoolin'
for the children".

"I learns 'em at home as much as I can. But I don't git a minute to
call me own; an' I'm ginerally that dead-beat at night that I'm fit for
nothink."

Mary had some of the children up now and then later on, and taught them a little. When she first offered to do so, Mrs Spicer laid hold of the handiest youngster and said –

"There – do you hear that? Mrs Wilson is goin' to teach yer, an' it's more than yer deserve!" (the youngster had been "cryin'" over something). "Now, go up an' say 'Thenk yer, Mrs Wilson.' And if yer ain't good, and don't do as she tells yer, I'll break every bone in yer young body!"

The poor little devil stammered something, and escaped.

The children were sent by turns over to Wall's to Sunday-school. When Tommy was at home he had a new pair of elastic-side boots, and there was no end of rows about them in the family – for the mother made him lend them to his sister Annie, to go to Sunday-school in, in her turn. There were only about three pairs of any-way decent boots in the family, and these were saved for great occasions. The children were always as clean and tidy as possible when they came to our place.

And I think the saddest and most pathetic sight on the face of God's earth is the children of very poor people made to appear well: the broken wornout boots polished or greased, the blackened (inked) pieces of string for laces; the clean patched pinafores over the wretched threadbare frocks. Behind the little row of children hand-in-hand – and no matter where they are – I always see the worn face of the mother.

Towards the end of the first year on the selection our little girl came. I'd sent Mary to Gulgong for four months that time, and when she came back with the baby Mrs Spicer used to come up pretty often. She came up several times when Mary was ill, to lend a hand. She wouldn't sit down and condole with Mary, or waste her time asking questions, or talking about the time when she was ill herself. She'd take off her hat – a shapeless little lump of black straw she wore for visiting – give her hair a quick brush back with the palms of her hands, roll up her sleeves, and set to work to "tidy up". She seemed to take most pleasure in sorting out our children's clothes, and dressing them. Perhaps she used to dress her own like that in the days when Spicer was a different man from what he was now. She seemed interested in the fashion-plates of some women's journals we had, and used to study them with an interest that puzzled me, for she was not likely to go in for fashion. She never talked of her early girlhood; but Mary, from some things she noticed, was inclined to think that Mrs Spicer had been fairly well brought up. For instance, Dr Balanfantie, from Cudgeegong, came out to see Wall's wife, and drove up the creek to our place on his way back to see how Mary and the baby were getting on. Mary got out some crockery and some table-napkins that she had packed away for occasions like this; and she said that the way Mrs Spicer handled the things, and helped set the table (though she did it in a mechanical sort of way), convinced her that she had been used to table-napkins at one time in her life.

Sometimes, after a long pause in the conversation, Mrs Spicer would say suddenly —

"Oh, I don't think I'll come up next week, Mrs Wilson."

"Why, Mrs Spicer?"

"Because the visits doesn't do me any good. I git the dismals afterwards."

"Why, Mrs Spicer? What on earth do you mean?"

"Oh, I-don't-know-what-I'm-talkin'-about. You mustn't take any notice of me." And she'd put on her hat, kiss the children — and Mary too, sometimes, as if she mistook her for a child — and go.

Mary thought her a little mad at times. But I seemed to understand.

Once, when Mrs Spicer was sick, Mary went down to her, and down again next day. As she was coming away the second time, Mrs Spicer said —

"I wish you wouldn't come down any more till I'm on me feet, Mrs Wilson. The children can do for me."

"Why, Mrs Spicer?"

"Well, the place is in such a muck, and it hurts me."

We were the aristocrats of Lahey's Creek. Whenever we drove down on Sunday afternoon to see Mrs Spicer, and as soon as we got near enough for them to hear the rattle of the cart, we'd see the children running to the house as fast as they could split, and hear them screaming —

"Oh, marther! Here comes Mr and Mrs Wilson in their spring-cart."

And we'd see her bustle round, and two or three fowls fly out the front door, and she'd lay hold of a broom (made of a bound bunch of "broom-stuff" — coarse reedy grass or bush from the ridges — with a stick stuck in it) and flick out the floor, with a flick or two round in front of the door perhaps. The floor nearly always needed at least one flick of the broom on account of the fowls. Or she'd catch a youngster and scrub his face with a wet end of a cloudy towel, or twist the towel round her finger and dig out his ears — as if she was anxious to have him hear every word that was going to be said.

No matter what state the house would be in she'd always say,

"I was jist expectin' yer, Mrs Wilson." And she was original in that, anyway.

She had an old patched and darned white table-cloth that she used to spread on the table when we were there, as a matter of course ("The others is in the wash, so you must excuse this, Mrs Wilson"), but I saw by the eyes of the children that the cloth was rather a wonderful thing to them. "I must really git some more knives an' forks next time I'm in Cobborah," she'd say. "The children break an' lose 'em till I'm ashamed to ask Christians ter sit down ter the table."

She had many Bush yarns, some of them very funny, some of them rather ghastly, but all interesting, and with a grim sort of humour about them. But the effect was often spoilt by her screaming at the children to "Drive out them fowls, karnt yer," or "Take yer maulies [hands] outer the sugar," or "Don't touch Mrs Wilson's baby with them dirty maulies," or "Don't stand starin' at Mrs Wilson with yer mouth an' ears in that vulgar way."

Poor woman! she seemed everlastingly nagging at the children. It was a habit, but they didn't seem to mind. Most Bushwomen get the nagging habit. I remember one, who had the prettiest, dearest, sweetest, most willing, and affectionate little girl I think I ever saw, and she nagged that child from daylight till dark — and after it. Taking it all round, I think that the nagging habit in a mother is often worse on ordinary children, and more deadly on sensitive youngsters, than the drinking habit in a father.

One of the yarns Mrs Spicer told us was about a squatter she knew who used to go wrong in his head every now and again, and try to commit suicide. Once, when the stationhand, who was watching him, had his eye off him for a minute, he hanged himself to a beam in the stable. The men ran in and found him hanging and kicking. "They let him hang for a while," said Mrs Spicer, "till he went black in the face and stopped kicking. Then they cut him down and threw a bucket of water over him."

"Why! what on earth did they let the man hang for?" asked Mary.

"To give him a good bellyful of it: they thought it would cure him of tryin' to hang himself again."

"Well, that's the coolest thing I ever heard of," said Mary.

"That's jist what the magistrate said, Mrs Wilson," said Mrs Spicer.

"One morning," said Mrs Spicer, "Spicer had gone off on his horse somewhere, and I was alone with the children, when a man came to the door and said —

"'For God's sake, woman, give me a drink!'

"Lord only knows where he came from! He was dressed like a new chum – his clothes was good, but he looked as if he'd been sleepin' in them in the Bush for a month. He was very shaky. I had some coffee that mornin', so I gave him some in a pint pot; he drank it, and then he stood on his head till he tumbled over, and then he stood up on his feet and said, 'Thenk yer, mum.'

"I was so surprised that I didn't know what to say, so I jist said, 'Would you like some more coffee?'

"'Yes, thenk yer,' he said – 'about two quarts.'

"I nearly filled the pint pot, and he drank it and stood on his head as long as he could, and when he got right end up he said, 'Thenk yer, mum – it's a fine day,' and then he walked off. He had two saddle-straps in his hands."

"Why, what did he stand on his head for?" asked Mary.

"To wash it up and down, I suppose, to get twice as much taste of the coffee. He had no hat. I sent Tommy across to Wall's to tell them that there was a man wanderin' about the Bush in the horrors of drink, and to get some one to ride for the police. But they was too late, for he hanged himself that night."

"O Lord!" cried Mary.

"Yes, right close to here, jist down the creek where the track to Wall's branches off. Tommy found him while he was out after the cows. Hangin' to the branch of a tree with the two saddle-straps."

Mary stared at her, speechless.

"Tommy came home yellin' with fright. I sent him over to Wall's at once. After breakfast, the minute my eyes was off them, the children slipped away and went down there. They came back screamin' at the tops of their voices. I did give it to them. I reckon they won't want ter see a dead body again in a hurry. Every time I'd mention it they'd huddle together, or ketch hold of me skirts and howl.

"'Yer'll go agen when I tell yer not to,' I'd say.

"'Oh no, mother,' they'd howl.

"'Yer wanted ter see a man hangin',' I said.

"'Oh, don't, mother! Don't talk about it.'

"'Yer wouldn't be satisfied till yer see it,' I'd say; 'yer had to see it or burst. Yer satisfied now, ain't yer?'

"'Oh, don't, mother!'

"'Yer run all the way there, I s'pose?'

"'Don't, mother!'

"'But yer run faster back, didn't yer?'

" 'Oh, don't, mother.'

"But," said Mrs Spicer, in conclusion, "I'd been down to see it myself before they was up."

"And ain't you afraid to live alone here, after all these horrible things?" asked Mary.

"Well, no; I don't mind. I seem to have got past carin' for anythink now. I felt it a little when Tommy went away — the first time I felt anythink for years. But I'm over that now."

"Haven't you got any friends in the district, Mrs.Spicer?"

"Oh yes. There's me married sister near Cobborah, and a married brother near Dubbo; he's got a station. They wanted to take me an' the children between them, or take some of the younger children. But I couldn't bring my mind to break up the home. I want to keep the children together as much as possible. There's enough of them gone, God knows. But it's a comfort to know that there's some one to see to them if anythink happens to me."

One day — I was on my way home with the team that day — Annie Spicer came running up the creek in terrible trouble.

"Oh, Mrs Wilson! something terrible's happened at home! A trooper" (mounted policeman — they called them "mounted troopers" out there), "a trooper's come and took Billy!" Billy was the eldest son at home.

"What?"

"It's true, Mrs Wilson."

"What for? What did the policeman say?"

"He — he — he said, 'I — I'm very sorry, Mrs Spicer; but — I — I want William.'"

It turned out that William was wanted on account of a horse missed from Wall's station and sold down-country.

"An' mother took on awful," sobbed Annie; "an' now she'll only sit stock-still an' stare in front of her, and won't take no notice of any of us. Oh! it's awful, Mrs Wilson. The policeman said he'd tell Aunt Emma" (Mrs Spicer's sister at Cobborah), "and send her out. But I had to come to you, an' I've run all the way."

James put the horse to the cart and drove Mary down.

Mary told me all about it when I came home.

"I found her just as Annie said; but she broke down and cried in my arms. Oh, Joe! it was awful! She didn't cry like a woman. I heard a man at Haviland cry at his brother's funeral, and it was just like that. She came round a bit after a while. Her sister's with her now. . . . Oh, Joe! you must take me away from the Bush."

Later on Mary said —

"How the oaks are sighing tonight, Joe!"

Next morning I rode across to Wall's station and tackled the old
man; but he was a hard man, and wouldn't listen to me — in fact,
he ordered me off the station. I was a selector, and that was
enough for him. But young Billy Wall rode after me.

"Look here, Joe!" he said, "it's a blanky shame. All for the sake of
a horse! And as if that poor devil of a woman hasn't got enough to
put up with already! I wouldn't do it for twenty horses. I'll tackle
the boss, and if he won't listen to me, I'll walk off the run for the
last time, if I have to carry my swag."

Billy Wall managed it. The charge was withdrawn, and we got
young Billy Spicer off up-country.

But poor Mrs Spicer was never the same after that. She seldom
came up to our place unless Mary dragged her, so to speak; and
then she would talk of nothing but her last trouble, till her visits
were painful to look forward to.

"If it only could have been kep' quiet — for the sake of the other
children; they are all I think of now. I tried to bring 'em all up
decent, but I s'pose it was my fault, somehow. It's the disgrace
that's killin' me — I can't bear it."

I was at home one Sunday with Mary and a jolly Bush-girl
named Maggie Charlsworth, who rode over sometimes from Wall's
station (I must tell you about her some other time; James was
"shook after her"), and we got talkin' about Mrs Spicer. Maggie was
very warm about old Wall.

"I expected Mrs Spicer up today," said Mary. "She seems better
lately."

"Why!" cried Maggie Charlsworth, "if that ain't Annie coming
running up along the creek. Something's the matter!"

We all jumped up and ran out.

"What is it, Annie?" cried Mary.

"Oh, Mrs Wilson! Mother's asleep, and we can't wake her!"

"What?"

"It's — it's the truth, Mrs Wilson."

"How long has she been asleep?"

"Since lars' night."

"My God!" cried Mary, *"since last night?"*

"No, Mrs Wilson, not all the time; she woke wonst, about daylight this mornin'. She called me and said she didn't feel well, and
I'd have to manage the milkin'."

"Was that all she said?"

"No. She said not to go for you; and she said to feed the pigs and calves; and she said to be sure and water them geraniums."

Mary wanted to go, but I wouldn't let her. James and I saddled our horses and rode down the creek.

Mrs Spicer looked very little different from what she did when I last saw her alive. It was some time before we could believe that she was dead. But she was "past carin'" right enough.

The Chosen Vessel

Barbara Baynton

She laid the stick and her baby on the grass while she untied the
rope that tethered the calf. The length of the rope separated them.
The cow was near the calf, and both were lying down. Feed along
the creek was plentiful, and every day she found a fresh place to
tether it, since tether it she must, for if she did not, it would stray
with the cow out on the plain. She had plenty of time to go after it,
but then there was her baby; and if the cow turned on her out on
the plain, and she with her baby, – she had been a town girl and
was afraid of the cow, but she did not want the cow to know it.
She used to run at first when it bellowed its protest against the
penning up of its calf. This satisfied the cow, also the calf, but the
woman's husband was angry, and called her – the noun was cur.
It was he who forced her to run and meet the advancing cow,
brandishing a stick, and uttering threatening words till the enemy
turned and ran. "That's the way!" the man said, laughing at her
white face. In many things he was worse than the cow, and she
wondered if the same rule would apply to the man, but she was
not one to provoke skirmishes even with the cow.

It was early for the calf to go to "bed" – nearly an hour earlier
than usual; but she had felt so restless all day. Partly because it
was Monday, and the end of the week that would bring her and
the baby the companionship of his father, was so far off. He was a
shearer, and had gone to his shed before daylight that morning.
Fifteen miles as the crow flies separated them.

There was a track in front of the house, for it had once been a
wine shanty, and a few travellers passed along at intervals. She
was not afraid of horsemen; but swagmen, going to, or worse
coming from, the dismal, drunken little township, a day's journey
beyond, terrified her. One had called at the house to-day, and
asked for tucker.

That was why she had penned up the calf so early. She feared more from the look of his eyes, and the gleam of his teeth, as he watched her newly awakened baby beat its impatient fists upon her covered breasts, than from the knife that was sheathed in the belt at his waist.

She had given him bread and meat. Her husband she told him was sick. She always said that when she was alone and a swagman came; and she had gone in from the kitchen to the bedroom, and asked questions and replied to them in the best man's voice she could assume. Then he had asked to go into the kitchen to boil his billy, but instead she gave him tea, and he drank it on the wood heap. He had walked round and round the house, and there were cracks in some places, and after the last time he had asked for tobacco. She had none to give him, and he had grinned, because there was a broken clay pipe near the wood heap where he stood, and if there were a man inside, there ought to have been tobacco. Then he asked for money, but women in the bush never have money.

At last he had gone, and she, watching through the cracks, saw him when about a quarter of a mile away, turn and look back at the house. He had stood so for some moments with a pretence of fixing his swag, and then, apparently satisfied, moved to the left towards the creek. The creek made a bow round the house, and when he came to the bend she lost sight of him. Hours after, watching intently for signs of smoke, she saw the man's dog chasing some sheep that had gone to the creek for water, and saw it slink back suddenly, as if it had been called by some one.

More than once she thought of taking her baby and going to her husband. But in the past, when she had dared to speak of the dangers to which her loneliness exposed her, he had taunted and sneered at her. "Needn't flatter yerself," he had told her, "nobody 'ud want ter run away with yew."

Long before nightfall she placed food on the kitchen table, and beside it laid the big brooch that had been her mother's. It was the only thing of value that she had. And she left the kitchen door wide open.

The doors inside she securely fastened. Beside the bolt in the back one she drove in the steel and scissors; against it she piled the table and the stools. Underneath the lock of the front door she forced the handle of the spade, and the blade between the cracks in the flooring boards. Then the prop-stick, cut into lengths, held the top, as the spade held the middle. The windows were little more than portholes; she had nothing to fear through them.

She ate a few mouthfuls of food and drank a cup of milk. But she lighted no fire, and when night came, no candle, but crept with her baby to bed.

What woke her? The wonder was that she had slept – she had not meant to. But she was young, very young. Perhaps the shrinking of the galvanized roof – hardly though, since that was so usual. Yet something had set her heart beating wildly; but she lay quite still, only she put her arm over her baby. Then she had both round it, and she prayed, "Little baby, little baby, don't wake!"

The moon's rays shone on the front of the house, and she saw one of the open cracks, quite close to where she lay, darken with a shadow. Then a protesting growl reached her; and she could fancy she heard the man turn hastily. She plainly heard the thud of something striking the dog's ribs, and the long flying strides of the animal as it howled and ran. Still watching, she saw the shadow darken every crack along the wall. She knew by the sounds that the man was trying every standpoint that might help him to see in; but how much he saw she could not tell. She thought of many things she might do to deceive him into the idea that she was not alone. But the sound of her voice would wake baby, and she dreaded that as though it were the only danger that threatened her. So she prayed, "Little baby, don't wake, don't cry!"

Stealthily the man crept about. She knew he had his boots off, because of the vibration that his feet caused as he walked along the verandah to gauge the width of the little window in her room, and the resistance of the front door.

Then he went to the other end, and the uncertainty of what he was doing became unendurable. She had felt safer, far safer, while he was close, and she could watch and listen. She felt she must watch, but the great fear of wakening her baby again assailed her. She suddenly recalled that one of the slabs on that side of the house had shrunk in length as well as in width, and had once fallen out. It was held in position only by a wedge of wood underneath. What if he should discover that? The uncertainty increased her terror. She prayed as she gently raised herself with her little one in her arms, held tightly to her breast.

She thought of the knife, and shielded its body with her hands and arms. Even the little feet she covered with its white gown, and the baby never murmured – it liked to be held so. Noiselessly she crossed to the other side, and stood where she could see and hear, but not be seen. He was trying every slab, and was very near to that with the wedge under it. Then she saw him find it; and heard the sound of the knife as bit by bit he began to cut away the wooden support.

She waited motionless, with her baby pressed tightly to her, though she knew that in another few minutes this man with the cruel eyes, lascivious mouth, and gleaming knife, would enter. One side of the slab tilted; he had only to cut away the remaining little end, when the slab, unless he held it, would fall outside.

She heard his jerked breathing as it kept time with the cuts of the knife, and the brush of his clothes as he rubbed the wall in his movements, for she was so still and quiet, that she did not even tremble. She knew when he ceased, and wondered why, being so well concealed; for he could not see her, and would not fear if he did, yet she heard him move cautiously away. Perhaps he expected the slab to fall – his motive puzzled her, and she moved even closer, and bent her body the better to listen. Ah! what sound was that? "Listen! Listen!" she bade her heart – her heart that had kept so still, but now bounded with tumultuous throbs that dulled her ears. Nearer and nearer came the sounds, till the welcome thud of a horse's hoof rang out clearly.

"O God! O God! O God!" she panted, for they were very close before she could make sure. She rushed to the door, and with her baby in her arms tore frantically at its bolts and bars.

Out she darted at last, and running madly along, saw the horseman beyond her in the distance. She called to him in Christ's Name, in her babe's name, still flying like the wind with the speed that deadly peril gives. But the distance grew greater and greater between them, and when she reached the creek her prayers turned to wild shrieks, for there crouched the man she feared, with outstretched arms that caught her as she fell. She knew he was offering terms if she ceased to struggle and cry for help, though louder and louder did she cry for it, but it was only when the man's hand gripped her throat, that the cry of "Murder" came from her lips. And when she ceased, the startled curlews took up the awful sound, and flew wailing "Murder! Murder!" over the horseman's head.

"By God!" said the boundary rider, "it's been a dingo right enough! Eight killed up here, and there's more down in the creek – a ewe and a lamb, I'll bet; and the lamb's alive!" He shut out the sky with his hand, and watched the crows that were circling round and round, nearing the earth one moment, and the next shooting skywards. By that he knew the lamb must be alive; even a dingo will spare a lamb sometimes.

Yes, the lamb was alive, and after the manner of lambs of its kind did not know its mother when the light came. It had sucked the still warm breasts, and laid its little head on her bosom, and slept till the morn. Then, when it looked at the swollen disfigured face, it wept and would have crept away, but for the hand that still clutched its little gown. Sleep was nodding its golden head and swaying its small body, and the crows were close, so close, to the mother's wide-open eyes, when the boundary rider galloped down.

"Jesus Christ!" he said, covering his eyes. He told afterwards how the little child held out its arms to him, and how he was forced to cut its gown that the dead hand held.

It was election time, and as usual the priest had selected a candidate. His choice was so obviously in the interests of the squatter, that Peter Hennessey's reason, for once in his life, had over-ridden superstition, and he had dared promise his vote to another. Yet he was uneasy, and every time he woke in the night (and it was often), he heard the murmur of his mother's voice. It came through the partition, or under the door. If through the partition, he knew she was praying in her bed; but when the sounds came under the door, she was on her knees before the little Altar in the corner that enshrined the statue of the Blessed Virgin and Child.

"Mary, Mother of Christ! save my son! Save him!" prayed she in the dairy as she strained and set the evening's milking. "Sweet Mary! for the love of Christ, save him!" The grief in her old face made the morning meal so bitter, that to avoid her he came late to his dinner. It made him so cowardly, that he could not say good-bye to her, and when night fell on the eve of the election day, he rode off secretly.

He had thirty miles to ride to the township to record his vote. He cantered briskly along the great stretch of plain that had nothing but stunted cotton bush to play shadow to the full moon, which glorified a sky of earliest spring. The bruised incense of the flowering clover rose up to him, and the glory of the night appealed vaguely to his imagination, but he was preoccupied with his present act of revolt.

Vividly he saw his mother's agony when she would find him gone. Even at that moment, he felt sure, she was praying.

"Mary! Mother of Christ!" He repeated the invocation, half unconsciously, when suddenly to him, out of the stillness, came Christ's Name – called loudly in despairing accents.

"For Christ's sake! Christ's sake! Christ's sake!" called the voice. Good Catholic that he had been, he crossed himself before he dared to look back. Gliding across a ghostly patch of pipe-clay, he saw a white-robed figure with a babe clasped to her bosom.

All the superstitious awe of his race and religion swayed his brain. The moonlight on the gleaming clay was a "heavenly light" to him, and he knew the white figure not for flesh and blood, but for the Virgin and Child of his mother's prayers. Then, good Catholic that once more he was, he put spurs to his horse's sides and galloped madly away.

His mother's prayers were answered, for Hennessey was the first to record his vote — for the priest's candidate. Then he sought the priest at home, but found that he was out rallying the voters. Still, under the influence of his blessed vision, Hennessey would not go near the public-houses, but wandered about the outskirts of the town for hours, keeping apart from the towns-people, and fasting as penance. He was subdued and mildly ecstatic, feeling as a repentant chastened child, who awaits only the kiss of peace.

And at last, as he stood in the graveyard crossing himself with reverent awe, he heard in the gathering twilight the roar of many voices crying the name of the victor at the election. It was well with the priest.

Again Hennessey sought him. He was at home, the housekeeper said, and led him into the dimly lighted study. His seat was immediately opposite a large picture, and as the housekeeper turned up the lamp, once more the face of the Madonna and Child looked down on him, but this time silently, peacefully. The half-parted lips of the Virgin were smiling with compassionate tenderness; her eyes seemed to beam with the forgiveness of an earthly mother for her erring but beloved child.

He fell on his knees in adoration. Transfixed, the wondering priest stood, for mingled with the adoration, "My Lord and my God!" was the exaltation, "And hast Thou chosen me?"

"What is it, Peter?" said the priest.

"Father," he answered reverently; and with loosened tongue he poured forth the story of his vision.

"Great God!" shouted the priest, "and you did not stop to save her! Do you not know? Have you not heard?"

Many miles further down the creek a man kept throwing an old cap into a water-hole. The dog would bring it out and lay it on the opposite side to where the man stood, but would not allow the man to catch him, though it was only to wash the blood of the sheep from his mouth and throat, for the sight of blood made the man tremble. But the dog also was guilty.

"And Women Must Weep"

Henry Handel Richardson

"For men must work"

She was ready at last, the last bow tied, the last strengthening pin
in place, and they said to her — Auntie Cha and Miss Biddons — to
sit down and rest while Auntie Cha "climbed into her own togs":
"Or you'll be tired before the evening begins." But she could not
bring herself to sit, for fear of crushing her dress — it was so light,
so airy. How glad she felt now that she had chosen muslin, and
not silk as Auntie Cha had tried to persuade her. The gossamer-like
stuff seemed to float around her as she moved, and the cut of the
dress made her look so tall and so different from everyday that she
hardly recognized herself in the glass; the girl reflected there — in
palest blue, with a wreath of cornflowers in her hair — might have
been a stranger. Never had she thought she was so pretty . . . nor
had Auntie and Miss Biddons either; though all they said was:
"Well, Dolly, you'll *do*," and: "Yes, I think she will be a credit to
you." Something hot and stinging came up her throat at this: a
kind of gratitude for her pinky-white skin, her big blue eyes and
fair curly hair, and pity for those girls who hadn't got them. Or an
Auntie Cha either, to dress them and see that everything was
"just so"

Instead of sitting, she stood very stiff and straight at the window,
pretending to watch for the cab, her long white gloves hanging
loose over one arm so as not to soil them. But her heart was beating pit-a-pat. For this was her first real grown-up ball. It was to be
held in a public hall, and Auntie Cha, where she was staying, had
bought tickets and was taking her.

True, Miss Biddons rather spoilt things at the end by saying:
"Now mind you don't forget your steps in the waltz. One, two,
together; four, five, six." And in the wagonette, with her dress filling one seat, Auntie Cha's the other, Auntie said: "Now, Dolly,
remember not to look too *serious*. Or you'll frighten the gentlemen
off."

But she was only doing it now because of her dress: cabs were so cramped, the seats so narrow.

Alas! in getting out a little accident happened. She caught the bottom of one of her flounces – the skirt was made of nothing else – on the iron step, and ripped off the selvedge. Auntie Cha said: "My *dear*, how clumsy!" She could have cried with vexation.

The woman who took their cloaks hunted everywhere, but could only find black cotton; so the torn selvedge – there was nearly half a yard of it – had just to be cut off. This left a raw edge, and when they went into the hall and walked across the enormous floor, with people sitting all round, staring, it seemed to Dolly as if every one had their eyes fixed on it. Auntie Cha sat down in the front row of chairs beside a lady-friend; but she slid into a chair behind.

The first dance was already over, and they were hardly seated before partners began to be taken for the second. Shyly she mustered the assembly. In the cloakroom, she had expected the woman to exclaim: "What a sweet pretty frock!" when she handled it. (When all she did say was: "This sort of stuff's bound to fray.") And now Dolly saw that the hall was full of *lovely* dresses, some much, much prettier than hers, which suddenly began to seem rather too plain, even a little dowdy; perhaps after all it would have been better to have chosen silk.

She wondered if Auntie Cha thought so, too. For Auntie suddenly turned and looked at her, quite hard, and then said snappily: "Come, come, child, you mustn't tuck yourself away like that, or the gentlemen will think you don't want to dance." So she had to come out and sit in the front; and show that she had a programme, by holding it open on her lap.

When other ladies were being requested for the third time, and still nobody had asked to be introduced, Auntie began making signs and beckoning with her head to the Master of Ceremonies – a funny little fat man with a bright red beard. He waddled across the floor, and Auntie whispered to him . . . behind her fan. (But she heard. And heard him answer: "Wants a partner? Why, certainly.") And then he went away and they could see him offering her to several gentlemen. Some pointed to the ladies they were sitting with or standing in front of; some showed their programmes that these were full. One or two turned their heads and looked at her. But it was no good. So he came back and said: "Will the little lady do *me* the favour?" and she had to look glad and say: "With pleasure," and get up and dance with him. Perhaps she was a little slow about it . . . at any rate Auntie Cha made great round eyes at

her. But she felt sure every one would know why he was asking
her. It was the lancers, too, and he swung her off her feet at the
corners, and was comic when he set to partners — putting one
hand on his hip and the other over his head, as if he were dancing
the hornpipe — and the rest of the set laughed. She was glad when
it was over and she could go back to her place.

Auntie Cha's lady-friend had a son, and he was beckoned to next
and there was more whispering. But he was engaged to be married,
and of course preferred to dance with his fiancée. When he came
and bowed — to oblige his mother — he looked quite grumpy, and
didn't trouble to say all of "May I have the pleasure?" but just "The
pleasure?" While she had to say "Certainly," and pretend to be
very pleased, though she didn't feel it, and really didn't want much
to dance with him, knowing he didn't, and that it was only out of
charity. Besides, all the time they went round he was explaining
things to the other girl with his eyes . . . making faces over her
head. She saw him, quite plainly.

After he had brought her back — and Auntie had talked to him
again — he went to a gentleman who hadn't danced at all yet, but
just stood looking on. And this one needed a lot of persuasion. He
was ugly, and lanky, and as soon as they stood up, said quite rude-
ly: "I'm no earthly good at this kind of thing, you know." And he
wasn't. He trod on her foot and put her out of step, and they got
into the most dreadful muddle, right out in the middle of the floor.
It was a waltz, and remembering what Miss Biddons had said, she
got more and more nervous, and then went wrong herself and had
to say: "I beg your pardon," to which he said: "Granted." She saw
them in a mirror as they passed, and her face was red as red.

It didn't get cool again either, for she had to go on sitting out, and
she felt sure he was spreading it that *she* couldn't dance. She didn't
know whether Auntie Cha had seen her mistakes, but now Auntie
sort of went for her. "It's no use, Dolly, if you don't do *your* share.
For goodness sake, try and look more agreeable!"

So after this, in the intervals between the dances, she sat with a
stiff little smile gummed to her lips. And, did any likely-looking
partner approach the corner where they were, this widened till
she felt what it was really saying was: "Here I am! Oh, *please*, take
me!"

She had several false hopes. Men, looking so splendid in their
white shirt fronts, would walk across the floor and *seem* to be coming . . . and then it was always not her. Their eyes wouldn't stay
on her. There she sat, with her false little smile, and *her* eyes fixed
on them; but theirs always got away . . . flitted past . . . moved on.

Once she felt quite sure. Ever such a handsome young man looked as if he were making straight for her. She stretched her lips,
showing all her teeth (they were very good) and for an instant his
eyes seemed to linger . . . really to take her in, in her pretty blue
dress and the cornflowers. And then at the last minute they ran
away — and it wasn't her at all, but a girl sitting three seats further
on; one who wasn't even pretty, or her dress either. — But her
own dress was beginning to get quite tashy, from the way she
squeezed her hot hands down in her lap.

Quite the worst part of all was having to go on sitting in the front
row, pretending you were enjoying yourself. It was so hard to
know what to do with your eyes. There was nothing but the floor
for them to look at — if you watched the other couples dancing
they would think you were envying them. At first she made a
show of studying her programme; but you couldn't go on staring at
a programme for ever; and presently her shame at its emptiness
grew till she could bear it no longer, and, seizing a moment when
people were dancing, she slipped it down the front of her dress.
Now she could say she'd lost it, if anyone asked to see it. But they
didn't; they went on dancing with other girls. Oh, these men, who
walked round and chose just who they fancied and left who they
didn't . . . how she hated them! It wasn't fair . . . it wasn't fair.
And when there was a "leap-year dance" where the ladies invited
the gentlemen, and Auntie Cha tried to push her up and make her
go and said: "Now then, Dolly, here's your chance!" she shook her
head hard and dug herself deeper into her seat. She wasn't going
to ask them when they never asked her. So she said her head ached
and she'd rather not. And to this she clung, sitting the while wishing with her whole heart that her dress was black and her hair
grey, like Auntie Cha's. Nobody expected Auntie to dance, or
thought it shameful if she didn't: she could do and be just as she
liked. Yes, to-night she wished she was old . . . an old, old
woman. Or that she was safe at home in bed . . . this dreadful
evening, to which she had once counted the days, behind her.
Even, as the night wore on, that she was dead.

At supper she sat with Auntie and the other lady, and the son
and the girl came, too. There were lovely cakes and things, but
she could not eat them. Her throat was so dry that a sandwich
stuck in it and nearly choked her. Perhaps the son felt a little
sorry for her (or else his mother had whispered again), for afterwards he said something to the girl, and then asked *her* to dance.
They stood up together; but it wasn't a success. Her legs seemed
to have forgotten how to jump, heavy as lead they were . . . as

heavy as she felt inside . . . and she couldn't think of a thing to say. So now he would put her down as stupid, as well.

Her only other partner was a boy younger than she was — almost a schoolboy — who she heard them say was "making a positive nuisance of himself". This was to a *very* pretty girl called the "belle of the ball". And he didn't seem to mind how badly he danced (with her), for he couldn't take his eyes off this other girl; but went on staring at her all the time, and very fiercely, because she was talking and laughing with somebody else. Besides, he hopped like a grasshopper, and didn't wear gloves, and his hands were hot and sticky. She hadn't come there to dance with little boys.

They left before anybody else; there was nothing to stay for. And the drive home in the wagonette, which had to be fetched, they were so early, was dreadful: Auntie Cha just sat and pressed her lips and didn't say a word. She herself kept her face turned the other way, because her mouth was jumping in and out as if it might have to cry.

At the sound of wheels Miss Biddons came running to the front door with questions and exclamations, dreadfully curious to know why they were back so soon. Dolly fled to her own little room and turned the key in the lock. She wanted only to be alone, quite alone, where nobody could see her . . . where nobody would ever see her again. But the walls were thin, and as she tore off the wreath and ripped open her dress, now crushed to nothing from so much sitting, and threw them from her anywhere, anyhow, she could hear the two voices going on, Auntie Cha's telling and telling, and winding up at last, quite out loud, with: "Well, I don't know what it was, but the plain truth is, she didn't *take!*"

Oh, the shame of it! . . . the sting and the shame. Her first ball, and not to have "taken", to have failed to "attract the gentlemen" — this was a slur that would rest on her all her life. And yet . . . and yet . . . in spite of everything, a small voice that wouldn't be silenced kept on saying: "It wasn't my fault . . . it wasn't my *fault!*" (Or at least not except for the one silly mistake in the steps of the waltz.) She had tried her hardest, done everything she was told to: had dressed up to please and look pretty, sat in the front row offering her programme, smiled when she didn't feel a bit like smiling . . . and almost more than anything she thought she hated the memory of that smile (it was like trying to make people buy something they didn't think worth while). For really, truly, right deep down in her, she hadn't wanted "the gentlemen" any more than they'd wanted her: she had only had to pretend to. And they showed only too plainly they didn't, by choosing other girls, who were not even pretty, and dancing with them, and laughing and talking and enjoying them. — And now, the many slights and humiliations of the evening crowding upon her, the long repressed tears broke through; and with the blanket pulled up over her head, her face driven deep into the pillow, she cried till she could cry no more.

Happiness

Katharine Susannah Prichard

Nardadu, grandmother of Munga, was singing as she gazed before her over the red plains under blue sky. Singing, in a low wandering undertone, like wind coming from far over the plains at night:

> *Be-be coon-doo-loo*
> *Multha-lala coorin-coorin . . .* *

She was sitting beside the stockyard fence in the offal of a dead beast. There had been a kill the night before. A stench of blood and filth flowed through the air about her. On an old hide rotting in the sun, a little lizard lay quite still. Nardadu plucked over a length of entrail and set it aside. She reached for another, grey-green, and dark with blood.

A small squat woman, with broad square features, wide jaw-bone, short hair in greasy strands packed with mud and bound by a dirty white rag, she sat there singing, and picking over all that was left of the dead bullock. A gina-gina, blue for a length, almost black with dust and grease, showed her bony legs and feet. Her face all placid satisfaction, the black sticks of her arms and fingers swung backwards and forwards, disturbing flies. Flies clung at the sunken wells of her eyes; but she plucked on over the mess of blood and dung, singing:

> *Be-be coon-doo-loo, coon-doo-loo,*
> *Be-be, be-be coon-doo-loo,*
> *Multhalala, la-la, lala, lala,*
> *Coorin-coorin, coorin-coorin.*

Across a stretch of ironstone pebbles the buildings of Nyedee homestead were clear in the high light of early morning. There were trees round the long white house with verandahs where John Gray slept and ate with his women and children. Megga had

---

* Cuddle your nose into my breast
  And know happiness.

planted the trees long ago, the tall dark ones, those bushes with curds of blossom, and the kurrajongs whose leaves were light green and fluttering just now.

Megga had ridden and worked with John when he first camped by Nyedee well. Tall and gaunt and hard, she had cooked in the mustering and droving camps, driven men and beasts through long dry seasons. Eh-erm, she drove John. He was still her little brother.

Half a mile away, Nardadu could see every plank and post of the verandah; white hens stalking across it; harsh green of cabbages, onions, turnips surging beside the big windmill; the mill, its wheel and long fine lines ruled against the sky; and the little mill on mulga posts with gauge stuck out like the tail of a bird. Kinerra and Minyi came out from the house for water. Slight, straight figures in dungaree gina-ginas, they moved slowly to the little mill. But it was out of order: would not give water except in a high wind.

White hens scattered and flew before Megga as she came along the verandah, Meetchie behind her, John after them both. A shrill screaming and flow of women's voices reached Nardadu; the throb and deeper reverberation of John's voice, as he came between the women, throwing a word or two before him. Small and stiff as chalk drawings her people had made on rocks in the hills, John and the two women rocked and moved with sharp little gestures before the house.

Nardadu knew what it was all about. She had heard that screaming and quarrelling of women and the anger of John's voice so often before. She smiled to herself and went on with her singing. Winding and rumbling through her, on and on it went, the eerie, remote melody. Nardadu remembered her mother singing that song. It did not belong to Nyedee people. Nardadu had brought it with her to Nyedee from beyond those wild tumbled hills which stood on the edge of the plain, north-east. Her mother had sung the little song to Nardadu when she was a cooboo. Nardadu had sung it to Beilba and Munga. Always it came fluttering out of her when she was pleased or afraid.

She was pleased this morning to have found something she could cook in the ashes of her fire to satisfy the hunger of Munga when he came in from the dogging. All the men of the uloo had been out trapping dingoes while John was away. But John was home again, the men would be in soon. The old, high, four-wheeled, single-seated buggy in which John had come from Karara station, with Chitali and old Tommy, still stood red with dust, out before the shed. Horses which had drawn the buggy, rough hair streaked and matted with dust and sweat, were feeding beneath the acacias and mulga, beyond the stockyards.

The little windmill would be mended. There would be the good smell of meat roasted on ashes, in the evening air, down by the uloo. When the men had eaten, talk would be made of dingoes: of wild dogs caught, or too cunning for any trap. Wongana would make a song about a dingo, clicking kylies beside his camp-fire. There would be singing: singing and sleeping in the warm, starlit darkness.

On other stations Nardadu knew, men of the camp would not have gone dogging and left their women at the uloo. Wiah! A curse threaded the words of her song. But Nyedee was not like other places. John Gray left the uloo to the ways of the uloo. Megga? Eh-erm — Nardadu guessed Megga was responsible for that. By her will it was, John did not drink whisky until his legs would not carry him; or take a gin even when old men of the camp sent her to him.

Nardadu did not understand how a woman came to have such power with a man that her will should be stronger than his. But Megga — Nardadu understood something of her and her will, having lived so long with her. Had she not made men of the uloo even wear wandy-warra, and the women grass and leaves from a string round their waists, before there were gina-ginas or trousers and boots on Nyedee? But that John should come under her will so, John who was a man of men! Nardadu clucked and threw out her hands in the native gesture of surprise.

Master he might be of all the country which lay before her old brown eyes, from the wedge of red and yellow purple-riven hills along the west, to those wild and tumbled timbered ridges north and east, beyond which stretched the country of her people and the buck spinifex flats, away and away inland. Yet John he was to her: John the all-powerful to be sure, giver of food and clothing, whose anger and boot you avoided; but who laughed and made fun with you, good-humouredly, when all went well with him.

She had come through the gorge of Nyedee hills with him, how long ago? Nardadu could not count beyond three. "Plenty years," she would say it was since John Gray had first brought cattle through the gorge of Nyedee hills, over there where the great koodgeeda's eyes made a pool of fresh drinking-water. Trembling, she remembered the great silver lidless eye in the shadow of dark rocks. How it had flashed at her, glimmered from beneath the water when she went down with her jindie! They had camped quite near, and Wagola, her man, had sent her down to the pool for water because he said the koodgeeda would not hurt a gin. He had made her sleep on the side nearest the pool, too. How terrified she had been, plenty years ago, when she first came to Nyedee with John Gray!

Wagola, her man, had been speared over there on the range by one of her own people. Wagola's brother claimed her. She had grown Beilba then; and Munga was Beilba's son. Her eyes wavered to the creek gums and burying-ground of the uloo, railed places and mounds covered with bark and branches. Her voice had the shrill anguish of wailing for her daughter.

Now she was an old woman, had bulyas on her hands, and led the women's singing in the corroborees. She had no husband to concern herself about, only Munga, her grandson, who put up her low humpy of boughs and hide. And the cows. Nardadu was cow-woman on Nyedee, drove the milkers from their night wandering on wide plains where the windgrass was yellow, and acacias, in their young green, stood against hills blue as the dungaree of a new gina-gina.

While a coolwenda was putting his slow melodious notes across the vast spaces of hill and plain, and stars were still in the sky, she went scurrying after the cows, and brought them through the Two-mile gate to the yards, red heifers and calves, a huge white cow who charged whenever she got a chance, and the old red bull, lumbering and sulky. Nardadu ruled the cows. A drab gnomish figure in dirty gina-gina and the old felt hat which had been Wagola's, she shambled swiftly over the stones, banging two tins to make the cows hurry: proud of herself, of being on the strength of the station, old woman though she was, cow-tailer.

She had not been away since first she came to Nyedee. She had never been pink-eye; but then none of the Nyedee people went pink-eye. Other tribes came to pink-eye on Nyedee every year. There were corroborees, and youths for hundreds of miles about were made men in the wide-spreading scrub of mulga and minner-ichi which stretched to the foot of the dog-toothed range.

The hut of mud-bricks, baked in the sun, on the place where Nyedee homestead now stood – Nardadu had helped to build that. After its walls were up Megga had not ridden out with the men. She had stayed at the hut to watch the sinking of wells, raising of windmills and stockyards. Every plank was set under her eyes: the windmills, with their great wheels and wedge tails of blue-grey iron, stretched taut against the sky.

Then camels bringing stores and sheets of ribbed iron had come over the creek! Again and again they had come, the great beasts, so savage and evil-smelling, yet led by a little stick through the nose and rope reins, bringing more and more sheets of iron and painted wood, flour, sugar, tea, gina-ginas; trousers, boots and hats for the men who went riding with John, pipes, tobacco and boiled lollies. Such days they were, great days of bustle and excitement, from the first fluting of the butcher-bird before stars paled in the eastern sky, until the sun went away behind the back of the hills.

The first room of mud-bricks was kept for a kitchen and the new house grew out from it, with verandahs, doors, wire cages for rooms. Megga had sent old men, women and children from the uloo to gather white clay in a creek bed, miles away, and had showed them how to paint the house. But to Nardadu, it still seemed, that the long white house among trees had reared itself by magic on the floor of the dead sea. Far out across the plains she had seen a mirage lying across it, reflections of a house in the sky, and had sung her song as a movin against evil, any evil magic could do an old woman by stealing her wits, when she was minding cows by herself, far away from her kin and the uloo of her people.

Megga herself had worn white clothes when the house was finished. The gins washed them, hung them out to dry and pressed them smooth with irons made hot in the fire. She had gathered about herself, too, china dishes and pots which broke when you dropped them, bringing down Megga's wrath as nothing had ever done.

Then the chickens came. Small fluffy creatures Megga had loved and tended until they were neat white hens, which if a dog killed — eh-erm, there was hell to pay.

Nardadu remembered the killing of one of those hens by Midgelerrie, her own dog, a brindle kangaroo hound, as dear to her almost as Munga. There was no better hunter on Nyedee; but he had pounced on and devoured one of those hens. Lowering, Megga, she remembered, had sent John out with his gun and he had shot the dog. John had told everybody in the uloo he would shoot any dog if it ate Megga's hens; but Nardadu had never forgiven Megga for the shooting. She did not blame John. He did as he was told.

Nothing had been the same on Nyedee since the chickens came. Nardadu believed that Megga's hens were the cause of all that went awry on Nyedee afterwards. Nardadu's was not the only dog

John shot because he had eaten one of Megga's hens. The uloo
bore Megga a grudge because of her hens, and the dogs John had
shot for eating them.

It was beyond anything natural to men and women, Nardadu
had decided, the way John and Megga lived in their new house
among the trees, with an abundance of food and clothing, shade
from the sun and shelter from the rain. They looked about them
with pride and contentment. John strutted out from the house to
the stockyards and blacksmith's shop, and stretched reading on the
verandah when he was not away mustering, or on the road with
bullocks for market. Megga cooked, sewed, watched over her
china and sat on her chairs, teaching girls from the uloo to scrub,
polish, make gina-ginas for themselves. Only two of the youngest
gins were allowed into the house, after they had scrubbed their
heads and bodies all over with soap and water, every morning,
and put on fresh dresses. Other women from the uloo were permitted to sweep round the verandah, in turn, or to help with the
washing; but that was all. And always there were new sheds going
up, sheds for harness and tools, a butcher miah, shade miah for
the hens even.

The station was growing and prospering. John and Megga were
growing with the station; but still, there were no children on
Nyedee except children from the uloo who played about the stockyard and woodheap sometimes. Down at the uloo they were
concerned about it. The old women suggested that both John and
Megga should be advised to take a mate. But Megga, it was agreed,
was beyond the age of childbearing.

The men asked John why he did not get a woman. They did not
understand his not having a woman except his sister, who was not
a wife, to live with him. John laughed and said he had been too
busy making the station to think about a wife and family. Men of
the uloo believed what he said. They had seen him so often, after a
day's hard riding, eat, and sleep as soon as he rolled in a rug beside
his campfire. They understood he had thought of nothing but his
station and cattle for years.

But the seasons were good. It rained – how it rained that year!
It had not rained since on Nyedee as it had rained then. Nardadu
herself, and all the other old women in the camp, had gone down
to the creek and beaten it back with green branches when the
muddy water swirled over its banks towards the uloo. They had
been busy patching their huts to keep the rain out. Grass was
green on the plains in a day or so; thick and deep in no time. The
cows grew fat. Nardadu clucked with pleasure over their milk and

calves, thick-set and sturdy. Megga, busy and masterful, directed everybody and everything, looking stouter, more good-humoured, every day. Since the hens and chickens had come, she seemed to have nothing left to wish for.

John went off mustering after the rain, taking all the boys, two or three gins and most of the horses with him. The grass and herbage everywhere made him gay and light-hearted. He talked now and then in easy familiar fashion with Chitali and the boys as he rode along; or when they camped for the night, he by his fire, they by theirs, at a little distance.

They were chasing breakaways in the back hills when the boys came on tracks of wild blacks from the other side of the range. Nyedee boys said these were cousins of theirs. John Gray visited the camp, talked to the old men, and in the evening when Nyedee boys were sitting singing round the camp-fire of the strangers, a young gin was sent to John Gray's camp by way of courtesy to an honoured guest.

Nyedee boys marvelled when she did not return, immediately, as others had always done from John Gray's fireside.

And in the morning, John had presented the old men of the camp with pipes, tobacco, and a couple of blankets.

Somehow Megga heard of it. The boys talked when they got back to the uloo. They told their women and the old men, who chuckled, laughing, and smelling what was to follow.

Megga had been angry with Minyi for breaking a cup. Minyi, to make her angrier and to take her mind off the cup, had told Megga of the gin John kept by his camp-fire that night in the Nyedee hills. Megga was furious. The girls heard her talking to John about it. John had been angry, too, angry and sulky. He walked up and down the fence for hours afterwards. For many nights, he walked the fences, morose and restless. Out on the run it was just the same, the boys said. John did not sleep as he used to: threw wood on the fire half the night, and walked about.

The blacks watched him fight out his trouble. They knew well enough what was the matter with him. His mouth took a hard line. Nardadu had seen John striding backwards and forwards at night, sombre and angry as her old bull when he went moaning and bellowing along the fences, separated from the herd. John scowled at everybody who spoke to him during the day. He could not break the habits Megga had imposed on him; would not drink more whisky than he did usually, or have gins about him. But after he had been south with cattle that year he brought back the kurrie.

She was with him in the old high buggy he had driven over from Karara in; and John looked as pleased with himself as Megga had looked when the new house sat, all built-up and whitewashed, on the plains. He had got what he wanted.

And Megga! Nardadu saw Megga's face, as though by lightning, so bleached and stiff it was. Megga had not known John would bring this other woman with him to Nyedee. He kissed Megga and said:

"I've got a surprise for you, Meg. This is my wife."

Megga did not speak, while the other laughed, saying in a high, singy voice:

"My name's Margie!"

John went on, as if he had done something as much for Megga's sake as his own:

"It was getting a bit lonely for you, Meg, with no white woman to talk to. You and Margie'll be company for each other."

Nardadu could see and hear them still as if they were corroboreeing before her. Megga, fat and dumb, in front of the girl on slight, bare-looking legs; Meetchie — which was the uloo's way of saying "Mrs Margie" — in her light frock and hat, holding a red sunshade: John between them, proud and pleased with himself.

They were delighted with the kurrie at the uloo; delighted and excited by her light, brightly coloured dresses, patterned with flowers; her necklaces, high-heeled shoes, the songs she sang, and the tookerdoo she gave them, sweet stuff covered in brown, sticky loam. John himself stepped with a jaunty kick and swing as he walked; his eyes laughed out at you. Nardadu gurgled and chuckled after him, and men of the uloo were very satisfied. Nobody worked very much in those days; and John was easy to get on with. He went about whistling in a queer, tuneless way. Nardadu had even heard him trying to whistle her own little song:

Be-be coon-doo-loo, coon-doo-loo . . .

How the gins laughed, and he with them, though Nardadu blackguarded him furiously when he took her calves off their milk too soon, so that the kurrie shold have plenty of cream and milk in her tea! Black tea was all the gins ever tasted. But the chatter and giggling round the woodheap where they drank their tea and ate their hunks of bread and meat and jam when it was suspected why John was concerned about milk for the kurrie!

He was angry if Nardadu did not drive the cows through the Two-mile gate. Useless to explain she was afraid of the narlu who haunted the mulga thickets beyond the gate: the narlu who had led Wagola from the tracks and hunting-grounds of his people, along the dog-toothed range. John laughed and joked with her good-naturedly enough; but he would have the cows taken where the grass was good. To be sure, he had sent Munga to mind the cows with her, and such days they had been for Nardadu and her grandson, out there on the wide plains, yellow with wind-grass, or in the dove-grey mulga thickets, under blue skies, she teaching Munga how to pick up tracks, and the movins against evil spirits and bullets; to find water, snare bungarra and dig for coolyahs.

Good days! Only in Megga's face the satisfaction faded; and the kurrie became wan and sickly in the hot weather. Nobody saw her during the day; but in the evening, when the sun had gone down behind the hills, she wandered about the verandah and garden. Wandered, wailing and complaining about the heat, the dust-storms, flies and mosquitoes. Up and down she walked: wept and lamented.

John was very tender with the kurrie in her weakness and sickness; as kind as he knew how to be, trying to soothe her when she cried: "Take me away from this dreadful place, John. I loathe it. Life here, it's so bare, and hard and ugly!" although it hurt him to hear her talk like that about Nyedee. Nyedee, with its wells and windmills, comfortable homestead, garden and bathrooms! What more did a woman want?

Against Megga, though, he would hear no word of complaint. She was mistress of her brother's house; had always been; would always be, he said. She cooked, was storekeeper, accountant, provisioned the parties of well-sinkers, fencers, musterers, rationed the blacks, and saw the gins kept the house clean and in order. There was nobody like her. Two men could not do what she did. She knew every well and windmill and what stock they carried. Megga must go on as she had always done. Meetchie could never do what she did; but she was his boogeriga, his little green parrot, his love-bird.

When Meetchie went away to have her baby the days flowed on at Nyedee as they had always done. Long, quiet days, filled by the riding out, or riding in, of John and the boys with cattle or horses: the arrival and departure of gangs to repair windmills, sink new wells, make fences, while Megga baked bread, prepared the meals, salted meat after the first day of a kill, figured in her account-books, sewed, worked in the garden, read and slept.

Meetchie came back with her baby, bringing cretonne dresses and sweets for the gins. There was a new, older more obstinate look on her face. She did not wail so much or sing so often; but soon the end of the house was regarded as hers and the baby's.

Within a few years there were three children in those rooms at Meetchie's end of the house: one a girl with hair the colour of the tasselled mulga blossom, a little, fleet, wild creature who watched the plains for dust of John's horse when he had been away and ran to meet him when the gins cried: "John comin'!" No horse on Nyedee would have let John take the child on his saddle, or have stood while she flew up by his stirrup; but always John dismounted to meet his daughter, gave his reins to one of the boys, and, catching her up in his arms, carried her home on the back of his neck, his face as childishly joyous as hers.

But Megga and Meetchie barely spoke to each other. Years only deepened the animosity between them, although Megga loved the children as though they were her own; and Meetchie knew she loved them.

As Nardadu looked at it, the house seemed to be cramped down over one of those dark, slimy, fungus growths which poison the air about them. At the uloo, when the women quarrelled and fought together, their shrieks drifted away; bad feeling was lost in a day and forgotten. But there, in the house, misery and bitterness crouched and clung. You knew they were about when you went near the place and saw the women: Megga's face set to her contempt and repressed indignation: the young wife's face moody and resentful.

For ten days' tramping there was no other building like this John had made in the bed of a dead sea: no other house under those wide, blue skies: no other white women to talk to each other but those two.

John left the house to the women as much as possible. He was out on the plains and in the hills for weeks at a time. The shadow lifted from his face as soon as he was out of sight of the homestead, although he cried out in pain and anger sometimes as he slept under the stars.

The conflict which had been going on for years took a step forward when the kurrie seized Megga by the throat with her fierce white hands and would have crushed life out of her had not John come between them. Then Megga had gone to live in the old storeroom near the creek.

Meetchie said she could do all Megga had done. She would cook, manage the housekeeping, order stores, provision the camps, feed the blacks. For months she worked to convince John she could do as well as Megga; but she could not. She had neither strength nor liking for what she had undertaken: she struggled on, overburdened, distraught, screaming at the hens and the gins, losing her soft young beauty, becoming almost insane in her weariness and discontent. John took as much as possible out of her hands. But bread would not rise, store-orders were forgotten, tucker-bags lost. He was cross and impatient. Why couldn't Meetchie have left Megga to run the place as she had always done? The station could not afford to have its work messed up in this way.

And Megga, living alone in her hut by the creek, sat gazing over the plain, day after day, strong, capable hands idle before her; the light gone out of her eyes. Deprived of her work, what had she to live for? She had given everything she had to the station, helping it to grow. She had reared and trained it, as she had John. And the seasons were going from bad to worse. Would it ever rain again? She could see, and John knew only too well, how he would need her to relieve him of all the little odd jobs he did now round the homestead, in the dry season ahead. He would have to be out on the run, moving cattle from well to well, wherever there was a picking, all through the blazing heat and dust storms.

Nardadu could hear them talking over at the house, Megga, Meetchie and John. Their voices came to her, clashing and clanging against each other.

"Your sister means more to you than I do!"

"What is it you want?" John's voice was surly and menacing. "Meg has left you the house. You want her to clear off of Nyedee, is that it?"

Meetchie made a long wail of grievances. Megga was always interfering, setting the children against their mother, and the gins would only do as she said. Meetchie had told Kinerra to catch and kill a hen for the children's dinner, and Megga had said no more hens were to be killed. It was always the same. If Meetchie told the gins to do one thing and Megga told them to do another, they obeyed Megga. "Either she goes or I go!"

"Turn my sister out for you?" John shouted. "Not on your life! She went to the hut of her own accord. But further she shan't go."

John had left the house and was striding across the red earth and ironstone pebbles towards Nardadu.

Beside the little windmill Kinerra and Minyi, who had been listening to and watching the quarrel, turned to get water. There was no wind; the mill-fans hung motionless; Kinerra, climbing wooden stays of the mill, swung the wheel; Minyi pumped, and filled the fire-blackened kerosene buckets. Two slight, straight figures, buckets on their heads, the girls moved slowly back to the house.

John walked to the shed before which the buggy was still standing. Nardadu had her affections, superstitions. They stirred as she watched John coming from the house towards her. His back was straight: he swung along with as steady, direct steps as when she had first known him, although his body had thickened and swelled in the white moleskin pants and faded blue shirt beneath. But the face under his wide hat-brim, fatter, redder, was sullen and heavy now: the blue of his eyes, burned deeper for the years out there on the plains working cattle under bare skies, held only passion and defeat.

The beat of his heels and spurs, as they clicked on the pebbles with a little silver tinkling, made Nardadu shiver. She remembered she should have been away beyond the gates with her cows: that John would shake his fist and yell angrily, if he saw her. Her song quavered into a queer gurgling laughter.

But John did not see her. He was calling Chitali and old Tommy, who had driven over from Karara with him.

Nardadu listened. John told the boys to put horses in the buggy again.

When the buggy drew up before the house Meetchie hurried forward and climbed into it. John lifted the children in beside her. He took the reins and they drove away, Megga, standing on the verandah, watched them go. Nobody called to her. The buggy whirled off in dust.

"Wiah!" Nardadu muttered, getting to her feet. Her instinct, sure and sensitive, told her Megga had won, and lost, in the fight which had been going on so long in John's house. Megga had got back the place and work which was hers and driven the kurrie off.

But John had brought the kurrie to Nyedee because he wanted a kurrie. And there were the children. Had he not loved and played with his children as men of the uloo loved and played with their children?

More than ever now, he would wander along the fences at night, like that sulky old bull from the herd: his face turn to Megga as it did this morning: misery and bitterness crouch under the long, white house, with its back to the blue, wild hills.

Against the sky-film, thin, clear blue, soft as the ashes of mulga and minnerichi, dust moved.

A cry rose in Nardadu's throat. She watched that dust grow against the sky and the edge of mulga scratching the sky. The tagged tail of horsemen swept out from it. Men of the uloo were returning from the dogging.

They swerved in a wide curve towards the stockyards, young

horses before them. Nardadu could see Munga in charge of the
packhorses: Munga on his white horse, ginger with dust, packhorses before him. The bay mare, a bucket lashed to her back,
made for the troughs, and Munga, after her. The swing-in of
dark, slender legs and flying tails through red mist of dust; bodies
of men and horses joined, free-flying, galloping; all wildness and
grace! Nardadu exulted. The horseman her Munga would be! And
how pleased with the meat she had to feed him from her fire that
night, as though he were a man!

The song of her gladness trembled, ranged its high minor notes
and went wandering out to Munga:

Be-be coon-doo-loo, coon-doo-loo,
Multha-lala coorin-coorin.

The Triskelion

Christina Stead

Editor's Note: "The Triskelion" appears in Christina Stead's linked collection of stories, *The Salzburg Tales,* which follows the tradition of *The Decameron* and *The Canterbury Tales* whereby a group of people tell stories to one another. In *The Salzburg Tales* the tellers and audience are a number of people who have gathered together for the music festival at Salzburg. "The Triskelion", like other stories in the collection, has a "lead-in" of discussion amongst the group by way of introduction. Towards the end of the story one of the listeners, the Balkan lawyer, is able to add to it, and some other listeners comment on it.

The Doctress, who tells the main story of the Triskelion, is described at the opening of *The Salzburg Tales,* in a section called "The Personages", as "a Scottish woman from Inverness jolly, fresh-complexioned and round, tall. . . . She had gone into the Government medical service, gave lectures in schools to embarrassed adolescents and taught nose-blowing to kindergarteners. . . . The Doctress preferred scandalous stories and her ideas came out in a slipshod fashion, with an evident intention of pleasing only herself. . . . "

Curiously, the tale of the Scottish Doctress is set first in Australia and later in Vienna. The Australian setting (like the characters) is not overt, except for the mention of Tuggerah Lakes and Terrigal (north of Sydney), where the main part of the story is set.

The sun poured down over the castle of emerald and hornstone: light sounds blew overhead, and thick clouds rose and hung over the distant mountains. Three young, fair-haired, capuchin monks passed along a lower path, while the band in the café in the market-place down below played the "Pilgrims' Chorus" from Tannhaüser.

They sat still, watching evening approach. The Viennese

Conductor then looked at the red sunlight burning on the Doctress's russet hair, and on her white skin, and said to her with a smile:

"Will you speak now, dear lady? Some wild legend from your native country, some incident from the history of that gallant and intelligent people."

"O, I can't bear those Scottish girls with their moppings and mowings, those Lucias, those hielan' lassies," cried the Doctress, fluttered and flushing; "and I have no time for romance: that is my blind spot. Besides, one gets tired of it: people are so romantic in a clinic, but a plate of soup, the removal of the tonsils, or a good day of sunlight, has a curious way of dissipating all these mental fogs and showers of rain. A doctor can't be mystic. Besides, I have always been very matter-of-fact: it's my fault, I admit it. And you wouldn't like to hear a case history, I suppose!"

"Why not?" said the Master, smoothly. "Tell us one of your clinical romances."

The Doctress looked sharply round the group, knotted her brows and after a moment of silence, began to speak in a dry voice. But she presently forgot her embarrassment, as the dusk gathered slowly over the wide landscape and began to soften the faces of her audience.

The Doctress's Tale

Arnold, the blind youth, waited patiently in the Matron's office. From time to time both hands played over the table as if he were reading Braille. The Matron's pen went scratch, scratch, writing in a register. Through the open window came sounds of voices and steps on the gravel drive, but neither moved. Then the sounds were heard in the paved hall, and in a moment the hall attendant opened the door and said: "Matron, Mrs Jeffries, and Mr and Mrs Skelton, come for Arnold." Arnold went directly to the visitors, saying: "Good morning, grandmother; good morning, Aunt Sylvia and Mr Skelton."

He sniffed and said with his thick articulation: "You have got a nice scent to-day, Aunt Sylvia."

"It is only lavender," said the young woman indifferently.

"Smell mine," said the grandmother, drawing a coquettish handkerchief from her bag and flicking its heavy perfume under the youth's nose.

"I can smell," said Arnold, and sat down in his chair, fingering absently the pattern of the tablecloth, waiting till these creatures, supercilious because of their supernatural gift of sight, should think of him again and take him away.

He had been born blind. He had been five years a pupil in the Royal Institute for the Blind and now, at nineteen, having slowly and painfully learned a trade, he hoped to free himself from the bonds natural to his condition. His family was rich, but he wanted to be a workman: in the rare moments when he spoke of himself, he said: "When I am a workman, I will do – so-and-so . . . " imagining a workman to be free, richly paid and respected.

He listened. His grandmother was giving the Matron the address of the bootmaker to whom he was to be apprenticed, and with whom he would board. Mr Skelton said to his wife: "But I think the poor fellow should have a home: an orphan must feel lonely, and then to be always blind, alone in the dark . . . and never to have known his father and mother!" Arnold felt acutely, as the Matron saw dully, the singular look of animosity interchanged between the two women.

"He doesn't feel happy with us, you know that," said Sylvia to her husband. "Besides, how would he get to work?"

"Then with your mother, dear," said the man submissively.

Mrs Jeffries hastened to say: "I'm too old to be bothered with young men at my age."

"At your age? What are you talking about, mother?" said the son-in-law mildly. The boy wondered why these people thought he was deaf because blind, instead of realizing that he was all ear.

They had gone down the long drive to the car waiting at the gate, when Arnold came hurrying back, holding out his arms on both sides, to feel the bushes along the drive. He arrived at the stone verandah where we stood, and queried: "Doctor?"

"Here, Arnold!"

He pressed into my hand something which I thought was a shilling, and started back towards his family. I called: "Arnold, what is this? You have given me your 'three-legs!'"

He hesitated a moment, said: "Take it, take it, Doctor!" and went on.

I smiled, and showed the Matron the round gold medal which Arnold had found one day, long ago, making sand castles on the beach: it bore as device, three legs radiating from a small circle. It had been his pride. After feeling it carefully for days, he had been able to reproduce the design. I said to Matron: "Poor little 'workman'; he is putting away childish things!" The Matron, shading her eyes with her hand, looked at the car moving away and said: "Well, that's the closest family that ever I met: I never got a word out of them about Arnold's parents, or anything else, not even the birth certificate. I suppose there was something wrong with the old lady's son, that the grandson's so queer."

"Your medical report is birth certificate enough," I said sadly.

The Matron said: "I'd give a fair price to know who he is, all the same: there's a skeleton in the cupboard."

"Matron," I said laughing, "your imagination runs riot."

"All right, all right, I've got a long nose," she said, ruffled.

Two years after, the Matron, who had an insatiable curiosity about the seamy side of life, from natural leaning as well as professional habit, showed me a copy of one of the two blackmail sheets the rich lively city can afford to support. *The Public Guardian* had printed the following paragraph: "Mrs Sylvia Charteris Skelton, *née* Jeffries, or Jenkins, heiress to the Jenkins jam fortune, has left home, hubby and mother and gone to spend an indefinite holiday in New Zealand. What's the fly in the jam-pot?" Nothing more appeared on this subject, and the Matron, inconsolable, said: "I'll bet those Jenkinses, or Jeffries, paid up."

I went to see the grandmother to find out what Arnold was doing and found him in her house. Mrs Jeffries, a middle-aged woman of young appearance, formerly pretty and fresh, now showed marks of dissipation: she was clumsily rouged, a little flabby, talkative and had a number of tics which like little animals seemed to ravage her against her will. Arnold recognized my voice but did not move from his seat to greet me. I asked the grand-mother about his health, and, softening over tea, she told me in a whisper that Arnold had been married almost eighteen months; that his wife, a young immigrant servant girl "who married him for his money", had turned him out of the house; and that this event had sufficed to transform the boy completely. He sat about the place in a depressed, dull way, never answered his grand-mother, and scarcely spoke to me. His fingers, not now thinking in Braille, wandered about his person and I saw that he felt the restraints of polite company no more than a dog or bird.

They asked me to see Arnold's wife. I wrote to her with the hope of getting information which would help me to a treatment for him. She told me, cannily, that I might go to see *her*. I entered a small grocer's shop bearing the name Arnold Jeffries, and saw her, a good-humoured, sanguine, hefty little woman of about twenty. "Are you the doctor?" she said when she saw me. She showed me into her parlour, down two steps from the shop, curtained with coarse machine lace, red-clothed, with a canary, and old stuffed chairs, a perfect replica of parlours she must have admired as a little girl in the old country.

She came in without her apron and said cheerfully: "I know you came to ask me about Arnold. Well; I put him out and I ain't goin' to take him back. It would suit me in the business to have a husband with me, but he ain't a husband, he's a — he's sick. I suppose his mother told you he put up the money for the stock here? Well, so he did, and every month, too, I send him what's fair, if there's any profits. Only, I can't take him back."

"Why?" said I.

"Aw," she said, hesitating for the first time, "I just can't, he isn't natural."

"Why do you say that?"

"I really can't explain, doctor," she said, "even to a doctor."

I said: "You mean, he has a certain malady, or is not very strong?"

She opened her eyes. "Oh, no, with me he's very lively, that is, when it comes to kissing and that."

I was astonished now. "What then? Arnold is my old patient: I have known him since he was a child. Perhaps I can improve him, although he can't be cured. And now I am distressed to see him sitting there, half-dead, plucking his clothes. . . . "

She looked upset. Deciding, she said: "Arnold, he — well, I s'pose because he's blind, and can't see like other men, and he's so used to using his hands for eyes (but hands are like eyes that can see in the dark, and no matter where, and go into the smallest corners like a match) — and, why, he can sleep all day if he wants to, but I can't, I've got to run the shop, and if you can imagine what it's like when you never get any sleep. Besides, my family was always very religious and very decent."

I stared at the girl, and suddenly began to smile.

"It's no laughing matter," said the girl, with spirit. "It's a disease — cure it if you say you can. And all day and night his hands would be running, running, like a pyannist doing his scales."

I did not tell this last adventure of Arnold to the Matron. Arnold was now, besides, irretrievably degenerate, and I expected him to die when he reached the difficult age of thirty.

I saw his wife again and told her this. She said: "Do *they* treat him well?"

"Passably."

"I'm making some profits now," she concluded. "I'll give him a fine funeral: there's a funeral parlour down the road does it on time-payment. You let me know: they never would." She wiped her eye, and said: "I mean him no harm."

One day, not long after this, my friend, Kate de Lens Ormonde, the barrister, noticed Arnold's trinket on my bracelet and said:

"The triskelion!" There were tears in her eyes.

She continued: "Pardon my crying over it! I've had the habit since childhood of crying in the presence of the supernatural."

To my blank look she responded, "You shall hear something curious!

"When I was six, we went to Terrigal, and since that time, three things have haunted me in imagination: a wild bull, for there was one loose in the district that could be heard bellowing at all times of the day; a wild boar, for there was one which had eaten a baby in its cradle and escaped and was somewhere in the woods; and third, the Skillion. The Skillion or Penthouse, is the headland which rises from the dark, tarnished lagoon at Terrigal. No one in my family knew what the name meant, and it haunted me and was ranged in my mind alongside the Sphinx, the Chimera, the Beast 666 and the Roc. We lived a month in what seemed to me the gloomy and marshy country of the Skillion.

"When I was twelve my mother took me with my five young brothers to 'Ascalon', a fashionable boarding-house at the Lakes Entrance, at Tuggerah, which is not far from Terrigal. I saw, in anticipation, the familiar landscape drenched with romance.

"Now my mother and her maid were occupied with the little boys, so I had all the day to myself: and in the early morning I left the house, going through the thickets of she-oaks, banksias and ficuses, dwarfed by the sea-winds, and climbing the grass-cobbled dunes which overlooked the mangrove swamps of the upper lakes, and the seven-mile ocean beach. There I often sat all day in a hollow of the sand, returning only at lunch-time and in the evening, half deaf with the everlasting crash of the waves on the sand, the bellowing of cows, the thudding of horses exercised on the flats of the beach, and the perpetual conversation of the winds. The curlews cried by the lake, at dawn and dusk, and nothing was more appropriate to the dreary wastes of sand-rooted underbush, the overgrown shrubbery full of tarantulas, the dreary wastes of the turbulent ocean, always peaked and foamy, and the bleak and ravaged headlands. O, that distant time, happy, morbid, cud-chewing dawn of adolescence!

"The sun set one evening yellow and red over the woods and lakes, purple over the sea and in the eastern sky, bands of purple and red. The wind hurried along the deserted beaches in spirals and eddies, and the rising tide hummed along the shelving dunes. The sun went down with a last pale gleam on clouds torn to

ribbons. The light was lit in the Norah Head lighthouse and
blinked out to sea. I had at that time marvellously long sight, not
blunted and blinded as I am now, reading for examinations. Something moved in the obscurity under the distant head, at first I
thought a buggy, and next it was like a giant turning hand-springs
by the sea; then I saw a wheel with three spokes; it approached
rapidly, and last I saw there were three legs sprouting from a hub,
bound together at the ankles to form a wheel, by a twisted cord,
grey as spindrift, blanched as stranded seaweed, trundling along
at an unnatural rate towards the Entrance. The circumference of
the wheel was about twelve feet: the legs were whitish-brown,
thick and muscular, and all were from the right side. The appearance passed me with the speed of a racing chariot or faster, leaped
over the Entrance and sped into the darkness of the cliffs beyond.

"I sat for perhaps a quarter of an hour, while the swart sea
assaulted the beaches and rammed the dunes. I looked towards
the thickness now enveloping the cliffs of Norah Head to see if
another phenomenon would pursue the first, but there was
nothing, only the long billows still visible rearing far out, and
along the masked beach, waves drawn by the undertows, retreat-
ing from the sand. The white line of foam, invariable warning of
dirty weather, leaped insatiably round the bombora, a mile from
the Entrance, and the yellow lake water still striped the sea. The
stars began to appear faintly in the dishevelled heavens, to light
some grey-headed drop of spume or some belated leaf for a
moment on its unfated way.

"At last I picked up my legs and went home slowly through the
quiet undergrowth. When I reached the house, the gong was ringing for dinner and I went in preoccupied, but without a word: who
would believe me?

"It happened that that night, as the wind made it a little cold,
I went into the great kitchen, which was about fifty feet long, and
was allowed to make toast in front of the ovens. The cover was
removed, and I looked down into the fire, where wood, charcoal
and twigs burned. 'Look, look,' I cried, laughing, 'here is a Turk
with long beard, fierce, with purple eyes: here is a stuck pig
bleeding, here is a judge in ermine and red, and here is a barrister
with his hand lifted, in charcoal.'

"They came to see, the household servants, dinner being finished, the last dishes put in their places, and lassitude filling each
one. 'Yes, yes, so it is,' they said agreeably.

"'You're seeing things,' said my mother's cousin, Rhoda, the
proprietor of the boarding-house.

"'Imagine what I saw this evening on the beach, Rhoda!'

"'What?' she said languidly.

"'On the beach at dusk I saw a wheel made of three legs rolling fast as the wind.'

"'Get along with you,' said my cousin laughing heartily. 'That's an old story: someone told it to you.'

"'No, I saw it plain as day,' I said, and though my eyes were wet with superstitious tears, as now, I made it clear what I had seen. I looked at the flushed faces of the kitchen men and maids on the other side of the great mantelpiece.

"'Something is going to happen,' said Rhoda nervously, and went out of the kitchen. I heard her giving orders in the dining-rooms: 'No one is to promenade along the beach to-night, do you hear? No walks, no fishing, no going on the lake: put up a notice in the hall. Shut up the cows: perhaps they will break loose: there is going to be a storm.' There was a repressed bustle in the company for the rest of the evening, and the young folks, dancing and gossiping, would go off into explosions of laughter about 'General Rhoda', and Carlo, a young fellow tutoring for the University, who had enormous success with the company, told an absurd tale of a 'ghost train with ten bogies'. In the midst of this the loving couples stole out to consult the amiable stars.

"Rhoda was annoyed. She said to my mother: 'It is a sort of phantom: it is called a triskelion, and appears here just before a crime or other grisly accident occurs in the district. I shudder at the mere thought. For example, three brothers and a sister lived in a small house on the other side of the lake, and all were abnormally fat, horribly fat, so that they could scarcely walk. They sent for a quantity of that patent medicine, Antibese, supposed to be a sure cure for obesity: they took it and it made them fatter still, so that people could not bear to go near them, even the tradespeople, to give them food, or the postman with letters – monsters they seemed. The news spread and was authenticated that a young man had appeared to court the sister. He was thin, overdressed and spoke "plausibly", as the people say hereabouts: by that they mean something disagreeable. The brothers refused his demand in marriage and chased him from the door. The woman eloped with him and they were married. It turned out that he was a showman attached to a travelling circus, and intended to earn his living by her. He whipped her (she had a nature as soft as jelly), forced her to appear, and lived meanwhile with the tight-rope dancer. The showman was found murdered in his caravan one morning, and the girl missing. The brothers were convicted, one was hung, and the other two are doing time. The girl has to earn her living now, and under another name she travels with the same troupe. The night the couple eloped, the triskelion appeared on the mud bank in the middle of the lake and was seen by all the passengers in the ferry.'

"'Very commendable of it,' said mother, 'but why didn't it alight on the chimney of the fat people?'

"'Another time,' said Rhoda, 'a man and woman were found hanging from a fig-tree back there in the brushwood. It was supposed that they committed suicide, because they had been vagabonding over the country for months, until every door was sick of them and the dogs were set on them. The night they hung themselves, the triskelion appeared rolling quickly over the sea, and rested for a time like a tired sea-bird on the tops of the wood: darkness fell and it could no longer be seen.

"'A third time was last year, when the bar at the Entrance was thrown up so high that the flood-waters could not escape and the lake was seething here outside the house. In the night I looked out to see the level of the flood waters, and saw the sky flickering with lightning, although there was no thunder. In one of the flashes I saw the triskelion, on the submerged lawn there, by the she-oaks. I went round the whole house, into all the bedrooms, with a lamp to see if anything had happened in the house. The next morning people, and some of mine, were out boating on the rough waters, shooting the races and eddies, when suddenly the bar was broken through by the pressure of waters within, and the flood poured out through the Entrance in a fierce torrent. The boats were whirled over a mile in two or three minutes: they shot through the churning overfall at the mouth and were seen no more: wreckage was found along the beach and on the bombora. Eight persons were drowned that morning.

"'So you see I am anxious,' said Rhoda. 'Perhaps something will happen to the Jenkinses, who are coming late this evening. You know them, Thomas Jenkins, the jam man from Haviland Street. They have taken the large front room with the bow-window. Some of their luggage has come on already. They are staying for a month: and imagine that they have sent on already two cases of whiskey, one of liqueurs, one of champagne, and conserves, biscuits and fruits galore! They think they get nothing to eat here: or else, they expect us to be quarantined when they arrive! Provided they hand it round a little, and are sociable. . . . '

"At this moment we heard the distant siren of the ferry, and saw the lights across the water, now roughened by the rising wind.

The young guests gathered on the verandah under the tossing Chinese lanterns and shouted encouragingly. The Jenkins family disembarked with a quantity of boxes, valises and handbags. They were scrutinized in the lamplight in the usual comic spirit by the established guests.

"Mr Thomas Jenkins, known to everyone present by his jams, was at least fifty years old, prematurely decrepit it seemed, with a small, creased, bearded face, on which a lascivious little smile played. He inclined frequently in conversation towards the person talking and in all ways displayed obsequious manners. Mrs Thomas Jenkins seemed a little over thirty, thickening towards the forty-year, pleasant, partly the conserved coquette, partly the made-over country girl. Sylvia, a self-possessed girl perhaps fifteen years old, sprung up unseasonably, thin like a sapling, and yet large-breasted, moved in advance of her parents and looked to left and right, sizing up the company and her surroundings with composure. She passed before them into the room reserved for them.

"Sylvia had not been in the drawing-room more than a few minutes before the young men had all gathered round her, questioning her and laughing at her sage or cunning replies. They angled with delicacy to know her age, but she replied directly, 'I will be twelve next month: I am always taken for fourteen, at least!' She coughed a little and said she had a delicate chest. The boys, abashed by her youth, looked at that admirably moulded part and said, 'What a shame!' Her father came into the room after a few minutes, and softly, with numerous polite little smiles, called her to bed.

"'Only eleven — what bad luck,' said one: 'such a jolly kid.'

"'I don't believe it,' said Carlo, a puppy Don Juan, chief buck of the troupe: but in a moment to controvert him, the mother appeared, soft, young and pretty, to explain that Sylvia was 'only a baby', and had to rest, and that her father had gone out for a smoke.

"After the first day or two the Jenkins family spent little time with the other guests, walking alone, and even taking meals in its own room. The servants complained first, because they could never make the full tale of dessert knives and plates. There were always several in Mr Jenkins' room. Later the ladies found Sylvia too pert for her age, too indifferent to the dignity of married ladies, and too assured with the boys. And she was dressed far, far too well for a child.

"The mother of a dark-haired, dark-eyed, timid and confiding little girl called Jean, said with despite: 'Imagine that yesterday that child changed her dress three times, I counted: I can't see myself dressing Jean so. That girl Sylvia's a ball of fluff: a nice coquette!' The boys were far from being so severe.

"The Vandenbrighs, family of social distinction, without whom the social columns of the city newspapers could hardly have survived, 'cut' the Jenkinses entirely. My mother, a mild person, said shaking her head, to her maid, as they went over the boys' linen: 'I don't cotton on to Mrs Jenkins at all.' The report spread that 'the whole family drank': the boys said that old Jenkins' jokes, off colour from the first, were now 'too much of a good thing': solemn, excited little girls, guests in the house, brought to their mothers shillings and cakes given them by the old fellow, and were sent flying back to return these gifts. Rhoda said, 'I shan't have them again.'

"One day I lay under the boughs of a little hollow by the sand-hills, listening to the pleasant distant cries of the Vandenbrigh boys, who had a separate pavilion higher up towards the ocean beach, on the border of the swimming channel, on this side of the lake. The breeze rustled intermittently. I heard a prolonged rustling, and looking over my feet, saw Mr Jenkins peering like a satyr through the branches. I sat up and said nothing: I disliked him as if he were a piece of dirty rag. He smiled ingratiatingly and approached. He sat down facing me, cross-legged, and began scraping in the sand between us, in a curious manner. Presently, he took a shilling out of his pocket and offered it to me, without a word. I pushed it away, while my heart thumped hard. His two small eyes were reddish and ichorous, as if they were two little wounds looking on an interior ulcer. I jumped to my feet, murmured some excuse about seeing my mother, and left him sitting there in the little hollow. I did not know why I was scared.

"One night I slept very uneasily, and waking, found myself, although conscious, paralysed. The darkness sat over me like an incubus. I strained from side to side, as I imagined, and beat on the bed, doing all I could to utter a cry that would waken my mother. Suddenly, I heard that cry, a dreadful cry, ringing in my ears. I found myself at the same moment awake, and my mother sitting up in bed.

"'Did you hear that?'

"'Perhaps it was I,' I said. 'I tried to call out.'

"'I thought it came from outside, though.'

"'It was a dog, or a curlew in the swamps,' said my mother's maid, holding her knees, as she sat up in bed, with her curl-papers swarming round her head.

"'It seemed different from a curlew's cry, horrid as that is,' said my mother, discontentedly, 'but it may have been. How I hate those birds. And how I hate this everlasting gush and hiss of the sea, and those swishing trees. What, in heaven's name, possessed me to come to "Ascalon"? I hate nature: it is full of cries and tears like a female madhouse.' She settled herself back in bed, and I heard her sigh and mutter several times before her regular breathing began again.

"In the morning, Rhoda came knocking on our door, to get us out in a hurry: little Jean, the dark-haired girl, had been found in the channel at five o'clock in the morning, by the Vandenbrigh boys and the others, going swimming. She had been murdered, and then thrown in. There was something secret about the business that we could not know. The police had been telephoned, but had to come seven miles by the regular launch, and would take some time to get there. Rhoda was getting the guests up, to be dressed and have an informal breakfast. No one could leave the house. The children spoke in whispers, if they dared speak at all.

"The Jenkins family was also still asleep. Their curtains were drawn and they did not answer repeated knockings. Rhoda said, 'Pigs! They probably drank too much last night: I heard them talking late in their room: well, they've got to get up and look respectable before the police come.' She thought with despair of her lover, who went there for two or three weeks, every six months, getting away from his family to live quietly there with her, in the off-season, on the pretext of a rest-cure. He was a brilliant lawyer, a labour turncoat, and was expected to be Prime Minister at the next change of Government. He could not afford to be involved in any scandal of any kind, nor to visit a house whose reputation was not high. They beat on the door, with irons brought from the stove, and when they had no response, the kitchen-man and the scullion forced the lock, and stood timid in the warm sleeping-chamber.

"Listening, gratified, we heard exclamations and the voice of Rhoda, trying to rouse Mrs Jenkins. They came out leading her, dazed, in her nightgown. Rhoda wrapped her in a rug, saying meanwhile, in a rage: 'Pig, pig!'

"'Get yourself in hand,' said my mother: 'are the others like that too?'

"'The old fellow's lying in there weltering in his blood,' said Rhoda, in a businesslike voice. 'The little girl's nowhere to be seen. Provided she hasn't been murdered too. . . . ' My mother began to moan. 'Why should you cry?' said Rhoda brutally. 'I'm ruined by this affair. Who will come here now?'

"Two days later Sylvia was discovered living in a hotel in a large market town seven or eight miles away. She had given a false name, but her appearance and clothes betrayed her. The mother, confronted with the daughter, accused her of the murder of her father, out of *jealousy*. The daughter, cold and assured, accused the mother! Terrified, the wretched mother immediately confessed that the father and daughter had cohabited for three years, and that the father, growing more depraved with advancing age, had for some time given the masterful Sylvia cause for jealousy. Sylvia at last, breaking down, like the child she was, admitted that she had killed her father in his sleep, 'because he had betrayed her'. She had suspected from his furtive manner that night that it was so; she questioned him adroitly, a past-master in the horrid art, and had proved her suspicions when he fell asleep: she did not know of course that Jean was dead. She had intended to make her way to the capital, and with the money she had taken with her, take a boat 'somewhere'.

"Poor Carlo, tender Don Juan, attended the trial, hardly able to keep calm when Sylvia was attacked and questioned, and when she was proved guilty, saying miserably, 'How she must have suffered, how she must have suffered, to reach that point.' He was perhaps the only person in the whole country that pitied her. She was sentenced to a reformatory for ten years, to be released after that if her family gave proper guarantees. The father of Carlo, a judge, moved by his son's desperate pleas, arranged for her to be allowed to enter a private asylum. She was rich by her father's will, and would inherit the whole fortune when her mother died.

"She had a boy child some months after she went into this house of correction, and the boy was brought up by the widow of the murdered man."

"That boy," said the Doctress, "was unquestionably Arnold, the boy of the triskelion." She looked at the coin which dangled on her bracelet.

"You can bear to wear that dreadful thing?" said a young lady.

"Poor Arnold!" sighed the Doctress. "It is in memory of him."

"I liked to hear your story, both your stories," said the Balkan Lawyer. "There is a sequel to all that, too, which I know by chance. Last year, an oldish woman with her daughter, both widows, it was said, and both rich, came to Vienna and made rather a sensation in the fast set of the foreign colony. There they met Count Winkel, a penniless young man of good family, good looks, and scruples: when I say scruples, I mean he had scruples about the people he took money from; he would not take it from a bankrupt or a beggar, for example! Count Winkel danced attendance on both ladies, determined to catch one and either. They did all the lidos, casinos, and fashionable resorts. They lived *en famille* for a month on a certain islet in the Adriatic, where it is said, no woman can go without losing her virtue.

"The daughter, quite a pretty woman, but delicate, believed that he and she were engaged, wore a ring, and referred to him as 'my fiancé, Cornelius Count Winkel, you know'. They returned to Vienna. She waited for him one afternoon in the public gardens and presently saw him coming towards her, with her mother leaning on his arm. The mother radiant and triumphant, in pink organdie, rushed up and presented, with a little confusion, 'the new stepfather'. The marriage had just been celebrated.

"The daughter said nothing: the next morning the young man received by post the daughter's supposed engagement ring: the girl died forty-eight hours later from an 'overdose of sleeping draught', as they say.

"The inquiry, which brought out these details, forced the newly-married pair to leave the city, and revealed among other things, that the young lady was Mrs Sylvia Skelton, divorced for serious misdemeanours, and the mother, Mrs Thomas Jeffries, a widow. The vice certainly flowered in that family in all its forms!"

"What a three-legged history!" said the Doctress. "I begin to think it will never stop."

"And you can still bear to wear that ornament?" said the young lady, irritably.

"If I throw it away, I am afraid it will start rolling again, making more business for clerks, registrars and judges," said the Doctress seriously.

"There is still time, and it is warm now," remarked the Master. "Philosopher, it is getting dark: you might light us a little way with your lantern."

Short-Shift Saturday

Gavin Casey

It was Saturday morning, so there was only half a shift to do, but the bad taste of underground was in my mouth, and four hours of it seemed a lot too much. There was sunshine on the verandah boards, but it was early, and there was a nip in the air. After the short shift there would be a long week-end to live above ground, in clean clothes. It was hard to get out of bed, but it was good to climb into soft white underclothes and a good silk shirt that would only be taken off for four hours out of the next fifty-six.

Annie was in the kitchen, cold and busy and not too agreeable; and young Bill was out early and up to tricks, as usual. Annie had sleep in her eyes. Her hair was just bunched up out of the way. She was moving about with short steps, in a sort of trot, with her shoulders bent like an old woman who has run about a kitchen getting early breakfasts all her life. She didn't say anything when I came in — just gave me a look and went on with her work — but she went off at young Bill.

"Put it down!" she said. "Put it back, you young wretch. You know you're not to touch the knives."

Young Bill put the bread-knife back on the table. But he gave me a grin and a look as much as to say "You know, dad." Annie saw it, but she never said anything. She usually puts herself in the wrong by trying to translate looks and smiles and winks and talking about them instead of taking no notice. She was too cold that morning and too busy, I suppose.

I hadn't felt hungry with the bad flavour of dirt in my mouth, but the kitchen was full of the strong smell of frying bacon. It cut through the dust and made my mouth water. When Annie dropped the eggs in the hot fat it spluttered like a string of crackers. She put out the butter and cut some good thick slices of bread. I was ready for it, and it was good just standing as near the fire as I could without getting in her way and watching the hot food come out.

The food didn't taste as good as it had smelled and looked, but it was good and hot, and there was plenty of it. I ate bacon and eggs, and young Bill went slow with his porridge, while Annie poured tea and fussed about. "What time'll you be home!" she asked.

She made a challenge of it, like she always does. She has the hot dinner on Saturdays, and I'm generally late. She never *asks* me to come home early, always tightening her lips and sort of shooting the question through them. Perhaps she used to ask one time. But now she gets my back up the way she puts it.

"Oh, about the usual," I said, knowing that was the answer she didn't like.

"You and your usual!" she said. "Three o'clock, I suppose, and smelling like a brewery."

She turned her back and made a great noise with the pans. But her neck was red and angry. "I'll have to spend the afternoon keeping things hot while you make a beast of yourself," she said.

She'd said it all before. She has a bit to complain about, I suppose, and I feel sorry for her sometimes when I'm on my own. But when she's there, talking the way she does, and looking as spiteful as a snake, I can't ever feel anything but the hair bristling on the back of my neck. I want to hurt her, and I'm pretty good at it.

"Skip the dinner if that's how you feel," I said, knowing she'd rather cut her throat. "I'll be home in time for tea, anyway."

"C'n we go down town after tea, dad?" said young Bill. "C'n we go down th' street?"

That was one for her, because she takes him whether I go or not. He always does like me to come in spite of all her efforts to make him satisfied without me.

"Yes, son, we'll go to town," I said.

"If your father's capable," said Annie.

That was a hard thing to say to the boy. What we know, we know about each other, but I wouldn't ever say a thing about her that young Bill might hear and understand. Her coming out with it like that made me feel hot all over. My skin felt tight, as if all the muscles under it were aching to smash her. I couldn't say anything, or, anyway, I wouldn't, until young Bill had finished his breakfast and was out in the yard. I just sat there looking at the little bits of grease and yellow-stained bacon-rind on my plate, rolling a cigarette and waiting.

But by the time young Bill was gone there didn't seem to be any way to start on the matter. Annie had nothing more to say. She went on with the kitchen jobs, working hard and moving fast, her lips tight. She's the kind that makes you mad by always being right, and by working hard and doing her job, whatever other people do. She looked foolish, I thought, scuttling about the room carefully not taking any notice of me. She was irritating, and she was wrong saying a thing like that directly to young Bill. But I didn't want to hit her or hurt her any more. I wanted to get away, to leave her to her job and come back when I felt like it. I wanted to get out with other men − cobbers who took you as they found you and didn't want you to alter your way of living to suit them.

I went through to the bedroom and rolled up a big, clean towel, to use after my shower at the end of the shift. I always take a clean towel on Saturdays, and when I come up the shaft and put on the clean clothes for the week-end I feel a new man.

"You'll miss the tram," Annie called out from the kitchen, so I came out, though I knew there was plenty of time to walk to the corner.

Young Bill was playing about in the yard. He was racing up and down the fence in the track the dog had worn, and Digger was chasing after him, barking. They were both happy, and they looked healthy. Young Bill's legs were a good brown with the sun, and he had plenty of room to run and play in the big yard. He was growing. Up here on the fields he had plenty of sunshine and plenty of good food, as well as room to stretch his legs. It was good for him.

But Annie wanted the coast. There was nothing on the fields for a woman. Brown ground and dust-storms. No beaches, no hills. Early breakfasts one week, lonely nights the next. Nowhere to go. She had been glad enough to come, to regular paydays and a house of her own again; but for all that it didn't suit her. She wanted to get back where the earth was green, where people lived steady lives. Perhaps she didn't want to more than I did, for all that she thought and talked about it more, and was always complaining about the drink.

There wasn't a cloud outside, and though it was early most of the chimneys in the street were smoking. There were plenty of men crunching over the gravel to catch the tram, and there were chaps going off on their bikes to work. It was warm enough now, and would be hot later on, but always the same temperature underground and always the same gloom. All right for those who are brought up to it, I suppose, though many of them don't care for it much.

Tom was coming out of his front gate, and we fell in together. "G'day," he said. "How's tricks?"

"All right," I said. "Looks like a good week-end."

"Good for the first match," said Tom. "They'll get a big crowd tomorrow."

But neither of us was much interested in the football. We walked on without saying anything, and the tram was still three blocks away when we reached the corner. There were a few men at each street, and wisps of smoke from their pipes and cigarettes hung a long while in the still air. They all had towels, a lot of them clean towels to dry themselves for the week-end. There was plenty of talk. But I was thinking about Tom and me and the way we had come to the fields and the luck we had had since we arrived.

The tram was a big one, with two large trailers, and it did not stop, just slowing down for us to swing aboard. We got in the first dummy, and the tram bowled on, making a lot of noise on the worn, broken rails. It slowed at every corner to take a few more men aboard, and there was talk that broke through the clatter of wheels and steel in disconnected bits. " . . . so I says to him, 'money up or shut up', an' he shut up, just like th' bloody squib he is. . . " " . . . reckon th' whisky's old Dick's trouble. If he'd stick t' beer like th' rest of us . . . " " . . . thought I might as well be broke as th' way I was, so I doubled up on Scrivener fer th' fifth. Y' know what *he* paid. Then fer th' last old Johnson's boy says . . . " " . . . I c'n shift more dirt in a day than him, an' I got a fiver . . . " " . . . ain't made over wages since we was shifted. Y' never saw sich ground. . . . "

It was man's talk. Boasts about work and drink and women, things that happened here where the talkers were. It was the talk of men who had plenty to do and plenty to amuse them, who didn't have to speak and think about happenings and matters a long way off. " . . . she ain't got cause to put on airs. One night out at th' Miner's Arms Jim and I went out t' th' back an' what d' y' think we seen? . . . " "ought t' go on th' back line! Ought t' go out o' th' team, y' mean. Why, it's blokes like him . . . "

It had seemed good talk to Tom and me when we first arrived from the coast. Exciting talk suited to a busy, optimistic man's town. But the novelty'd worn off. We just sat there thinking our own thoughts.

We came to the goldfields the cheapest way, of course. Both of us out of work for over a year, and both married men, too. Real mugs, as well; Tom with nothing behind him but a gasworks job ever since he left school, and me with eight years at the warehouse. We started off walking and cadging lifts and odd jobs, but we soon found the best way to get anywhere was to take a ride without asking on a goods. When we tumbled to that we got to the fields in three easy stages.

Most of the people along the line didn't like us. They didn't go much on any of the chaps who were pushing in towards the fields without any kitty. There were plenty on the way, and no doubt it seemed to the people in the towns that they ought to have stayed at the unemployment camps or on relief at the coast. A nuisance, we were. We knew it, but we didn't worry. We got just as hungry as the people in the houses, and we filled our bellies. It didn't take Tom and me long to learn how to go about it. You can get a hand in most towns, and where you can't there are still ways. We learned a lot.

We learned more when we got to the fields. We lived a month in an old boiler behind a foundry, and then Tom had a bit of luck, and soon he worked me in on the Extended. There were plenty of others as good as us who kept on living in old boilers and rusty tanks until the cops got sick of the sight of them, and moved them on. Not that the cops were any harder than they had to be. But you've got to eat, even when you live in a tank. Chaps used to make things out of wire and pester people to buy them. People got sick of it. The chaps got sick of it, too. You get lazy – anyone gets lazy – with little to do, and that little no damn' good. It was just luck Tom and I got a break. We'd get tired of tramping around the mines listening to well-fed jokers say "No". We'd have been shifted on soon, but Tom found someone he knew in a staff job on the Extended. That's the way to do it – find someone you know! And it didn't take him long to work me in.

Those were the best times for a long while when we had both just found jobs. Then we brought our wives and youngsters up. Young Bill was just a baby then, and Annie was different. I suppose I've changed, too. She was eager to come, and I was eager for her. It felt good to be able to look after the pair of them again. I was in good nick, had hardly had a drink for months and was working hard. Annie used to look after herself in those days, and still looked like a young girl. She had no nice clothes, but it didn't need nice clothes to make her look good. But early breakfasts and dust-storms, and I suppose me drinking, have changed her. We don't have many good times now. Not even as many as we used to have at the coast when I was out of work and we were broke.

"We're set," I told her when she arrived. "I'm on good money, better than I got at the warehouse, and they all say this is a good town when you get used to it."

But it hasn't been too good to us. Annie never has got used to it, and, though I get a lot of fun one way and another, I doubt if it's good for me either. We don't jog along too well.

With Tom it's different. He drinks, and he and Clara have their rows. But Clara's different. She gets her trouble over and done with. Doesn't chew on it, and make the most of it, and stretch it out like Annie does. Perhaps that's only how it looks to me. Perhaps Tom could tell different. They look all right.

Tom was quiet in his seat in the tram, and I wondered what he was thinking about. But Tom and I know each other well enough not to have to talk. I looked through the window at the big, putty-coloured dumps with the poppet-legs and smoke-stacks poking out between. A nest of them so big that it made you dog-tired to walk around them looking for work. Underground like a honeycomb. Places that never see daylight. Bad places to work. And the week-end out of them would be just like all other week-ends on the gold-fields! Roam around and drink!

"Well, it's only a short one," said Tom cheerfully as we tramped between the dumps.

"Long enough," said I.

"They ought to cut it out," said Tom. "Waste of time."

I wasn't interested in the job. Not that day. I wanted to get away from it, that was all. We were tramping along a foot-track that wound between the dumps to the Extended change-room, and there were plenty of men, a lot of them going in the same direction. Since the boots had first started treading the path they had worn it down a couple of feet in places. I wondered what fraction of an inch mine had taken off it in five years, and how deep it would be trodden before I was finished with it.

Through the gaps in the dumps you could see workings everywhere. Big stacks and smart painted corrugated-iron, side by side with old rusty buildings and ancient condensers with their pipes twisted everywhere. There were mine-houses, too. Good, large, well-built places, where members of the staffs lived. Nice homes but dumped right in the middle of all the swirling dust that any wind peeled off the great loose piles around. Most of them had high iron fences, in the hope of keeping a bit of it out. They got it just the same. Underground it was just like a honeycomb. They said that if the barriers between leases were down you could walk over a mile from mine to mine. And there were plenty of other places where you'd only have to shift a few feet of earth to get through. Forty years of work for several thousand men, it all was. And they are still digging it out.

I was in a bad mood that day. I'd had a bad week, and though there hadn't been so much said the trouble with Annie in the morning seemed more serious than usual. That's how it seemed in my mind, but I wasn't so filled up with hatred of Annie that I couldn't regret the way things had gone and wonder why it had happened. I could remember when things were different, when we used to have a lot of fun together. It was the mines and the goldfields that were to blame. Perhaps it's all right for those who have been brought up to it, but it's a rotten, unnatural life for a man, and the fields are no place for a woman who has known anything else.

We were getting the money, but I was spending it, too. I must say that Annie always looked after what I gave her. What was the good of the money when you couldn't do any good with it? It would be better at the coast with half the pay. I wanted to get out of the place, but five years were tying me there. I didn't know how to go about it.

It's hard to be gloomy in a change-room. The one on the Extended is as big as a barn, with forms around the wall and racks for clothes above them and the hot showers next door. When Tom and I got there it was full of familiar faces, and bodies with hardly any clothes on, and steam from a leaky pipe, and noise.

As we got our pants on we roamed out into the sunshine to wait for the whistle. Tom and I were among the last, and at the door we ran into old Mace.

Mace was leaning against the wall taking his breath in strangled gasps. He'd found it heavy going uphill through the dumps from the tram. He wasn't white, because the best he could do through his skin was putty colour. "'Day," he said. "Th' boy. Left his clo'es. On the booze. Missus sent me for 'em."

Feeling as I was, I sort of jumped back from old Mace. Like you would from a leper. But, of course, there was nothing that infectious about him. He was just the result of thirty years under-ground. A nice, cheerful sight for a chap that can taste the Twelve-hundred-foot Level on his tongue every morning and can't shake off winter colds! With five years underground behind me, and feeling the way I was, old Mace made my stomach turn.

"Heavy goin', heavy goin' up th' dumps," said old Mace. "I thought it was one o' me good days, too."

Even five years back, when I'd come to the Extended, he'd been a big man, the old fellow. Six feet of him, but not just tall; arms as thick as your thigh, hair all over him, and a neck like a lump of a tree. I'd been his bogger when I started, and he was the chap to show you how to load trucks and unload them, too. He used to get sick of the machine and take a bit of exercise now and again. Never knew there was anything wrong with him. When he went up to the Health Laboratory for the usual examination and they gave him his "First Ticket" he laughed like hell.

"Bin underground thirty years," he said. "Bin examined ten times in th' last ten years, an' now them fellers reckon there's a spot on me lung! Git out o' th' mines be damned! I'll still be handlin' the old Holman on the Extended when that doctor bloke's dead of overstuffin' hisself."

But it got him. Fast. The very next examination they wiped him out for good. No more work on the mines! Out on a pension or a lump sum. He blustered a bit, but he didn't laugh. He disappeared out of the Extended. His boy Dick started bogging on the Twelve a few weeks later.

After that I didn't see Mace often. Just sometimes I'd spot him down at the pub. Moving a bit slower, looking a bit more sallow, dropping a pound or two of weight. With a breath like a bad rise — what I can taste on my tongue of a morning, only worse. A bit short of wind.

But now he was done for. He wouldn't see Christmas. When they talk about a man being all skin and bone they just mean thin. They ought to see someone in the last stages of miner's complaint. Old Mace was pretty near transparent in places. You couldn't help noticing the back of his hands. They still had black hair on them, but they were so bleached underneath that you could see the white flesh through the fur. His fingers were thin, delicate, with brittle-looking nails. His eyes were bright. Too bright. And his breath hooked up in his throat and whistled and wheezed. When he moved about, getting the parcel of clothes his boy had left in the change-room, he put each foot on the floor as if it hurt, and he automatically held on to things. You could smell his breath. Death in it. Something eating him up inside. The air he took in seeped through decay and bad flesh before it got out again. We didn't stay to yarn to him.

"Dirty times, them early days," said Tom. "No ventilation worth having. No regulations and inspections. No anything but dust when Mace did his first twenty years down below. We're luckier. Poor old cow!"

Tom didn't sound quite natural. I reckoned he was trying to convince himself, as well as me, that nothing like old Mace could possibly happen nowadays. I'd shoot myself, I thought, if it happened to me. I thought it the way you think things, not the way you talk them. I thought of Annie and young Bill, and of myself like that. I thought more of how I'd feel than how they would, but I felt bad again.

"The mines!" I said. "They're better, but still not so good."

"Better than being out of work," said Tom.

It was warm enough and lively outside. The surface men had started at seven-thirty, and they were all over the place. The men waiting to go underground sat and lay about like lords and watched them. There were some fitters up the poppet-legs measuring around the cracker, and the sailor gang was on the side of a mullock heap rigging gear for a winch and scoops to shift it. There were chips flying in the carpenter's shop, and in the fitting shop the compressed air was whistling between thuds as the blacksmith's big hammer dropped. Stackers were throwing five-foot bush wood off a line of trucks near the boilers, and the winder was pulling half a mile of cable on to the drums after dropping the first cageful of men to the bottom. A couple of surface labourers were rolling tins of carbide into the store.

The men waiting to go down looked funny. Lordly, leisurely attitudes, and rags and tatters; mostly with felt hats with the brims cut off. You don't need hat-brims to keep the sun out of your eyes down below; but if you go hatless your hair gets a lot dirtier than it has to. All wearing flannels instead of singlets. Flannels are compulsory underground. A lot with nothing on top. Some with old dungaree coats. One or two, going down to the bottom where the water's bad, with oilers on, and boils on their hands from the brackish wet. Tom and I went across to the carbide bin and filled our lamps.

When we got back to the shaft there was a bunch for our level squatting together smoking, and we went across. "Lofty" Tower and Sim Cherry, his mate, and a couple of pipe-fitters who were only putting in a few days there. Also a contracting party that was just about through with the dirty, risky work of putting up a rise, not so far from the face where Tom and I were. Herb Sutton and Joe Webb and Don Bell. A decent crowd.

Coming over, we could see them together in characteristic attitudes. Lofty on the flat of his back, with his hands behind his head, chewing his pipe and stretching pretty near from the shaft to the roasters. Sim prowling about, as restless as the big chap was lazy. The rest on their heels, with their backs against whatever was handy, and the hooks of their lamps stuck in their pockets, except for Don, who was standing up with his feet apart and his thumbs in his belt. They looked good and familiar and friendly as we walked over.

"G'day," I sang out when I was close enough.

They said hello, and I gravitated towards Don. "Well," I said, "you've nearly finished pullin' the ground out on top of you. S'pose you'll be after some easy stuff next time. A possie where there's a bit of fresh air."

But Don didn't say anything. He just looked at me. And when the rest of the bunch suddenly shut up altogether I realized that they hadn't been talking as loud and funny as usual. I realized I'd said something I shouldn't have to Don. It startled me, and I noticed tight skin around Don's mouth. "I'll git plenty fresh air, Bill," he said. "I've got me ticket."

I'd sent in another little punch to follow the big one that Don had already got. I looked at him straight, but I couldn't find the words to say anything that wouldn't make it worse.

"Yair," said Lofty from the flat of his back. "Right out o' the big black holes fer Don. Th' hardest work he'll do in a day after this'll be a bit o' street-corner bookmakin'. Surface fer good! Lucky cow!"

Of course no one thought Lofty really reckoned Don was lucky. They knew how they'd feel. But the long bloke rolled it off his tongue easy, making it light for me, and trying to kid Don it wasn't so serious.

"The best thing that ever happened to y'," barked Sim Cherry. "Tickets don't mean nothin'. Ben Jason went out with th' first bunch twelve years ago. Still drawin' half-pay. Will fer twenty more years."

"It ain't like it used t' be. Them quacks send y' out in time nowadays."

"Y'll git fat, loafin'. That's all that'll happen t' you, Don."

"Take a lump sum, boy, an' git hold of a slice o' ground down in th' hills."

"Remember old Jack Walters? Seen him at the coast last time I was on holidays, an' he reckons gettin' his ticket was th' best thing ever happened t' him."

But they talked fast and nervous, and didn't kid anyone.

"It'll be fast," said Don. "Never got a first ticket. Clean sheet last time, an' wiped off this time."

"If y' drop yer bundle, Don," pleaded Sim miserably. "Y' know it's droppin' yer bundle does th' damage. Y've seen it yerself."

The platman was roaring for us, wanting to know if we thought we were at the Ritz and he was the liftboy. The talk stopped suddenly, like it started, and we went across and piled in, half a dozen of us, chest to chest, and shoulder to shoulder. The cage dropped away and went down with a slither; air whizzed between us and the wet walls of the shaft. The lights on the plats dived up past us, and at one or two of the levels someone let out a cheerful roar. It doesn't take long to drop twelve hundred feet, but in the little time it does take you can think more than you can say in a week. No one said anything. It was the first time in five years that I'd ridden down with a cageful and not heard a word.

Don was a chap I liked. A man I never knew very well out of the shaft, but one I had a feeling for. He was the kind that can stop you from feeling sorry for yourself on your bad days and make even mines look funny. He could always crack a joke when the ground started to talk, or even when it stopped, which is worse. But he'd struck something he couldn't crack a joke about now. A short, thick fellow, well-fleshed. Very strong, he was; and in spite of underground he had plenty of colour. It used to be a treat to see him go cherry-red with joy over something he'd heard or told. It was good to watch him throw his Holman about when he was setting it up, with the muscles in his big arms playing hide-and-seek. It was horrible to think of the meat fading away from him, his broad hands turning into transparent claws like those of old Mace. Don, with feverish, bright eyes, moving carefully, as weak as a baby, and with the stench of death in his breath. The idea nearly made me sick. Physically sick.

At the Twelve the cage stopped. It bounced on the end of its rope for a moment, and we all piled out on to the plat. There was fresh steel there, heaped beside the water-tank. Electric light, yellow and hopeless-looking, shining down on the truckrails and the mouth of the ore-chute to the bin. Mining regulations and bell signals stuck up, but ancient and dirty. Logs and bags, where we sat at crib-time and while we were waiting for the cage. Black mouths of tunnels on both sides of the shaft, with air-pipes lost in the gloom. All in solid rock, the kind you've got to go down a thousand feet to find. A place to work where they can't have the roof half skylights, and where they can't do much more for ventilation than see you get enough clean air to make it only possible, instead of probable, that the dust will get you.

We always have a smoke on the plat before we go in. That day, nobody wanted to. But we couldn't skip it, or Don would know why. We rolled our makings, lit them and stood about waiting for someone to start talking about something.

"Somethin' t' show y' down our way," said Lofty to one of the pipe-fitters. "Bad leak."

"Them pipes was only put in a couple of weeks ago," said the fitter.

"Can't help it. They leak," said Lofty.

"Well, we'll have a look at 'em Monday," said the fitter.

"What's wrong with today?" asked Lofty.

"What th' hell!" said the fitter. "What's it matter to you, anyway? We're takin' it easy this mornin'."

"Matter t' me!" said Lofty. "It matters a hell of a lot t' me. I ain't loafin' fer wages like you blokes. I'm on contract, see? Air means money t' me, see?"

"Bull!" said the fitter. "Them new pipes can't be leakin' that bad you're short o' pressure at th' drill. They're on'y new. Don't be dopey."

Lofty was only kidding them along. He'd found something to talk about. But the pipe-fitter didn't savvy. He started to get sore.

"We're in hard ground," said Lofty. "We need all th' air. Them pipes must've been fitted lousy, anyway."

"Lousy!" yelled the fitter. "I'll bet the bloody leak wouldn't blow up a toy balloon. You talk about air, y' flamin' flamingo! Th' only place you'd ever git enough air'd be if you was sent on top fer good."

It wasn't anything, really; but six pairs of eyes flickered to Don, and the fitter suddenly swallowed his Adam's apple and shut up. It was no good. There wasn't anything to talk about.

Without saying anything, Herb Sutton set off along the rails with a truck, and we all followed him, bar the fitters, who went the other way. We went off into the dark, with our lamps cutting little holes in it, without saying anything more. I saw Don looking up at the rock, and perhaps he was wondering why some of it couldn't have fallen on him some time during the last twelve months. It made me feel bad, the way he looked at the stone when we were going through the big stope. The big stope is a hole in the rock so big you could chuck three or four two-storey hotels in it. But in parts it's low, and the ground's so bad there's half a forest in use holding it up. Don and his mates turned off to reach their job, and Tom and I went on the few yards to our face alone.

"Poor bloody Don!" said Tom.

I didn't say anything.

"She's a cow of a game," said Tom. "Did you ever see anythin' like poor old Mace? Horrible!"

"I remember him before," I said.

"He dropped his bundle," said Tom. "No doubt about it, Sim was right. If they drop their bundles they're gone a million. They don't all go that way. For some blokes th' ticket's just second-class to an easy living."

"For some of 'em it's a ticket to hell," I said.

Tom looked queer and sober in the vague light against the big rocks. "I reckon you're right," he said after a while.

Then we got on with the job without saying any more, and we worked extra hard all that morning, and left it as late as we could to go out to the plat.

It was a bad half-shift. I kept thinking of the way I'd seen Don look at the stone in the big stope. I kept thinking of him working in a rise. In a rise you're driving straight up. Awkward, dangerous work. You're on a flimsy platform, with the machine trying to tear your wrists off, and whenever you start a hole bits of ground flake away and fall on you. You've got to keep an eye on it, and be out from under at times when the bits weigh a couple of tons or so. It was bad ground where Don was, and he wouldn't be in a careful mood. I hadn't liked his look. He might be worse than careless.

I got myself into a nervy state. I thought about Don coming down fifty feet, with truck-loads of black jagged rock on top of him. If he went out that way he'd make a joke of it, if he had a breath left when they dug him clear. It was only the dust he couldn't laugh at. Perhaps he was thinking as I was. Perhaps it would be good if he was.

I cursed the mines, in my mind, and the silent stone that surrounded Tom and Don and myself and all the rest of us. A treacherous mass that blunted steel and resisted all your efforts to overcome its solidness. Until one day it gave a grunt and a mouth opened in it and grinned at you, before the lot of it came down and snuffed you out. Or it played a waiting game. Let you tear it about with fracteur and cart it and haul it and crush it. But it left its poison, the poison you couldn't see, and could only taste in your mouth in the mornings, in the still air.

I got back to Don. I didn't know anything about him away from the mine. I didn't know if he was married, who else he had besides himself. I didn't know much about how he thought, though I'd always liked him. Cheery, that's how we all thought of him. But that was only his main characteristic, not the whole of him. And he wasn't cheery now. He'd dropped his bundle. He was frightened and miserable. And he was putting in his last day underground working bad dirt in a rise! I couldn't stop imagining things happening to Don. I worked with an ear cocked for shouts.

Tom may have felt that way, too. We didn't talk about it, but he toiled furiously. Usually you don't go too hard on a half-shift. He looked more serious than usual. He was thinking about it, along some line or other, anyway.

By the time the watch said we were through our flannels were wet. My forehead was wet, too. We looked at each other and we each knew that the other felt curious and afraid. We finished up, and went out to the plat without saying anything more than a few words. Very matter-of-fact we were. But once we got moving we walked fast along the drive.

Everyone was at the plat except Don and his mates. They weren't saying much. Just sitting smoking. When we came out of the gloom, from the direction from which Don would come, they were all staring hard. They looked disappointed that it was us. We knew how they felt and how they had been thinking. We sat down, too, and made smokes for ourselves.

Then Don and his mates came out, and we all started to talk. We laughed a lot. Some of the things we said weren't very sensible. When they weren't we laughed at each other. Don looked surprised, but after a while seemed to work out something in his mind and looked grateful and pretty miserable.

The shower was good. The change-room was full of men, and all the six sprays in the shower-room were kept busy. We had a lot of fun, the chief joke being to turn on the hot-water tap harder, until steam hissed through some of the holes in the sprays, and anyone underneath jumped for safety. It was a trick that had been worked plenty of times, but never lost its point, in the roomful of naked men, all jumping and sloshing about, and claiming bits of soap, and slipping on other bits on the wet floor. I waited until most of them had finished so I could really enjoy it.

And I did enjoy it. I got the temperature just right, and used plenty of soap. I lathered until I looked like a snow man, and then washed it all off and lathered again. The last time I got under I turned on a bit of extra hot for luck, and it made my skin red all over. Then I rubbed with the good clean towel. I put on the soft clean singlet and underpants, and they felt good, and when I had got into the shirt and a pair of lightweight grey pants, and had brushed my hair, I felt better than I had all day, or all the week, for that matter. I thought about Don a bit, but I couldn't do without my week-end wash, even to feel sorry for him.

Tom got impatient waiting, like he always does. "What the hell are you up to?" he said a couple of times. "You'll rub yourself away."

But he waited all the same, like the good sort he is, and we went down to the pub together.

There were plenty of men still going down the tracks between the dumps, all clean and spruce and ready for the week-end. There were still a few going up to the mines for the short afternoon shift from twelve to four o'clock, but most of them were on the job, and had gone down in the cages that brought us up. We day-shift chaps were all through for the week, and it was good. Some of us were moving along leisurely, making the most of nothing to do, and others were scooting away from the mines as if they didn't intend to miss a moment of their free time. There were young fellows who weren't worrying about the future, or miner's complaint, or the price of gold, as long as they could spend the night with some girl or other, and there were old blokes who had given over worrying about anything. There'd be trots and whippet racing, and pictures in the evening, as well as just walking about the town, but just at present most of us were making for the one place. The pub.

In the night time there's enough on on Saturdays on the fields, and they have the football in winter on Sunday afternoon. But Saturday afternoon's a bit on the dull side. There are plenty of people in the street, but it's no good roosting in the gutter like a shag on a rock. Everyone oozes in and out of the pubs. And there's nothing like getting an early start as soon as you knock off. Anyway, you need a couple of good big ones to wash the taste of underground out of your mouth.

There's only one pub within walking distance of the mines, and there's more money in it than there is in most of the leases. It doesn't have a saloon bar, because it doesn't need one. It only has to cater for pot-size thirsts, and at change of shift the barmen have to move fast to manage it. When Tom and I arrived they were sweating. There were parcels of "blueys", rolled in towels, all over the place, and men five-deep at the counter. There was plenty of noise, since no one on the fields seems to be able to talk as if they weren't yelling down a shaft. We had to wait a while, but then we got in, and put ourselves outside a couple in good style. A pair of twelve-ounce pots tasted all right after the hard half-shift, but insufficient. When we emptied the second, Tom looked at me and I looked at him.

"I think we'll just have another one," said Tom. "Just one more and then we'll go home."

"Only one, then," I said. "We'll only have one more, so we'll make it a sixpence in."

"Don't worry about the zac," said Tom.

We were just kidding ourselves along, anyway. I knew that if it didn't stop at two it wouldn't stop at four or five or six, either. I knew a couple should be enough, and that it would be better for us to get off home. But if you drink a lot regularly you only need a taste and you really want a lot. You want it badly, in a way that makes dinner seem not worth worrying about. The other things you were looking forward to doing don't seem worth worrying about until you've had a few more. In a pub, drinking beer, you don't have any problems, and it's about the only time you don't. A pub is hard to leave. Fellows who have big beanos every now and again, and not very much in between, don't know what it's like when you get used to the steady drinking on the fields. You never get very drunk and you never get very sober when you're not working. Your inside gets a good lining and you don't suffer much from after effects. When you do, it's easy to fix. A hair of the dog that bit you. But you finish up having the whole dog and a few others of the same breed. That's the trouble.

Anyway, the beer was good and we were thirsty. The minutes didn't seem so very valuable, with the whole week-end ahead, so we started on a short course of steady drinking, hanging on to our possies at the bar and letting the mob push about and roar for drinks behind us.

Sam O'Connor and Winch, who worked with Tom and me when we were at the Six, closed in next to me. Someone tossed down a couple of bob, and the four of us had a round together. I was getting enough in me to make me feel good. Enough to make me bright and normal, not drunk. But we went around the four of us and started to do it again, and my belt got tight, and I started to feel warm. The mob around the bar was thinning down, with chaps grabbing their bundles and going off home. I wouldn't have minded getting away, too, but it was a long way to travel in the tram and I was late, anyway. I thought another one or two wouldn't do any harm, and that I might as well be hung for a sheep as a lamb.

"What're you jokers doing tonight?" asked Winch. "Like to come to a party?"

"What sort of a party?" asked Tom.

"She'll be a good 'un," promised O'Connor. "Over at Syd's place. We got an eighteen, and plenty o' bottles coming over."

"Some good sorts," said Winch. "Y' don't even have to bring that along yourself. Three from th' show, and Millie and her cobber from the Metropole."

"Nice work," said Tom. "We better be in it, Bill."

I was thinking hard about the party and I wanted to go, but I wasn't game. I've never had anything to do with women since Annie and I got married, and I didn't know what might happen if I started. I'd bought a lot of drink from Millie's bar, and there's something about her, and they say she doesn't talk. She'd never looked at me as if she didn't like me, and Annie'd done a lot of that lately. I reckoned Millie and I would get along fine at Winch's party, and, if it was easy, so much the better. You lose your enthusiasm for high fences when you grow up. I'd have liked to get Millie out on her own better than at a party, but I'd never do that. I was frightened of the party, too, and what might happen to me and Annie and young Bill if I went. It almost sobered me up, wanting to go to the party and being so frightened of it. "Aw, beer and women don't go well together," I said. "I like 'em one at a time."

"One *all* th' time," said Winch.

That didn't come well from him, standing there, like he does, with his hat pulled over his eyes and his shirt and pants fitting on his lean body easily, without any bulges, like they always do. It's one most of the time with him, too. Only the other one. I might be frightened of it and he might know, but I felt contempt for his sort. Perhaps I felt a bit jealous, too, but I couldn't think of anything to say, and I wasn't going to stand it from him, so I took a crack at his face.

All I did was hit the air, he got out of the way so quickly. I went after him, but Tom got my arms. Tom didn't know what it was all about. He hadn't worked it out yet, and couldn't see any insult. Winch was back against the wall with an empty pot in each hand. "Let me go, Tom," I said.

"Let him go," said Winch, waving his hands, "and I'll put one of these pots through his fat head."

But Tom wouldn't let go. The barman came over and hung on, too, though why they picked me instead of Winch I don't know. The chaps in the bar were all yelling out advice, and they all reckoned that if Winch was a man he'd put the pots down and have a fair go. O'Connor was looking sick and sorry for himself, and ashamed to have been with Winch. But Winch said he'd put the pots down on the nose of anyone who tried to take them away from him. Then, when things got calmer, he threw them both on the floor and walked out, and after a while Tom and the barman let me go.

They didn't know what started the argument, but they all reckoned I was right. I hadn't picked up any pots to start fighting with. We had a couple more drinks, but they didn't taste good. I was glad they hadn't let me get at Winch. You can't settle that sort of argument by punching people on the nose. And Winch was right that I was frightened of women, and that I drank too much. I dare say he was right to grab something hard and heavy to keep off a bigger chap like me, though the mob wouldn't think so. Only I still felt contempt for him. And for myself, too.

I felt sorry for myself all the way home in the tram. Tom had a hunch that his luck was in, and went off to the two-up school, but I didn't want to go along. I don't gamble much. There must be something in what Winch said about it being one thing all the time for me: beer. I was a bit drunk, then, going home in the tram. Not doing or saying anything silly or feeling out of control, but just sweating with a tight belt and a little bit fuzzy and very sorry for myself.

It was no good, I thought. I should have said yes when Winch first suggested the party and there would have been no trouble, and I'd most likely have got to know Millie properly and had a good time. What might have happened wouldn't matter. Perhaps it would be better for Annie and me if there was something like that to make a quick break of it. We were just wearing each other out. I was a bloody fool, drinking and thinking too much. It would have been better if I'd gone to the two-up with Tom. I didn't want to go home. It was after two o'clock and everyone else had gone off somewhere. There was nowhere else to go but home. It wasn't like going home down at the coast of a Saturday afternoon to stretch out and rest and read on the lawn, or go on the river. There was nothing to do here. The week-end I'd been looking forward to had started and I knew I was just going home to loaf about until I got thirsty again and then go out. There was no fun in it. There was no fun in anything.

The only thing to do would be to have it out with Annie. Like I'd had it out with Winch (and with just about as much satisfaction, I thought). What was wrong with me was that I didn't have any guts. Big size and a bad temper, that was all I had. If I'd had any guts I wouldn't have quarrelled with Winch. I'd have gone to his party and had a hell of a good time, and if Annie had ever found out I'd have told her to wipe the sour look off her face if she wanted me to stay home with her. She'd perhaps have respected me more than she did a drunk. If she split with me, who'd care?

Then I thought about the young chap — young Bill — and my ideas changed. You couldn't do anything wrong to a kid like young Bill, I decided, and however low I got I couldn't help remembering that. I could never have gone to Winch's party with young Bill home. I pretty nearly persuaded myself that it was because I'd thought of young Bill that I'd turned it down, not because I was frightened of it. I was drunker than I thought, and I sat on my own, never even noticing who got on and off when the tram stopped, and just feeling sorry for myself, until it reached my street. Then I went along to the house and I was ready for trouble, because I thought I wasn't being treated properly.

The dinner was ready and hot, as it always is, and Annie put it out on a clean cloth. It was a good roast, with vegetable and gravy, and I could tell how good it must be, though I couldn't taste the best of its flavour through all the beer I'd had. Annie didn't say a word. She'd had her dinner and she just moved about, serving up mine, like a restaurant waitress. I didn't say anything, either, for a long while, but I got wild eating and considering how she treated me. That sort of a greeting was different to the one I'd have had from the girls at Winch's party, I thought. I was glad that young Bill had finished his dinner and was out in the yard somewhere, playing.

"Spuds are hard," I said after a while.

"They won't stay soft if they have to be kept," said Annie.

I knew that, of course. I knew it was my own fault, but I was in the mood to look for trouble.

"You can keep 'em without keeping on cooking 'em," I said. "Just keep 'em warm."

"Perhaps I could if I sat over them, watching them, for two hours," said Annie. "But I think I do enough as it is."

"You don't," I said. "Why the hell don't you smile occasionally?"

"You don't give me much to smile about," she said.

It was true, come to that. But I wasn't in the mood to admit it. Things hadn't been going right with me, and I was half-drunk and I wanted to take it out on her. If I'd been sober I'd have known she hadn't had the taste of underground in her mouth that morning, or seen old Mace wheezing his life out in the change-room, or had Don on her mind all through a bad half-shift in bad ground, or made a fool of herself in a row with a rat like Winch. I felt bad afterwards about what I said.

"I could give you plenty to smile about," I said. "I could go out to-night to a meet that'd give you something to laugh at if I wanted to.

It's only because I promised young Bill to go down the street that I'm not."

She got the drift of it and she looked startled. She'd never heard me talk that way before, even when drunk, and for a minute she looked sick and dizzy. She looked bad in her old kitchen clothes, with her hair untidy and her worn face with a helpless, terrified look. Scoring so well wasn't such a good feeling as I'd thought it would be. I felt angry with her and myself, too. I grabbed the paper and went out on to the back verandah.

"Riots in Paris". That was the first heading I saw. What the hell did riots in Paris matter to a man who'd just said a thing like that to his wife for the first time? Nothing in the paper mattered to me. The local news was all rubbish, and seventy-eight deaths in an oil-well explosion in Texas didn't mean a thing to me alongside what was happening to Annie and myself and young Bill there in our own house.

I was feeling more sober after the good feed, but I wasn't feeling good. I dropped the paper on the verandah and sat there on the deck-chair watching young Bill playing. He was building a little goldmine in the corner with tobacco-tins for vats and poppets made with his meccano set, and dumps and little roads all over the place. I got interested. "You need some sheds, Bill," I said. "You need a change-room and a fitting shop and a store."

After a while I went down and showed him where they all went on the Extended, and soon we had a rough little model of the mine, and young Bill was pleased. "Make us underground, too, dad," he said. "Make us underground, too."

"We'd have to get some ants and train them to dig it for us, Bill," I said. "We're not small enough."

He didn't understand and I started to explain all about under-ground. I showed him how we could push a stick into the ground and it would make a little shaft the right size for our mine, but that we couldn't get down it to dig out the levels and make the stopes and winzes and rises. It was too little.

"I'll get the shovel, then, dad," said young Bill, "and y' can dig it out big."

That made me laugh, and then I had to explain why. I got on my heels and started to draw it on the tin fence with the end of a burnt stick. I had the shaft there and I was making a drive. The face I was working on got too far away and I leaned over to reach it with the stick. I shifted my foot, nearly on top of young Bill's poppet-legs, and he let out a yell. Trying to dodge his things I got off balance and fell over on my side.

Annie was on the back verandah and she laughed. She didn't say anything about my falling over, but the laugh said a good deal. Then, when I was getting up, she said: "I'd think you'd teach him about something other than mines. I hope he won't be satisfied with mines."

That was just what I needed to make me get over feeling sorry for her. I knew she was wrong on both counts. I hadn't fallen over because I was drunk, and God knew if there was anyone not satisfied with mines it was me. She'd put it that way that there was no answer, as she often does, but I was right. I was just playing with the nipper and we were both enjoying it. But there wouldn't be any fun in it any more. I went back to the deck-chair on the verandah and young Bill was disappointed for a while, but soon got over it and went on with the game on his own.

I sat in the sunlight watching him and feeling pretty miserable. He was building himself a mine, but most likely when he grew up the only part he'd be able to take in that sort of thing would be on the end of a shovel. All his mother's big ideas, and mine, too, wouldn't keep him off the handle of a banjo if that was what he was suited for. It made me shiver to think of some of the things that might happen to young Bill. A man thinks a lot about his nippers, but if Don, for instance, had any he wouldn't be thinking clear and right about them that day.

Don had slipped out of my mind, but he came back. I didn't know now what I'd do if I was in his position. Not many men's minds are strong enough to come out of a hole like that. Those who ought to shoot themselves aren't game, and those who shouldn't, think too fast and muddled, and go and do it. But I wasn't just thinking about myself and what I'd do. I suddenly felt concerned about Don.

I sweated like I had in the mine that morning when he was somewhere else underground, feeling bad and working a rise in dangerous ground. It hadn't been right to wash and drink and almost forget about him like I had. He'd come up the shaft feeling bad four hours ago, and I didn't know now where he was. What were my troubles compared with his? I had a lot of sympathy for Don. More than I had for Annie, though I can see when I'm thinking clear that I'm not right there. It was just that Don and I were frightened of the same thing.

Sitting there in the sun, with no one about except the boy playing in the yard and Annie away back inside the house, I worked out most of what was wrong with me. And I knew how to fix it, too. I knew how to start and how to keep going, and I worked out some pretty big moves for the future. The first thing for me to do would be to get up and go under the cold shower and stay there until I shivered. That'd do me good, and when I came out I'd have to do my best to grin like I used to five years ago. If I couldn't quite manage it I'd have to keep on making the effort and using cold showers instead of beer, and –

But I never even made the first move. It was hot in the sun and my limbs wouldn't stir themselves. It would be better to think the whole thing out more thoroughly here where it was comfortable and lazy. I was thinking about what I could do when I got back some of the kick I'd had before we left the coast, when I went to sleep and forgot about the lot of it.

You reach a half-dead state sleeping in the sun. The easiest way to get comfortable again seems to be to stay and go back to sleep. You hate every moment of time, creeping back to being wide awake, but you can't turn back. You dislike anyone who tries to speak to you.

I heard Annie saying she wanted some wood chopped, and I saw young Bill standing in front of me with the axe. I didn't like either of them as they stood there trying to get me properly awake. But they were there, and my mouth was dry and all the rest of me wet. I took the axe, blinking in the strong light, and went down to the woodheap with young Bill.

"You carry it up," I said to young Bill. The axe seemed to weigh a ton, and my clean, fresh clothes were crumpled and wet and dirty. I was thirsty. I couldn't remember anything pleasant from before I'd gone to sleep, and the free time I'd looked forward to wasn't turning out well. I might as well be down below, bogging out Tom's dirt, I thought. It's always the way, the things you look forward to go wrong.

"Your tea's ready," said Annie.

But I didn't feel like food. I got more clean clothes and went to the bathroom and had the shower I should have had two or three hours before. The water was fresh and good, and when I came out I felt better. The effect of the drink I'd had was gone and I was ready for a meal.

Annie looked sour, but I didn't care about Annie. I'd got over being angry with her and I didn't feel sorry any more over what I'd said. I looked at her bustling about, and felt sorry for her but not in a personal way. She wasn't having too good a time, but neither was I. Neither was Don Bell nor old Mace.

No one was having too good a time. My young Bill was there, and he was all right. But God knew what'd happen to him later on. It wouldn't be any worse than the things that were happening to most people, anyway. It was a silly way to think, perhaps, but that was how I felt. It didn't make me get cheerful, but I felt less sick of myself. I didn't want to hurt Annie any more, but I wasn't worrying about the hurts she had, either. I felt superior, as if I knew something that not many people did. They said "It'll be all the same in a hundred years' time," but they didn't mean it. I did. I didn't worry to say anything, but I wasn't stopping quiet through being surly. Annie didn't understand. She thought I was sulking, but I didn't care. Then Tom and Clara came in, and I had to get back into the game again.

"We're going down th' street," said Tom. "We just dropped in to see what you were doing."

"We're going down town, too," I said.

"Well, we'll all go in together," said Tom, "and you and I can have a couple while they look at th' shops."

The women were in a clatter of talk before we got started, and to look at Annie you'd never have thought there was anything between her and me or anything on her mind at all. She wasn't worrying, she wasn't hurt so badly after all, I thought. Then I remembered. I hoped no one could see anything wrong with me, and I thought perhaps Annie wasn't as pleased as she looked. The kids were getting together, too, Tom's two and my one. Tom and I lit up cigarettes and went into the front room and talked the way we always do.

"We'll have a quieter time than if we'd gone to Winch's party," said Tom.

"Yes," I said.

"Won't do any harm," said Tom. "A bit o' peace after Don Bell's trouble this morning and then you an' Winch nearly getting stuck into each other at the pub."

"I made a fool of myself," I said.

"Not a bit of it!" said Tom. "You was right. I seen what he was gettin' at and I wouldn't let a squib like him put that over me. You was right."

It was no use going into it with Tom. If I'd said I should have gone to Winch's party he'd have reckoned I was mad after having done what I did. He'd have reckoned it was O.K. to have gone or to have done what I did, but he'd have thought it silly to have been doubtful about it.

"How'd you go at the two-up?" I asked.

"Aw, I got a spin," said Tom. "They only owe me a couple of quid since Christmas now. I was holdin' a score but I dropped most of it."

"Much of a mob?" I said.

"Hell of a crowd," said Tom. "You'd have thought it was payday."

"I should have come out," I said.

"What'd you do?" asked Tom.

"Just hung about the house," I said. "Went to sleep on the back verandah."

"What a life!" said Tom. "I dunno how y' can put in the time doing nothing."

We went on talking that way about nothing very important for a long time. It was easy talk, just like a rest, thinking enough to stop you thinking about anything else, but not enough to overwork your head. We could hear the women outside, and Clara was laughing a lot, like she always does. Annie's voice sounded lively and interested, and I thought that perhaps it was easy talk for her, too. Different to what passes between us two most of the time. The kids were making a row, wanting to be off down the street, and after a while young Bill came into the front room, looking blue. "They ain't going down town, dad," he said. "They reckon it's too late. I told 'em you promised me we'd go down town."

The women followed him in. "It's half-past eight," said Annie.

"We might as well all stop here now," said Clara. "We'd just have to go down and come almost straight back."

"I'm easy," said Tom.

"I want to go down the street," said young Bill.

Young Bill was looking at me, and I remembered what I had promised that morning. Annie was looking at me, too, and I remembered what she'd said. Clara was watching us both as if she knew something was wrong. I got obstinate.

"It's ridiculous," said Annie. "We don't have to go to town just because we intended to. We're more comfortable here."

"I promised the kid we'd go," I said. "We'll have to go in for a while."

"Oh, well, it doesn't matter," said Clara. "We can go in for an hour. It won't do us any harm."

Annie opened her mouth to say something and I was ready to tell her I was "capable" and young Bill and I were going whether they came or not. I'd forgotten about Tom and Clara being visitors. I was ready to walk out and start feeling sorry for myself again, I suppose. But Annie changed her mind and shut her mouth again, and after Tom had grumbled a bit we all got ready and went.

There's plenty of fun in town on Saturday nights for those that
want it. Talkies, of course, and dances for the kids. The place is
bright and crowded and there are long lines of motor-cars parked
outside the shows and plenty of other cars scooting about. There
aren't many places for the drivers to go, but they use a lot of petrol
and from the footpath they look to be having a good time. The
louts hang about on the corners as they do in any town, but on the
fields there seem to be more of them and they seem cheekier.
They look undersized to me, but perhaps they'll grow to be as big
as the chaps I went to school with.

We walked along the street, the bunch of us, and I was thinking
that there were a lot like us. There seemed to be plenty of fun for
the youngsters and for the heads with their motors, but not much
for the married men like Tom and me. The single chaps about our
age were all having a good time, but they were only drinking.
There were plenty of married men with their wives and children
wandering about like us, looking in the shop windows and
wondering what to do next. Every now and again a couple of the
parties would come together. The women would all chatter, and
the men always seemed to stand in the background without much
to say unless they could get away for a pot. The women would go
on and on about their children and their illnesses and the prices of
things and their troubles, and the men — and the kids, too —
would stand about and look a bit silly. But perhaps the women
weren't having such a gay time, either, in spite of all their talk.

Our crowd wandered about, and Tom and I were better off than
most because we were together. The women went on ahead talking nineteen to the dozen and the kids were with us. But we
handed the nippers over for half an hour and slipped into the
Metropole and had four good pots each. Annie didn't approve, but
Clara didn't seem to care much.

"Well, we'll go straight on up the street and back on the other
side and we'll expect you to meet us before we get back," said
Annie.

"Oh, we'll meet them somewhere," said Clara. "It's not such a big
town as that."

It was good in the Metropole, and we sucked the fresh beer into
us and enjoyed it. It was half-time at the pictures and there was a
big, noisy mob in the bar. There were a lot of chaps among them
who'd been there since after tea and were arguing or singing or
just emptying pots and looking dopey. There were a lot of good,
expensive clothes on big blokes with hard, broken hands, and
there were some lads, just old enough to get served by the look of

them, putting on a silly show. Millie wasn't behind the bar, of course, and it set me thinking of Winch's party and what might be going on there. Tom's mind went the same way. "Wonder what's happenin' to Millie now," he said. "How does this compare with Winch's party?"

"Suits me all right," I said.

"A man's a fool," said Tom.

Most likely he was criticizing his own thoughts. It seemed to me he'd hit the nail on the head. A man was a fool, I thought, and the question was, was he a bigger fool for going flat out for a good time like Winch, or for hanging on to the good things that were crumbling up, like I was? Winch or Tom or myself or any of us might get what was coming to us tomorrow. Anyone underground might poke the point of a drill into a live charge or be under bad ground at the wrong moment. Or he may get it the worst way of all, like Don Bell had. I reckoned Winch would fall to pieces if he ever found himself in Don's position. But it gave me a knock to remember that Don was "cracking up", too. I didn't know much about Don out of the shaft, but I knew he was different to Winch. My kind, I'd always thought. It would have been better if it had been Winch who had got his ticket and been left with a wheezy lung to leak some of the cocksureness out of him.

But there was Don rattled and sick and desperate and myself chewing the sock and thinking and thinking and getting into dirty, uncivil moods, while Winch was probably having a hell of a good time. I wished I'd gone after Winch at lunch-time and smashed him up, queered his pitch for a while, anyway, and given him something to think about while his face got back to normal. I should have done it, I thought. But the trouble with me was I never did anything, I just thought about it. I wondered where Don was and if he had any real cobbers out of the shaft who would stick around and kid him along until he got used to the idea of being a crock. I wondered if he had a wife and what she was like. I got a bit of a shock when I realized that inside me I reckoned Annie would be all right in a case like that, even if we weren't running so well together now when things were good. I wished I had known Don better so that I could have picked him up after the half-shift and gone off with him and kept an eye on him. A merry bloke like Don was sure to have plenty of cobbers, but perhaps they wouldn't know; he wouldn't tell them.

We finished our fourth drink and I was still thirsty. I didn't want to go outside because bars are the most cheerful places I know. "Have another?" I said to Tom.

"Hell, no!" said Tom. "Keep out of trouble. We're with the women."

He was right, too, so we went out and picked our families up a few doors down looking at some hats, and I got a nasty look from Annie for being away so long. Clara wasn't worrying. She's not the worrying kind. "Now you'll have to buy us some," she said cheerfully. "You've had your drink, so now you've got to buy us all a spider at Smith's."

"O.K.," said Tom. "I'm easy, only we'll walk about a bit first so Bill and I can have one, too, without spoiling our beer."

We went up the street again and it was a bit quieter. The crowd was back in the pictures and lots of families who had been in the street with young kids had gone off home. There were still plenty about, though, flappers trotting along in dance frocks, louts on the corners and a few drunks, none of them too bad. I hung on to young Bill's fist and wondered what he'd think of his dad if he knew as much about him as I did.

Since things came good during the years when the rest of the country was in a bad way, the main street has turned into a funny place. It's patchy. In between new, modern, well-lit shop fronts there are poky little old places. Some of the old ramshackles have had new paint and paper and are respectable, though different. Nowadays every second shop seems to be a ladies' hairdresser and every third one a restaurant. The drapers' displays are big and flash, and there are plenty of frock shops. The street is wide. The place was planned in the first place for twenty thousand people. It's a well-lit street and a fairly interesting one until you've walked up and down it so often that you're sick of the sight of it.

That's how I was, and Tom was pretty bored, too, though the women were all right, yapping as usual and enjoying the things in the windows. I got thirsty again. I hadn't stopped being thirsty, but it came on me harder than ever and I didn't want to go back and sit in Smith's and drink silly coloured muck with ice-cream floating in it with the family. I'd have to do it, I supposed, but, anyway, it would be over before long and there'd be plenty of time for a couple more drinks before the pubs shut at eleven.

We were wandering along talking about nothing, and when we were getting near the Ballarat I saw there was some sort of trouble going on inside. There was a lot of noise. A copper on the other side of the street stopped walking opposite the pub and stood there waiting for something to happen. It sounded big, and he took a

look up and down the road to see if there were any other policemen in sight. There weren't any, but he didn't go away. He must
have known the town, because he just waited where he was to see
what would happen and if the trouble would blow out before he
got mixed up in it. Then the swing doors of the bar bulged out and
someone inside shot a bloke into the gutter.

The chap reeled over the footpath and wrapped his arms around
a verandah-post to keep himself up. His shirt was half-off and
there was blood on his face and hands. He was a stocky build with
big arms, and fury and beer had equal grips on him. He didn't look
pretty with the dirt and sawdust off the bar floor and blood all
over him, and but for the beer, which wouldn't let him stand
properly, he would have looked damned dangerous. He was roaring defiantly when he shot through the door, and he kept on roaring as he hung on to the post.

It was Don Bell.

"Who says a ticket makes any difference t' me?" he yelled. "Good
as ever I was. Lotta bloody rot. Who says I ain't? Come out 'ere an'
I'll bloody well kill 'im."

"Beast!" said Annie. She turned around to go back, away from
the pub, and even Clara didn't look too pleased with Don Bell.
Only Tom looked at me and I looked at Tom, and each of us could
see the kick the other got out of seeing poor old Don skiting drunk
and ready to defy the whole world and a dirty lung into the
bargain. Tom and I can't get under each other's skin with words,
but Tom tumbles to things so quick it surprises me sometimes.

"What's he goin' to do now, dad?" yelped young Bill, fairly jumping with excitement. "Are th' men goin' to come out an' hit 'im,
dad?"

"Come here, Billy," said Annie.

I wanted to hop in and help Don, and I whispered it to Tom. But
he said no, and he was right. The copper was coming across the
road and Don was heaving himself back towards the pub to kill
someone. Don was swearing and skiting, but he wasn't going to be
much trouble for the John.

"He'll be right," said Tom. "Cooler's th' best place for him."

It was, too. Waking up in jail with a head too big for the cell
never killed anyone yet. It takes your mind off other things.
It would put Don right. I wondered if it had just happened or if
some of his cobbers had filled him with beer and set him on the
warpath for the good of his soul. It was something I'll always
remember as a good sight, seeing Don get chucked out of the
Ballarat and carted off to the boob with blood and dirt all over
him. It made me laugh, though not like you laugh at a joke.

"What fun men get out of making such pigs of themselves I can't understand," said Annie.

That was just it, I thought. She couldn't understand. But I felt good and happy, and I didn't hear much of what was said as we all walked down to Smith's.

Smith's is large and white, with plenty of fans, and the things they sell there generally fascinate young Bill so much you can't get a word out of him until he's finished eating and drinking. But that night he was excited with what he'd seen, or nearly seen. "What'd they done to th' man, daddy?" he asked. "Why was he so wild?"

"Aw, it was just some chaps'd been slinging off at him," I said.

"What was he goin' to do to them?" said young Bill, his eyes goggling. "What was he all wobbly for?"

"Here!" said Annie. "Drink up your ginger beer or mummie will have it."

Young Bill grabbed his glass, but he wasn't going to be put off that way. "What was the policeman goin' to do?" he asked. "Why couldn't we stay an' watch?"

"Because the man was being very silly and not at all nice," said Annie.

"Wasn't he nice? He was funny," said young Bill.

"What a place for a child!" said Annie.

But I didn't think it was worse than any other place. Young Bill would work things out for himself wherever he was. He would think a man's way, not like a woman. I felt sorry for Annie, thinking how she couldn't help but lose trying to keep young Bill thinking the way she did. "The man'd been in trouble, Bill," I said. "He worried so much it made him go out and get a bit drunk and silly."

Annie gave me a nasty look. "It doesn't take much worry to make a man get drunk in this town," she said.

A few hours earlier I'd have taken that badly, but now I didn't feel bad against anyone. I just laughed.

Then Tom paid for the drinks out of the fiver he'd won at the two-up and we all went out. There was nothing to do and it was late. Later than the time the kids usually go to bed. We got out of the bright street, heading for home, and before long Tom had his younger kid in his arms. Young Bill stopped chattering and began to "wobble" like poor old Don had, so I picked him up, too, and he was asleep as soon as his legs stopped moving. There was a high sky full of stars, like there almost always is on the fields.

There wasn't much said. Perhaps we were all a bit tired, like the kids. I'd got back all the punch that had been oozing out of me. My good, clean, soft week-end clothes felt fine and I hadn't any thirst. It was good tramping along, weary, but not too weary, with young Bill solid and warm in my arms. We left Tom and Clara at their gate and had only a few houses to go to our own place. It looked warm and cosy. The dark had rubbed out its drab colours and you didn't notice how bare the yard was in the night time.

Annie went in and switched the lights on, and after I'd put young Bill in his bunk and she'd undressed him without waking him and we were both in the kitchen, I wanted to say something nice to Annie. Only I didn't know how to go about it. I wanted to tell someone all that had been in my mind, but she was busy opening windows, putting out the milk jug, winding the clock. "How'd it be if we all went to the football tomorrow?" I said.

"It'd be nice for Billy," said Annie.

But she didn't think we'd really go. She reckoned I'd get down town and have a few pots in the morning and then want more in the afternoon. I wondered if she'd really like to go. She doesn't like football much, but I guessed she'd rather go there than stop home. Anyway, she thought she'd be stopping home. It was no use using words on her.

We got undressed and tumbled into bed. Through the window I could see plenty of clear sky and I lay thinking. Annie switched out the light and snuggled under the blankets, getting off to sleep as quickly as possible like she always does. I lay there and wanted to tell her all about everything. But it was too big a job. It'd take the night, or half of it. The words were not in me. It was so long since I'd talked to her about what I thought that I couldn't start now.

I remembered when we were first married living at the coast. We'd often talked half the night and let each other know things you could never find words for in the daytime. In those days we'd say what was in us and know each other better in the morning. I couldn't locate the time when either of us had started to change, but we were a long way from it now. She looked after me and she looked after young Bill, and we were both fond of the kid. I was fond of her, too, in a way, but it was different. It wasn't like the old times.

I wanted the old times back but I couldn't get them. I wanted to touch her, to make some sort of contact with her that might help the words to come. But there was so much time between now and the last time I'd spoken that I knew I could never fill it in. I'd grown new ways of thinking, and so had she.

Josie

Vance Palmer

It was drowsy in school that afternoon. We woke up only when
the teacher stopped talking and went out on to the verandah to
speak to a boy who had ridden up on a bicycle. Those who could
see from the back seats said it was young Paton, who worked in
the brickfields near the station. Young Paton, Josie's brother!
There was a buzz of whispering, a scuffle among the class standing
round the blackboard, all wanting to get a look out of the window.
No one was tall enough without standing on the teacher's chair.

When he came back he had taken off his spectacles, and his eyes
had the pale, uneasy look we always noticed in them when the
inspector was about or someone's father was coming to speak to
him.

"You can go back to your seats," he said to the class on the floor.

And then, rapping with his cane on the table and calling for
silence, he began in a queer voice that seemed to come from the
back of his throat, "I have some sad news for you, children. Death
— it is a solemn thought — death has visited our little community
for the first time since this school was opened. You will be grieved
to hear that your little playmate, Josie Paton, passed away this
morning. There will be no more school this afternoon. Those of
you who haven't had your homework already set can leave it till
Monday."

There had never been such quiet in the school before. No one
wanted to move; no one wanted to look round. Even the small
children in the front desks sat as still as if they were holding their
breath to listen to the clock tick. We had nearly forgotten about
Josie. She had been taken off to the township hospital three weeks
before because the nurse said there was no room for anyone sick
down at Paton's. She would be away till the next holidays, they
told us.

It wasn't till we had marched out and were getting our bags from the hooks on the verandah that our voices came back, and then only in whispers.

"It's dip. The nurse said it was dip."

"She never. She on'y said it might be."

"They can't tell at first. You get a sore throat and then it swells."

"I know. It swells till you can't swaller, and then you choke."

"Dip! It ain't catching, is it?"

"Not catching? Oo, listen; he says it ain't catching!"

Everyone wanted to go past Paton's on the way home, yet not to go too near. There it stood by the edge of the railway, a little slab-sided place, with no gutters on the tin roof and a chimney half brick and half wood. There was a dog-leg fence round it and a pepper-tree droooping over the wood heap. No garden. Paton was a ganger on the line, and grew his vegetables on a patch inside the wires, like the other navvies. They brought home sacks of them when they came home from work. And they all lived in bare little houses like this one of Paton's, with no paddocks or yards, though usually there were a few spindly lemon- or peach-trees at the back.

Most of us had passed the place that morning, but now a change had come over it. It had grown quiet and strange; even the fowls, rooting in the dust, looked as if they might know something we didn't. An axe stood fixed in the chopping block near the door. The broken shutter over the front window seemed like a squinting eye.

And though the place was shut up we had a feeling that Josie was somewhere inside. Lurking there as she had a way of doing under the school verandah when the teacher had given her leave to go out. How well we remembered her sitting in the sand, letting handfuls of it filter through her fingers as she hunted for the ant lions that squatted at the bottom of their little pits, and ready to make a face at anyone who caught her!

"Where's Josie Paton?" the teacher was always asking. "Didn't she answer the roll this morning?"

And one of us would be sent out to look for her.

No one had ever liked Josie very much. There was her moony look, her way of cleaning her slate with her tongue, the silly grin she always gave when she was found picking at the lunch in other girls' bags. Often there was a fight about sitting next to her in class. They said she had things in her hair. And more than once she had had ringworm.

But it seemed wicked to think of all that now. Josie would be lying still and cold in her room at the township hospital, her eyes

closed and her face turned to wax. Yet not all of her would be
there. That was what made you feel uneasy in thinking about her.
When anyone died, they said, the spirit was set free. And Josie's
might be somewhere about, able to overhear not only what you
said, but what you thought. It might be in the house, this spirit;
it might be flickering about through the air like a yellow butterfly.
There was something creepy about the Paton's place, with the
broken shutter giving it a watching look, and the fowls staring
one-eyed at the closed door.

All that afternoon the thought of having to die clung to us as we
played about the cow-sheds and down by the creek. Never before
had it come so near, though we had all heard about Bob Sheddan,
the butcher's offsider. He had been frightening to meet when he
was drunk, his eyes all bloodshot and his horse dancing round as
he laid about him with his whip, cutting the cattle coming out of
the railway trucks. But they said that before he hit the ground he
had muttered "God be merciful to me a sinner", and that had saved
him in the end.

"God be merciful to me a sinner." For months afterwards we had
been haunted by these words, wondering fearfully whether we
would have time to get them out if the worst happened. They were
always on the tip of our tongues: they came back to us every night
before our eyes closed: sometimes we gabbled them beneath our
breath when we were running to take off from the high bank at
the swimming-hole or preparing for a jump from the leaning tree
behind the school.

And they were in the air about us now as we trailed round the
paddocks, waiting for the long afternoon to pass, waiting for it to
be time to bring in the cows and get ready for tea. There seemed so
many ways in which death might trip you up. Every black, snaky-
looking stick in the grass made your heart jump; the sleepy
draught-horses by the bails looked as if they might lash out
suddenly and catch you in the stomach.

Overhead, when you lay in the grass, the sky seemed empty and
far away. Eternity? What did it mean? Was there really another
life that went on for ever and ever, without change? And would
there be a meeting-place where you could find your family and
the people you knew, or was there a risk of being left wandering
by yourself as you sometimes were in dreams? If you tried to think
about it you felt the world flowing away from you: you were left
in some soundless place where you were cold, frightened and
hopelessly lost.

And that was not the worst. There were the woodcuts in the

illustrated Bible with the red cover – a world grey-black instead
of dazzling white. Wicked people sitting on thunderclouds adrift
in space; pits of darkness you looked down upon from the peaks of
bare mountains; hordes of grinning figures with the wings of bats
and the feet of goats.

They did not bear thinking about, those pictures. No, you would
lie awake all night listening for sounds in the dark if you kept
thinking of them. It was better to rush about heedlessly, jumping
over every patch of grass where a snake might lie hidden, giving
the heels of the draught-horses a wide berth, and keeping the
magic words ready on your tongue, "God be merciful to me a
sinner." After all, lots of people did grow up to be old, and your
chance was as good as any.

That evening, when tea was finished, mother called us out to
look at the sky. It was filled with small clouds the colour of tinned
salmon, massed together lightly like plucked feathers, but parted
in the middle to leave a path of pearly blue. Far, far away into
another world that path took you. The sun had just set, and there
was a gentle look about everything – the cropped paddocks, the
cows lying by their penned calves, the soft trees touched with
gold.

No one wanted to speak. We were thinking of Josie – Josie
squatting in the dust under the school steps; Josie letting the spit
run down her slate in class; Josie lying now, white as wax, her
hands folded on her chest, in a room that smelt of lilies.

And above were the soft clouds, parted in a pearly-blue opening,
as if they had been brushed aside by a feather, letting the faint
stars show through. Beautiful, it looked, shedding an awe upon
the heart. It was the path, mother said, made by the angels' wings
as they carried Josie up to heaven.

We felt sad and tender about Josie. We were glad the angels
didn't know as much about her as we did.

Trees Can Speak

Alan Marshall

I heard footsteps and I looked up. A man carrying a prospector's dish was clambering down the bank.

"This man never speaks," the store-keeper in the town three miles away had told me. "A few people have heard him say one word like 'Hullo' or something. He makes himself understood by shaking or nodding his head."

"Is there something wrong with him?" I asked.

"No. He can talk if he wants to. Silent Joe, they call him."

When the man reached a spot where the creek widened into a pool he squatted on his heels and scooped some water into the dish. He stood up and, bending over the dish, began to wash the dirt it contained by swinging it in a circular motion.

I lifted my crutches from the ground and hopped along the pebbles till I stood opposite him across the pool.

"Good day," I said. "Great day."

He raised his head and looked at me. His eyes were grey, the greenish grey of the bush. There was no hostility in his look, just a searching.

They suddenly changed their expression and said, as plainly as if he had spoken, "Yes."

I sat down and watched him. He poured the muddy water into the clear pool.

It rolled along the sandy bottom, twisting and turning in whorls and convolutions until it faded into a faint cloud, moving swiftly with the current.

He washed the residue many times.

I crossed over above the pool and walked down to him.

"Get anything?"

He held the dish towards me and pointed to three specks of gold resting on the outer edge of a layer of sand.

"So that's gold," I said. "Three specks, eh! Half the troubles of this world come from collections of specks like those."

He smiled. It took a long time to develop. It moved over his face slowly and somehow I thought of an egret in flight, as if wings had come and gone.

He looked at me with kindliness and, for a moment, I saw the bush, not remote and pitying, but beckoning like a friend. He was akin to trees and they spoke through him.

If I could only understand him I would understand the bush, I thought.

But he turned away and, like the gums, was remote again, removed from contact by his silence which was not the silence of absent speech, but the eloquent silence of trees.

"I am coming with you," I said.

We walked side by side. He studied the track for my benefit. He kicked limbs aside, broke the branches of wattles drooping over the pad that skirted the foot of the hill.

We moved into thicker timber. The sun pierced the canopy of branches and spangled our shoulders with leaf patterns. A cool, leaf-mould breath of earth rose from the foot-printed moss. The track dipped sharply down into a gully and ended in a small clearing.

Thin grass, spent with seeding, quivered hopelessly in a circle of trees.

In the centre of the clearing a mound of yellow clay rose from around the brink of a shaft. A windlass, erected on top of the mound, spanned the opening.

A heavy iron bucket dangled from the roller.

"So this is your mine!" I said.

He nodded, looking at it with a pleased expression.

I climbed to the top of the mound and peered down into darkness. A movement of air, dank with the moisture from buried rocks and clay, welled up and broke coldly on my face. I pushed a small stone over the edge. It flashed silently from sight, speeding through a narrow darkness for a tense gap of time, then rang an ending from somewhere deep down in the earth.

"Cripes, that's deep!" I exclaimed.

He was standing beside me, pleased that I was impressed.

"Do you go down that ladder?" I asked. I pointed to a ladder of lashed saplings that was wired to a facing of timber.

He nodded.

"I can climb ladders," I murmured, wondering how I could get down, "but not that one."

He looked at me questioningly, a sympathetic concern shading his face.

"Infantile paralysis," I explained. "It's a nuisance sometimes. Do you think you could lower me down in that bucket? I want to see the reef where you get the gold."

I expected him to demur. It would be the natural reaction. I expected him to shake his head in an expressive communication of the danger involved.

But he didn't hesitate. He reached out across the shaft and drew the bucket to the edge. I placed my crutches on the ground and straddled it so that my legs hung down the sides and the handle lay between my knees. I grasped the rope and said, "Righto," then added, "You're coming down the ladder, aren't you?"

He nodded and caught hold of the bucket handle. He lifted and I was swung out over the shaft. The bucket slowly revolved, then stopped and began a reversing movement. He grasped the wind-lass, removed a chock. I saw him brace himself against the strain. His powerful arms worked slowly like crank-shafts. I sank into the cold air that smelt of frogs.

"What the hell did I come down here for?" I thought. "This is a damn silly thing to do."

The bucket twisted slowly. A spiralling succession of jutting rock and layers of clay passed my eyes. I suddenly bumped the side. The shaft took a turn and continued down at an angle so that the opening was eclipsed and I was alone.

I pushed against the side to save my legs from being scraped against rocks. The bucket grated downwards, sending a cascade of clay slithering before it, then stopped.

A heavy darkness pressed against me. I reached down and touched the floor of the shaft. I slid off the bucket and sat down on the ground beside it.

In a little while I heard the creak of a ladder. Gravel and small stones pattered beside me. I was conscious of someone near me in the dark, then a match flared and he lit a candle. A yellow stiletto of flame rose towards his face, then shrank back to the drooping wick. He sheltered it with his hand till the wax melted and the shadows moved away to a tunnel that branched from the foot of the shaft.

"I'm a fool," I said. "I didn't bring my crutches."

He looked at me speculatively while candle shadows fluttered upon his face like moths. His expression changed to one of decision and I answered the unspoken intention as if it had been conveyed to me in words.

"Thanks very much. I'm not heavy."

He bent down and lifted me to his back. Beneath his faded blue shirt I could feel his shoulder muscles bunch then slip into movement.

He crouched low as he walked so that my head would not strike the rocks projecting from the roof of the tunnel. I rose and fell to each firm step.

The light from the candle moved ahead of us, cleansing the tunnel of darkness.

At the end of the drive he stopped and lowered me gently to the ground.

He held the candle close to the face and pointed a heavy finger at the narrow reef which formed a diagonal scar across the rock.

"So that's it!" I exclaimed.

I tried to break a piece out with my fingers. He lifted a small bar from the ground and drove it into the vein. I picked up some shattered pieces and searched them in the light of the candle. He bent his head near mine and watched the stone I was turning in my fingers. He suddenly reached out his hand and took it away. He licked it then smiled and held it towards me. With his thumb he indicated a speck of gold adhering to the surface.

I was excited at the find. I asked him many questions. He sat with his hands clasped around his drawn-up knees and answered with eloquent expressions and shakes of the head.

The candle flame began to flutter in a scooped stub of wax.

"I think it's time we left," I said.

He rose and carried me back to the foot of the shaft, I tied my knees together with string and placed my legs in the bucket this time. I had no control over the right leg, which fell helplessly to one side if not bound to its stronger neighbour. I sat on the edge of the bucket clasping the windlass rope and waited. The candle welled into sudden brightness then fluttered and died. I could hear the creaks of the tortured ladder, then silence.

In all the world only I was alive. The darkness had texture and weight like a blanket of black. The silence had no expectancy. I sat brooding sombrely, drained of all sunlight and song. The world of birds and trees and laughter was as remote as a star.

Without reason, seemingly without object, I suddenly began to rise like a bubble. I swung in emptiness; I moved in a void, governed by planetary laws over which I had no control.

Then I crashed against the side and the lip of the bucket tipped as it caught in projecting tongues of stone. The bottom moved up and out then slumped heavily downwards as the edge broke free.

I scraped and bounced upwards till I emerged from a sediment of darkness into a growing light. Above my head the mouth of the shaft increased in size.

I suddenly burst into dazzling sunlight. An arm reached out; a hand grasped the handle of the bucket. There was a lift and I felt the solidity of earth beneath me. It was good to stand on something that didn't move, to feel sun on your face.

He stood watching me, his outstretched arm bridging him to a grey box-tree that seemed strangely like himself.

I thanked him then sat down on the rubble for a yarn. I told him about myself and something about the people I had met. He listened without moving, but I felt the power of his interest drawing words from me as dry earth absorbs water.

"Goodbye," I said before I left him, and I shook his hand.

I went away, but before I reached the trees I turned and waved to him.

He was still standing against the grey box like a kindred tree, but he straightened quickly and waved in return.

"Goodbye," he called, and it was as if a tree had spoken.

The Persimmon Tree

Marjorie Barnard

I saw the spring come once and I won't forget it. Only once. I had
been ill all the winter and I was recovering. There was no more
pain, no more treatments or visits to the doctor. The face that
looked back at me from my old silver mirror was the face of a
woman who had escaped. I had only to build up my strength. For
that I wanted to be alone, an old and natural impulse. I had been
out of things for quite a long time and the effort of returning was
still too great. My mind was transparent and as tender as new
skin. Everything that happened, even the commonest things,
seemed to be happening for the first time, and had a delicate
hollow ring like music played in an empty auditorium.

I took a flat in a quiet, blind street, lined with English trees.
It was one large room, high ceilinged with pale walls, chaste as a
cell in a honey comb, and furnished with the passionless,
standardized grace of a fashionable interior decorator. It had the
afternoon sun which I prefer because I like my mornings shadowy
and cool, the relaxed end of the night prolonged as far as possible.
When I arrived the trees were bare and still against the lilac dusk.
There was a block of flats opposite, discreet, well tended, with a
wide entrance. At night it lifted its oblongs of rose and golden light
far up into the sky. One of its windows was immediately opposite
mine. I noticed that it was always shut against the air. The street
was wide but because it was so quiet the window seemed near.
I was glad to see it always shut because I spend a good deal of time
at my window and it was the only one that might have overlooked
me and flawed my privacy.

I liked the room from the first. It was a shell that fitted without
touching me. The afternoon sun threw the shadow of a tree on my
light wall and it was in the shadow that I first noticed that the bare
twigs were beginning to swell with buds. A water colour, pretty
and innocuous, hung on that wall. One day I asked the silent

woman who serviced me to take it down. After that the shadow of
the tree had the wall to itself and I felt cleared and tranquil as if I
had expelled the last fragment of grit from my mind.

I grew familiar with all the people in the street. They came and
went with a surprising regularity and they all, somehow, seemed
to be cut to a very correct pattern. They were part of the mise en
scene, hardly real at all and I never felt the faintest desire to
become acquainted with any of them. There was one woman I
noticed, about my own age. She lived over the way. She had been
beautiful I thought, and was still handsome with a fine tall figure.
She always wore dark clothes, tailor made, and there was reserve
in her every movement. Coming and going she was always alone,
but you felt that that was by her own choice, that everything she
did was by her own steady choice. She walked up the steps so
firmly, and vanished so resolutely into the discreet muteness of
the building opposite, that I felt a faint, a very faint, envy of anyone who appeared to have her life so perfectly under control.

There was a day much warmer than anything we had had, a
still, warm, milky day. I saw as soon as I got up that the window
opposite was open a few inches, "Spring comes even to the careful
heart," I thought. And the next morning not only was the window
open but there was a row of persimmons set out carefully and
precisely on the sill, to ripen in the sun. Shaped like a young
woman's breasts their deep, rich, golden-orange colour seemed
just the highlight that the morning's spring tranquillity needed.
It was almost a shock to me to see them there. I remembered at
home when I was a child there was a grove of persimmon trees
down one side of the house. In the autumn they had blazed deep
red, taking your breath away. They cast a rosy light into rooms on
that side of the house as if a fire were burning outside. Then the
leaves fell and left the pointed dark gold fruit clinging to the bare
branches. They never lost their strangeness – magical, Hesperi-
dean trees. When I saw the Fire Bird danced my heart moved
painfully because I remembered the persimmon trees in the early
morning against the dark windbreak of the loquats. Why did I
always think of autumn in springtime?

Persimmons belong to autumn and this was spring. I went to the
window to look again. Yes, they were there, they were real. I had
not imagined them, autumn fruit warming to a ripe transparency
in the spring sunshine. They must have come, expensively packed
in sawdust, from California or have lain all winter in storage. Fruit
out of season.

It was later in the day when the sun had left the sill that I saw the window opened and a hand come out to gather the persimmons. I saw a woman's figure against the curtains. *She* lived there. It was her window opposite mine.

Often now the window was open. That in itself was like the breaking of a bud. A bowl of thick cream pottery, shaped like a boat, appeared on the sill. It was planted, I think, with bulbs. She used to water it with one of those tiny, long-spouted, hand-painted cans that you use for refilling vases, and I saw her gingerly loosening the earth with a silver table fork. She didn't look up or across the street. Not once.

Sometimes on my leisurely walks I passed her in the street. I knew her quite well now, the texture of her skin, her hands, the set of her clothes, her movements. The way you know people when you are sure you will never be put to the test of speaking to them. I could have found out her name quite easily. I had only to walk into the vestibule of her block and read it in the list of tenants, or consult the visiting card on her door. I never did.

She was a lonely woman and so was I. That was a barrier, not a link. Lonely women have something to guard. I was not exactly lonely. I had stood my life on a shelf, that was all. I could have had a dozen friends round me all day long. But there wasn't a friend that I loved and trusted above all the others, no lover, secret or declared. She had, I suppose, some nutrient hinterland on which she drew.

The bulbs in her bowl were shooting. I could see the pale new-green spears standing out of the dark loam. I was quite interested in them, wondered what they would be. I expected tulips, I don't know why. Her window was open all day long now, very fine thin curtains hung in front of it and these were never parted. Sometimes they moved but it was only in the breeze.

The trees in the street showed green now, thick with budded leaves. The shadow pattern on my wall was intricate and rich. It was no longer an austere winter pattern as it had been at first. Even the movement of the branches in the wind seemed different. I used to lie looking at the shadow when I rested in the afternoon. I was always tired then and so more permeable to impressions. I'd think about the buds, how pale and tender they were, but how implacable. The way an unborn child is implacable. If man's world were in ashes the spring would still come. I watched the moving pattern and my heart stirred with it in frail, half-sweet melancholy.

One afternoon I looked out instead of in. It was growing late and the sun would soon be gone, but it was warm. There was gold dust in the air, the sunlight had thickened. The shadows of trees and buildings fell, as they sometimes do on a fortunate day, with dramatic grace. *She* was standing there just behind the curtains, in a long dark wrap, as if she had come from her bath and was going to dress, early, for the evening. She stood so long and so still, staring out – at the budding trees, I thought – that tension began to accumulate in my mind. My blood ticked like a clock. Very slowly she raised her arms and the gown fell from her. She stood there naked, behind the veil of the curtains, the scarcely distinguishable but unmistakeable form of a woman whose face was in shadow.

I turned away. The shadow of the burgeoning bough was on the white wall. I thought my heart would break.

Mother

Judah Waten

When I was a small boy I was often morbidly conscious of
Mother's intent, searching eyes fixed on me. She would gaze for
minutes on end without speaking one word. I was always dis-
concerted and would guiltily look down at the ground, anxiously
turning over in my mind my day's activities.

But very early I knew her thoughts were far away from my
petty doings; she was concerned with them only in so far as they
gave her further reason to justify her hostility to the life around
us. She was preoccupied with my sister and me; she was for ever
concerned with our future in this new land in which she would
always feel a stranger.

I gave her little comfort, for though we had been in the country
for only a short while I had assumed many of the ways of those
around me. I had become estranged from her. Or so it seemed to
Mother, and it grieved her.

When I first knew her she had no intimate friend, nor do I think
she felt the need of one with whom she could discuss her inner-
most thoughts and hopes. With me, though I knew she loved me
very deeply, she was never on such near terms of friendship as
sometimes exist between a mother and son. She emanated a kind
of certainty in herself, in her view of life, that no opposition or
human difficulty could shrivel or destroy. "Be strong before
people, only weep before God," she would say and she lived up to
that precept even with Father.

In our little community in the city, acquaintances spoke deris-
ively of Mother's refusal to settle down as others had done, of
what they called her propensity for highfalutin day-dreams and of
the severity and unreasonableness of her opinions.

Yet her manner with people was always gentle. She spoke
softly, she was measured in gesture, and frequently it seemed she
was functioning automatically, her mind far away from her body.

There was a grave beauty in her still, sad face, her searching, dark-brown eyes and black hair. She was thin and stooped in carriage as though a weight always lay on her shoulders.

From my earliest memory of Mother it somehow seemed quite natural to think of her as apart and other-worldly and different, not of everyday things as Father was. In those days he was a young-looking man who did not hesitate to make friends with children as soon as they were able to talk to him and laugh at his stories. Mother was older than he was. She must have been a woman of nearly forty, but she seemed even older. She changed little for a long time, showing no traces of growing older at all until, towards the end of her life, she suddenly became an old lady.

I was always curious about Mother's age. She never had birthdays like other people, nor did anyone else in our family. No candles were ever lit or cakes baked or presents given in our house. To my friends in the street who boasted of their birthday parties I self-consciously repeated my Mother's words, that such celebrations were only a foolish and eccentric form of self-worship.

"Nothing but deception," she would say. "As though life can be chopped into neat twelve-month parcels! It's deeds, not years, that matter."

Although I often repeated her words and even prided myself on not having birthdays I could not restrain myself from once asking Mother when she was born.

"I was born. I'm alive as you can see, so what more do you want to know?" she replied, so sharply that I never asked her about her age again.

In so many other ways Mother was different. Whereas all the rest of the women I knew in the neighbouring houses and in other parts of the city took pride in their housewifely abilities, their odds and ends of new furniture, the neat appearance of their homes, Mother regarded all those things as of little importance. Our house always looked as if we had just moved in or were about to move out. An impermanent and impatient spirit dwelt within our walls; Father called it living on one leg like a bird.

Wherever we lived there were some cases partly unpacked, rolls of linoleum stood in a corner, only some of the windows had curtains. There were never sufficient wardrobes, so that clothes hung on hooks behind doors. And all the time Mother's things accumulated. She never parted with anything, no matter how old it was. A shabby green plush coat bequeathed to her by her own mother hung on a nail in her bedroom. Untidy heaps of tattered books, newspapers, and journals from the old country mouldered in corners of the house, while under her bed in tin trunks she kept her dearest possessions. In those trunks there were bundles of old letters, two heavily underlined books on nursing, an old Hebrew Bible, three silver spoons given her by an aunt with whom she had once lived, a diploma on yellow parchment, and her collection of favourite books.

From one or other of her trunks she would frequently pick a book and read to my sister and me. She would read in a wistful voice poems and stories of Jewish liberators from Moses until the present day, of the heroes of the 1905 Revolution and pieces by Tolstoy and Gorki and Sholom Aleichem. Never did she stop to inquire whether we understood what she was reading; she said we should understand later if not now.

I liked to hear Mother read, but always she seemed to choose a time for reading that clashed with something or other I was doing in the street or in a near-by paddock. I would be playing with the boys in the street, kicking a football or spinning a top or flying a kite, when Mother would unexpectedly appear and without even casting a glance at my companions she would ask me to come into the house, saying she wanted to read to me and my sister. Sometimes I was overcome with humiliation and I would stand listlessly with burning cheeks until she repeated her words. She never reproached me for my disobedience nor did she ever utter a reproof to the boys who taunted me as, crestfallen, I followed her into the house.

Why Mother was as she was only came to me many years later. Then I was even able to guess when she was born.

She was the last child of a frail and overworked mother and a bleakly pious father who hawked reels of cotton and other odds and ends in the villages surrounding a town in Russia. My grandfather looked with great disapproval on his offspring, who were all girls, and he was hardly aware of my mother at all. She was left well alone by her older sisters, who with feverish impatience were waiting for their parents to make the required arrangements for their marriages.

During those early days Mother rarely looked out into the streets, for since the great pogroms few Jewish children were ever to be seen abroad. From the iron grille of the basement she saw the soles of the shoes of the passers-by and not very much more. She had never seen a tree, a flower, or a bird.

But when Mother was about fifteen her parents died and she

went to live with a widowed aunt and her large family in a far-away village. Her aunt kept an inn and Mother was tucked away with her cousins in a remote part of the building, away from the prying eyes of the customers in the tap-rooms. Every evening her aunt would gaze at her with startled eyes as if surprised to find her among the family.

"What am I going to do with you?" she would say. "I've got daughters of my own. If only your dear father of blessed name had left you just a tiny dowry it would have been such a help. Ah well! If you have no hand you can't make a fist."

At that time Mother could neither read nor write. And as she had never had any childhood playmates or friends of any kind she hardly knew what to talk about with her cousins. She spent the days cheerlessly pottering about the kitchen or sitting for hours, her eyes fixed on the dark wall in front of her.

Some visitor to the house, observing the small, lonely girl, took pity on her and decided to give her an education. Mother was given lessons every few days and after a while she acquired a smattering of Yiddish and Russian, a little arithmetic, and a great fund of Russian and Jewish stories.

New worlds gradually opened before Mother. She was seized with a passion for primers, grammars, arithmetic and story books, and soon the idea entered her head that the way out of her present dreary life lay through these books. There was another world, full of warmth and interesting things, and in it there was surely a place for her. She became obsessed with the thought that it wanted only some decisive step on her part to go beyond her aunt's house into the life she dreamed about.

Somewhere she read of a Jewish hospital which had just opened in a distant city and one winter's night she told her aunt she wanted to go to relatives who lived there. They would help her to find work in the hospital.

"You are mad!" exclaimed her aunt. "Forsake a home for a wild fancy! Who could have put such a notion into your head? Besides, a girl of eighteen can't travel alone at this time of the year."

It was from that moment that Mother's age became something to be manipulated as it suited her. She said to her aunt that she was not eighteen, but twenty-two. She was getting up in years and she could not continue to impose on her aunt's kindness.

"How can you be twenty-two?" her aunt replied greatly puzzled.

A long pause ensued while she tried to reckon up Mother's years. She was born in the month Tammuz according to the Jewish calendar, which corresponded to the old-style Russian calendar month of June, but in what year? She could remember being told of Mother's birth, but nothing outstanding had happened then to enable her to place the year. With all her nieces and nephews, some dead and many alive, scattered all over the vastness of the country only a genius could keep track of all their birthdays. Perhaps the girl was twenty-two, and if that were so her chance of getting a husband in the village was pretty remote; twenty-two was far too old. The thought entered her head that if she allowed Mother to go to their kinsmen in the city she would be relieved of the responsibility of finding a dowry for her, and so reluctantly she agreed.

But it was not until the spring that she finally consented to let her niece go. As the railway station was several miles from the village Mother was escorted there on foot by her aunt and cousins. With all her possessions, including photographs of her parents and a tattered Russian primer tied in a great bundle, Mother went forth into the vast world.

In the hospital she didn't find that for which she hungered; it seemed still as far away as in the village. She had dreamed of the new life where all would be noble, where men and women would dedicate their lives to bringing about a richer and happier life, just as she had read.

But she was put to scrubbing floors and washing linen every day from morning till night until she dropped exhausted into her bed in the attic. No one looked at her, no one spoke to her but to give her orders. Her one day off in the month she spent with her relatives who gave her some cast-off clothes and shoes and provided her with the books on nursing she so urgently needed. She was more than ever convinced that her deliverance would come through these books and she set about swallowing their contents with renewed zest.

As soon as she had passed all the examinations and acquired the treasured diploma she joined a medical mission that was about to proceed without a moment's delay to a distant region where a cholera epidemic raged. And then for several years she remained with the same group, moving from district to district, wherever disease flourished.

Whenever Mother looked back over her life it was those years that shone out. Then she was with people who were filled with an ardour for mankind and it seemed to her they lived happily and freely, giving and taking friendship in an atmosphere pulsating with warmth and hope.

All this had come to an end in 1905 when the medical mission was dissolved and several of Mother's colleagues were killed in the uprising. Then with a heavy heart and little choice she had returned to nursing in the city, but this time in private houses attending on well-to-do ladies.

It was at the home of one of her patients that she met Father. What an odd couple they must have been! She was taciturn, choosing her words carefully, talking mainly of her ideas and little about herself. Father bared his heart with guileless abandon. He rarely had secrets and there was no division in his mind between intimate and general matters. He could talk as freely of his feelings for Mother or of a quarrel with his father as he could of a vaudeville show or the superiority of one game of cards as against another.

Father said of himself he was like an open hand at solo and all men were his brothers. For a story, a joke, or an apt remark he would forsake his father and mother, as the saying goes. Old tales, new ones invented for the occasion, jokes rolled off his tongue in a never-ending procession. Every trifle, every incident was material for a story and he haunted music-halls and circuses, for he liked nothing better than comedians and clowns, actors and buskers.

He brought something bubbly and frivolous into Mother's life and for a while she forgot her stern precepts. In those days Father's clothes were smart and gay; he wore bright straw hats and loud socks and fancy, buttoned-up boots. Although she had always regarded any interest in clothes as foolish and a sign of an empty and frivolous nature Mother then felt proud of his fashionable appearance. He took her to his favourite resorts, to music-halls and to tea-houses where he and his cronies idled away hours, boastfully recounting stories of successes in business or merely swapping jokes. They danced nights away, though Mother was almost stupefied by the band the bright lights and looked with distaste on the extravagant clothes of the dancers who bobbed and cavorted.

All this was in the early days of their marriage. But soon Mother was filled with misgivings. Father's world, the world of commerce and speculation, of the buying and selling of goods neither seen nor touched, was repugnant and frightening to her. It lacked stability, it was devoid of ideals, it was fraught with ruin. Father was a trader in air, as the saying went.

Mother's anxiety grew as she observed more closely his mode of life. He worked in fits and starts. If he made enough in one hour to last him a week or a month his business was at an end and he went off in search of friends and pleasure. He would return to business only when his money had just about run out. He was concerned only with one day at a time; about tomorrow he would say, clicking his fingers, his blue eyes focused mellowly on space, "We'll see."

But always he had plans for making great fortunes. They never came to anything but frequently they produced unexpected results. It so happened that on a number of occasions someone Father trusted acted on the plans he had talked about so freely before he even had time to leave the tea-house. Then there were fiery scenes with his faithless friends. But Father's rage passed away quickly and he would often laugh and make jokes over the table about it the very same day. He imagined everyone else forgot as quickly as he did and he was always astonished to discover that his words uttered hastily in anger had made him enemies.

"How should I know that people have such long memories for hate? I've only a cat's memory," he would explain innocently.

"If you spit upwards, you're bound to get it back in the face," Mother irritably upbraided him.

Gradually Mother reached the conclusion that only migration to another country would bring about any real change in their life, and with all her persistence she began to urge him to take the decisive step. She considered America, France, Palestine, and finally decided on Australia. One reason for the choice was the presence there of distant relatives who would undoubtedly help them to find their feet in that far-away continent. Besides, she was sure that Australia was so different from any other country that Father was bound to acquire a new and more solid way of earning a living there.

For a long time Father paid no heed to her agitation and refused to make any move.

"Why have you picked on Australia and not Tibet, for example?" he asked ironically. "There isn't much difference between the two lands. Both are on the other side of the moon."

The idea of leaving his native land seemed so fantastic to him that he refused to regard it seriously. He answered Mother with jokes and tales of travellers who disappeared in balloons. He had no curiosity to explore distant countries, he hardly ever ventured beyond the three or four familiar streets of his city. And why should his wife be so anxious for him to find a new way of earning a living? Didn't he provide her with food and a roof over her head? He had never given one moment's thought to his mode of life and he could not imagine any reason for doing so. It suited him like his gay straw hats and smart suits.

Yet in the end he did what Mother wanted him to do, though even on the journey he was tortured by doubts and he positively shouted words of indecision. But he was no sooner in Australia than he put away all thoughts of his homeland and he began to regard the new country as his permanent home. It was not so different from what he had known before. Within a few days he had met some fellow merchants and, retiring to a café, they talked about business in the new land. There were fortunes to be made here, Father very quickly concluded. There was, of course, the question of a new language but that was no great obstacle to business. You could buy and sell – it was a good land, Father said.

It was different with Mother. Before she was one day off the ship she wanted to go back.

The impressions she gained on that first day remained with her all her life. It seemed to her there was an irritatingly superior air about the people she met, the customs officials, the cab men, the agent of the new house. Their faces expressed something ironical and sympathetic, something friendly and at the same time condescending. She imagined everyone on the wharf, in the street, looked at her in the same way and she never forgave them for treating her as if she were in need of their good-natured tolerance.

Nor was she any better disposed to her relatives and the small delegation of Jews who met her at the ship. They had all been in Australia for many years and they were anxious to impress new-comers with their knowledge of the country and its customs. They spoke in a hectoring manner. This was a free country, they said, it was cultured, one used a knife and fork and not one's hands. Everyone could read and write and no one shouted at you. There were no oppressors here as in the old country.

Mother thought she understood their talk; she was quick and observant where Father was sometimes extremely guileless. While they talked Father listened with a good-natured smile and it is to be supposed he was thinking of a good story he could tell his new acquaintances. But Mother fixed them with a firm, relentless gaze and, suddenly interrupting their injunctions, said in the softest of voices, "If there are no oppressors here, as you say, why do you frisk about like house dogs? Whom do you have to please?"

Mother never lost this hostile and ironical attitude to the new land. She would have nothing of the country; she would not even attempt to learn the language. And she only began to look with a kind of interest at the world round her when my sister and I were old enough to go to school. Then all her old feeling for books and learning was re-awakened. She handled our primers and readers as if they were sacred texts.

She set great aims for us. We were to shine in medicine, in literature, in music; our special sphere depended on her fancy at a particular time. In one of these ways we could serve humanity best, and whenever she read to us the stories of Tolstoy and Gorki she would tell us again and again of her days with the medical mission. No matter how much schooling we should get we needed ideals, and what better ideals were there than those that had guided her in the days of the medical mission? They would save us from the soulless influences of this barren land.

Father wondered why she spent so much time reading and telling us stories of her best years and occasionally he would take my side when I protested against Mother taking us away from our games.

"They're only children," he said. "Have pity on them. If you stuff their little heads, God alone knows how they will finish up." Then, pointing to us, he added, "I'll be satisfied if he is a good carpenter; and if she's a good dressmaker that will do, too."

"At least," Mother replied, "you have the good sense not to suggest they go in for business. Life has taught you something at last."

"Can I help it that I am in business?" he suddenly shouted angrily. "I know it's a pity my father didn't teach me to be a professor."

But he calmed down quickly, unable to stand for long Mother's steady gaze and compressed lips.

It exasperated us that Father should give in so easily so that we could never rely on him to take our side for long. Although he argued with Mother about us he secretly agreed with her. And outside the house he boasted about her, taking a peculiar pride in her culture and attainments, and repeating her words just as my sister and I did.

Mother was very concerned about how she could give us a musical education. It was out of the question that we both be taught an instrument, since Father's business was at a low ebb and he hardly knew where he would find enough money to pay the rent, so she took us to a friend's house to listen to gramophone records. They were of the old-fashioned, cylindrical kind made by Edison and they sounded far away and thin like the voice of a ventriloquist mimicking far off musical instruments. But my sister and I marvelled at them. We should have been willing to sit over the long, narrow horn for days, but Mother decided that it would only do us harm to listen to military marches and the stupid songs of the music-hall.

It was then that we began to pay visits to musical emporiums. We went after school and during the holidays in the mornings. There were times when Father waited long for his lunch or evening meal, but he made no protest. He supposed Mother knew what she was doing in those shops and he told his friends of the effort Mother was making to acquaint us with music.

Our first visits to the shops were in the nature of reconnoitring sorties. In each emporium Mother looked the attendants up and down while we thumbed the books on the counters, stared at the enlarged photographs of illustrious composers, and studied the various catalogues of gramophone records. We went from shop to shop until we just about knew all there was to know about the records and sheet music and books in stock.

Then we started all over again from the first shop and this time we came to hear the records.

I was Mother's interpreter and I would ask one of the salesmen to play us a record she had chosen from one of the catalogues. Then I would ask him to play another. It might have been a piece for violin by Tchaikowsky or Beethoven or an aria sung by Caruso or Chaliapin. This would continue until Mother observed the gentleman in charge of the gramophone losing his patience and we would take our leave.

With each visit Mother became bolder and several times she asked to have whole symphonies and concertos played to us. We sat for nearly an hour cooped up in a tiny room with the salesman restlessly shuffling his feet, yawning and not knowing what to expect next. Mother pretended he hardly existed and, making herself comfortable in the cane chair, with a determined, intent expression she gazed straight ahead at the whirling disc.

We were soon known to everyone at the shops. Eyes lit up as we walked in, Mother looking neither this way nor that with two children walking in file through the passageway towards the record department. I was very conscious of the humorous glances and the discreet sniggers that followed us and I would sometimes catch hold of Mother's hand and plead with her to leave the shop. But she paid no heed and we continued to our destination. The more often we came the more uncomfortably self-conscious I became and I dreaded the laughing faces round me.

Soon we became something more than a joke. The smiles turned to scowls and the shop attendants refused to play us any more records. The first time this happened the salesman mumbled something and left us standing outside the door of the music-room.

Mother was not easily thwarted and without a trace of a smile she said we should talk to the manager. I was filled with a sense of shame and humiliation and with downcast eyes I sidled towards the entrance of the shop.

Mother caught up with me and, laying her hand upon my arm, she said. "What are you afraid of? Your mother won't disgrace you, believe me." Looking at me in her searching way she went on, "Think carefully. Who is right – are they or are we? Why shouldn't they play for us? Does it cost them anything? By which other way can we ever hope to hear something good? Just because we are poor must we cease our striving?"

She continued to talk in this way until I went back with her. The three of us walked into the manager's office and I translated Mother's words.

The manager was stern, though I imagine he must have had some difficulty in keeping his serious demeanour.

"But do you ever intend to buy any records?" he said after I had spoken.

"If I were a rich woman would you ask me that question?" Mother replied and I repeated her words in a halting voice.

"Speak up to him," she nudged me while I could feel my face fill with hot blood.

The manager repeated his first question and Mother, impatient at my hesitant tone, plunged into a long speech on our right to music and culture and in fact the rights of all men, speaking her own tongue as though the manager understood every word. It was in vain; he merely shook his head.

We were barred from shop after shop, and in each case Mother made a stand, arguing at length until the man in charge flatly told us not to come back until we could afford to buy records.

We met with rebuffs in other places as well.

Once as we wandered through the university, my sister and I sauntering behind while Mother opened doors, listening to lectures for brief moments, we unexpectedly found ourselves in a large room where white-coated young men and women sat on high stools in front of arrays of tubes, beakers and jars.

Mother's eyes lit up brightly and she murmured something about knowledge and science. We stood close to her and gazed round in astonishment; neither her words nor what we saw conveyed anything to us. She wanted to go round the room but a gentleman wearing a black gown came up and asked us if we were looking for someone. He was a distinguished looking person with a florid face and a fine grey mane.

Repeating Mother's words I said, "We are not looking for anyone; we are simply admiring this room of knowledge."

The gentleman's face wrinkled pleasantly. With a tiny smile playing over his lips he said regretfully that we could not stay, since only students were permitted in the room.

As I interpreted his words Mother's expression changed. Her sallow face was almost red. For ten full seconds she looked the gentleman in the eyes. Then she said rapidly to me, "Ask him why he speaks with such a condescending smile on his face."

I said, "My mother asks why you talk with such a superior smile on your face?"

He coughed, shifted his feet restlessly and his face set severely. Then he glared at his watch and without another word walked away with dignified steps.

When we came out into the street a spring day was in its full beauty. Mother sighed to herself and after a moment's silence said, "That fine professor thinks he is a liberal-minded man, but behind his smile he despises people such as us. You will have to struggle here just as hard as I had to back home. For all the fine talk it is like all other countries. But where are the people with ideals like those back home, who aspire to something better?"

She repeated these words frequently, even when I was a boy of thirteen and I knew so much more about the new country that was my home. Then I could argue with her.

I said to her that Benny who lived in our street was always reading books and papers and hurrying to meetings. Benny was not much older than I was and he had many friends whom he met in the park on Sunday. They all belonged to this country and they were interested in all the things Mother talked about.

"Benny is an exception," she said with an impatient shrug of her shoulders, "and his friends are only a tiny handful." Then she added, "And what about you? You and your companions only worship bats and balls as heathens do stone idols. Why, in the old country boys of your age took part in the fight to deliver mankind from oppression! They gave everything, their strength and health, even their lives, for that glorious ideal."

"That's what Benny wants to do," I said, pleased to be able to answer Mother.

"But it's so different here. Even your Benny will be swallowed up in the smug, smooth atmosphere. You wait and see."

She spoke obstinately. It seemed impossible to change her. Her vision was too much obscured by passionate dreams of the past for her to see any hope in the present, in the new land.

But as an afterthought she added, "Perhaps it is different for those like you and Benny. But for me I can never find my way into this life here."

She turned away, her narrow back stooped, her gleaming black hair curled into a bun on her short, thin neck, her shoes equally down at heel on each side.

The Incense-Burner

John Morrison

It was a one-way trip, and I paid off in London in the middle of winter with twenty pounds in cash, a wristwatch worth fifteen pounds, and a good kit of clothes, half on my back and half in a suitcase. And a fair bit of experience for my nineteen years.

I put up at somebody's "Temperance Hotel" near King's Cross Station because I was sick of the drunken orgies that had marked every port of call coming over from Australia, and was knocked up at eleven o'clock the first night by a housemaid innocently armed with dust-pan and empty bucket who asked me if there was anything I wanted. There wasn't. That also was something I'd got sick of on the way over.

At the end of a fortnight I had added something to my experience and was down to thirty shillings, a pawn-ticket in place of the watch, and the suitcase, still with contents. So I left the hotel, took a room in a seamen's lodging-house down near the East India Docks, and started to look for a ship home.

I wasn't long in finding out that I'd left my gallop a bit late. In 1929 a seaman looking for a ship out of London needed something better than thirty shillings and a brand-new discharge book. I had only one entry in my book, and Second Engineers and shipping officials weren't impressed. Thousands of good men were haunting the docks every day. Real seamen, with lifetimes of experience behind them, and rubbed old books to prove it. I came to the conclusion after a few days that my book was more of a handicap than a help. I'd had enough of London, and I wanted a ship bound for Australia and nowhere else. And my book made it all too clear. Second Engineers and Second Mates used to flick it open, drop the corners of their lips, and pass it back to me with a dry smile. I had it written all over me — Adelaide to London. They wanted men for a round voyage, not homesick Australians who would skin out at the first port touched.

I lasted two weeks; ten shillings a week for my room and ten shillings the fortnight for food. I did it by getting in sweet with a ship's cook, a Melbourne man, on one of the *Bay* ships laid up for repairs. I got breakfast out of the black pan every blessed day of the fortnight. Sometimes tea, too, until he told me not to make it too hot.

There were some good feeds, but not nearly enough, and it was all very irregular, and I was only nineteen, and as fit as they come, and walking up to fifteen miles every day, and I got hungrier and hungrier. There were days when I could have eaten my landlady. She was a skinny, sad-looking woman with bulging fish's eyes and a rat-trap mouth. I thought she was the toughest thing I'd ever met in my life. I was out all day every day, and on the rare occasions when I saw her she didn't seem to care whether she spoke to me or not. I used to turn in fairly early and lie reading, and until a late hour every night I could hear the thumping of a smoothing-iron in the kitchen at the far end of the passage. She was a widow; with only one other lodger, a pensioner, she had to support herself by taking in washing. It was a dark, silent, dismal hole of a place, smelling perpetually of wet clothes and yellow soap.

I saw the other lodger only once, an old man in a beard and long overcoat, vanishing into his room as I came in one night. I heard him often enough though. Too often. He had one of those deep, rumbling coughs that seem to come all the way up from the region of the stomach. He would go for minutes on end without stopping. He used to wake me up every night. Sometimes I thought he was going to suffocate.

His name was Burroughs – "old Burroughs" to Mrs Hall. I knew nothing about him – or about Mrs Hall either, if it came to it – until my last day in the house. I had sevenpence-ha'penny left, and the rent of my room was due that night. It was a cold, raw day with skies you could reach up and touch, and a threat of snow. In the morning I did the usual round of the docks, missed out on a last feed on the *Bay* ship, and went back to Finch Street to tell Mrs Hall I was leaving. I'd had to recognize the fact that I was well and truly on the beach; that there was nothing for it now but the Salvation Army "Elevator", an institution about which I'd heard plenty in the past two weeks.

I was to learn that day that my landlady's forbidding manner was nothing more than a front deliberately built up over years of contact with tough London seamen. She had a heart of gold, but like a lot of good people had become afraid to let the world see it.

She talked to me at the kitchen door, and as I told her what I was going to do she stared past me down the length of the short passage with her grim little mouth tightly shut and an expression of sullen bitterness on her dour face. I felt I was telling her an old and familiar and hated story. She must have seen a lot of defeated men in her time. Behind her was a table piled with washing; two or three ramshackle chairs, a linoleum with great holes rubbed in it, and a stove with several old-fashioned irons standing at one side.

"It's a damned shame, that's what it is," she burst out with a vehemence that startled me. "Good, clean, respectable, young men walking the streets." She sniffed and tossed her head. For a moment I thought she was going to cry. Instead she asked me in for a cup of coffee. "I was just going to make one. It'll warm you up."

It was the worst coffee I'd ever tasted, half a teaspoonful of some cheap essence out of a bottle, mixed with boiling water. And a slice of bread to eat with it. Stale bread spread thinly with greasy margarine. But I was cold and hungry, and friendly words went with it. God help her! It was all the hospitality she could offer me. One glance around that wretched room convinced me that I had been living better than her.

I told her I didn't want to take any good clothes into the hostel with me, and asked could I leave my suitcase with her until my luck turned.

"You can leave anything you like. Only no responsibility, mind you." She went on to tell me that she never knew from one day to another who she was going to have under her roof, and in the middle of it there came a muffled sound of coughing from along the passage. She stopped to listen, holding her breath and pulling a face, as if she were actually experiencing some of the old man's distress. "I'm not saying anything about *him*. He's all right. I can go out and leave anything lying around. Poor old soul! There's many a time I give him a cup of coffee, and I'll swear to God it's the only thing that passes his lips from morn till night. Where he gets to when he goes out . . . "

"He's pretty old, isn't he, Mrs Hall?"

"Not that old. He was in the war. He's a sick man, that's what's wrong with him. One of these days I'll wake up and find I've got a corpse on my hands. You just ought to be here when he gets one of his foreign parcels."

"Foreign parcels?"

Mrs Hall finished her coffee, got up, and began sorting the things on the table. "Don't ask me where it comes from. He never tells me anything, and I never stick my nose into another body's business. But he's got somebody somewhere that hasn't forgotten him. Every few months he gets this parcel. Not much – a pair of underpants or socks, or a muffler – just bits of things. And a little bundle of dry leaves, herbs for his cough I suppose. My God, you just ought to smell them! He burns them in a bit of a tin pan he's got. They stink the house out. And there he sits and just sucks it in. It's beyond me how he can stand it. I've got to get out till he's finished."

Mrs Hall sniffed and blew, as if the smell of the herbs from the foreign parcel were in her nostrils even then. "He's been here twelve months, and if it wasn't for that I wouldn't care if he stopped for three years. He never bothers nobody, and he keeps his room like a new pin. I've never yet seen him with drink in, and that's a change from some of them I get here, you mark my words. I know *you're* not the drinking kind, otherwise I wouldn't have asked you in here."

Poor Mrs Hall!

She wished me good luck and promised to keep my suitcase in her own room until I came back for it.

Travelling light, I walked all the way to the Salvation Army headquarters in Middlesex Street, stated my case to a "soldier" just inside the door, and was sent over to an elderly grey-haired "officer" seated at a desk piled with papers. All this happened a long time ago, and many of the details are hazy, but I'm left with an impression of newness, of spacious floors, of pleasant faces, of friendly efficiency.

The officer asked me what it was I wanted them to do for me. I told him.

"I'm an Australian. I worked my way over as a ship's trimmer. I wanted to see London; you know how it is. Now I'm broke, and I'm looking for a passage back home. I've got to find somewhere to live while I look for a ship."

"Where have you been living?" Nothing inquisitorial about the question. He was taking quiet stock of me all the time. I had no reason to deceive him, but I felt it would be a waste of time anyway, that I was dealing with a man full of experience.

"In lodgings down in Custom House near the East India Docks. I've got to get out tonight, though; I haven't a shilling left."

"You didn't jump your ship, did you?"

Only a man who knew sailors would have asked me that. "No, I've got a clean book." My hand went to my pocket, but he stopped me with a gesture.

"It isn't necessary for me to pry into your affairs, my boy. You understand that if you go into the Elevator you won't have much time to look for a ship?"

"I know I'll have to work, but that's all right. I could get some time off now and then, couldn't I?"

"Yes, as long as you did your task. But that's the responsibility of the commandant down there." He reached out and picked a form off a little pile at his side. "I'll give you a note to take down. I can't promise he'll have room for you, but it's worth while trying. What's your name?"

"Thomas Blair."

"Do you know where Old Street is?"

They took me in, and for a little over three weeks I earned food and lodging by sorting waste string at the establishment known as the Elevator, down in Spitalfields.

It was the strangest three weeks I have ever experienced, and the most generally hopeless company of men I was ever mixed up with. There were about forty of us, of whom perhaps twenty were professional tramps wintering in. Of the others, fellows in circumstances more or less similar to my own, I got an impression that only a few were still trying to get their heads above water again. Conversation was not primarily around the prospect of finding employment, as I expected it to be, but around the petty incidents of the day, that evening's bill of fare, a certain current murder trial, and every triviality of hostel administration they could think up. At the time I was thoroughly contemptuous of it all, but I understand better now. Those men had had a lot more of London than I had; I was still fresh to the struggle . . .

We worked nine hours a day; seven-thirty in the morning until five-thirty in the evening, with an hour off for dinner.

I was never able to find out why they called the place the Elevator, unless because it was intended as an elevator of fallen men. That's likely enough, but I'm not sure that it worked out in practice. I'm not questioning the good faith of the Salvation Army officers charged with its administration, but the prevailing atmosphere was far from elevating. On the first morning a short conversation with my immediate bench-mate served to reveal in a flash the spirit permeating the entire establishment.

"Been in before?" he asked me.

"No."

"Stopping long?"

"No longer than I can help."

"That might be longer than you think, chum. Y'ought to try and get on the staff. It's a sitter if they don't know you."

"What staff?"

"Here, and up at the hostel. Sweeping out, making beds, cooking and serving. They're all chaps that come in off the streets, like you. Not much money in it, but everything's turned on free. All you got to do is get saved."

"Saved?"

"Go out to the penitent form at one of the prayer meetings. Give your heart to Jesus . . . "

And that was it. It was a home for the destitute, largely run by some of the destitute. And if you weren't particularly anxious to move on, and were sufficiently unscrupulous, you could be one of the running brigade. And the way to muscle into the running brigade was simply to get "saved". I discovered that some of the old hands got saved every year as soon as the winter winds began to blow and the roads frosted up.

All the charge-hands at the Elevator were such brands clutched from the burning, and a more foxy-looking crowd I never set eyes on. They were on a sweet thing, and in their anxiety to stick to it they took good care that precious little of the spirit of Army benevolence got beyond the corner of the building where the commandant had his little office. Beggars-on-horseback, they ran the place with much of the efficiency, and even less of the humanity, of an ordinary factory.

The Elevator was simply a depot for the collecting and sorting and repacking of waste paper, rags and string. All day long motor-trucks, horse-drawn lorries and handcarts kept coming in heaped with salvage, which was unloaded and dragged to various parts of the great concrete floor for sorting out.

I was put onto the string bench, and each morning was given a one-hundredweight bag of odds and ends of string which I had to disentangle and distribute into a row of boxes marked "cotton", "sisal" – I forget the other names.

That was my task for the day, the price I paid for three meals and a bed to sleep in at night. Anything I did over and above that was paid for, if I remember correctly, at the rate of half-a-crown a hundredweight. In the three weeks I was there I earned just enough cash to keep me in cigarettes, carefully rationed, and nothing more. And there was no getting out of it if you wanted those three feeds and the bed. I tried, on the very first day – seizing a moment when I thought nobody was looking, and ramming a double handful of unsorted string into the sisal box. But one of the foxes saw me from a distant part of the floor and made me drag it out again under the threat of instant expulsion.

We didn't live at the Elevator. An old shop next door had been converted into a dining-room, and every day at twelve o'clock we trooped in and received dinners served from hot-boxes brought down from some Army cookhouse. And at the end of the day's work each man was given three tickets on the hostel in Old Street a mile or so away, one for tea, one for bed, and one for breakfast next morning.

The Old Street hostel was one of the biggest in London, and was run on much the same lines, and in much the same spirit, as the Elevator. There was a washhouse with neither soap nor towels, dormitories – barrack-like but quite clean – and a spacious dining-room where the men could sit for the rest of the evening after eating. I understood that most of the food – "leftovers" of some kind or other – was donated or bought cheaply from hotels, cafes, shops and bakehouses. But it was priced so low that a man could usually eat plenty; it was dished up with every appearance of cleanliness, and I can't say I ever found it anything but appetizing. Meal tickets were valued at 1s. 3d, and we could choose what we liked from the bill of fare stuck up at the end of the serving counter: slice of bread and margarine 1d, pot of tea or coffee 1d, soup 2d, roast beef or mutton 3d, stew 3d, kippers 1d each, vegetables 2d, apple tart 3d.

All a bit primitive, if you like, but I had a two weeks' hunger to work off, and they were the most enjoyable meals I ever had in my life. Food was, indeed, the only thing that made life at all worth living just then. I would open my eyes every morning thinking of breakfast, and when it was over I'd grit my teeth and stagger through the next four hours sustained only by thoughts of dinner. And when that was over there came thoughts of tea.

One red-letter day I cashed two tea tickets. My neighbour on the string-bench got on to something better for that evening, and gave me his. When I lined up at the counter the second time the fox in the white apron gave me a cold stare.

"What's this? I've served you once."

"Don't be funny," I replied. "How many tickets d'you think we get?"

Still staring, he became positive, threw the ticket into the tray, and turned to the next man in line, dismissing me with a curt: "Move on, chum, you've had it."

He should have known better, because there are two things for which a man is always prepared to fight, and food is one of them. I reached out and seized his wrist.

"Come up with it, Mister! I'm in the Elevator. I worked for that ticket – "

He shook himself free, but I must have looked as savage as I felt because he served me without further argument.

I was like that all the time, hostile on the whole infernal world and ready to take it out on anybody. Each week I got leave off for half a day and went the familiar round of the docks, but a ship seemed to be as far off as ever. I hated London as I'd never hated any place before, began to lose hope, and fell into a mood of gloomy self-pity that made me impatient and contemptuous of everybody around me. Those men didn't talk much about their private affairs, and with the egotism and intolerance of youth I assumed that none of their troubles was as great as mine. A man with youth and good health, and no responsibilities, should find any tussle an exhilarating adventure, but some of us don't realize that until youth is past. I used to try to cheer myself up by comparing my circumstances to those of old Burroughs coughing his life away down in the hovel in Finch Street, but that only made matters worse. Visions of the old man creeping along the dark passage, or crouched over his periodical burning of the herbs, positively frightened me. For he also had had a youth, and somewhere in the past there had been a beginning to the road that led to Finch Street, and that assuredly would go on from there nowhere but to the grave.

The hostel was full of them, shivering watery-eyed old men, who wandered the streets all day, and stumbled in at nightfall to stand for a long time studying the bill of fare with a few miserable coppers clutched in their stiff fingers. Nobody took any notice of them. No doubt they would have envied old Burroughs, for nobody ever sent *them* parcels with mufflers and "bits of things" in them. All the same, they moved me to horror and fear more than to pity, for were they not life-members of a fraternity of which I had become a novitiate?

And if during the day all my dreams were of food, then at night-time all my dreams were of home. The coughing of old Burroughs had nothing on the wheezings and mutterings of that refuge of lost men. Sleep came to me slowly, and was often broken, and in the wakeful moments I would lie with wide eyes and tight lips, deliberately torturing myself with nostalgic longings.

Some building close by had a clock that chimed the hours, and whenever I heard it I would think carefully and call up a scene in Australia that I knew was true and exact of that very moment.

At midnight I would say to myself: it's ten o'clock in the morning, and the hotels down Flinders Street are just opening and the wharfies coming away from the first pick-up are crossing from

the Extension and dropping into the Hotham and the Clyde for a
quick one before going home to lunch. And there's a white sky and
a smell of dust, and trembling pavements which by noon will be
hot enough to fry eggs on. And down at St Kilda beach lazy little
waves are lapping in, and some of the Fortunate Ones are crossing
the Promenade from the big apartment houses and spreading their
towels on the sand for a brown-off. And even though it's a week-
day, the Point Nepean Highway down the Peninsula is already
lively with cars heading for the bush and more distant beaches.
And there's a place down there in the heath country where my
mates and I used to go rabbiting on Sunday afternoons. And the
big loose-limbed manna-gum where we found the parrot's nest is
still there, its thin foliage hard and sharp against the sky in that
way that always reminded me of the figures on a Japanese willow-
pattern plate. And somewhere on the scrubby slope that runs up
to the road a wallaby sits with drooping paws and pricked ears.
And the air is full of the scent of the paperbarks down in the
swamp, and of the whistlings and twitterings of grey thrushes and
honeyeaters and blue wrens. And every now and then, on the
breathlike puff of a breeze that comes out of the north, there is
another smell that I know well, and over in a saddle of the distant
Dandenongs a column of smoke marks where the bushfire is
burning . . .

For three weeks.

Then – suddenly, like most things – it was all over.

One morning at breakfast time I got talking with a stranger who
turned out to be a sailor. And within a few minutes he knew what
I was looking for.

"Why don't you give the *Tairoa* a go?" he asked me. "Ever done a
trip as a steward?"

"No. What about the *Tairoa?*"

"She's leaving for Australia today, and they were signing on
single-trippers yesterday. A lot of the New Zealand Company's
packets do it. They go out stuffed with emigrants in the 'tween-
decks. At the other end they dismantle the accommodation and fill
up with cargo for home. They only want most of the stewards one
way."

"How is it I've never heard about this? I've walked those docks
– "

"Well, you wouldn't be looking for Chief Stewards with that
book, would you? Anyway, the Shore Superintendent's the chap
you want to see. He's got an office down at the East India somewhere. You'll have to look lively if you want to try the *Tairoa* –
she's up for noon . . . "

She's up for noon – oh, the friendly, intimate jargon of the sea! There was a promise in the familiar phrase that raised my excitement to fever-heat. I never met that seaman again, but I'll love him till the day I die.

It took me two hours to find the Shore Superintendent, and less than five minutes to get the ship. He was a busy man all right. I was at his office by half-past eight, but they told me he had just left for a certain ship, and it was half-past ten before I caught up with him. I can't at this distance of time trace my wanderings in those two hours, but I must have visited at least six vessels at widely separated berths, always just a few minutes behind him. However, I was after something that drew me like the very Holy Grail, and I nailed him at last just as he was about to get into his car. I knew I was on the right track as soon as he stopped to listen to me.

"We don't want trimmers," he said after a glance at my book. "We want stewards."

"That's all right with me," I replied. "I want the passage. I'll sign as a steward. I've worked in hotels."

He passed the book back, taking me in from head to feet.

"Where's your gear?"

I could hardly speak for excitement. "Up in my room in Custom House – "

"You'd have to be aboard by twelve o'clock."

"I can do that. Where's she lying?"

He told me. "Give us your name." He pulled out a pocket-book. "Report to the Second Steward and give him this note."

She's up for noon . . .

Finch Street was two miles away, but I'll swear I made it in twenty minutes. There was plenty of time, but I had it in mind there was a suitcase to lug over the return trip, and I wasn't taking any chances. It was a cold foggy morning, but I was sweating from the long chase and the fever of success. And the grey buildings, and the shrouded figures that passed me on the pavement, were like things seen through the enchanted mists of fairyland. All the world had become beautiful, and I strode along puffed with triumph and springing on my toes with physical well-being. I told myself that youth and strength and pertinacity had to tell in the long run. You couldn't keep a good man down. Not when he had something big to struggle for. Those old men of the hostel had lacked the spur, inspiration, a vision . . .

No more Elevator. No doubt I wore a silly smile, because more than once I caught a curious glance directed at me as I hurried on.

Perhaps my lips were moving too, because the magical phrase "she's up for noon" rang in my head until it took on the tune of a well-known military march. I could have danced to it, shouted it aloud.

She's up for noon . . .

I remember afterwards holding back to let an ambulance pass me as I was about to cross into Finch Street, but the fact that it was an ambulance didn't register at the time — only a car of some kind, and in a hurry.

But I did observe instantly the women out at their doors all along both sides, and the little knot of gossipers in front of my old lodgings.

I thought first of Mrs Hall, then of old Burroughs. But the humour of pitiless superiority was still on me, and I hardly quickened my pace. I'd come back for a suitcase, that was all, and in a few minutes these people . . .

They turned their heads and watched me as I came up. I saw Mrs Hall in the doorway, her popping eyes red with weeping.

"It's the old man, sailor. They've just took him off. The poor old soul."

Some of the arrogance and detachment left me. I wasn't interested in old Burroughs, but this woman had given me a cup of coffee and a few words of sympathy when I needed them most. The other women stood aside, and I moved into the passage, taking the landlady by her elbow and drawing her after me. Something tickled my nostrils, but all my attention was on something else.

"He's an old man, you know, Mrs Hall. What happened?"

"They think it's a stroke." She began to weep again, dabbing her nose with the lifted end of her tattered apron. "God help him! He tried to talk to me. He got one of them parcels this morning, them herbs. He's been sitting there — you got a ship, sailor?"

She could think of me too.

"Yes, I'm going aboard in an hour. Where've they taken him?"

But I didn't hear her reply.

Because that something which had been tickling my nostrils got right inside, and I lifted my head like a parched bullock scenting water, and stared along the passage, and sniffed, and licked my lips — and drew in a mighty inhalation that filled my lungs and sent me dizzy with the sickness that had been eating into me for five mortal weeks. I seized Mrs Hall with a violence that made her stare at me in sudden fright.

"Mrs Hall! — that smell — those herbs — where did they come from?"

As if I didn't know!

"Sailor – "

Burning gum-leaves! Oh, shades of the bush and smell of my home!

Pushing her from me, I was down the passage in two frenzied leaps and throwing open the door.

But nothing was left save the belongings of a lonely old man, a wisp of blue smoke rising from a tin set on an upturned box, and a digger's hat hanging on a nail driven into the mantel-piece.

Shadow

Peter Cowan

Outside the rain drove across the streets and smeared the windows near her table like other, opaque, glass pressed against the squared frames. In the room she heard the phone ring without real awareness. One of the girls said, "It's for you, Beth."

She walked across to the phone, conscious of the other girls, uneasy, the convention of the conversation shared with the room an art she could not master, hating the revelation of the stated words she must make casual like some denial.

His voice seemed to hold impatience. "I had to ring now — I'll be out on a job this afternoon."

"It's all right," she said.

"How about tonight?"

"Yes."

"What time?"

"At nine?" she said.

"That's pretty late."

"I can't help it, Alan."

"You couldn't not go tonight?"

"You know I must."

"It wouldn't hurt for once, surely."

She did not answer, aware of the others close to her, knowing, the routine of their day faintly enlivened by the small vicarious struggle.

He said, "I told them we'd be there at eight."

She let bitterness edge her tone. "It won't be for very much longer."

"I'll have to go," he said. "The truck's waiting. Eight o'clock?"

"I can't, Alan."

"So I'll have to get away about nine and come round and see if you're there?"

"I'll be at the corner," she said.

"Well, I'd hope so."

She went over to her table. From the window, standing, she could see the clouds moving quickly behind the buildings, and below the dark streets with the quick streaks of the moving vehicles slashed along the wet blackness. The other girls, carefully, were not looking at her. She sat down and her hands shifted the sheets of paper before her.

In the house she hung the damp tea-towel on the rack and walked down the passage to the front room. The man did not look up, and she said, "I'll be going in a minute."

He moved his paper impatiently. "I'll come a bit later."

She said, "You will come?"

"There's no sense in it," he said. "She doesn't know me half the time."

"Sometimes she does. It's not so much to do."

"I'll come later," he said.

She went into her room and changed quickly. Outside the wind swept the rain along the darkened street and she ran down towards the bus stop. But the clouds were broken, swift-moving, darker patches of clear sky behind their shifting shapes, and when she reached the corner the rain had stopped.

She had become in some measure accustomed now to the hospital, the first sense of finality, of fear, dulled by the daily contact with its corridors and wards, its cleanliness and order and anonymity, the quality of living held as if in suspense, unimportant beyond the wide tiled entrance and glass doors.

Looking up from the bed, the woman saw the girl's shape move slowly to individuality, as though shifting from the strange hours that had lost all the qualities of recognition, making the day's divisions unfamiliar and unreal, her mind finding peace now only in the past. The girl's hair as she leant over the bed held drops of moisture shining in the light and her words came: "It's raining – I was caught coming down the road" – uncertain like the woman's faint smile that might have indicated knowledge of the words or have been greeting. For the rain had come greyly up the slope and from the window she had seen him begin to walk ahead of it towards the house. His feet kicked through the fallen fern he had been cutting, the fronds lifting before him. In the small clearing, stretching only a short distance down the slope from the house, almost she could have seen him wherever he worked. Near the building the rain closed about him and he quickened his pace, running up the steps onto the verandah. He saw her standing on the chair before the window of the front room and he stepped inside, from the doorway seeing her twist sideways towards him, her arms stretched upwards, holding the curtain rod.

"I've nearly finished the curtains," she said. "How do you think they'll look?"

"All right," he said.

"I like them."

"They won't be bad."

He came towards the window. She pushed the curtains, looking outside.

"It's heavy, the rain."

"Yes."

Down the slope towards the timber she could see the patch of fallen fern where he had been cutting.

"You're getting through it."

He nodded. "Slow, though. And they come up as fast as you cut them. But it's too wet out there now."

"It's set in."

He stepped close to her as she stood balanced on the chair, and his arms went suddenly round her.

"You'll tip me off."

His hold tightened, his head pressing against her thighs. She put her hands on his shoulders, holding him against herself. He lifted her, carrying her across the room, herself still held upright as she had been standing on the chair, and he lowered her gently, looking down at her.

The rain had fallen steadily, and she had listened to it on the iron roof. She lay looking at the new curtains she had been putting up, seeing that they hung unevenly, a gap down the centre where they had not been pulled together. She moved her hand slightly, thinking to shift her arm, on which his head was resting. She could not see his face, but his hair, black and dry and thick, was against her cheek when she turned her head. The rain came with a steady sound like something that could never cease, and it seemed to her she could not imagine a time when its noise had not been heavy and persistent in the small room. She lay, comfortable in the warmth of their bodies, the sound of the rain like a presence that drove out thought and left her mindless, both of them lifted beyond time and all immediacy. She let her eyes close, in warmth, in pleasure, into the drift of sleep. When she woke the rain was lighter and through the window she could see a break in the heavy sky, a long pale streamer of light above the trees. The man moved, his head pressing against her arm, and slowly through the sense of her tenderness came the edge of uncertainty. She waited, not speaking, afraid for what came sometimes now like denial between them. He stretched himself slowly, and turned over, lying on his back.

"My arm's gone to sleep," she said. She lifted it, the flesh creased where his head had lain. He drew her arm down and let it rest so that his lips moved over the ridged flesh, and his fingers smoothed it slowly.

"The rain's stopping," she said softly.

"Yes."

She wanted to get up while there was the affection and tenderness between them.

"Nearly a whole afternoon. And look at my curtains still not hung."

"Sorry?"

"No."

The rain had stopped, the room strangely quiet.

"It was the rain," she said.

Her eyes sought the girl sitting by the bed and in her hair there were the drops of rain.

She was aware suddenly that he had appeared beside them, and her eyes closed in a quietness like something she welcomed and had long prepared herself for. He stood looking down at her, not speaking, and he forgot suddenly the ward and its strangeness that seemed somehow like a threat that made him uneasy and embarrassed and he looked at her and thought how it had come to this, that she should lie there, himself seeing her in this place that was beyond all their experience, in which they must part as strangers, and he wondered if she knew any better than he did. He saw suddenly that she was watching him, her eyes no longer closed, and for a moment he thought to speak, to put it before her, to make some stay of this time, but he became aware again of the ward and of the other people, and the words could never be said between them.

Looking up at him, she saw his slack reddened face, and his eyes, and her hand moved vaguely, as if to have taken his, but he was holding his hat clasped before him, clumsily, in both hands, and her gesture wavered into stillness.

He stood for a time close to the bed, opposite the girl, and then as it seemed the woman slept again he said he would wait outside and went awkwardly down the ward.

Among the beds in the smaller ward no one seemed to speak

loudly, or to laugh, and the girl sat touching her mother's hand until quite suddenly the woman's lips moved and she leant towards her, and quite clearly her mother asked her to close the window – the bathroom window was banging, would she close it? – and the girl thought suddenly of the small weatherboard structure that had been built onto the back verandah to form a bathroom. In it were box shelves and an old cupboard that held clothes, against the wall the big galvanized-iron tub that was moved outside on wash-days, and was as often left on the verandah or by the shed where the copper stood as returned to the bathroom, so that they must run looking for it while the bathwater cooled in the kerosene tins and the wide saucepan. Cooled in the draught from the window whose frame had become warped by the weather so that it did not close properly, and at night with the wind often banged until someone got up to shut it, dragging it tight into the frame. One of the girl's earliest memories was of the persistent banging of the window, loud in the small house, imperative, pregnant with some meaning that would never be revealed on the nights when the wind beat against the weatherboard walls and drove the rain against the iron roof in sound that filled her whole world until she could not have dared to leave her bed, and then of someone stumbling in the darkness to shut it. Or when sometimes it was unaccountably ignored and in the morning the glass was broken and there was her father's futile anger, and for a long time the glass would remain cracked, with sharp pointed pieces splintered from it, until one Saturday he would bring a new pane back from the town and it would be mended. But no mending remedied the warped frame, and the wind could still blow the window back from the wire catch that had been fitted inside until the catch became loose, and the fastening of it no more than a gesture.

She said, "I wonder if it is the same now. We've never been back, have we?" and the woman smiled faintly and then abruptly she asked for him. The girl rose and told her she would be only a moment and went out to find him, not knowing if he might perhaps have gone. But he was in the large waiting-room, sitting near the door. He rose when he saw her as if to go, but followed her back into the ward, walking stiffly, as though he tried not to see those about him. He stood by the bed, looking down at the woman, his hat in his hands, the black coat of his suit creased and shiny, and as the girl's eyes lifted towards him he saw quickly a near hatred in them, yet with it a kind of puzzlement, so that he looked beyond them both, standing at the foot of the bed, until, since it was clear the woman would not wake, he went without words.

Outside, the rain had stopped, though the wind was cold as she walked down the pavement towards the intersection. Near the corner she saw him standing by the lighted shop windows, his overcoat collar turned up, his hands in his pockets. He was looking down at the pavement, not seeming aware of the people brushing close to him, banking up on the corner as the traffic went against them, and she slowed in her walk, screened by those who had left the hospital when she had at the close of the visiting hour, seeing him move suddenly, impatiently, his thin figure in the overcoat buttoned about him. She turned suddenly, pausing on the edge of the pavement, moving quickly between the cars out into the centre of the road, and then across to the other side, shielded now by the people about her and the traffic, turning away down the cross-street, not looking back at the crowded intersection where he waited.

A Double
Because It's Snowing

Hal Porter

Scene: *Saloon bar of Saint Ives, uphill from Salamanca Place, Hobart, the waterfront.*
Saint Ives: *Steep-roofed railway-station Gothic — quaint and cosy to sea-people. Ship-stewards, wireless operators, sometimes a purser or a ham-pink engineer, climb up Montpelier Retreat past the freestone Georgian cottages with their fan-lights, gig-houses, area railings and plots of Dusty Miller.*
Outside: *Snow, intensifying, rice-like, rakishly thrown for some singular marriage far above which the organ-piped granite of Mount Wellington seems about to explode an eccentric voluntary.*
Time: *7 p.m., recently enough; maybe two, maybe three, years ago.*
Inside: *A newly-arrived friend has been greeted by a man who appears older and younger. His face too controlled, he is dressed in pied neatness, furtive richness. White shirt — white face. Dark tie — dark lips. He is speaking*:

If you want to talk tonight you must listen; you see it's snowing. I listened to you last time. Didn't I now, when you were. . . . Autumn, wasn't it? "It was autumn and the golden leaves were falling" — early Hedda Hopper that from a Lonsdale play called . . . . Eh? Of course I'm drunk, of course, of course. Eyes mum as cats now but in two hours they'll be running about like mice. Yes, it's snowing again so I'm drunk and hate my mother, hate her more again.

Nonsense, why not me? Hate is thicker than water.

You know, when it began snowing, the scales of my mind tilted, I began to watch her. Obliquely and, oh, skilfully. Do you sometimes watch something, say a — a horse, un-assessing it, neutralizing associations so that presently it seems new, out-of-drawing and. . . .

You don't? You really don't?

I do. I did. A tame horse that once bit too deep. A horse one hates, and waits warily to hate more. So I left the horse, the hearse, the house. No horses here. After an hour I telephoned you, wanting your ear, a nice ear, red and kind.

A *double* brandy, you urk, you traitor, my only friend and ear. A double because it's snowing.

Let me, for God's sweet sake, get drunk.

All *right*, drunk-*er*.

I'll do and do decorously, and you drive me home when Elvie says, "Ten o'clock, gentlemen", and takes off her plastic apron, and out blink the teeny-tiny fairy-lights around the liqueur bottles, and that affected fire relaxes. My eyes are still still as two cats, eh? Two nasty moggies.

My mother.

She was a hotel chambermaid. You knew?

No?

She doesn't really look like a horse or chambermaid, more a lady teddy-bear with a Pond's Cream skin. Something from Beatrix Potter. Cuddly. Motherly.

Father's a bookmaker. *That* you knew.

I have never − I say this with conviction, from experience, without malice − met two more vulgar people. Not merely common. Vulgar. Vulgar emotionally, vulgar morally, vulgar parentally, vulgar from A to Z in triplicate. Plenty of pelf − stinking oodles of mug's money, dreamer's money − and not an aitch between them except for haitch. Don't smoke. Don't drink. Don't fritter. They garner.

They garner me. They've garnered a succession of me's from peeing babyhood to piddling manhood: the brilliant and astonishing fruit of their loins lecturing with every aitch on at that scrubby university perched on yet another foothill. Hobart and its humps and hollows! Rome is *flat*.

Indeed, Elvie, the same *sorts* of drinks, please and thank you.

Hills! Up-and-down, skew-whiff, nothing straight except the mountain shadow slicing down toward the Estuary. I daily want to run before it, be scraped off into a liner, a launch, a coracle, to escape.

What do I want to escape? You don't mean that!

You do?

Morbid, unoriented, ungrateful boy I am − I want to escape them. Vulgarity and them. I am *the* bird in *the* gilded cage.

The cage looks attractive, you say?

The proportions of that Regency cage are superb, serene, et cetera, because John Lee Archer designed it to the last valance-

board for some colonial bigwig. Inside – Christ! A looney-bin of
possessions, of unbelievable mines and thines. Theatre-lounge
carpets, crammed china-cabinets, battalions of statuettes, of Wool-
worth figurines, ebony elephants, Majolica plaques, love-birds,
gold-fish, fixed cats . . . everything inside to be fondled, tallied,
ranged *seriatim*. Tutankhamen's tomb by Dali! a firsthand second-
hand shop! – I the central *objet d'art*, the chilli in the pickle-bottle.
Even Summer, Autumn, Winter and Spring, marble statues that
lived under the garden-trees and had for nearly a century, were
gentled into the conservatory. Oxalic acid baths keep *those* seasons
in order. Couldn't get the trees inside – so – "T-i-m-b-e-r!" Now,
lawns everywhere and lousy contemporary annuals. Let the scent-
less bastards but bloom, and *snip*, inside with them, water and
Aspros, alum for them in some hand-painted atrocity. Chambermaid's delight! No escape from loving care, from being dusted and
owned.

I'll whisper this . . . my mother has a ceaseless hand soft as a
feather duster.

Your ear does not pale?

But I did escape once. Once, and for nearly a year.

Mesmerize Elvie away from the hearty shellbacks. I talk too
much. I'm parched.

Thank you, Elvie, thank you, thank you and thank you.

A-a-ah!

Escape was ten years ago. Oh, I looked no younger. I look no
older. What could make me look older? I am the apple of a
chambermaid's eye. The core doesn't show. All spit-and-polish,
me. No older. Except when it's snowing. And it's snowing. Oh,
indeed, it's snowing.

It's been tabulated so often and scrupulously and with such
verve, why does one never learn . . . the printed pages of other
hearts, the maps of sorrow, the impeccable diagrams of anguish,
the soundings, the graphs . . . why? Why never?

How I raked up courage to get a travelling lectureship despair
alone knows; all was irreversibly setted before my mother knew;
she had little time to do it but I was a virtual matricide by the time
I stubbornly escaped to Japan to lecture to the troops, telling men,
who knew more about life than I'll ever know, all about life. I, the
solitary man in the Chinese café, the lone stranger peering at the
name-plates on trees in Botanical Gardens, the dipper-into Gideon
bibles in single bedrooms in middle-class pubs.

Land of the Rising Sun!

After a couple of months I was at Shimoda – the Townsend

Harris place, the first foreign settlement after all those un-Westernized centuries of . . . well, never mind.

Shimoda.

Education-types from Tokyo had guided me there educationally with copious Suntory whisky and several million of those little salty biscuit-things with seaweed in. It was spring. It was *accidentally* spring; the Pacific was treacherously pacific outside the inn-shutters.

Your turn to buy but I'll buy. I'll buy your ear a stimulant.

How large your ears! How small your alcoholic needs!

I insist. I'm as dry as a briquette.

Nonsense! Brandy dehydrates.

Fiddlededee *and* poppycock – I *insist*, and shall only lower my voice if. . . .

Ah, you resemble Marie Antoinette, Elvie. Before execution naturally. The Petit Trianon days maybe.

Decidedly a double, *altessa*. . . .

Shimoda . . . spring-time . . . Suzuki. . . .

Suzuki was one of half a dozen local almost-geisha engaged to amuse the Tokyo gents on their intellectual ran-tan. I . . . let me drink this . . . fell in love with her.

One never learns. All I'd studied, all I'd taught the descendants of ticket-of-leave men and Cockney go-getters, all those poetic accuracies and searing details . . . pouf!

The girls did their turns – the sing-song, the meticulous paper-folding, the corny fan-balancing – mysteriously boring. The education boys were as merry as grigs: giggles, hot flushes *et tout cela*. My yawns were just not showing. Then Suzuku did the dance of O-Kichi.

O-Kichi was Townsend Harris's woman, the first Foreigner's Woman if you count out the missus of poor shipwrecked Will Adams a couple of centuries before, and give Francis Xavier and his gaunt mates the benefit of the doubt.

There we all were, half-molo or as pissed as minks, squatting on the padded floor. Night and the sea immediately outside; the night with its back turned; the sea shushing itself: *"Thalassa! Thalassa!"* One of the dolls was slicing with an outsize plectrum rather like an ivory battle-axe-head at the samisen, a hellishing long banjo with the round part square and covered with cat-skin. Distraught music; pentatonic, I fear. Convincing though. Suzuki danced the story of O-Kichi. She danced with expressionless face – the Greek theatre mask idea – the thickly-whitened face must show nothing; gesture tells the story, hands, fan, the floor-touching

kimono sleeves. There was dead-pan Suzuki of the Port of
Shimoda being dead O-Kichi to the life. Sleeves, fan, wrists,
fractional movements of her white cloven booties illustrated
everything.

She was . . . was . . . heartbreaking.

Did I really say that?

First she shuffled with her young lover along the shelly beaches
of rapture, entrancing butterfly O-Kichi. Then — she danced
horror at the village elder's command to be Harris's plaything. You
know, I should write for Hutchinson's. She pleaded; the plectrum
slashed restlessly and remorselessly at the nerves of the samisen.
At the nerves; yes, at the nerves. Pleading and horror were
useless, were replaced by agony as her lover was torn from her.
Next came repulsion as she was pawned — get that "pawned"! —
into the arms of the hairy red-skinned barbarian. Weariness now,
alone with her loathsome master through odious days and obligat-
ory nights. Yes . . . yes . . . I *should* write for the shoe-shop girls.

Don't ask how I understood it. Suzuki was O-Kichi.

I understood.

I understand more now.

Finally, Harris having been recalled to America, she danced her
relief and, more movingly than anything, her elated but timid
emergence into the village. And now her shuddering sleeves and
hands revealed the loneliness of the tainted woman, the fruit with
the blemish, the classic outcast. She ran from the thrown stones.
At this point, at the crux of horror, the snow began to fall . . .
blinding snow, scorching snow. She acted this, she did, she did,
so that I saw snow, *saw* it. She faltered through it, up Shimoda's
minor Fuji-san, to suicide.

Poor O-Kichi.

Suzuki — poor Suzuki.

The dance was ended; the party whinnied and groped and spilt
on. But I could not take my eyes from. . . .

Another drink, please. My eyes steady? Look, still snowing outside. . . .

Thanks. And *grand merci mille fois.*

Brandy is handy.

Suzuki became my house-girl. During the Occupation that was
too possible: a half-word there and there . . . and there we were!

The remainder months were ecstasy. God! an Honours Degree
and all one does is re-state a cliché in a cliché. Of course, I'd fallen
in love with O-Kichi rather than Suzuki. At first, that is . . .
mother-ridden male virgin falls in love with art-form. Suzuki

herself, the real one, may have been as common as my mother; she was a house-girl, a sort of personal inn-sister which is the Jap equivalent of chambermaid. And I wouldn't know if she dropped Nipponese aitches or had an accent like a Queenslander.

But not vulgar.

Never, never, never, never, never . . . Lear!

It wasn't, you understand, until we'd travelled yon and hither together for a month that I . . . well. . . .

I was lecturing around Kyoto. High summer. Suzuki had met me, and we'd walked to our hotel together through streets shaded with split-bamboo awnings – flicker-flicker the skinny zebra shadows; little fountains had gurgled in wooden tubs filled with melons and ice; glass wind-bells everywhere. . . .

We were staying in one of those inns in Kiyamachi Gojo along the Kamo River that divides Kyoto. At this spot, inns on one side, brothels on the other, between them the river like lemonade fizzing and hurdling over stones. Opposite our shutters, shabby-green electric trains shot through the mugwort, past the brothels, and now and then screeched – a perforating cry, a scalding cry, poverty-stricken, infinitely pathetic.

We had dined. Twilight. I was in the cotton kimono hotels supply guests with. She was in the blue-and-white summer robe that all young women there wear. Cool-making designs on it . . . waves, reeds, clouds, willows. All undulant. You know? The Kamo was making the same sound the Rivulet does as it escapes through Hobart. The same: sometimes on wet nights I walk down past John Lee Archer's jail. . . . Exclamation mark! My parents' house *and* the jail . . . what an architect for posterity, tourists and cages! I walk, as poisoner Wainewright must often have walked, to the Palladio and lean there, as he must have leant, on the same balustrade, to listen. What poor little Wainewright was listening for with his convict's ears, who knows? I listened for the Kamo and – would it be happiness?

Of course, fill 'em up. I'm much more articulate full than half, much more nostalgic, happier than when reputedly happier. Moreover, notice please, I acquire the same elegant lisp Wainewright had. . . .

Paper shutters open: heat, a lantern moon floating above all the brothel lanterns and garish fluorescents, the acetylene lamps of the noodle-soup stalls: occasionally a train squalling in the very voice of twilight Japan . . . oh, sad, sad. It was then, there, that I knew I needed Suzuki for fulfilment and peace. It was there, then, that Suzuki split away like the half of a philippina from O-Kichi, and I felt for the first time like other men, like dinkum effing Aussies, like blokes.

Flourish of hautboys: I had a girl of my own!

I can remember . . . ah, Marie Antoinette, your condescension is timely. For friend and self, please. A double for self. And one for you or a chinchilla stole.

My friend ungraciously declines?

He has to pilot the motoring-cart? I don't. I dee oh en apostrophe tee.

Now Elvie's returned to her roaring porky seafarers tell me why they're all tattooed on their great ruddy hands. A ploy between bar and brothel? Bloodhouse, brothel, tattooery − the ports of the world fringed with 'em!

I'm aware my eyes resemble garnets. Next time the reds of my eyes will be white, I'll be the dull friend and listen to you.

Suzuki and manhood.

What?

I was saying, "I can remember . . . "? Was I now? Was I indeed?

I can remember a long addition sum of fascinations and delights. Before fleeing *maman* I'd imperfectly pictured Japan: eaves entangled in cherry-blossom, women lithe as irises, rococo croquet-hoops of bridges − all the floating-world colour-print stuff. Not like that. Not the design on the bread-and-butter plate at 'all, at all. More . . . oh, skip it. Contentment between male and female doesn't need local colour, either plate or fact, doesn't need illustration, eulogy.

Just happiness, day after day till the last day. . . .

A son, at first, doesn't estimate the omnipotence of perverted maternity, doesn't credit its additional senses. My letters must have stunk of joy, maybe I'd written with naive cunning that I was planning a job in Tokyo University when my lecture year was up. Anyway the atom-bomb cable: *Mother gravely ill, return at once. Ill,* you see − she's the sort who says it too. She'd never been sick. Never has − physically.

I am a fool. Was a fool. Was the Pope of fools. Hadn't foreseen that lie, hadn't conceived a mother would play motherhood like an ace of bloody hearts, didn't realize how tenaciously vulgar she . . . is. Then I made my greatest mistake, I. . . .

No, my friend, not that, nothing psychic or so masterful even as hedging. Dutiful son caught the next plane from Haneda. Home in three days with a hangover head that could have been Baudelaire's to be met by a mother strong as a horse stamping expensive hooves in aitchless victory. Back to Hobart, back to the Rowlandson alley-ways, the butchers' displaying blowflies and minced kangaroo, the hilltop university, the hill with KEEN'S CURRY monstrous on it in whitewashed rocks, the streets that go uphill then down. . . .

O.K., Queen of France, I shan't sing if you replenish. Shan't lose my head if you don't lose yours.

Yes. Back to the mountain and the mountain-shadow moving like a blade towards the Estuary, back to the bucket of ashy ice hung at the bottom of a bitter world.

Eh?

My greatest mistake? Didn't I tell?

My, I must stop tippling in the next few decades.

Suzuki and I were in Yokohama when the cable arrived. I grabbed a jeep and – the mistake – drove her home to Shimoda. A lack-lustre day. All those fabled towns – Fujisawa, Oiso, Odawara. Snow began to fall on the sloping streets of Atami, kept on falling, falling along the haunted shores of the Sea of Sagami, went leaping down Suicide Cliff, fell on Ito, on the camellia orchards of Kawana, on a hundred and fifty miles of disciplined agony to Shimoda. No tears; control like a mockery of plate-glass between us and the truth. Because of snow we travelled slowly; my time was running out; the plane to obligation would start in five hours. One last kiss under the snowy pines outside Shimoda Inn – pure Hiroshige the scene. By the street-braziers men and women in snow-caked hats watched us unmovingly, unblinkingly – foreigner and foreigner's woman. We tore ourselves apart.

As the jeep leapt forward she cried out savagely, squawked like an electric train, shattering the glass of self-restraint, and began to run after the jeep, arms outstretched in the snow, screaming my name while I shouted through tears at the road ahead, "Good-bye, O-Kichi!"

O-Kichi! Dead for so long.

I shouted it for miles.

Who said *Es ist nichts auf dieser Erde so still wie der Schnee?* Nothing on this earth so still as snow – liar! The snow wailed and sobbed, cried my name and stumbled behind the jeep stretching out its hopeless arms . . . the snow . . . the lonely snow. . . .

Sir Ear, how charming of you. . . .

I *could* drink an-oth-er doub-le brand-y. Then, at your be-hest, be-*hest*, I'll come qui-et-ly even if thoshe – *those* – two Marie An-toin-ettes are not ready yet to turn out the twinkly fairy-lights and us. My eyes are now sprucely darting about like wet mice . . . aren't they sprucely? aren't they?

It was much later when they left Saint Ives and reached the beautiful house with its hideous garden.

As the friend's car slid away, the man, older now, talked-out, crunched with stately care to the conservatory, its nineteenth-century panes replaced by plate-glass. Within stood four immaculate statues.

With a savage cry he had heard somewhere before, with deadly power, he pushed Spring, Summer and Autumn through the glass.

There was less noise than he expected, or his sobbing drowned it.

Wantonly celebrating, the snow hissed in as he stood embracing Winter, head battering her breast as through demanding admission.

When his mother reached the conservatory from upstairs to stand sweetly saying, "Come now, Boysie, I've kep' y' dinner 'ot. Don't worry, Boysie, y' dinner's 'ot", he and the icy marble woman he was gutturally and fiercely addressing were already crusted with snow, the gritty confetti of a crippled, bygone and unavailing nuptial.

Down at the Dump

Patrick White

"Hi!"

He called from out of the house, and she went on chopping in the yard. Her right arm swung, firm still, muscular, though parts of her were beginning to sag. She swung with her right, and her left arm hung free. She chipped at the log, left right. She was expert with the axe.

Because you had to be. You couldn't expect all that much from a man.

"Hi!" It was Wal Whalley calling again from out of the home.

He came to the door then, in that dirty old baseball cap he had shook off the Yankee disposals. Still a fairly appetizing male, though his belly had begun to push against the belt.

"Puttin' on yer act?" he asked, easing the singlet under his armpits; easy was policy at Whalleys' place.

"'Ere!" she protested. "Waddaya make me out ter be? A lump of wood?"

Her eyes were of that blazing blue, her skin that of a brown peach. But whenever she smiled, something would happen, her mouth opening on watery sockets and the jags of brown, rotting stumps.

"A woman likes to be addressed," she said.

No one had ever heard Wal address his wife by her first name. Nobody had ever heard her name, though it was printed in the electoral roll. It was, in fact, Isba.

"Don't know about a dress," said Wal. "I got a idea, though."

His wife stood tossing her hair. It was natural at least; the sun had done it. All the kids had inherited their mother's colour, and when they stood together, golden-skinned, tossing back their unmanageable hair, you would have said a mob of taffy brumbies.

"What is the bloody idea?" she asked, because she couldn't go on standing there.

"Pick up a coupla cold bottles, and spend the mornun at the dump."

"But that's the same old idea," she grumbled.

"No, it ain't. Not our own dump. We ain't done done Sarsaparilla since Christmas."

She began to grumble her way across the yard and into the house. A smell of sink strayed out of grey, unpainted weatherboard, to oppose the stench of crushed boggabri and cotton pear. Perhaps because Whalleys were in the bits-and-pieces trade their home was threatening to give in to them.

Wal Whalley did the dumps. Of course there were the other lurks besides. But no one had an eye like Wal for the things a person needs: dead batteries and musical bedsteads, a carpet you wouldn't notice was stained, wire, and again wire, clocks only waiting to jump back into the race of time. Objects of commerce and mystery littered Whalleys' back yard. Best of all, a rusty boiler into which the twins would climb to play at cubby.

"Eh? Waddaboutut?" Wal shouted, and pushed against his wife with his side.

She almost put her foot through the hole that had come in the kitchen boards.

"Waddabout what?"

Half-suspecting, she half-sniggered. Because Wal knew how to play on her weakness.

"The fuckun *idea!*"

So that she began again to grumble. As she slopped through the house her clothes irritated her skin. The sunlight fell yellow on the grey masses of the unmade beds, turned the fluff in the corners of the rooms to gold. Something was nagging at her, something heavy continued to weigh her down.

Of course. It was the funeral.

"Why, Wal," she said, the way she would suddenly come round, "you could certainly of thought of a worse idea. It'll keep the kids out of mischief. Wonder if that bloody Lummy's gunna decide to honour us?"

"One day I'll knock 'is block off," said Wal.

"He's only at the awkward age."

She stood at the window, looking as though she might know the hell of a lot. It was the funeral made her feel solemn. Brought the goose-flesh out on her.

"Good job you thought about the dump," she said, out-staring a red-brick propriety the other side of the road. "If there's anythun gets me down, it's havin' ter watch a funeral pass."

"Won't be from 'ere," he consoled. "They took 'er away same evenun. It's gunna start from Jackson's Personal Service."

"Good job she popped off at the beginnun of the week. They're not so personal at the week-end."

She began to prepare for the journey to the dump. Pulled her frock down a bit. Slipped on a pair of shoes.

"Bet *She*'ll be relieved. Wouldn't show it, though. Not about 'er sister. I bet Daise stuck in 'er fuckun guts."

Then Mrs Whalley was compelled to return to the window. As if her instinct. And sure enough there She was. Looking inside the letter-box, as if she hadn't collected already. Bent above the brick pillar in which the letter-box had been cemented, Mrs Hogben's face wore all that people expect of the bereaved.

"Daise was all right," said Wal.

"Daise was all right," agreed his wife.

Suddenly she wondered: What if Wal, if Wal had ever. . . . ?

Mrs Whalley settled her hair. If she hadn't been all that satisfied at home – and she was satisfied, her recollective eyes would admit – she too might have done a line like Daise Morrow.

Over the road Mrs Hogben was calling.

"Meg?" she called. "Mar*gret*?"

Though from pure habit, without direction. Her voice sounded thinner today.

Then Mrs Hogben went away.

"Once I got took to a funeral," Mrs Whalley said. "They made me look in the coffun. It was the bloke's wife. He was that cut up."

"Did yer have a squint?"

"Pretended to."

Wal Whalley was breathing hard in the airless room.

"How soon do yer reckon they begin ter smell?"

"Smell? They wouldn't let 'em!" his wife said very definite. "You're the one that smells, Wal. I wonder you don't think of takin' a bath."

But she liked his smell, for all that. It followed her out of the shadow into the strong shaft of light. Looking at each other their two bodies asserted themselves. Their faces were lit by the certainty of life.

Wal tweaked her left nipple.

"We'll slip inter the Bull on the way, and pick up those cold bottles."

He spoke soft for him.

Mrs Hogben called another once or twice. Inside the brick entrance the cool of the house struck at her. She liked it cool, but not cold, and this was if not exactly cold, anyway, too sudden. So now she whimpered, very faintly, for everything you have to suffer, and death on top of all. Although it was her sister Daise who had died, Mrs Hogben was crying for the death which was waiting to carry her off in turn. She called: "Me-ehg?" But no one ever came to your rescue. She stopped to loosen the soil round the roots of the aluminium plant. She always had to be doing something. It made her feel better.

Meg did not hear, of course. She was standing amongst the fuchsia bushes, looking out from their greenish shade. She was thin and freckly. She looked awful, because Mum had made her wear her uniform, because it was sort of a formal occasion, to Auntie Daise's funeral. In the circumstances she not only looked, but was thin. That Mrs Ireland who was all for sports had told her she must turn her toes out, and watch out — she might grow up knock-kneed besides.

So Meg Hogben was, and felt, altogether awful. Her skin was green, except when the war between light and shade worried her face into scraps, and the fuchsia tassels, trembling against her unknowing cheek, infused something of their own blood, brindled her with shifting crimson. Only her eyes resisted. They were not exactly an ordinary grey. Lorrae Jensen, who was blue, said they were the eyes of a mopey cat.

A bunch of six or seven kids from Second-Grade, Lorrae, Edna, Val, Sherry, Sue Smith and Sue Goldstein, stuck together in the holidays, though Meg sometimes wondered why. The others had come around to Hogbens' Tuesday evening.

Lorrae said: "We're going down to Barranugli pool Thursday. There's some boys Sherry knows with a couple of Gs. They've promised to take us for a run after we come out."

Med did not know whether she was glad or ashamed.

"I can't," she said. "My auntie's died."

"Arr!" their voices trailed.

They couldn't get away too quick, as if it had been something contagious.

But murmuring.

Meg sensed she had become temporarily important.

So now she was alone with her dead importance, in the fuchsia bushes, on the day of Auntie Daise's funeral. She had turned fourteen. She remembered the ring in plaited gold Auntie Daise had promised her. When I am gone, her aunt had said. And now it had really happened. Without rancour Meg suspected there hadn't been time to think about the ring, and Mum would grab it, to add to all the other things she had.

Then that Lummy Whalley showed up, amongst the camphor laurels opposite, tossing his head of bleached hair. She hated boys with white hair. For that matter she hated boys, or any intrusion on her privacy. She hated Lum most of all. The day he threw the dog poo at her. It made the gristle come in her neck. Ugh! Although the old poo had only skittered over her skin, too dry to really matter, she had gone in and cried because, well, there were times when she cultivated dignity.

Now Meg Hogben and Lummy Whalley did not notice each other even when they looked.

> Who wants Meg Skinny-leg?
> I'd rather take the clothes-peg . . .

Lum Whalley vibrated like a comb-and-paper over amongst the camphor laurels they lopped back every so many years for firewood. He slashed with his knife into bark. Once in a hot dusk he had carved I LOVE MEG, because that was something you did, like on lavatory walls, and in the trains, but it didn't mean anything of course. Afterwards he slashed the darkness as if it had been a train seat.

Lum Whalley pretended not to watch Meg Hogben skulking in the fuchsia bushes. Wearing her brown uniform. Stiffer, browner than for school, because it was her auntie's funeral.

"Me-ehg?" called Mrs Hogben. "Meg!"

"Lummy! Where the devil are yer?" called his mum.

She was calling all around, in the woodshed, behind the dunny. Let her!

"Lum? Lummy, for Chris*sake!*" she called.

He hated that. Like some bloody kid. At school he had got them to call him Bill, halfway between, not so shameful as Lum, nor yet as awful as William.

Mrs Whalley came round the corner.

"Shoutin' me bloody lungs up!" she said. "When your dad's got a nice idea. We're going down to Sarsaparilla dump."

"Arr!" he said.

But didn't spit.

"What gets inter you?" she asked.

Even at their most inaccessible Mrs Whalley liked to finger her children. Touch often assisted thought. But she liked the feel of them as well. She was glad she hadn't had girls. Boys turned into men, and you couldn't do without men, even when they took you for a mug, or got shickered, or bashed you up.

So she put her hand on Lummy, tried to get through to him. He was dressed, but might not have been. Lummy's kind was never ever born for clothes. At fourteen he looked more.

"Well," she said, sourer than she felt, "I'm not gunna cry over any sulky boy. Suit yourself."

She moved off.

As Dad had got out the old rattle-bones by now, Lum began to clamber up. The back of the ute was at least private, though it wasn't no Customline.

The fact that Whalleys ran a Customline as well puzzled more unreasonable minds. Drawn up amongst the paspalum in front of Whalleys' shack, it looked stolen, and almost was – the third payment overdue. But would slither with ease a little longer to Barranugli, and snooze outside the Northern Hotel. Lum could have stood all day to admire their own two-tone car. Or would stretch out inside, his fingers at work on plastic flesh.

Now it was the ute for business. The bones of his buttocks bit into the boards. His father's meaty arm stuck out at the window, disgusting him. And soon the twins were squeezing from the rusty boiler. The taffy Gary – or was it Barry? had fallen down and barked his knee.

"For Chrissake!" Mrs Whalley shrieked, and tossed her identical taffy hair.

Mrs Hogben watched those Whalleys leave.

"In a brick area, I wouldn't of thought," she remarked to her husband once again.

"All in good time, Myrtle," Councillor Hogben replied as before.

"Of course," she said, "if there are *reasons*."

Because councillors, she knew, did have reasons.

"But that home! And a Customline!"

The saliva of bitterness came in her mouth.

It was Daise who had said: I'm going to enjoy the good things of life – and died in that pokey little hutch, with only a cotton frock to her back. While Myrtle had the liver-coloured brick home – not a single dampmark on the ceilings – she had the washing machine, the septic, the TV, and the cream Holden Special, not to forget her husband. Les Hogben, the councillor. A builder into the bargain.

Now Myrtle stood amongst her things, and would have continued to regret the Ford the Whalleys hadn't paid for, if she hadn't been regretting Daise. It was not so much her sister's death as her life Mrs Hogben deplored. Still, everybody knew, and there was nothing you could do about it.

"Do you think anybody will come?" Mrs Hogben asked.

"What do you take me for?" her husband replied. "One of these cleervoyants?"

Mrs Hogben did not hear.

After giving the matter consideration she had advertised the death in the *Herald*:

> MORROW, Daisy (Mrs), suddenly, at her residence,
> Showground Road, Sarsaparilla.

There was nothing more you could put. It wasn't fair on Les, a public servant, to rake up relationships. And the *Mrs* – well, everyone had got into the habit when Daise started going with Cunningham. It seemed sort of natural as things dragged on and on. Don't work yourself up, Myrt, Daise used to say; Jack will when his wife dies. But it was Jack Cunningham who died first. Daise said: It's the way it happened, that's all.

"Do you think Ossie will come?" Councillor Hogben asked his wife slower than she liked.

"I hadn't thought about it," she said.

Which meant she had. She had, in fact, woken in the night, and lain there cold and stiff, as her mind's eye focused on Ossie's runny nose.

Mrs Hogben rushed at a drawer which somebody – never herself – had left hanging out. She was a thin woman, but wiry.

"Meg?" she called. "Did you polish your shoes?"

Les Hogben laughed behind his closed mouth. He always did when he thought of Daise's parting folly: to take up with that old scabby deadbeat Ossie from down at the showground. But who cared?

No one, unless her family.

Mrs Hogben dreaded the possibility of Ossie, a Roman Catholic for extra value, standing beside Daise's grave, even if nobody, even if only Mr Brickle saw.

Whenever the thought of Ossie Coogan crossed Councillor Hogben's mind he would twist the knife in his sister-in-law.

Perhaps, now, he was glad she had died. A small woman, smaller than his wife, Daise Morrow was large by nature. Whenever she dropped in she was all around the place. Yarn her head off if she got the chance. It got so as Les Hogben could not stand hearing her laugh. Pressed against her in the hall once. He had forgotten that, or almost. How Daise laughed then. I'm not so short of men I'd pick me own brother-in-law. Had he pressed? Not all that much, not intentional, anyway. So the incident had been allowed to fade, dim as the brown-linoleum hall, in Councillor Hogben's mind.

"There's the phone, Leslie."

It was his wife.

"I'm too upset," she said, "to answer."

And began to cry.

Easing his crutch Councillor Hogben went into the hall.

It was good old Horrie Last.

"Yairs . . . yairs . . . " said Mr Hogben, speaking into the telephone which his wife kept swabbed with Breath-o'-Pine. "Yairs . . . Eleven, Horrie . . . from Barranugli . . . from Jackson's Personal . . . Yairs, that's decent of you, Horrie."

"Horrie Last," Councillor Hogben reported to his wife, "is gunna put in an appearance."

If no one else, a second councillor for Daise. Myrtle Hogben was consoled.

What could you do? Horrie Last put down the phone. He and Les had stuck together. Teamed up to catch the more progressive vote. Hogben and Last had developed the shire. Les had built Horrie's home, Lasts had sold Hogbens theirs. If certain people were spreading the rumour that Last and Hogben had caused a contraction of the Green Belt, then certainly people failed to realize the term itself implied flexibility.

"What did you tell them?" asked Mrs Last.

"Said I'd go," her husband said, doing things to the change in his pocket.

He was a short man, given to standing with his legs apart.

Georgina Last withheld her reply. Formally of interest, her shape suggested she had been made out of several scones joined together in the baking.

"Daise Morrow," said Horrie Last, "wasn't such a bad sort."

Mrs Last did not answer.

So he stirred the money in his pocket harder, hoping perhaps it would emulsify. He wasn't irritated, mind you, by his wife – who had brought him a parcel of property, as well as a flair for real estate – but had often felt he might have done a dash with Daise

Morrow on the side. Wouldn't have minded betting old Les
Hogben had tinkered a bit with his wife's sister. Helped her buy
her home, they said. Always lights on at Daise's place after dark.
Postman left her mail on the verandah instead of in the box. In
summer, when the men went round to read the meters, she'd ask
them in for a glass of beer. Daise knew how to get service.

Georgina Last cleared her throat.

"Funerals are not for women," she declared, and took up a cardigan she was knitting for a cousin.

"You didn't do your shoes!" Mrs Hogben protested.

"I did," said Meg. "It's the dust. Don't know why we bother to
clean shoes at all. They always get dirty again."

She stood there looking awful in the school uniform. Her cheeks
were hollow from what she read could only be despair.

"A person must keep to her principles," Mrs Hogben said, and
added: "Dadda is bringing round the car. Where's your hat, dear?
We'll be ready to leave in two minutes."

"Arr, Mum! The hat?"

That old school hat. It had shrunk already a year ago, but had to
see her through.

"You wear it to church, don't you?"

"But this isn't church!"

"It's as good as. Besides, you owe it to your aunt," Mrs Hogben
said, to win.

Meg went and got her hat. They were going out through the
fuchsia bushes, past the plaster pixies, which Mrs Hogben had
trained her child to cover with plastic at the first drops of rain.
Meg Hogben hated the sight of those corny old pixies, even after
the plastic cones had snuffed them out.

It was sad in the car, dreamier. As she sat looking out through
the window, the tight panama perched on her head lost its power
to humiliate. Her always persistent, grey eyes, under the line of
dark fringe, had taken up the search again: she had never yet
looked enough. Along the road they passed the house in which her
aunt, they told her, had died. The small, pink, tilted house, standing amongst the carnation plants, had certainly lost some of its life.
Or the glare had drained the colour from it. How the mornings
used to sparkle in which Aunt Daise went up and down between
the rows, her gown dragging heavy with dew, binding with bast
the fuzzy flowers by handfuls and handfuls. Auntie's voice clear
as morning. No one, she called, could argue they look stiff when

they're bunched tight eh Meg what would you say they remind
you of? But you never knew the answers to the sort of things
people asked. Frozen fireworks, Daise suggested. Meg loved the
idea of it, she loved Daise. Not so frozen either, she dared. The sun
getting at the wet flowers broke them up and made them spin.

And the clovey scent rose up in the stale-smelling car, and smote
Meg Hogben, out of the reeling heads of flowers, their cold stalks
dusted with blue. Then she knew she would write a poem about
Aunt Daise and the carnations. She wondered she hadn't thought
of it before.

At that point the passengers were used most brutally as the car
entered on a chain of potholes. For once Mrs Hogben failed to
invoke the Main Roads Board. She was asking herself whether
Ossie could be hiding in there behind the blinds. Or whether,
whether. She fished for her second handkerchief. Prudence had
induced her to bring two − the good one with the lace insertion
for use beside the grave.

"The weeds will grow like one thing," her voice blared, "now that
they'll have their way."

Then she began to unfold the less important of her handkerchiefs.

Myrtle Morrow had always been the sensitive one. Myrtle had
understood the Bible. Her needlework, her crochet doilys had
taken prizes at country shows. No one had fiddled such pathos out
of the pianola. It was Daise who loved flowers, though. It's a moss-
rose, Daise had said, sort of rolling it round on her tongue, while
she was still a little thing.

When she had had her cry, Mrs Hogben remarked: "Girls don't
know they're happy until it's too late."

Thus addressed, the other occupants of the car did not answer.
They knew they were not expected to.

Councillor Hogben drove in the direction of Barranugli. He had
arranged his hat before leaving. He removed a smile the mirror
reminded him was there. Although he no longer took any risks in
a re-election photograph by venturing out of the past, he often
succeeded in the fleshy present. But now, in difficult circumstances, he was exercising his sense of duty. He drove, he drove,
past the retinosperas, heavy with their own gold, past the lager-
stroemias, their pink sugar running into mildew.

Down at the dump Whalleys were having an argument about
whether the beer was to be drunk on arrival or after they had
developed a thirst.

"Keep it, then!" Mum Whalley turned her back. "What was the point of buyin' it cold if you gotta wait till it hots up? Anyways," she said, "I thought the beer was an excuse for comin'."

"Arr, stuff it!" says Wal. "A dump's business, ain't it? With or without beer. Ain't it? Any day of the week."

He saw she had begun to sulk. He saw her rather long breasts floating around inside her dress. Silly cow! He laughed. But cracked a bottle.

Barry said he wanted a drink.

You could hear the sound of angry suction as his mum's lips called off a swig.

"I'm not gunna stand by and watch any kid of mine," said the wet lips, "turn 'isself into a bloody dipso!"

Her eyes were at their blazing bluest. Perhaps it was because Wal Whalley admired his wife that he continued to desire her.

But Lummy pushed off on his own. When his mum went crook, and swore, he was too aware of the stumps of teeth, the rotting brown of nastiness. It was different, of course, if you swore yourself. Sometimes it was unavoidable.

Now he avoided by slipping away, between the old mattresses, and boots the sun had buckled up. Pitfalls abounded: the rusty traps of open tins lay in wait for guiltless ankles, the necks of broken bottles might have been prepared to gash a face. So he went thoughtfully, his feet scuffing the leaves of stained asbestos, crunching the torso of a celluloid doll. Here and there it appeared as though trash might win. The onslaught of metal was pushing the scrub into the gully. But in many secret, steamy pockets, a rout was in progress: seeds had been sown in the lumps of grey, disintegrating kapok and the laps of burst chairs, the coils of springs, locked in the spirals of wirier vines, had surrendered to superior resilience. Somewhere on the edge of the whole shambles a human ally, before retiring, had lit a fire, which by now the green had almost choked, leaving a stench of smoke to compete with the sicklier one of slow corruption.

Lum Whalley walked with a grace of which he himself had never been aware. He had had about enough of this rubbish jazz. He would have liked to know how to live neat. Like Darkie Black. Everything in its place in the cabin of Darkie's trailer. Suddenly his throat yearned for Darkie's company. Darkie's hands, twisting the wheel, appeared to control the whole world.

A couple of strands of barbed wire separated Sarsaparilla dump from Sarsaparilla cemetery. The denominations were separated too, but there you had to tell by the names, or by the angels and

things the RIPs went in for. Over in what must have been the
Church of England Alf Herbert was finishing Mrs Morrow's grave.
He had reached the clay, and the going was heavy. The clods fell
resentfully.

If what they said about Mrs Morrow was true, then she had
lived it up all right. Lum Whalley wondered what, supposing he
had met her walking towards him down a bush track, smiling. His
skin tingled. Lummy had never done a girl, although he pretended
he had, so as to hold his own with the kids. He wondered if a girl,
if that sourpuss Meg Hogben. Would of bitten as likely as not.
Lummy felt a bit afraid, and returned to thinking of Darkie Black,
who never talked about things like that.

Presently he moved away. Alf Herbert, leaning on his shovel,
could have been in need of a yarn. Lummy was not prepared to
yarn. He turned back into the speckled bush, into the pretences of
a shade. He lay down under a banksia, and opened his fly to look
at himself. But pretty soon got sick of it.

The procession from Barranugli back to Sarsaparilla was hardly
what you would have called a procession: the Reverend Brickle,
the Hogbens' Holden, Horrie's Holden, following the smaller of
Jackson's hearses. In the circumstances they were doing things
cheap – there was no reason for splashing it around. At Sarsaparilla Mr Gill joined in, sitting high in that old Chev. It would have
been practical, Councillor Hogben sighed, to join the hearse at
Sarsaparilla. Old Gill was only there on account of Daise being his
customer for years. A grocer lacking in enterprise, Daise had stuck
to him, she said, because she liked him. Well, if that was what you
put first, but where did it get you?

At the last dip before the cemetery a disembowelled mattress
from the dump had begun to writhe across the road. It looked like
a kind of monster from out of the depths of somebody's mind, the
part a decent person ignored.

"Ah, dear! At the cemetery too!" Mrs Hogben protested. "I
wonder the Council," she added, in spite of her husband.

"All right, Myrtle," he said between his teeth. "I made a mental
note."

Councillor Hogben was good at that.

"And the Whalleys on your own doorstep," Mrs Hogben
moaned.

The things she had seen on hot days, in front of their kiddies too.

The hearse had entered the cemetery gate. They had reached

the bumpy stage toppling over the paspalum clumps, before the thinner, bush grass. All around, the leaves of the trees presented so many grey blades. Not even a magpie to put heart into a Christian. But Alf Herbert came forward, his hand dusted with yellow clay, to guide the hearse between the Methoes and the Presbyterians, onto Church of England ground.

Jolting had shaken Mrs Hogben's grief up to the surface again. Mr Brickle was impressed. He spoke for a moment of the near and dear. His hands were kind and professional in helping her out.

But Meg jumped. And landed. It was a shock to hear a stick crack so loud. Perhaps it was what Mum would have called irreverent. At the same time her banana-coloured panama fell off her head into the tussocks.

It was really a bit confusing at the grave. Some of the men helped with the coffin, and Councillor Last was far too short.

Then Mrs Hogben saw, she saw, from out of the lace handkerchief, it was that Ossie Coogan she saw, standing the other side of the grave. Had old Gill given him a lift? Ossie, only indifferently buttoned, stood snivelling behind the mound of yellow clay.

Nothing would have stopped his nose. Daise used to say: You don't want to be frightened, Ossie, not when I'm here, see? But she wasn't any longer. So now he was afraid. Excepting Daise, Protestants had always frightened him. Well, I'm nothing, she used to say, nothing that you could pigeonhole, but love what we are given to love.

Myrtle Hogben was ropeable, if only because of what Councillor Last must think. She would have liked to express her feelings in words, if she could have done so without giving offence to God. Then the ants ran up her legs, for she was standing on a nest, and her body cringed before the teeming injustices.

Daise, she had protested the day it all began, whatever has come over you? The sight of her sister had made her run out leaving the white sauce to burn. Wherever will you take him? He's sick, said Daise. *But you can't*, Myrtle Hogben cried. For there was her sister Daise pushing some old deadbeat in a barrow. All along Showground Road people had come out of homes to look. Daise appeared smaller pushing the wheelbarrow down the hollow and up the hill. Her hair was half uncoiled. *You can't! You can't!* Myrtle called. But Daise could, and did.

When all the few people were assembled at the graveside in their good clothes, Mr Brickle opened the book, though his voice soon suggested he needn't have.

"I am the resurrection and the life," he said.

And Ossie cried. Because he didn't believe it, not when it came
to the real thing.

He looked down at the coffin, which was what remained of
what he knew. He remembered eating a baked apple, very slowly,
the toffee on it. And again the dark of the horse-stall swallowed
him up, where he lay hopeless amongst the shit, and her coming at
him with the barrow. What do you want? he asked straight out.
I came down to the showground, she said, for a bit of honest-to-
God manure, I've had those fertilizers, she said, and what are you,
are you sick? I live 'ere, he said. And began to cry, and rub the snot
from his snively nose. After a bit Daise said: We're going back to
my place, What's-yer-Name — Ossie. The way she spoke he knew
it was true. All the way up the hill in the barrow the wind was
giving his eyes gyp, and blowing his thin hair apart. Over the
years he had come across one or two lice in his hair, but thought,
or hoped he had got rid of them by the time Daise took him up.
As she pushed and struggled with the barrow, sometimes she
would lean forward, and he felt her warmth, her firm diddies
pressed against his back.

*"Lord, let me know mine end, and the number of my days: that I may
be certified how long I have to live,"* Mr Brickle read.

Certified was the word, decided Councillor Hogben looking at
that old Ossie.

Who stood there mumbling a few Aspirations, very quiet, on the
strength of what they had taught him as a boy.

When all this was under way, all these words of which, she knew,
her Auntie Daise would not have approved, Meg Hogben went
and got beneath the strands of wire separating the cemetery from
the dump. She had never been to the dump before, and her heart
was lively in her side. She walked shyly through the bush. She
came across an old suspender-belt. She stumbled over a blackened
primus.

She saw Lummy Whalley then. He was standing under a
banksia, twisting at one of its dead heads.

Suddenly they knew there was something neither of them could
continue to avoid.

"I came here to the funeral," she said.

She sounded, well, almost relieved.

"Do you come here often?" she asked.

"Nah," he answered, hoarse. "Not here. To dumps, yes."

But her intrusion had destroyed the predetermined ceremony of
his life, and caused a trembling in his hand.

"Is there anything to see?" she asked.

"Junk," he said. "Same old junk."

"Have you ever looked at a dead person?"

Because she noticed the trembling of his hand.

"No," he said. "Have you?"

She hadn't. Nor did it seem probable that she would have to now. Not as they began breathing evenly again.

"What do you do with yourself?" he asked.

Then, even though she would have liked to stop herself, she could not. She said: "I write poems. I'm going to write one about my Aunt Daise, like she was, gathering carnations early in the dew."

"What'll you get out of that?"

"Nothing," she said, "I suppose."

But it did not matter.

"What other sorts of pomes do you write?" he asked, twisting at last the dead head of the banksia off.

"I wrote one," she said, "about the things in a cupboard. I wrote about a dream I had. And the smell of rain. That was a bit too short."

He began to look at her then. He had never looked into the eyes of a girl. They were grey and cool, unlike the hot, or burnt-out eyes of a woman.

"What are you going to be?" she asked.

"I dunno."

"You're not a white-collar type."

"Eh?"

"I mean you're not for figures, and books, and banks and offices," she said.

He was too disgusted to agree.

"I'm gunna have me own truck. Like Mr Black. Darkie's got a trailer."

"What?"

"Well," he said, "a semi-trailer."

"Oh," she said, more diffident.

"Darkie took me on a trip to Maryborough. It was pretty tough goin'. Sometimes we drove right through the night. Sometimes we slept on the road. Or in places where you get rooms. Gee, it was good though, shootin' through the country towns at night."

She saw it. She saw the people standing at their doors, frozen in the blocks of yellow light. The rushing of the night made the figures for ever still. All around she could feel the furry darkness, as the semi-trailer roared and bucked, its skeleton of coloured

lights. While in the cabin, in which they sat, all was stability and
order. If she glanced sideways she could see how his taffy hair
shone when raked by the bursts of electric light. They had brought
cases with tooth-brushes, combs, one or two things – the pad on
which she would write the poem somewhere when they stopped
in the smell of sunlight dust ants. But his hands had acquired such
mastery over the wheel, it appeared this might never happen. Nor
did she care.

"This Mr Black," she said, her mouth getting thinner, "does he
take you with him often?"

"Only once interstate," said Lummy, pitching the banksia head
away. "Once in a while short trips."

As they drove they rocked together. He had never been closer to
anyone than when bumping against Darkie's ribs. He waited to
experience again the little spasm of gratitude and pleasure. He
would have liked to wear, and would in time, a striped sweat-shirt
like Darkie wore.

"I'd like to go in with Darkie," he said, "when I get a trailer of me
own. Darkie's the best friend I got."

With a drawnout shiver of distrust she saw the darker hands,
the little black hairs on the backs of the fingers.

"Oh well," she said, withdrawn, "praps you will in the end," she
said.

On the surrounding graves the brown flowers stood in their jars of
browner water. The more top-heavy, plastic bunches had been
slapped down by a westerly, but had not come to worse grief than
to lie strewn in pale disorder on the uncharitable granite chips.

The heat made Councillor Last yawn. He began to read the
carved names, those within sight at least, some of which he had
just about forgot. He almost laughed once. If the dead could have
sat up in their graves there would have been an argument or two.

"In the midst of life we are in death," said the parson bloke.

JACK CUNNINGHAM

BELOVED HUSBAND OF FLORENCE MARY,

read Horrie Last.

Who would have thought Cunningham, straight as a silky-oak,
would fall going up the path to Daise Morrow's place. Horrie used
to watch them together, sitting a while on the verandah before
going in to their tea. They made no bones about it, because every-

body knew. Good teeth Cunningham had. Always a white, well-ironed shirt. Wonder which of the ladies did the laundry. Florence Mary was an invalid, they said. Daise Morrow liked to laugh with men, but for Jack Cunningham she had a silence, promising intimacies at which Horrie Last could only guess, whose own private life had been lived in almost total darkness.

Good Christ, and then there was Ossie. The woman could only have been at heart a perv of a kind you hadn't heard about.

"Forasmuch as it hath pleased Almighty God of his great mercy to take unto himself the soul . . . " read Mr Brickle.

As it was doubtful who should cast the earth, Mr Gill the grocer did. They heard the handful rattle on the coffin.

Then the tears truly ran out of Ossie's scaly eyes. Out of darkness. Out of darkness Daise had called: What's up Ossie, you don't wanta cry. I got the cramps, he answered. They were twisting him. The cramps? she said drowsily. Or do you imagine? If it isn't the cramps it's something else. Could have been. He'd take Daise's word for it. He was never all that bright since he had the meningitis. Tell you what, Daise said, you come in here, into my bed, I'll warm you, Os, in a jiffy. He listened in the dark to his own snivelling. Arr, Daise, I couldn't, he said, I couldn't get a stand, not if you was to give me the jackpot, he said. She sounded very still then. He lay and counted the throbbing of the darkness. Not like that, she said — she didn't laugh at him as he had half expected — besides, she said, it only ever really comes to you once. That way. And at once he was parting the darkness, bumping and shambling, to get to her. He had never known it so gentle. Because Daise wasn't afraid. She ran her hands through his hair, on and on like water flowing. She soothed the cramps out of his legs. Until in the end they were breathing in time. Dozing. Then the lad Ossie Coogan rode again down from the mountain, the sound of the snaffle in the blue air, the smell of sweat from under the saddle-cloth, towards the great, flowing river. He rocked and flowed with the motion of the strong, never-ending river, burying his mouth in brown cool water, to drown would have been worth it.

Once during the night Ossie had woken, afraid the distance might have come between them. But Daise was still holding him against her breast. If he had been different, say. Ossie's throat had begun to wobble. Only then, Daise, Daise might have turned different. So he nuzzled against the warm darkness, and was again received.

"If you want to enough, you can do what you want," Meg Hogben insisted.

She had read it in a book, and wasn't altogether convinced, but theories sometimes come to the rescue.

"If you want," she said, kicking a hole in the stony ground.

"Not everything you can't."

"You can!" she said. "But you can!"

She who had never looked at a boy, not right into one, was looking at him as never before.

"That's a lot of crap," he said.

"Well," she admitted, "there are limits."

It made him frown. He was again suspicious. She was acting clever. All those pomes.

But to reach understanding she would have surrendered her cleverness. She was no longer proud of it.

"And what'll happen if you get married? Riding around the country in a truck. How'll your wife like it? Stuck at home with a lot of kids."

"Some of 'em take the wife along. Darkie takes his missus and kids. Not always, like. But now and again. On short runs."

"You didn't tell me Mr Black was married."

"Can't tell you everything, can I? Not at once."

The women who sat in the drivers' cabins of the semi-trailers he saw as predominantly thin and dark. They seldom returned glances, but wiped their hands on Kleenex, and peered into little mirrors, waiting for their men to show up again. Which in time they had to. So he walked across from the service station, to take possession of his property. Sauntering, frowning slightly, touching the yellow stubble on his chin, he did not bother to look. Glanced sideways perhaps. She was the thinnest, the darkest he knew, the coolest of all the women who sat looking out from the cabin windows of the semi-trailers.

In the meantime they strolled a bit, amongst the rusty tins at Sarsaparilla dump. He broke a few sticks and threw away the pieces. She tore off a narrow leaf and smelled it. She would have liked to smell Lummy's hair.

"Gee, you're fair," she had to say.

"Some are born fair," he admitted.

He began pelting a rock with stones. He was strong, she saw. So many discoveries in a short while were making her tremble at the knees.

And as they rushed through the brilliant light, roaring and lurching, the cabin filled with fair-skinned, taffy children, the youngest of whom she was protecting by holding the palm of her hand behind his neck, as she had noticed women do. Occupied in this way, she almost forgot Lum at times, who would pull up, and she would climb down, to rinse the nappies in tepid water, and hang them on a bush to dry.

"All these pomes and things," he said, "I never knew a clever person before."

"But clever isn't any different," she begged, afraid he might not accept her peculiarity and power.

She would go with a desperate wariness from now. She sensed that, if not in years, she was older than Lum, but this was the secret he must never guess: that for all his strength, all his beauty, she was, and must remain the stronger.

"What's that?" he asked, and touched.

But drew back his hand in self-protection.

"A scar," she said. "I cut my wrist opening a tin of condensed milk."

For once she was glad of the paler seam in her freckled skin, hoping that it might heal a breach.

And he looked at her out of his hard blue Whalley eyes. He liked her. Although she was ugly, and clever, and a girl.

"Condensed milk on bread," he said, "that's something I could eat till I bust."

"Oh, yes!" she agreed.

She did honestly believe, although she had never thought of it before.

Flies clustered in irregular jet embroideries on the backs of best suits. Nobody bothered any longer to shrug them off. As Alf Herbert grunted against the shovelfuls, dust clogged increasingly, promises settled thicker. Although they had been told they might expect Christ to redeem, it would have been no less incongruous if He had appeared out of the scrub to perform on altars of burning sandstone, a sacrifice for which nobody had prepared them. In any case, the mourners waited – they had been taught to accept whatever might be imposed – while the heat stupefied the remnants of their minds, and inflated their Australian fingers into foreign-looking sausages.

Myrtle Hogben was the first to protest. She broke down – into the wrong handkerchief. *Who shall change our vile body?* The words were more than her decency could bear.

"Easy on it," her husband whispered, putting a finger under her elbow.

She submitted to his sympathy, just as in their life together she had submitted to his darker wishes. Never waiting more than peace, and one or two perquisites.

A thin woman, Mrs Hogben continued to cry for all the wrongs that had been done her. For Daise had only made things viler. While understanding, yes, at moments. It was girls who really understood, not even women – sisters, sisters. Before events whirled them apart. So Myrtle Morrow was again walking through the orchard, and Daise Morrow twined her arm around her sister; confession filled the air, together with a scent of crushed fermenting apples. Myrtle said: Daise, there's something I'd like to do, I'd like to chuck a lemon into a Salvation Army tuba. Daise giggled. You're a nut, Myrt, she said. But never *vile*. So Myrtle Hogben cried. Once, only once she thought how she'd like to push someone off a cliff, and watch their expression as it happened. But Myrtle had not confessed that.

So Mrs Hogben cried, for those things she was unable to confess, for anything she might not be able to control.

As the blander words had begun falling, *Our Father*, that she knew by heart, *our daily bread*, she should have felt comforted. She should of. Should of.

Where was Meg, though?

Mrs Hogben separated herself from the others. Walking stiffly. If any of the men noticed, they took it for granted she had been overcome, or wanted to relieve herself.

She would have liked to relieve herself by calling: "Margaret Meg wherever don't you hear me Me-ehg?" drawing it out thin in anger. But could not cut across a clergyman's words. So she stalked. She was not unlike a guinea-hen, its spotted silk catching on a strand of barbed-wire.

When they had walked a little farther, round and about, anywhere, they overheard voices.

"What's that?" asked Meg.

"Me mum and dad," Lummy said. "Rousin' about somethun or other."

Mum Whalley had just found two bottles of unopened beer. Down at the dump. Waddayaknow. Must be something screwy somewhere.

"Could of put poison in it," her husband warned.

"Poison? My arse!" she shouted. "That's because *I* found it!"

"Whoever found it," he said, "who's gunna drink a coupla bottlesa hot beer?"

"I am!" she said.

"When what we brought was good an' cold?"

He too was shouting a bit. She behaved unreasonable at times.

"Who wanted ter keep what we brought? Till it got good an' hot!" she shrieked.

Sweat was running down both the Whalleys.

Suddenly Lum felt he wanted to lead this girl out of earshot. He had just about had the drunken sods. He would have liked to find himself walking with his girl over mown lawn, like at the Botanical Gardens, a green turf giving beneath their leisured feet. Statues pointed a way through the glare, to where they finally sat, under enormous shiny leaves, looking out at boats on water. They unpacked their cut lunch from its layers of fresh tissue-paper.

"They're rough as bags," Lummy explained.

"I don't care," Meg Hogben assured.

Nothing on earth could make her care — was it more, or was it less?

She walked giddily behind him, past a rusted fuel-stove, over a field of deathly feltex. Or ran, or slid, to keep up. Flowers would have wilted in her hands, if she hadn't crushed them brutally, to keep her balance. Somewhere in their private labyrinth Meg Hogben had lost her hat.

When they were farther from the scene of anger, and a silence of heat had descended again, he took her little finger, because it seemed natural to do so, after all they had experienced. They swung hands for a while, according to some special law of motion.

Till Lum Whalley frowned, and threw the girl's hand away.

If she accepted his behaviour it was because she no longer believed in what he did, only in what she knew he felt. That might have been the trouble. She was so horribly sure, he would have to resist to the last moment of all. As a bird, singing in the prickly tree under which they found themselves standing, seemed to cling to the air. Then his fingers took control. She was amazed at the hardness of his boy's body. The tremors of her flinty skin, the membrane of the white sky appalled him. Before fright and expectation melted their mouths. And they took little grateful sips of each other. Holding up their throats in between. Like birds drinking.

Ossie could no longer see Alf Herbert's shovel working at the earth.

"Never knew a man cry at a funeral," Councillor Hogben complained, very low, although he was ripe enough to burst.

If you could count Ossie as a man, Councillor Last suggested in a couple of noises.

But Ossie could not see or hear, only Daise, still lying on that upheaval of a bed. Seemed she must have burst a button, for her breasts stood out from her. He would never forget how they laboured against the heavy yellow morning light. In the early light, the flesh turned yellow, sluggish. What's gunna happen to me, Daisy? It'll be decided, Os, she said, like it is for any of us. I ought to know, she said, to tell you, but give me time to rest a bit, to get me breath. Then he got down on his painful knees. He put his mouth to Daise's neck. Her skin tasted terrible bitter. The great glistening river, to which the lad Ossie Coogan had ridden jingling down from the mountain, was slowing into thick, yellow mud. Himself an old, scabby man attempting to refresh his forehead in the last pothole.

Mr Brickle said: "*We give thee hearty thanks for that it hath pleased thee to deliver this our sister out of the miseries of this sinful world.*"

"No! No!" Ossie protested, so choked nobody heard, though it was vehement enough in its intention.

As far as he could understand, nobody wanted to be delivered. Not him, not Daise, anyways. When you could sit together by the fire on winter nights baking potatoes under the ashes.

It took Mrs Hogben some little while to free her *crêpe de Chine* from the wire. It was her nerves, not to mention Meg on her mind. In the circumstances she tore herself worse, and looked up to see her child, just over there, without shame, in a rubbish tip, kissing with the Whalley boy. What if Meg was another of Daise? It was in the blood, you couldn't deny.

Mrs Hogben did not exactly call, but released some kind of noise from her extended throat. Her mouth was too full of tongue to find room for words as well.

Then Meg looked. She was smiling.

She said: "Yes, Mother."

She came and got through the wire, tearing herself also a little.

Mrs Hogben said, and her teeth clicked: "You chose the likeliest time. Your aunt hardly in her grave. Though, of course, it is only your aunt, if anyone, to blame."

The accusations were falling fast. Meg could not answer. Since joy had laid her open, she had forgotten how to defend herself.

"If you were a little bit younger" – Mrs Hogben lowered her voice because they had begun to approach the parson – "I'd break a stick on you, my girl."

Meg tried to close her face, so that nobody would see inside.

"What will they say?" Mrs Hogben moaned. "What ever will happen to us?"

"What, Mother?" Meg asked.

"You're the only one can answer that. And someone else."

Then Meg looked over her shoulder and recognized the hate which, for a while, she had forgotten existed. And at once her face closed up tight, like a fist. She was ready to protect whatever justly needed her protection.

Even if their rage, grief, contempt, boredom, apathy, and sense of injustice had not occupied the mourners, it is doubtful whether they would have realized the dead woman was standing amongst them. The risen dead – that was something which happened, or didn't happen, in the Bible. Fanfares of light did not blare for a loose woman in floral cotton. Those who had known her remembered her by now only fitfully in some of the wooden attitudes of life. How could they have heard, let alone believed in, her affirmation? Yet Daise Morrow continued to proclaim.

Listen, all of you, I'm not leaving, except those who want to be left, and even those aren't so sure – they might be parting with a bit of themselves. Listen to me, all you successful no-hopers, all you who wake in the night, jittery because something may be escaping you, or terrified to think there may never have been anything to find. Come to me, you sour women, public servants, anxious children, and old scabby, desperate men. . . .

Physically small, words had seemed too big for her. She would push back her hair in exasperation. And take refuge in acts. Because her feet had been planted in the earth, she would have been the last to resent its pressure now, while her always rather hoarse voice continued to exhort in borrowed syllables of dust.

Truly, we needn't experience tortures, unless we build chambers in our minds to house instruments of hatred in. Don't you know, my darling creatures, that death isn't death, unless it's the death of love? Love should be the greatest explosion it is reasonable to expect. Which sends us whirling, spinning, creating millions of other worlds. Never destroying.

From the fresh mound which they had formed unimaginatively in the shape of her earthly body, she persisted in appealing to them.

I will comfort you. If you will let me. Do you understand?

But nobody did, as they were only human.

For ever and ever. And ever.

Leaves quivered lifted in the first suggestion of a breeze.

So the aspirations of Daise Morrow were laid alongside her small-boned wrists, smooth thighs and pretty ankles. She surrendered at last to the formal crumbling which, it was hoped, would make an honest woman of her.

But had not altogether died.

Meg Hogben had never exactly succeeded in interpreting her aunt's messages, nor could she have witnessed the last moments of the burial, because the sun was dazzling her. She did experience, however, along with a shiver of recollected joy, the down laid against her cheek, a little breeze trickling through the moist roots of her hair, as she got inside the car, and waited for whatever next.

Well, they had dumped Daise.

Somewhere the other side of the wire there was the sound of smashed glass and discussion.

Councillor Hogben went across to the parson and said the right kind of things. Half-turning his back he took a note or two from his wallet, and immediately felt disengaged. If Horrie Last had been there Les Hogben would have gone back at this point and put an arm around his mate's shoulder, to feel whether he was forgiven for unorthodox behaviour in a certain individual – no relation, mind you, but. In any case Horrie had driven away.

Horrie drove, or flew, across the dip in which the dump joined the cemetery. For a second Ossie Coogan's back flickered inside a spiral of dust.

Ought to give the coot a lift, Councillor Last suspected, and wondered, as he drove on, whether a man's better intentions were worth, say, half a mark in the event of their remaining unfulfilled. For by now it was far too late to stop, and there was that Ossie, in the mirror, turning off the road towards the dump, where, after all, the bugger belonged.

All along the road, stones, dust, and leaves, were settling back into normally unemotional focus. Seated in his high Chev, Gill the grocer, a slow man, who carried his change in a little, soiled canvas bag, looked ahead through thick lenses. He was relieved to realize he would reach home almost on the dot of three-thirty, and his wife pour him his cup of tea. Whatever he understood was punctual, decent, docketed.

As he drove, prudently, he avoided the mattress the dump had spewed, from under the wire, half across the road. Strange things had happened at the dump on and off, the grocer recollected. Screaming girls, their long tight pants ripped to tatters. An arm in a sugar-bag, and not a sign of the body that went with it. Yet some found peace amongst the refuse: elderly derelict men, whose pale, dead, fish eyes never divulged anything of what they had lived, and women with blue, metho skins, hanging around the doors of shacks put together from sheets of bark and rusty iron. Once an old downandout had crawled amongst the rubbish apparently to rot, and did, before they sent for the constable, to examine what seemed at first a bundle of stinking rags.

Mr Gill accelerated judiciously.

They were driving. They were driving.

Alone in the back of the ute, Lum Whalley sat forward on the empty crate, locking his hands between his knees, as he forgot having seen Darkie do. He was completely independent now. His face had been reshaped by the wind. He liked that. It felt good. He no longer resented the junk they were dragging home, the rust flaking off at his feet, the roll of mouldy feltex trying to fur his nostrils up. Nor his family – discussing, or quarrelling, you could never tell – behind him in the cabin.

The Whalleys were in fact singing. One of their own versions. They always sang their own versions, the two little boys joining in.

Show me the way to go home,
I'm not too tired for bed.
I had a little drink about an hour ago,
And it put ideas in me head . . .

Suddenly Mum Whalley began belting into young Gary – or was it Barry?

"Wadda *you* know, eh? Wadda *you?*"

"What's bitten yer?" her husband shouted. "Can't touch a drop without yer turn nasty!"

She didn't answer. He could tell a grouse was coming, though. The little boy had started to cry, but only as a formality.

"It's that bloody Lummy," Mrs Whalley complained.

"Why pick on Lum?"

"Give a kid all the love and affection, and waddayaget?"

Wal grunted. Abstractions always embarrassed him.

Mum Whalley spat out of the window, and the spit came back at her.

"Arrrr!" she protested.

And fell silenter. It was not strictly Lum, not if you was honest. It was nothing. Or everything. The grog. You was never ever gunna touch it no more. Until you did. And that bloody Lummy, what with the caesar and all, you was never ever going again with a man.

"That's somethink a man don't understand."

"What?" asked Wal.

"A caesar."

"Eh?"

You just couldn't discuss with a man. So you had to get into bed with him. Grogged up half the time. That was how she copped the twins, after she had said never ever.

"Stop cryun, for Chrissake!" Mum Whalley coaxed, touching the little boy's blowing hair.

Everything was sad.

"Wonder how often they bury someone alive," she said.

Taking a corner in his cream Holden Councillor Hogben felt quite rakish, but would restrain himself at the critical moment from skidding the wrong side of the law.

They were driving and driving, in long, lovely bursts, and at the corners, in semi-circular swirls.

On those occasions in her life when she tried to pray, begging for an experience, Meg Hogben would fail, but return to the attempt with clenched teeth. Now she did so want to think of her dead aunt with love, and the image blurred repeatedly. She was superficial, that was it. Yet, each time she failed, the landscape leaped lovingly. They were driving under the telephone wires. She could have translated any message into the language of peace. The wind burning, whenever it did not cut cold, left the stable things alone: the wooden houses stuck beside the road, the trunks of willows standing round the brown saucer of a dam. Her too candid, grey eyes seemed to have deepened, as though to accommodate all she still had to see, feel.

It was lovely curled on the back seat, even with Mum and Dad in front.

"I haven't forgotten, Margaret," Mum called over her shoulder.

Fortunately Dadda wasn't interested enough to inquire.

"Did Daise owe anything on the home?" Mrs Hogben asked. "She was never at all practical."

Councillor Hogben cleared his throat.

"Give us time to find out," he said.

Mrs Hogben respected her husband for the things which she, secretly, did not understand: Time the mysterious, for instance, Business, and worst of all, the Valuer General.

"I wonder Jack Cunningham," she said, "took up with Daise. He was a fine man. Though Daise had a way with her."

They were driving. They were driving.

When Mrs Hogben remembered the little ring in plaited gold.

"Do you think those undertakers are honest?"

"Honest?" her husband repeated.

A dubious word.

"Yes," she said. "That ring that Daise."

You couldn't very well accuse. When she had plucked up the courage she would go down to the closed house. The thought of it made her chest tighten. She would go inside, and feel her way into the back corners of drawers, where perhaps a twist of tissue-paper. But the closed houses of the dead frightened Mrs Hogben, she had to admit. The stuffiness, the light strained through brown holland. It was as if you were stealing, though you weren't.

And then those Whalleys creeping up.

They were driving and driving, the ute and the sedan almost rubbing on each other.

"No one who hasn't had a migraine," cried Mrs Hogben, averting her face, "can guess what it feels like."

Her husband had heard that before.

"It's a wonder it don't leave you," he said. "They say it does when you've passed a certain age."

Though they weren't passing the Whalleys he would make every effort to throw the situation off. Wal Whalley leaning forward, though not so far you couldn't see the hair bursting out of the front of his shirt. His wife thumping his shoulder. They were singing one of their own versions. Her gums all watery.

So they drove and drove.

"I could sick up, Leslie," Mrs Hogben gulped, and fished for her lesser handkerchief.

The Whalley twins were laughing through their taffy forelocks.

At the back of the ute that sulky Lum turned towards the opposite direction. Meg Hogben was looking her farthest off. Any sign of acknowledgment had been so faint the wind had immediately blown it off their faces. As Meg and Lummy sat, they held their sharp, but comforting knees. They sank their chins as low as they would go. They lowered their eyes, as if they had seen enough for the present, and wished to cherish what they knew.

The warm core of certainty settled stiller as driving faster the wind payed out the telephone wires the fences the flattened heads of grey grass always raising themselves again again again.

The Mateship Syndrome

Thelma Forshaw

He had been nicknamed "The Ace" by his mates because — that's the way he was: fanatically efficient, passionately perfectionist, plus a certain cockiness his class of Australian has. In Australia, you tend to call such people "The Ace". You don't much like them, you feel you should, you square it with a pseudo-complimentary title.

He dared to bear himself proudly. He walked tall. ("Kids himself, The Ace does.") When he was not in his working-clothes with the welder's mask covering his face and neck — a mask that looked oddly like Ned Kelly's helmet — he dressed fastidiously and well. For his part he was a husky male, but he knew enough already to put mateship before his lust for women.

Behind a curtained window of her small wooden house, his sister watched him stride up the path to her front door. Something was wrong. She never saw him except when he had a problem, although, after her divorce, she had come to live only a few streets away from where he "boarded", in a bustling, sprawling, outer-Sydney suburb. People with problems sought her out, and this gave her a sybilline feeling she enjoyed. For the rest, she emptied herself into diaries, and this endowed her with the seemingly tranquil air of the expressed. She too had a mask — one known as "silence, exile and cunning". This mask was emphasized, or thickened, by a hoarse, uncouthly accented voice — chosen rather than innate. One shoulder had a placating tilt as though to say: "I'm quite harmless. I wouldn't offend you for worlds." The disguise had been built up over a long period of seeming to give offence by her very nature. You could say she had been shocked into disguise. Shocks of self-discovery induced by the reactions of those around her.

When she opened the door The Ace seemed unaware of the schizoid personality before him. He looked about at the ice-clean living-room with its lack of either joyous slapdashness or achieved elegance.

"Well, yer a lot tidier than yer used to be," he said approvingly. Because she was his senior by eight years, he made up the difference by asserting his standards. His perfectionism was outward, hers inward, though he did not know this. He only knew that she was "booky and highbrow" and had done a bit of writing earlier in her life. She had scared him when he was a boy. Now he considered her, in some way, beached. Still, a man could confide in her, and even get a bit of sense out of her. She was a lot nicer than she used to be. Not so talky. Not so big-headed. The way a woman ought to be, in fact.

He looked indulgently at the bookshelves. "Still the old reader, eh? Trying to solve the riddle of the universe." He laughed, and she smiled — delighted with his pleasantry.

"Well, now, I got a little problem," said The Ace carelessly, as if it were really of no moment. He reached between his thighs and pulled a chair under him. He had thudded a damp brown-paper package on the table and now drew from it a bottle of beer. His sister filled two glasses, then she took the shape of what could only be called acute listening. She contracted to a focused point that could draw stammering confessions from people as a thorn is drawn from an animal's paw. She prized this. It was all she believed herself good for — all she was valued for, that is: the listener to whom all things may be said. She could not communicate her own true self; but she was overjoyed when, selfishly and heedlessly, people used her to volley forth their own secrets or pain, or bewilderment. She was not deluded. She sensed indifference behind their not caring what *she* thought of their revelations. Fronts were kept up for people whose good opinion you wanted. Terrible secrets were told to strangers — or the declassed. In her diary she had commented ironically: "I realize my function is little better than that of an emetic."

The Ace began to tell her about the talk with the boss — The Trump, he called him — and how, later in the bar last night he had felt the blokes were different the moment he walked in. He had drunk down a schooner of beer before he felt able to speak to the man next to him.

He mimed everything, he quoted the men in a racy, dramatic way that revealed his intensity. He re-lived rather than recounted what had taken place.

"So I just up and says, 'Watsa matter, Blue? You pipped about something?' and Blue, he says, 'No, why? *Should* I be?' Real sarcastic.

"'You're not like usual.'

"'Who's not like usual?'

"'You're not, Blue. You and the others — you're different since The Trump offered me that job.'

"'*We're* not bloody different. It's *you* that's bloody different — not me.'

"'Me! What's got into yer? It's youse that're different — not me.'

"'*We* got nothing to be different about — it's you that has.' Then: 'Ah, turn it up, for Christ's sake, and quit belly-aching. You got what yer wanted, ha'n't yer!'"

Then Blue had muttered something and turned back to his drink and the yarns of his mates, who, throughout, had carefully looked away from where The Ace was standing and talked together in undertones.

His heart had leapt when The Trump had summoned him to the office and offered him the position of shop manager. "Give it a burl, Ace," he'd said. "I know you've got it in you."

A boss. And his first duty to fire three men — his mates and drinking partners — because the firm wanted to retrench. He was offered the position of a boss. That's why they were different last night at the pub. They knew what he had to do. But men had been fired before and always would be. It was not *only* that that made them change towards him.

"They's good as called me a crawler and a boss's man." He was bitterly silent, then spoke as if to himself. "But it ain't that — I got the tickets to show what I can do. I don't need to crawl — " He added, "except to *them*," in a low voice. Then he threw up his head as if to defy something. Setting down his glass, he leant forward and tapped the back of his sister's hand emphatically.

"I look at it this way — you're okay as long as yer stay put, see? Then nobody can do enough for yer. Don't get the idea I'm dumb because I don't read like you. I think a lot. You gotta stay put and not get ahead of anyone." He hesitated, then said aggressively: "Am I right, Lil?"

His sister was far away, gazing at him, gazing straight through his face at a montage of the past. She was remembering the time of her detribalization, when she had been quite young and begun to show signs of being — different to those around her; that is, bookish, free-thinking, shockingly frank. In the country of the blind the one-eyed man is king, the saying went. She had discovered that in the country of the blind the one-eyed man is an *offence*, a deviation. The one-eyed woman even more so. She had been dealt with. Buffeted by mockery; gales of mockery had blown her out of the warm safety of the herd. Lacking the arrogant self-containment of the solitary, she had grown from childhood wanting to be hailed with friendliness, approached without guardedness and looked at amiably as if whatever she stood for was . . . perfectly natural, the way it was with those around her. She had wanted that badly, terribly. She had given years of her life to the study and impersonation of what seemed acceptable. She had expended all her energies acquiring, and then projecting, the approved antipodean attitudes, learning to conceal her passion for what was intellectual and analytical, cultivating a good-natured mindlessness, mimicking the way they joked the truth out of existence. Somehow it had not worked. They always saw she was a "ring-in", and heard a "foreign" accent in her voice — so that her imitation of them was seen not as flattering, not as indicative of her desire to be one of them, but as a calculated ridicule.

She had lived a life of shame, in a way — by rights she was no different from those Frenchwomen of the last war who'd had their heads shaved by their compatriots for fraternizing with the enemy. Only — who *was* the enemy? Was it them? — or her exiled self? According to her exiled self, she had committed shameful capitulations, abdicated from ideals she held in order to embrace theirs, agreed with patent nonsense, condoned larrikinism and stupidity as "fair dinkum", and humbly admired, even loved, those who judged her by jeer or cold shoulder. She had defected from all she'd believed in. She had as good as said: "I will do anything, anything, if you will only make me one of you." She had thrown the fight, like a crooked boxer who valued something else more than conquest.

It was mateship she craved. The fellowship and moral support of the class into which she had been born. She had still not accepted defeat — not even when her marriage had ended in a welter of scorn: "You and your ratbag ideas! You and your long words! Jesus, why didn't somebody *tell* me!" Another of her impersonations that had broken down. Yet she had gone on pursuing the beloved people who wanted none of her. She had not accepted defeat by finding a place for herself among a minority. To aspire — (and this the minority would have demanded of her) — to reach beyond the realm of the dead-level was considered a form of treason against the egalitarian idea, and so she had chosen to do nothing that could alienate her further from her class.

That's what The Ace was up against now. The montage receded, and she saw that he had refilled both their glasses.

"You can see I got the qualifications, can't yer, Lil? You can see I could go places. I beat university-trained blokes in a welding contest, know that? Three were Yanks. Take The Trump even. You know, he can't answer me on questions of welding theory! He can't bloody well answer me! He can't do what I can do."

His voice had grown fast, excited. His suppressed pride and aspiration unfolded before her. He assessed himself freely, triumphantly, throwing her the burden of his heresy. There was a striving in him that, in defiance of his place and company, made love-wrought artefacts. Not for him Blue's slapdash let's-get-it-over-and-go-for-a-quickie attitude.

"Look" — he fumbled in his pocket — "here's some of me tickets. Just to prove to yer . . . Done it all at night after work — and that's only a few of them."

She fingered the papers he flung on the table: Supervisor Cert. DLI; "A" Grade Cert. AWI; Pipeline Cert. API — more followed, thrown down one after another. Was he standing at the border showing some menacing official the papers that proved his right to enter another country ? Or was he challenging something, fighting something *through* her? Perhaps the certificates flung down on the table were his gauntlet. The Trump had taken up his gauntlet and engaged him in the battle he demanded. It was not sufficient. Precious intangibles were involved and must be made secure — or propitiated? — before he could ride forth. What was it he wanted from *her?* — she, the tame bear who no longer danced to her own drum. What part of her did he call on for his answer? Was she, for him, a priestess dedicated to the will of the god Demos they had both been brought up to worship — and were the papers on the table his plea for release from a creed outgrown? Had he simply run to a woman's skirts in his dilemma as men often did? Or did he want to hear the dare-all cry of the valkyrie that some women can utter for a man who needs its goad?

His fire, his anger, his fear struck at her slouched shoulders, her dreaming apathy, the ambiguity that allowed anyone to make of her whatever scapegoat they needed. All this passivity, this non-resistance, sprouted out of a sub-soil of national attitudes the flower of which was the creed of mateship. That flower she had never been able to pluck; for mateship was not a reward for what you *did*, though what you did may be sacrificed in its name — but for what you *were*, and you were one of us — or you were not. The smell of self-betrayal was detected at once.

She gazed at him, and her two selves wrestled for him. She stirred from her slumped position, made uneasy by the ferment of this divided man. Eyes behind her eyes watched him, pity in the dual gaze.

How often as now did the tough-male glare — a sort of mask —
drop from his grey eyes and anxiety and fear gaze out? Hoping
perhaps for an "All clear"? Needing permission to commit the
treason of excelling his mates. How to pass this cruel snare that
lay between mediocrity and being The Ace and, some day — if he
would — The Trump? Was that what he needed to know?

"How much do you want it?" she asked in the roughened voice
which was now habitual. "How much do you want to be a boss,
and go up and up — all the time farther away from them?"

In his eyes the dread of loneliness and of betraying a creed —
dread of being shut out from all he had known. She saw the power
in his face at war with the dread in his eyes. He was a man who
wanted to realize his full potential. He wanted his head above the
crowd, to have status but, not being born to it, he must first reach
for it with his own hands, confront painful choices — above all be
ruthless enough to discard those who would stand in his way. The
social climate in which he lived did not favour such bold and
kingly growth. Rather, the artificial dwarfing called *bonsai* was
practised upon men's spirits when it seemed they might overtop
their fellows. He would get no help from those who had moulded
him.

He said slowly: "Trouble is — it'll put a barrier between us.
Me mates would have to treat me different and I'd have to treat
them different. I seen it already. That's how it is with bosses."
He looked into his glass, turning it absently. "It'd be lonely as hell
being shop manager . . . perhaps having to fire blokes that are me
mates. There'd be The Trump, but . . . " But The Trump belonged
to a class in which men struggled against each other with grim zest
and paid only a smiling lip-service to allegiance. A colleague
might be many things — he was not a "mate".

The Ace had mates. He was close to his own people. To her that
was the crown of life. That was the Holy Grail *she* still wistfully
pursued. They called him The Ace. That was status enough — for
all its wryness.

"I wonder what a man oughta do?" he said into his glass, seeming
not to ask her.

The eyes behind her eyes glared brilliant a moment — a night-
mare's silent shout through sealed lips. He did not see, or he might
have taken his answer then. He only heard her voice saying,
"I'd give it the go-by. Ambition isn't everything. You have your
mates — stick to them."

"Praps you're right. Big dough, and authority like — " his voice
grew slower and slower. "All that — it's okay. But you can't be

with your mates in the old way. Wouldn't be much of a life, would it?" He repeated "*Would* it?" on a note of strong inquiry.

"No, it's better — *far* better — to have your mates." At that moment she was not speaking to him at all. She was running up a flag, watching it flutter, saluting its emblem of two hands clasped in mateship. She heard a drum roll . . . but it was not her drum.

"Yeah . . . well . . . I reckon I'll have to knock it back."

His shoulders sagged. The excitement had gone out of him. She thought for a moment he looked . . . quenched. But it was the relief of the decision, the slackening of strain. Fondly, she imagined the boisterous approval of his mates when they knew: "Ar, good on yer, Acey!" Drawing him back to them again, proud of him now, the boilermaker who beat university-trained blokes — three of them Yanks — yet who chose to prove their rightness and their power rather than prove himself. The Ace who was still on their side, who would not leave them for . . . well, for all the bloody tea in China!

He would be happy now. One had to choose. It was painful. But he would settle down and be glad after a while. He just didn't know how lucky he was to be one of them. It was only his foolish egotism and ambition that had led to the rift between them. He would soon see that he had made the right choice, the happy choice, the honourable choice.

He got up, looked at her coolly, free now of his necessity. "You live a lonely sorta life, don't yer?" Half curious, half contemptuous. She was a bloody queer bird, you couldn't get away from it. Still, a man could talk to her, tell her things he couldn't tell others.

"I like it," she said too quickly. The wound of human failure touched.

"Okay, to each his own. Be seeing yer, Lil."

As she watched him go down the path towards the street, she said to herself, rejecting the illusion of closeness and companionship of the past hour: An emetic — that's all. He's brought it all up. He goes . . . back to his real life. I'm as shameful as a confessional — to be concealed like a visit to the psychiatrist. She thought she was being realistic, facing facts. She did not recognize her self-flagellation, or that the flail she used had been passed to her long ago by others, as an outcast Japanese is handed the weapon of hari-kiri . . . and left alone. In the country of the blind the one-eyed man is an offence. . . .

It was six months before she saw The Ace again. It would have

been better for her had she not seen him, if he had gone his way
and never returned, letting her believe all his problems had been
solved.

She had settled down for the evening to write in her diary, retiring to the secret retreat where there were no taboos against ways
of being, and the only mockery was – she believed – her own,
not realizing it was a borrowed mockery, that she herself endorsed
it – thought it as true a part of herself as her demotic voice.

There came a thunderous knocking on the door, which continued until she ran to open it. The Ace lurched past her, slamming
the door, gasping as if after hard running.

"Yer gotta hide me! Hide me, Lil!"

His usually immaculate clothing was torn and begrimed.

"You've been in an accident!"

"I dunno if I've killed the bastard – the cops are after me – I
gotta hide. . . . " He was half laughing.

"But what's the good of hiding if they saw you come here?"

"They'll run me in. They run me in six or seven times past few
months. Bastards. . . . "

"What have you been doing to yourself? My God, you look
terrible!"

He lurched about the room, running his hand unsteadily along
the walls, the shelves of books. "You and yer bloody books! You
know bugger-all, Lil. Bugger-all – "

The sound of heavy boots pounding up the path.

"Jeez, there they *are!*"

The Ace flattened himself against the wall, his mouth hardened,
tight shut, he snorted laughter.

A hammering on the door. "Okay, open up! Police!"

She shrugged helplessly and went to open the door. As the two
big men moved in towards The Ace, he reached behind him and
hurled book after book into their faces – a barrage of books, some
of which struck his sister, while he laughed – "You know bugger-
all! Read what the experts say – find out about me – bugger-all!"

The two officers lunged at The Ace, their forearms raised
against the hurtling books, and as they grappled with him he
began furiously to punch and struggle. It was over in a few
minutes of harsh, heavy breathing and unthinkable language
streaming from The Ace's hate-filled mouth. When the huge
bodies straightened she saw with a shock that The Ace was hand-
cuffed.

"But what's he done?" she cried out.

"Beat up one of his mates – the man's in hospital, not expected to live. We've had enough of this trouble-maker. Believe me, lady, it's not the first time we've tangled with him."

"But he's drunk. He didn't mean it. He couldn't — "

The Ace shouted, "I meant it! Jesus, I meant it!"

All her borrowed theory and idealism reeled.

"Come on, you." The officers hauled at him roughly. "You've cooked your goose this time."

The Ace wrenched them to a standstill in the doorway. He stared at his sister. He said with a new self-mockery: "Yer know, Lil, I reckon I coulda been something." They pulled him away. The grief broke through. "Y'hear me, Lil? I coulda *been* something! I coulda. . . . "

The Unicorn

Dal Stivens

"You're a virgin, of course?" he asked. I said I was. If he was silly
enough to believe he'd seen a unicorn, he could believe I was *virgo
intacta*.

"I've seen it," he said. "Him, I mean. Several times. Out in the
Red Desert. But I can't get near him. You will be able to. A virgin
always can. That's how they used to catch unicorns in the past."

I wanted to laugh out loud. I thought then he was mad as they
come. Ten years of hunting for rare animals in East Africa must
have done it. He was about forty, fat, bald and with broken teeth.
The sweat was wriggling tadpole-fashion down his yellow crinkled
face. He'd picked me up in the white-washed adobe bar where I'd
been drinking solidly for three hours and I thought it was the same
old story. Loneliness to be staved off for a brief respite in a mesh-
ing of the flesh, in a fierce short obliteration of the mind. But I was
wrong. He wasn't seeking that.

I hadn't wanted to drink with him at first. And I don't know why
I agreed to go on his unicorn hunt. For laughs, I suppose.

I was thirty and I'd reached a bit of a crisis. Not one thing but a
lot of things . . . the bomb, what could I believe in, what should I
do or was anything worthwhile. And I'd given up painting. I'd
left my husband, too. It wasn't his fault. I was too bitchy. I'd
some wild idea that I might recover something in the Red Desert.
So I'd left London and gone to East Africa where I drank rather too
much. Backhaus — he said he was a zoologist — was saying:

"I've been hunting for unicorns for ten years. Say you'll come!"

"All right," I said.

"He's the most beautiful thing you ever saw," he said. "The
purest white — new snow isn't in it — and that single twisted
horn."

"Like the lefthand tusk of the narwhal?" I asked.

"Why, yes," he said.

"And a goat's beard?"

"Yes," he said.

"And the hindquarters of an antelope?"

"Yes," he said. "But how do you know? Could it – could it be you have seen him?"

"I've read about unicorns. A weird zoological mixture they were called."

"Not weird," he said, crossly. "Anyway they are only rough resemblances – the hindquarters are merely of the most delicate slenderness." He began murmuring, almost as though for his ears alone:

> I once did see
> In my young travels through Armenia,
> An angry unicorn in his full career
> Charge with too swift a foot a jeweller
> That watch'd him for the treasure of his brow:
> And ere he could get shelter of a tree
> Nail him with his rich antler to the earth.

"George Chapman," I said.

He beamed delightedly. "You'll do it," he said. "You appreciate unicorns and he'll respond to that. His fierceness will be tamed."

"He'll put his head in my virgin lap," I said.

He nodded gravely. I was shaking inside with laughter so much it was a wonder he couldn't see or hear it. The whole business was zany and the zaniest was to come. He really had found a unicorn deep in the desert back of the seaport, as I found four days later.

We stood with our native safari on a stony ridge under the sparse shade of some thorny bushes. The unicorn was about three hundred yards off, gleaming white, his hooves lost in shimmer of the noonday heat.

"But how?" I asked, incredulous. "How did you find him?"

I hadn't bothered to ask during the dreary trek into the interior in three four-wheel drive vehicles.

"My Schliemann approach," he said, smiling. "Schliemann, as you know, studied Homer and found Troy. I have studied the old writings about unicorns. Aristotle said the unicorn was the Indian ass but I began to suspect that he should have written African. There were other indications."

The unicorn must have seen us or smelled us. He began pawing the red dust with his front legs. The dust hung in the air and drifted slowly behind him. Backhaus was excited: "The paraclete," I murmured to myself.

"Isn't he magnificent?"

And he was beautiful too. Breathlessly so. I was sorry now —
not for the virgin jape but because Backhaus had that lousy cage
all ready and waiting. And if there was a unicorn then that virgin
business would probably work sometime.

"Off you go," he said. "You have nothing to fear."

I started out over the loose red sand, the soles of my shoes
squeaking and the glare stabbing my eyes. The air I breathed was
hot. Behind me Backhaus and the natives were wheeling out the
cage. When I was one hundred yards out the unicorn faced me,
tossing his head and neighing fiercely. I don't know why I kept on
going. I kept remembering that bit, "Nail him with his rich antler
to the earth." I'd no chance to get shelter of a tree. But I walked on,
my shorts clinging to my crutch. If he's ever seen a virgin she'd
have been wearing a frock, I thought. The unicorn suddenly
threw up his head and galloped towards me.

I didn't run though I was quaking. He came right on, of surpass-
ing beauty and fleet power. When he had only a little way to
cover, I saw his wonderful golden eyes fiery with his rage.

Backhaus called out to me to run. I couldn't move. Anyway it
was far too late.

The unicorn stopped suddenly, digging in his polished black
hooves. Red dust rose. Then he came on quietly and put his milky
white head on my breast and those magnificent eyes, silent subtle
mirrors of his mind, were now gentle and chivalrous. I knew it
then as assuredly as if he had spoken that he had seen through me
but had decided to act magnanimously. Why he should I couldn't
understand. I didn't deserve any generosity. He allowed himself
to be caged, nuzzling my hands with his velvety black muzzle.
He shone luminescently within the bars. I wanted to cry.

I even addressed him: "Why did you do it? If you didn't want to
kill me, why didn't you just run away?" And then, not quite knowing what I was saying, "You can't help me. No one can."

Backhaus cut in, "There's no record of unicorns understanding
human speech." He was beside himself with excitement. I didn't
argue with Backhaus but I wasn't so sure the unicorn didn't take it
in.

"The biggest zoological discovery of all time," he exulted. "You
thought I was mad, didn't you? I knew you weren't a virgin."

"You were bright," I said sarcastically.

"I banked on the animal being generous," he said. "There are old
records of similar benign behaviour."

"You'll let him go?" I asked but without any hope.

He didn't bother to answer.

We started back the same day. The unicorn, as proud and relucent as ever, was towed by one of the vehicles. I'll swear the unicorn knew he wasn't trapped. I saw it in his golden eyes − a princely disdain, an occasional fiery opalescent flash but always succeeded by benevolence. I was sure he could kick down the bars any time he wanted. Backhaus might know a lot about ordinary animals but I was sure he'd underestimated this one. I wondered if there were other unicorns in the desert. There'd have to be, I suppose, but anything was possible.

"The treasure of his brow," I said to Backhaus, reproachfully that evening when we made camp.

How it might have ended I don't know if Backhaus hadn't made a pass at me that night. I put up a fight and I wasn't in any real trouble but the unicorn began neighing and lashing out with his hooves at the cage. He got free quickly and charged Backhaus who ended up like Chapman's jeweller with the rich antler through his head. Then the wonderful beast stood waiting, his twisted horn dripping blood. The head boy got a gun but I wouldn't let him use it. I sat down. I was feeling weak. The unicorn put his head in my lap. He stayed for ten minutes and then went off into the night.

I suppose you'll say this story was sure to end this way. But you're only half right. It was a bit of chicanery on the unicorn's part. I think he did it this way because although he didn't mind my tricking him, he didn't like Backhaus doing it, too.

Well, the end was I went back to London. Not to my husband − I wasn't as magnanimous as the unicorn − but I took up painting again, not with much enthusiasm but more to keep faith with the unicorn.

Crabs

Peter Carey

Crabs is very neat in everything he does. His movements are almost fussy, but he has so much fight in his delicate frame that they're not fussy at all. Lately he has been eating. When Frank eats one steak, Crabs eats two. When Frank has a pint of milk, Crabs drinks two. He spends a lot of time lying on his bed, groaning, because of the food. But he's building up. At night he runs five miles to Clayton. He always means to run back, but he always ends up on the train, hot and sweating and sticking to the seat. His aim is to increase his weight and get a job driving for Allied Panel and Towing. Already he has his licence but he's too small, not tough enough to beat off the competition at a crash scene.

Frank drives night shift. He tells Crabs to get into something else, not the tow truck game, but Crabs has his heart set on the tow trucks. In his mind he sees himself driving at eighty mph with the light flashing, arriving at the scene first, getting the job, being interviewed by the guy from 3UZ's Night Watch.

At the moment Crabs weighs eight stone and four pounds, but he's increasing his weight all the time.

He is known as Crabs because of the time last year when he claimed to have the Crabs and everyone knew he was bullshitting. And then Frank told Trev that Crabs was still a virgin and so they called him Crabs. He doesn't mind it so much now. He's not a virgin now and he's more comfortable with the name. It gives him a small distinction, character is how he looks at it.

Crabs appears to be very small behind the wheel of this 1956 Dodge. He sits on two cushions so he can see properly. Carmen sits close beside him, a little shorter, because of the cushions, and around them is the vast empty space of the car — leopard skin stretching everywhere, taut and beautiful.

The night is sweet, filled with the red tail lights of other cars, sweeping headlights, flickering neon signs. Crabs drives fast, keeping the needle on the seventy mark, sweating with fear and excitement as he chops in and out of the traffic. He keeps his small dark eyes on the rear-vision mirror, half hoping for the flashing blue lights that will announce the arrival of the cops. Maybe he'll accelerate, maybe he'll pull over. He doesn't know, but he dreams of that sweet moment when he will plant his foot and all the power of this hotted-up Dodge will roar to life and he will leave the cops behind. The papers will say: "An early model American car drew away from police at 100 mph".

Beside him Carmen is quiet. She keeps using the cigarette lighter because she likes to use it. She thinks he doesn't see her, the way she throws away her cigarettes after a few drags, so she can use the cigarette lighter again. The cigarette lighter and the leopard skin upholstery make her feel great.

The leopard skin upholstery is why they're going to a drive-in tonight. Because Carmen whispered in his ear that she'd like to do it on the leopard skin upholstery. She was shy. It pleased him, those small hot words blowing on his ear. She blushed when he looked at her. He liked that.

He didn't tell Frank about the leopard skin. He didn't think it was good for Frank to know how Carmen felt about it. Anyway Frank hates the leopard skin. He normally keeps it covered with a couple of old grey blankets. He didn't tell Frank about the drive-in either because of the Karboys.

The Karboys have come about slowly and become more famous as the times have got worse. With every strike they seem to grow in strength. And now that imports are restricted and most of the car factories are closed down they've got worse. A year ago you only had to worry if your car broke down on the highway or in a tough suburb. They'd come and strip down your car and leave you with nothing but the picked bones. Now it's different. If you buy a used car part (and you try and get a *new* carbie, say, for a 1956 Dodge) it's sure to come from some Karboy gang or other and who's to say they didn't kill the poor bastard who owned the Dodge it came off. Every time Frank buys a part he crosses himself. It's a big joke with Frank, crossing himself. Crabs too. They both have this big thing going about crossing themselves. It's a joke they have. Carmen doesn't get it, but she never was a Catholic anyway.

The official word is not to resist the Karboys, to give them all your car if you have to, but you don't see a man giving his car away that easily. So a lot of drivers are carrying guns, mostly sawn off .22s. And if you've got any sense you keep your doors locked and windows up and you keep your car in good nick, so you don't get stranded anywhere. The insurance companies have altered the wars and civil disturbances clauses to cover themselves, so you take good care of your car because you'll never get another one if you lose it.

And you don't go to drive-ins. Drive-ins are bad news. You get the odd killing. The cops are there but they don't help much. Last week a cop shot another cop who was knocking off a bumper bar. He thought the cop was a Karboy but he was only supplementing his income.

So Crabs hasn't told Frank what he's doing tonight. And he's got some of Frank's defensive gear out of the truck. This is a sharpened bike chain and a heavy duty spanner. He's got them under the front seat and he's half hoping for a little trouble. He's scared, but he's hoping. Carmen hasn't said anything about the Karboys and Crabs wonders if she even knows about them. There's so much she doesn't know about. She spends all day reading papers but she never takes anything in. He wonders what she thinks about when she reads.

There are more cars at the drive-in than he expected and he drives around until he finds the cop car. He plans on parking nearby, just to be on the safe side. But Carmen is very edgy about the police, because she is only just sixteen and her mother is still looking for her, and she makes Crabs park somewhere else. In the harsh lights her small face seems very pale and frightened. So Crabs finds a lonely spot up in the back corner and combs his thick black hair with a tortoise-shell comb while he waits for the lights to go out. Carmen arranges the blankets over the windows. Frank has got this all worked out, from the times when he went to drive-ins. There are little hooks around the tops of all the windows so they can be curtained with towels or blankets. Frank is ingenious. In the old days he used to remove all the inside door handles too, just in case his girl friends wanted to run away.

They put down the layback seats and Carmen unpins her long red hair. She only pinned it up because Crabs said how he liked her unpinning it. He sits like a small Italian buddha in the back seat and watches her, watches her hair fall.

She says, you're neat, you know that, very neat.

When she says that he doesn't know how to take it. She means that he is almost dainty. She says, you're sort of . . . She is going to say "graceful" but she doesn't.

Crabs says, shut-up, and begins to struggle with the buckle of his motorcycle boots. Crabs never had a motorbike, but he bought the boots off Frank who was driving one night when there was a bike in a prang. He got them from the ambulance driver for a packet of fags. Crabs bought them for three packets of Marlborough. There was a bit of blood, but he covered it up with raven oil.

Crabs really likes heavy things. Also he dislikes laces. All his shoes have zips, buckles, or slip on. When he was at the tech they used to tie him to the chain wire fence by his shoe laces, every lunch time. They tied him to the fence right in front of the Principal's window and the only way he could ever get out was to break the laces, because he couldn't bend down − if he bent down they kicked him in the arse. Crabs's father was always coming up to see the Principal and complaining about the shoe laces but it never did any good. Once Crabs came to school with zip-up boots and they stole them from him so he had to wear the laces, for his own protection.

The first film is crackling through the loud speaker and Carmen sits up near the front window with only her black pants on, her hair down, covered with a heavy sweet perfume she always wears. Crabs shyly eyes her breasts which are small and tight. He would like her to have big boobs, like the girls in *Playboy*. That is the only way he would like to improve her, for her to have big boobs, but he never says anything about this, even to himself. He says, help me with my boots. He is embarrassed to ask her. He knew this would happen and it was worrying him. He says, just pull. Normally Frank pulls off his boots for him. The boots are one size too small but they don't hurt too much.

Crabs lies back with his shirt off, his black jeans down, and one sock off while Carmen pulls at the second boot. Crabs is coming on fuzzy as he watches Carmen stretched back, her face screwed up with concentration and effort. He watches the small soft muscle on the inside of her thigh and the small soft hollow it has, just where it disappears into her pants.

She says, hey careful. The boot is still half on the foot.

He is on top of her and she, giggling and groaning, manoeuvres sweetly below him, reciting nursery rhymes with her arse. He thinks, for the hundredth time, of the change that comes over her when she screws. Until now she is nothing much, talking dumb or sleeping or listening to the serials on the radio. It is only now she wakes up. And you could never guess, no matter how much you knew, that this girl would turn on like this. She sits around all day eating peanut butter and honey sandwiches or reading the

Women's Weekly or reading the Tatt's results or the grocery adver-
tisements. Crabs feels he is drowning in a sea of honey. He says,
"humpty-dumpty". Carmen, swerving, swaying, singing beneath
him says, "Wha?"

Crabs says, bang, bang-bang-bang.

Carmen, her mascara-smudged eyes blinking beneath his
mascara-smudged lips giggles, groans, arches like a cat.

Crabs says, bang, bang, bang-bang.

Carmen arches. Crabs thinks she will break in half. Him too.
She falls. He rolls and keeps rolling down to the left hand side of
the car. He says shit, oh *shit!*

The car is on one side, listing sharply. Carmen lies on her back,
smiling at the ceiling. She says, mmm.

Crabs says, Jesus Christ, someone's knocked off the wheels,
Jesus CHRIST.

Carmen turns on her side and says, the Karboys. So she knew
about them all the time. She sounds pleased.

Crabs says, you'll stain the upholstery. He searches for the other
boot and the bike chain.

He runs through the cars. He doesn't know what he is looking for,
just those two wheels, one will do because he has the spare. His
white jacket is weighed down by the chain. He runs through the
cars. Sometimes he stops. He knocks on windows but no-one will
answer. Everyone's too scared.

He rounds the back of a late model Chevvy and comes face to
face with the cop car. One of the cops is putting something in the
boot. Crabs is convinced that it's the wheels. He keeps going past
the car, walks round the perimeter of the drive-in and returns to
the Dodge. Carmen has taken the blankets down and is watching
the film. He tells her his theory about the cops and she says,
shh, watch.

The manager fills out the two forms and gives them meal
tickets. He is a slow fat man with a worn grey cardigan. He
explains the meal ticket system – the government will supply
them with ten dollars' worth of meal tickets each week, these
tickets can be spent at the Ezy-Eatin right here on the drive-in.
If they run out of tickets, that's too bad, because it's all they'll get.
If they want blankets they have to sign for them now. Carmen
asks about banana fritters. The manager looks at her feet and
slowly raises his half-shut eyes until they meet hers. He says that
banana fritters are only made at night, but she can purchase anything sold in the cafeteria.

The manager then asks if there's anyone they want to notify. Crabs begins to give him Frank's name and then stops. The manager waits and licks the stubby pencil he is using. Crabs says, it doesn't matter. The manager says, that's your decision. Crabs says, no it doesn't matter, forget it. He can see Frank when he gets the notification, when he learns that his Dodge has lost two wheels, when he learns Crabs took it to a drive-in. He'd come out and kill them both.

Carmen says, we'll walk home next Saturday.

The manager sighs loudly and scratches his balls. Crabs wonders if he should hit him. He's got the chain in his jacket. The manager is saying, "Now this time listen to what I tell you. First, you ain't got no public transport . . . "

Carmen says, I didn't *mean* public transport. I . . .

" . . . you don't have a bus or a train because buses and trains don't come to the Star Drive-in. They've got no reason to, do they? Secondly, you can't walk down that highway, young lady, because it's an 'S' road. And if you know the laws of the land you ain't permitted to walk on or near an 'S' road."

He looks across at Crabs and says, "And dogs aren't allowed on 'S' roads, or bicycles or learner drivers. So we're not allowed to let you out of that gate until this bloody government finds a bus that they can spare to get you all home. There are now seventy-three people in your situation. I don't like it either. I don't make a profit from you so don't think I want you around. So we'll all have to wait until something is done. And we all pray to God that something's done soon." He crosses himself absently and Carmen laughs.

The manager stares at her blankly. Crabs would like to lay that chain across his fat face. The man says, "You want me to notify your mother?" and Carmen becomes very quiet and smoothes her skirt with great concentration. She says "no" very quietly.

The manager is standing up. He shakes them both by the hand. He advises them to sign for blankets but they say no, they have some. He has become very fatherly. At the door he shakes their hands again and says he hopes they can make themselves comfortable.

It is bright sunlight outside. Carmen says, he seemed nice.

Crabs says, he's a bastard. I'll get him.

Carmen says, for what?

Crabs says, for being a bastard.

Carmen takes his hand and they walk to the Ezy-Eatin, dodging in and out of the temporary clothes lines that have sprung up since

last night. There are about thirty cars scattered throughout the
drive-in. Some kids are playing on the swings beneath the screen.
In front of the Ezy-Eatin a blonde woman of about forty is hanging
out her washing and wearing a grey blanket like a cape. She
smiles at them. Crabs scowls. When they pass she calls out,
"Honey-mooners", and a man laughs. Crabs takes his hand out of
Carmen's but she grabs it back.

The woman at the Ezy-Eatin explains to Carmen about the
banana fritters, that they only have them at night, so she has an
ice cream sundae instead. Crabs has a chocolate malted with
double malt. The woman takes the coupons. Carmen says, isn't it
lovely, like a picnic.

It takes him a week to collect the bricks for the back wheel. When
he has enough he chocks them under the rear axle and then puts
the spare on the front. Carmen reads comics and listens to the
music they play through the speakers. Crabs goes looking for
another Dodge to get a wheel from. There aren't any.

At night he wanders round the drive-in tapping on car windows.
He plans to get a lift out, get a wheel somehow, and return. But
no-one will open their windows.

He begins to collect petrol caps and hub caps, just to keep
himself occupied. When he has enough he'll find a Karboy to swap
his lot for a wheel. He feels heavy and dull and spends a lot of
time sleeping. Carmen seems happy. She eats banana fritters at
night and watches the movie. Crabs strips down the engine and
puts it together again. A lot of the day he spends balancing the
flow through the twin carbies, until, one afternoon at about four
o'clock, he runs out of petrol.

There is no way out. Carmen tells him this every day. Each day
she comes back from the Ladies' with new reasons why there is no
way out. At the Ladies' they know everything. They stand and
squat for hours on end, their arms folded, holding up their breasts.
At the Men's it is the same. But Crabs shits in silence with his ears
disconnected. He has no wish to know why there is no way out.

He is waiting for the arrival of a 1956 Dodge. He eats little, sav-
ing his coupons to exchange for a wheel and hubcap he will need.
There are dozens of other wheels he could use, but he wants to
return Frank's Dodge in perfect condition. So he waits, lying on
the leopard skin upholstery he has come to hate. He tries not to

think of Frank but he has nothing else to think of. He is not used
to this, doing nothing. He has always been busy before, getting fit,
or going to the pictures or out in the truck with Frank. And all day
he has worked, delivering engravers' proofs in the Mini Minor.
He hated that Mini. He misses that hate. He misses driving it,
knocking shit out of its piddling little engine, revving it hard
enough to burst, waiting for the day when he would work at Allied
Panel and Towing.

But his mind keeps coming back to Frank and every day the
pain is worse. He tries to think of reasons why Frank will forgive
him. He can't think of any. He tries to make Frank's big spud face
smile at him and say, forget it, mate, it happens to the best of us.
But the face contorts, the big knobbly jaw juts and he sees Frank
take out his teeth, ready for a fight. Or he sees Frank's hand holding the shifting wrench.

Frank said, you get a nice car, people respect you when you got
a nice car. You go somewhere, a motel, and you got a nice car,
they look after you. Frank looked after Crabs. Frank said, you
build up your body, then you can stand up for yourself anywhere.
You build up your body and you can walk in anywhere and know
how to look after yourself. He gave him the chest expanders and
an old photo he had of Charles Atlas. Frank said, that man is a
genius.

Crabs hid in the Dodge and tried to keep his mind free of all
these things. He tried to keep his mind free by keeping busy with
Carmen but she didn't like doing it in the daylight.

Carmen lies on the roof, sunbaking while Crabs hides in the
Dodge. He makes plans for getting out and he tells them to
Carmen. But the wire is now electrified. But the drive-in is closed
to visitors. But the security cars circle the perimeter all night.

Crabs walks through the drive-in each morning after breakfast,
looking for the Dodge he is sure will arrive, somehow, one night.
He picks his way through the clothes lines, around the temporary
toilet facilities, skirts round the rubbish disposal holes, edged by
the card games and temporary cricket pitches. It is like the beach
when he was a kid. Everybody is doing something. He would like
to blow them all up.

He looks at Carmen's face and tries to see exactly what has
happened to it. It is older. Her sweater is covered with small
"pills" of wool. Her hair is pulled back and done in a plait but
doesn't hold in her ears which seem to stick out. She has got fatter.

Her mouth is full of hamburger while she tells him. He knows. He has seen it. He watched it all. She knows he saw it. She wipes her mouth clean of hamburger grease with the arm of her sweater, and tells him about what happened last night.

He says, I know, I saw.

But she tells him, because she feels he sees nothing. She has told everyone at the Ladies' about him and they've come to gaze at him, individually and in groups. He puts up the blankets to keep out their stares, but Carmen invites them in. Their husbands come and invite him to cricket or two-up. He thinks of Frank and the Dodge that will come.

He says, I saw.

He saw, last night, the convoy of trucks come in through the main gate of the drive-in. Everybody went to look. Crabs went afterwards and stood on the edge of the crowd. For some reason they cheered, they cheered the trucks and the drivers as if they were liberating troops. But the trucks only held more cars, cars without wheels, cars without engines, crippled cars, cars unable to move. Crabs watched silently, wondering what it meant.

He watched while the huge mobile crane shifted the cars from the trucks to the ground. He watched the new cars being arranged in lines, in vacant spaces. And when everyone else had lost interest he still watched. He saw the prefabricated Nissen huts come on a huge Mercedes low-loader. He watched the Nissen huts unloaded under the harsh glare of searchlights that had been mounted on top of the old projection room, on top of the Ezy-Eatin.

And he was still there at dawn, when the low-loaders, the cranes, and the other trucks had gone, he was there when the buses began to arrive.

He was there, removing two wheels from a 1956 Dodge.

Everybody goes to stare at the arrivals. Carmen is frantic, she begs him to come. He has never seen her so happy, so angry. Her eyes are sharp and clear. He would like to screw her but he is busy. He would love to hold her, to calm her, warm her, cool her. But he has two wheels from a 1956 Dodge and he is busy. In the corner of his eyes he sees exotic things: cloaks, robes, dark skin, swarthy complexions. He hears voices he doesn't understand, he thinks of the towel of Babel and then he thinks of the Sunday School where he heard about the tower of Babel and then he thinks about peppercorn trees and then he thinks of the two wheels and he tells Carmen, soon, I'll come soon.

The jack is in good shape. He has kept it in good shape. He jacks up the back of the car and removes the bricks. Then he puts on the new wheel. The tyre is a little flat. He guesses at about fifteen pounds per square inch, but it is good enough. Then he removes the front wheel, and puts it back in the spare compartment, and then he puts on the new front wheel.

He will need petrol. Maybe oil too.

He feels as if he is alive again. He will bring the car back to Frank. He will tell a story to him, a fantastic story. He was driving in the country. He was forced off the road by a Mercedes low-loader, and cut off by a jeep. They lifted the Dodge onto the low-loader with Crabs and Carmen inside, and drove off to a country rendezvous. There was a gang. Crabs joined the gang. At night they drove off with the low-loaders. Crabs drove one of them, a Leyland. They stole cars from off the highway. Made the drivers walk home. Crabs became their leader after a fight. He regained the Dodge. Rebuilt it. Then he escaped and brought it back here, to you, Frank.

He is happy. There is tumult around him. He will need to check the oil and petrol. He lifts the bonnet and has the dip stick half out when he notices the carbies are missing. He stops, frozen. Then, slowly he begins the check. The generator is gone. The distributor also. The fan and fan belt. The battery together with the leads. Both radiator hoses and the air cleaner.

Something inside him goes very taut. Some invisible string is taken in one more notch.

He walks, very slowly, back to the newly arrived Dodge. There are people in it. He ignores them. He opens the door and tugs the bonnet release catch. Someone pulls at his clothing. He knocks them off. He opens the bonnet and looks in, looking for the parts he will salvage. There is nothing there. No engine. A dirty piece of plywood has been placed inside to give the engine compartment a floor. Some small chickens, very young, are drinking water from a bowl in the middle.

He lies back on the leopard skin and gazes at the sights outside. Carmen is beside him. She is snuggled up against him. She is saying a lot. Slowly Crabs begins to see what his eyes see.

A large group of Indians, dressed in saris, are gathered around a battered blue Ford Falcon. One of them, an old man, squats on the roof. The Ford Falcon was delivered last night. A group of men, possibly Italians, lean against the front of Frank's Dodge. They are laughing. They seem to be playing a game, taking turns to throw a small stone so that it lands near the front wheel of a bright yellow

Holden Monaro. Small children, black, with swollen bellies run past shouting, chased by a small English child with spectacles.

Carmen is crying. She is saying, they are everywhere. They stare at me. They want to rape me.

Crabs has been thinking. He has been thinking very deeply. Things have been occurring to him and he has reached a conclusion. He has formed the conclusion into a sentence and he tells Carmen the sentence.

Crabs says, to be free, you must be a motor car or vehicle in good health.

Carmen is crying. She says, you are mad, mad. They all said you were going mad.

Crabs says, no, not mad, think about the words – to be free, you . . .

She puts her hand over his mouth. She says, it stinks. It stinks. The whole place stinks of filthy wogs. They're dirty, filthy, everything is horrible.

Crabs sees a car moving along the lane that separates this line of cars from the next. It is a 1954 Austin Sheerline. Inside is the manager, he sits behind the wheel stiffy, looking neither left nor right. It is moving. Crabs is excited for a moment, wondering if he can buy the car with his meal tickets. The car narrowly misses the Indian family and, as it passes in front of him, he sees that the Austin is being pushed by an English family, a man, a woman, and three young boys.

Crabs says, a motor car or vehicle in good health.

Flags, some of them ragged and dirty, flutter in the evening breeze. With every step Crabs smells a different smell, a different dish, a different excretion. He walks slowly along the dusty lanes filled with bustling people. Carmen is in the Dodge. He left her with the bicycle chain and the doors locked.

The situation has become such that no progress is possible. Crabs is now formulating a different direction. Movement is essential, it is the only thing he has ever believed. Only a motor car can save him and he is now manufacturing one. Crabs has decided to become a motor vehicle in good health.

As yet, as he walks, he is unsure of what he will be. Not a Mini Minor. He would like something larger, stronger. He begins to manufacture the tyres, they are large and fat with heavy treads. He can feel them, he feels the way they roll along the dusty lanes. He feels them roll over an empty can and squash into the dust.

Then the bumper bars, huge thick pieces of roughly welded steel
to protect him in case of collision. Mud guards, large and curving.
They feel cool and smooth in the evening breeze. There is something that feels like a tray, a tray at the back. He can feel, with his
nerve ends, an apparatus, but as yet he doesn't know what the
apparatus is. The engine is a V8, a Ford, he feels the rhythm of its
engine, the warm, strong vibratings. A six-speed gearbox and
another lever to operate the towing rig. That is what the apparatus
is, a towing rig.

He feels whole. For the first time in his life Crabs feels
complete. He shifts into low gear and cruises slowly between the
lanes of wrecked cars, between the crowds, the families preparing
their evening meals.

And he knows he can leave.

He has forgotten Carmen. He is complete. He changes into
second and turns on the lights, turning from one lane into the
next, driving carefully through the maze of cars and Nissen huts,
looking for the gate. The drive-in seems to have been extended
because he drives for several miles in the direction of the south
fence. He turns, giving up, and shifting into third looks for the
west fence where the gate was.

It is late when he finds it. His headlights pick up the entry
office. No-one seems to be on guard. As he comes closer he sees
that the gates are open. He changes down to second, accelerates,
and leaves the drive-in behind in a cloud of dust.

On the highway he accelerates. He feels the light on top of him
flashing and, for the pure joy of it, he turns on the siren. The truck
has no governor and he sits it on ninety-two mph, belting down
the dark highway with the air blasting into the radiator, the cool
radiator water cooling his hot engine.

He has gone for an hour when he realizes that the road is empty.
He is the only motor vehicle around. He drives through empty
suburbs. There are no neon signs. No lights in the houses. A
strong headwind is blowing. He begins to take sideroads. To turn
at every turn he sees. He feels sharp pains as his tyres grate,
squeal, and battle for grip on the cold hard roads. He has no sense
of direction.

He has been travelling for perhaps three hours. His speed is
down now, hovering around thirty. He turns a corner and enters a
large highway. In the distance he can see lights.

He feels better, warmer already. The highway takes him

towards the lights, the only lights in the world. They are closer. They are here. He turns off the highway and finds himself separated from the lights by a high wire fence. Inside he sees people moving around, laughing, talking. Some are dancing. He drives around the perimeter of the wire, driving over rough unmade roads, through paddocks until, at last, he comes to a large gate. The gate is locked and reinforced with heavy duty steel.

Above the gate is a faded sign with peeling paint. It says, "Star Drive-in Theatre. Please turn off your lights."

Ore

Murray Bail

The list of publications Wes Williams read carefully, especially between the lines.

Petroleum Intelligence Weekly
Wolfrom's Commodity Digest
Financial Review
London Financial Times (Sat. only)
Sugar Review
Tin International
Skinner's Mining International Yearbook
Rydge's
Pamphlets from chartists. Annual Reports.
Statements from as far away as Detroit – when America catches a cold the rest of the world gets pneumonia. Sundry newspapers.

In the saloon bar, legs apart, he spoke with a kind of mechanical earnestness, looking over the heads of the others. He and his friends wore the short-sleeve shirt; with a tie of course. They could have been tennis players showered and combed after a match. In fact, they were from the one office. Wes has pale blue eyes like the water in one of those Sydney swimming pools, a small mouth, and large wrist knuckles. About thirty odd.

They were talking about the gold price.

"It was a cert. It was on the cards. The Americans had to let it go," Wes said simply.

Each was familiar with the other's arguments, predictions, yet never tired of hearing them. "Shares" were an infectious, endlessly comforting disease. It affected the nasal passages. If someone changed the subject, even to cars, Wes would look around, restless, till it returned.

Wes had a few sugar shares – bought on the crest of the nickel boom. Everybody knew that. But Wes had recently moved into gold as well. He was keeping quiet about that, though anyone

could tell, if they opened their eyes, he had assumed the complac-
ent, almost deaf, manner of an "insider".

"Tell you what, copper'll go next."

Ha, ha. Wes was always on about copper.

"The currency crisis," Wes went on. "It'll affect the commodities.
Copper's fucking low anyway."

"The Cobar mine's doing all right."

Wes smacked his lips.

"Give me Mt Isa any day."

Gazing over their heads he threw in a tonnage and price/earnings
ratio. Then bulging his stomach, pressing his chin to his chest, he
gave two short belches: something he always did after the first
few mouthfuls of beer. It was a free country.

The trouble was, the others could only go on about iron ore.
The finer arguments on gold, copper and silver, their relationships
to the dollar and so forth, were beyond them. Really, completely.

Wes Williams first became aware he was different shortly after he
had his teeth filled. Since buying his sugar shares he'd chewed
sweets whenever he could and put too much sugar in people's tea,
including his own; and one day actually leaned on his secretary's
morning cake, destroying it "accidentally": all in his own way to
help raise, or at least hold, the world sugar price. He had only —
what — forty-one ordinary shares, but it was the largest sugar
company in the Southern Hemisphere. The distant logic that
"every grain must count" had spread throughout his mind to his
arms and eyes, the way sugar itself is altered by moisture. He
thought of the sugar that went into wedding cakes, and enjoyed all
marriages. Empty trays in delicatessen windows caught his eye.
Chewing gum in a gutter was another good sign. These things can
add up. A really pleasant dream, one he replayed in broad daylight, was of a line of trucks leaving a refinery, each with a hole in
the floor, the precious stuff running out like sand, or Time,
unknown to the driver, until the trucks arrived empty — although
Williams was yet to hear of such a case. He took a keen interest in
hurricanes if any were reported heading towards the Caribbean
Islands.

His dentist went busy and grim. Williams needed seven gold
fillings.

The 1969–70 mining boom possessed its own mythology now.
It was incredible. Poseidon had been written up in *Time* magazine.
"Great Boulder", "Carr Boyd Rocks", "Western Mining" were names

similar in feeling to "Burke and Wills", "Leichhardt", "Ayers Rock", their modern equivalents perhaps, although that wasn't why Wes preferred them to the industrials.

The following day the price of gold fixed at US$35 an ounce was allowed to float. The wealth in Williams' mouth doubled overnight.

Hectic scenes were photographed at the Sydney stock exchange — men shouting and waving papers. Some experts were talking about $130 an ounce. Meanwhile his friends stood around talking, and looked small-time.

He could scarcely contain himself.

Up to $117 in no time.

Williams ran his tongue around his mouth. Main gold producing countries: Russia, South Africa. If the blacks went mad now, destroyed a few mines . . .

Wes nodded carefully.

"It'll crack a hundred and fifty, no worries."

The spread in holdings made him feel diversified, secured successfully. It seemed there were more things of interest in the world, more to occupy his mind. At home he had "files" and a book where he kept track of his shares. Regularly he added up the dividends collected so far. Wes was a bit tight. Even Judith, his wife, could get irritated. But it wasn't a bad flat. At six you needed sunglasses in the lounge.

She had a part-time job somewhere, which helped.

No, you had to be on the look-out. Since the nickel boom he'd missed — Christ — the land boom, the cocoa boom, and the rubber boom. So had his friends. And they were looking the other way when Persian carpets, then paintings by Australian artists, took off. Australiana books Wes knew nothing about; brass beds he'd heard were a good thing but already high; original bushranger posters few and far between. You never know. There was the chance of stumbling across a pair of real convict handcuffs one day. Abo axe-heads. Where could you get hold of them now?

Literally, the world consisted of objects beckoning, about to leap in value.

"Mt Isa" seemed to be waving from the share lists, signalling before it was too late. That was what it was like: a name detached itself with its stark pithead, geologist's camp, future prospects . . .

On the 27th, a Friday, gold topped $148 an ounce.

Williams could think of nothing else. Much of his job at the office was done automatically, the attention he paid his wife became distracted noticeably. Food was tasteless.

Mt Isa also had silver, lead. A large slab of the capital was held by the US parent. See, these were the factors his friends never took into account.

Arriving home one night he told Judith about the market, as matter-of-factly as possible. He even sketched out the gold tier-system for her. She was painting her toenails. "Isn't 'bamboo' the most beautiful word in the world?" she asked, not looking up. He noticed then she was naked.

"What are you doing like this?" he shouted.

She wasn't listening.

"What's this you're reading?"

He picked up *Lasseter's Last Ride*.

"Ion Idriess?"

"Give it back please."

He was about to, and would have chucked it; but he couldn't put it down.

Wes sat up with a headache and the taste of old pennies in his mouth. This was funny. He'd never felt crook in his life before.

"You were talking in your sleep," his wife complained.

"Nothing dirty, I hope."

This bloody headache!

"Something about Mary Kathleen," said Judith in a flat voice.

Perhaps no man can absorb as many numerical figures as Williams did at that time. While Judith was talking he studied his teeth in the bathroom and farted. That was better. He carried the world's copper reserves around in his head, and much valuable supporting data, including core samples and lode depths, "promising situations". Ordinary news failed to register. There was no room. Occasionally, he squeezed in a political movement from Zambia or Chile; but that was tied up with copper. Optical wonders such as an iron ball swinging through one of the city's old buildings passed without his mouth opening.

The headache came in waves. Stranger was the taste of pennies. It reminded him of the ore piled up outside Mt Isa; but then so did mould on his cheese at lunch one day. His head continued its slow cracking.

No need to tell the wife.

He found a doctor. Here was an eminent specialist, an expert in his field. He had a paisley handkerchief almost falling out from his lapel pocket. He wore tortoise-shell glasses.

As he shined a torch down Wes's mouth he constantly changed the shape of his own mouth.

"And you've been off appetite?"

Before Williams could nod a thermometer rose from his mouth. Mercury! Interesting, mysterious metal. How about mercury? Not traded enough though, not in the big league. Wes subsided. And he'd caught sight of the doctor's cuff links: solid gold.

"How long have you been out?" Wes asked, stretching his legs. "I take it you're from the UK?"

Macquarie Street, thought Wes. He'd be doing all right.

The doctor took the thermometer to the window.

"It was actually a Friday morning, August 1969."

"Just in time," Wes called out. "Poseidon, Western Mining. I s'pose you got some shares?"

Everyone else did.

"You seem to have a fever," the doctor said, shaking the thermometer. "Yes, I did as a matter of fact."

"Still goddem?"

Wes relaxed. One of the things about the mining boom was its spontaneous camaraderie.

"Still goddem?"

"I am afraid so."

"Copper," said Wes loudly, in case he was speaking here with a man disillusioned with the market. "That's going to move."

The doctor smiled.

"You think so?"

"Well, I'd buy now," Wes advised him. "Hang on. Whoow," he said, suddenly sitting down. "I'm as dizzy as buggery. Fuck this!"

Copper broke through the psychological £500 barrier at the London Metal Exchange; the Australian producers quickly followed. Big fall in warehouse stocks. The Zambian railway cut. China was reported buying.

The taste in Wes's mouth became so strong Judith must have noticed. On top of her he found he could hold off by picturing the lay-out of a famous open-cut mine. On the other hand, his head was so full of figures it rejected breakfast.

At the doctor's now he noticed the *Financial Review* alongside *Punch* and *The Autocar*.

Wes thought he could slap him on the back; because of the terrific mood just then.

"There you are, six hundred and fifty this morning. What did I tell you?"

It left sugar for dead.

The doctor gazed at him, tapping his teeth with a pencil.

"Several of my colleagues," he said, "have expressed an interest."

Wes wasn't sure what he was getting at.

"We shall have to take a sample. A smallish operation. Your permission is required, of course."

"Well, you're the experts," said Williams loudly.

In case he was seriously ill or something he stumbled on, "I'd say it was a moot point whether to buy a copper share now, or a ton of the metal itself."

To his existing reserves Williams added discoveries of low grade ore in Indonesia and Iran. Against that he put the latest consumption figures of the Industrialized West; added acres of future cars and motor bikes, colour TV sets, fridges: eating into the known reserves. And what if Red China's economy took off? He rubbed his hands.

On the day, the doctor was unusually jovial yet didn't introduce him: nodded at Wes to lie down.

The others were "specialists". Each had the *Financial Review* under his arm. One wore a cork helmet. Another a handlebar moustache and cigar, though it was not yet ten o'clock in the morning. The third carried a superb English walking stick — worth a lot of money — but was actually a theodolite. He was red in the face but grinning.

"Hello, old boy."

"Pip, pip."

"What?"

"I say."

They crowded around.

"Standing at $2.70, with a yield of 6.3," Wes began. He was a bit annoyed. They were now all calling him "Mr Williams". All part of their act.

They ignored his toneless predictions; lowered the bright lights, and murmured to each other. Some had their sleeves rolled up.

The first exploratory drilling encountered grey matter, nothing else.

The telephone rang.

"788."

"5.6"

The third and the fourth holes struck ore of major density, just below the surface. Further intersections proved the reserves. Open-cut was feasible. They all agreed. They had the equipment. It became a rapid large-scale operation. Wes's babbling went quieter, the figures became smaller, even dubious, until he was silent.

"That will be all. Thank you. You might take these tablets if you feel anything."

Wes felt vaguely grateful. The others had gone; where were the others?

"No headache now? Good. Thank you, then."

The doctor turned his back and began writing. Wes searched around for the taste of copper in his mouth. It too had gone.

Macquarie Street outside was sharply defined and noisy. Another hot day. The bar was empty, but Wes thought he'd wait there for the lunch crowd. Nothing else he could do. He looked around. No worries though. He adjusted himself on the stool. Diamond drilling intersected ore of major density.

The Airport, the Pizzeria, the Motel, the Rented Car, and the Mysteries of Life

Frank Moorhouse

In the airport lounge we embraced. We embraced under the international ideograms. I am hungry. I want to go to the lavatory. I need an interpreter. Where is the doctor. This way out. They spoke to me and I to them above and beyond my greetings to my ex-wife after seven years. I should have listened to them.

I stood in my Breton holiday cap and stared after the people suspended in Transit. I wanted to be with them in Transit. A destination ahead. The place you've come from, well behind you. Suspended. No badgering choices. No possessions. All services present. A true state of purity.

"Well."

"Well."

"After all these years."

"It's been a long time."

As I looked into her eyes the droning of the airport called to me. Translated English came through, calling to me, from the comforting, depersonalized Public Address System. A voice filtered of all human evil, threat, mood with a hypnotic cadence. Another purity.

We got straight into the mysteries where we had left off those years before in the milk bars of our Australian city suburb.

"I had déjà vu just then," she said, my ex-wife, in the airport lounge.

"Oh yes?" I said.

"Do you ever have déjà vu?"

"Yes, I've had déjà vu."

"Doesn't it affect you. I mean, doesn't it serve as a reminder?"

"A reminder?" What had I forgotten? "I'm sorry, I'm not with you."

"A reminder that all cannot be explained. Suggestions of our pre-existence."

I used a smiling head movement to say, no one denies, some things are difficult, come on now that's no mystery, and who the hell talks like that, and what for instance.

"There are explanations of sorts," I said in words.

"What explanations?" she demanded, courteously petulant.

"Oh, physiological − retinal skip − optical paramnesia − something like that."

"I won't accept that," she said, like a quiz gong.

I waved a generous hand, "What does it matter − it's certainly a weird sensation," not wanting grit in the eye of our first meeting.

"I think it's evidence that we have lived before," she said, "I know you'll scoff but it has never been explained to my satisfaction."

"Now . . . " I said, almost choking on scoff, "where is that fiery atheist from Concord High School?"

It helps to remember that we all came from High Schools.

"Even you have to admit there are things that cannot be explained," she said, "and anyhow I hate people who have explanations."

Now what do I say? Is it something to do with women being denied the scientific tradition, denied a role in the affairs of the world, that leads them to superstition? Or maybe I attract this sort of person, or maybe I bring it out in them, maybe this is their rebellion against my personality and its oppression. I have known a number of women who hold on to some mystical gemstone, secretly, sometimes ashamedly, usually when it is sensed, and prised out, like a stone from a hoof, they are embarrassed. But they continue to hold on to it, say a belief that there are card tricks that cannot be explained. That one person in the world is imbued with supernatural power, Uri Geller, albeit rather useless power. Something like that.

I said, "We cannot explain some things," wondering if I was giving too much away, "only because we don't have the explanations. I know this is going to sound bad, but I find life pretty simple to explain, especially human motivation. I don't think there is much to it . . . to life." I shrugged my shoulders. That was how it seemed to me then.

"I find that dreadfully arrogant," she said, putting a smile on top of her criticism to ease it, "I think there are eternal mysteries, déjà vu, our dreams, dualism." She took my hand, "Our coming together after seven years, the number seven, after you disappeared without so much as a word."

Dualism? Where'd she get that? That's what I'd told Hestia. I blinked. I was with my ex-wife in Portugal. Not with Hestia.

We formally kissed; "Now let's get out of here," she said, "I hate airports."

I love airports. I love the opera of airports. People weeping, and how soon people stop their tears. The flare of excessive interest in someone because they are coming or going. Everyone audience to the person. Speechy conversation which no one can remember afterwards, everyone over-laughing. Families with high-gloss airport emotion, a linkage of smiles, tears, and touching. A moratorium on malice, air-conditioned goodwill. When the airport sanctuary is left, the automatic doors open into the sweaty heat and blown litter, and they also re-open the wounds of the family and the dust blows into the lacerations.

I did not want to leave the airport.

In the pizzeria we held hands. We held hands before the repetition. Each pizza thrown perfectly together. Parts of life have reached perfection ahead of the rest. Pizza-making is one. Thrown together with unthinkable dexterity, artlessly sculptured. Perfectly repeated.

"It's been a long time since we ate a meal together," I said, with a squeezed cheeriness.

"It has been a long time. I can't say, though, I call this a meal. Here you are in a new country and the first thing you eat is a pizza from a take-away food chain."

"I want to begin with the familiar," I said, "I *know* the pizza. New experiences have to be stalked."

"I wish you had let me take you to Enrico's."

"Remember," I said, "those river picnics."

"Very dearly."

"Remember doing it on the rock."

She frowned, as though not remembering.

"It was our first time – you gave me your virginity for my birthday."

"No, I didn't."

"Yes, yes you did," I said, insistently, hanging perilously on my effort at sentimentality. Had I got it wrong?

Was it with someone else. Some other time. In another existence?

"No," she said, "we didn't do *it* and I didn't give you my virginity – I gave you *me*."

"Oh yes, that's what I meant."

"Did you know that you and Paul have the same birthday. Did

you know that? I think that's incredible. Two men in my life and they should have the same birthday."

"Two pizza specials, please."

"My astrologist, oh . . . " she stopped on the word, putting her hand to her mouth to hold the rest in, "I remember, you don't talk about astrology."

"Of course I do, of course I talk about astrology."

"You don't take it seriously. You attacked me in the letters."

"Two pizza specials, yes."

"In some ways you've become more narrow, less open to life," she said, pensively, "I don't mean to be offensive."

"No – that's alright."

I wanted to watch the pizza-making.

"Look, ahem . . . " I milled around, "ahem, well, look, it seems to me the problem of astrology is what to do with this knowlege of the future."

She looked besieged.

I didn't mean to besiege her.

"I mean, that is, if you accept predestination it doesn't mean that you can alter it – and if you could, wouldn't your attempts to alter it and their outcome also be, well, foreseeable?"

She did not reply.

"You may as well not know about it," I mumbled, to soften it, mumble, mumble, "gypsies think it is a curse to be able to see the future – not a gift."

"It is possible that magnetic forces at the time of your birth somehow programme your brain cells," she said, unhappily.

She thought "magnetic" and "programme" were words which might appeal to me.

"If on the other hand," I said, nodding at what she had said, "if on the other hand you believe in the forewarning – which events do you change – can't fate outwit you?"

"I don't like your approach to life – you used to be more reverent, less arrogant."

"I'm sorry."

The pizza came as expected, hot, boxed, honest, as promised.

"I hate take-away food," she said.

"I love it," I said fiercely, recklessly, which wasn't really as true as I made it sound. But it was too late. I was away – riding an unbroken horse.

"I love Kentucky Fried Chicken. Children love take-away food above all else – they hate the food at home – children have to be force-fed – did you realize that? – for the first years they are physically force-fed and beaten until they eat the lousy food their mothers dish up."

I knew she harboured a Rousseauian theory that children were instinctively wise and that given no adult guidance they would choose in their best interest. She harboured bad theories, like escaped criminals, in the cellars and attics of her mind. I knew they were there. I remembered now.

"They are propagandized," she said, "given the choice without all the pressures they'd do what was right."

Why do they believe the propaganda? Why don't they know it to be false after the first bite of take-away food? Tell me that. Why doesn't the instinctively wise child believe reality over propaganda?

"Why!" I said, "take-away food is the beginning of the communal kitchen," I ripped on, "most people cook so badly they love take-away food."

I had flown a thousand miles for one of her smiles at a very high altitude and here we were embattled over take-away food. The pizzas in their boxes were complaining, burning me through the cardboard. I shifted them from hand to hand.

The people in the suburbs, I told her, were already learning that it was better to share the services of a professional cook. That's what take-away food is all about. At last, I blurted, we are getting rid of a million little women in a million little kitchens stirring a million little pots. Saint-Simon.

Then I came up with something else. I told her I thought that children preferred take-away food because they feared poisoning at the hands of basically hostile, frustrated, unliberated mothers. The traditional mother is an anti-mother. They punish their husbands and themselves by punishing the child.

Why do I ride these unmanageable horses?

"Do you have a theory about everything," she asked tiredly.

In the motel we fought. We fought over the idea of "motel sex" and the miracle of creation.

"I don't know why but it makes me feel debased — furtive."

"What you feel," I said, to my ex-wife, straining to make our personalities meet in the middle, also our bodies, "is that a motel lacks the 'ambience of true living', that motels contain no personal 'detritus'."

"Yes, you always have a cold word for everything," she said, "you were always the master of the clinical expression."

She sat in what should have been the comfortable relaxing chair for weary travellers. I lay on the vibrator bed. The motel met my every expectation and I thanked it. I had on the musak and the television without sound. The English-language newspapers would be delivered. I could monitor reality. Systematized comfort, cushioned by media.

I have been in a hundred motel rooms in many countries. I like the morning concourse, bags humping into luggage compartments of dusty cars. The clatter of breakfast trays.

"Have you read the short story called *The St Louis Rotary Convention 1923, recalled*," I asked. She shook her head and said something about it being a good title.

"In that story a character called Becker sings a song of praise to the motel."

"We should have stayed with my friend Pieta."

"I didn't want to stay with your friend Pieta. I wanted to be alone with you where we could be intimate."

"A motel room!" she sneered but it didn't sneer properly, she was too nice.

"Yes I feel *at home* in a motel," I said.

"We should be with Chris – our child. Your daughter."

"*Your* child," I said, "I fathered her but she is totally your child. For godsake I haven't seen her since birth."

"Why don't you want to be with Chris," she said plaintively, tenderly.

"Because I want to be with you. We couldn't have had sex with her about."

"Chris is me."

"Crap."

"You wouldn't understand – you've become so . . . It only hides your fear of life, you know. I am not a single person. It is no use getting accustomed to me. I am a combination of myself and my children."

"Holy jesus."

"Why are you so abusive."

"Breeding is a rapidly depreciating virtue," I said.

"Oh I see," she said, "so having children is – how would you say it? – invalid?"

"Yes, you don't need children – unless you're a dairy farmer."

"How unloving you've become – and I think, a little sick."

"This patient enjoys his illness."

I brooded and vibrated.

"You don't sound convincing," she said, caringly.

"Children," I began again, "were once an economic necessity and then a religious obligation – now nothing more than a suburban convention."

"I don't wish to talk about it in those terms."

"Why did the State and the Church have to work so hard to convince people to have children – suppressing birth control information – why? – I'll tell you why – because people preferred not to have children. That's why."

She had closed her eyes, as if to the words. Then she said, "You must miss so much – I feel really sorry for you – oh, I know you've achieved so much – you lead what you call a free life but so much pleasure in life comes from having commitments and trials and worries."

I watched her closely during her speech, the bed vibrating away under me.

"I like my life to be a warm muddle," she said, "you wouldn't, I'm afraid, understand that."

I shook my head vigorously.

How clever the living process was. Oh bloody clever. You couldn't really make a mistake. Whatever you did, wherever you ended up, the mind reshaped to accommodate and even celebrate it. Except for the intrusion, now and then, of ideal forms. Our tormented gift of being able to visualize perfection.

Then I listened to her mundane certificates of life – her two deeply meaningful love relationships (including those early years with me – before I changed),

– her three "creative" children,

– her four uncomplicated working class friends,

– her five well-worn railings of inaccurate commonsense,

– her six conversational mysteries.

How correct all the black things of life then seemed. How basically good and decent pornography was. All the perversity and ornery, difficult people who messed up formulations about "full life" and "loving interpersonal relationships". All that American love.

I told her that Anatole France said that volupté was the only solace.

Dispiritedly, she said, "What?"

"Volupté! Sensual pleasure! Evil sensuality!"

She said that all she sought from life – now that I'd brought it up – was the warmth of the hearth and "the sticky fingers of loving children".

I stared at the ceiling.

"I guess," I said, brightly, "that really I'm for Sin and against Motherhood."

I thought that was glib enough summing up, so while she was in the bathroom, probably weeping into the sanitized wash basin, I soundlessly left. The second time in seven years.

In the rented car I breathed freely. A rented car is not an extension of self in quite the same way as a car you own. You are free of the bonds of ownership. The rented car is not your ego, rusting away, corroding, scratched. A rented car renews itself at each renting and renews you with it. Certain things, I said, can be best and freely used when not owned. People? Then they are not tangled with your ego.

Ah!! Give me the technological life.

I am a simple non-spiritual man, I said to myself, leading a simple rented life.

I spoke to all the international ideograms at the airport, and took the advice of the wine glass.

Disconsolation joined me at the bar some fifteen or twenty minutes later when I began to ponder on how difficult and confounding it was to find volupté which Anatole France said was the only solace.

I pulled my Breton cap over my disconsolate brow.

Where *was* this volupté when you needed it???

Green Grow the Rushes

T. A. G. Hungerford

The de Blore place stood on a high ridge of sandstone looking out over the river to the city on the other side. Its enormous weatherboard and lacy-iron pile used up sufficient space and material for the twenty 1975-type family-kennel "units" which, in fact, now occupy the site. Framed and shaded by huge old trees, with pergolas of wisteria and bignonia, it overshadowed the low-lying riverside paddocks where we lived, topographically as well as socially only a rung or two above the multi-coloured swathe of vegetable gardens established by the industrious Chinese left-overs from early goldrushes on the crescent of deep, rich black soil built up by a million years of flood deposits on the southern bank of the river. It offered us a two-sided message — for our elders, what they had missed out on, and for us, what we might attain to: it was in its heyday at a time when youngsters still planned to attain something other than retirement and the pension.

I used to go up there with my father. He was a piano-tuner, come down in life — as my mother used to remind him whenever the opportunity presented itself. Although now I wonder if she was reminding him, or informing us that there had been a time when things had been better. Not that he didn't make a reasonable living for those days, even though it was early in the Depression. It seemed as if every second person then had a piano of some sort, and of course every piano needed tuning now and then. He had his daily bit of business, and there were the occasional dances and wedding breakfasts and twenty-first birthday parties in the Mechanics Institute Hall. Also, he played Saturday nights at the old Bijou, that incredible old fleapit where, nevertheless, overture and entr'acte were studiously observed, and sometimes after interval a visiting tenor would sing "Roses in Picardy" and "A Wandering Minstrel". With one thing and another my father made ends meet, and without my mother going out to work. Wood stove, outside copper for the washing, four kids and part responsibility for the vegetable garden must have kept her from wondering what she might have been if she hadn't fallen for my father's winning Irish ways. I don't recall ever having been hungry, other than the just-home-from-school emptiness we filled immediately with bread-and-jam or bread-and-dripping, so undermining our health that I near the end of five decades without ever having seen the inside of any but a military hospital – and what I was in there for was certainly not brought on by any diet deficiency.

My father used to take me up to the de Blore place to recite. It earned me the envy of every youngster in the district – not that I could recite, but that it got me access to what was, in a way, the enchanted castle of our immediate neighbourhood. Old de Blore bestrode our affairs like a great pot-bellied colossus. He was legendary around the large country town that Perth then was, and for a couple of thousand miles north of it, as a first-in drover and now station-owner who had physically battled the blacks for their territory. He had spear-wounds in his back to prove it, some said. He had been a prospector and a mine promoter, a pearler and a camel-master and god-only-knows-what else – and had made money at all of them. A big part of the legend, for us, was that Aborigines from his stations were employed in his house and in his garden and his stables. Since Mrs de Blore had died years before in a cyclone in Broome, perhaps even before I was born, there was quite a lot of conjecture, which I didn't understand at the time, as to his relationship with the Aboriginal women. They worked exclusively in the house and seemed happy enough, but the moment they became aware of the presence of outsiders – my father and me, for instance – they would simply disappear: or if they didn't disappear, they would hang their heads so that their curly brown hair made a curtain before their faces, and you could see their eyes glinting at you from behind. I never saw the men who worked in the stables, but the gardeners always seemed to be standing around, only half-visible in flecked sunlight under the trees, or ever so slowly dragging rakes or barrows across the lawns and among the roses. Sometimes, in their moleskin trousers and huge felt hats, they squatted in groups on the paths, smoking stick-thin roll-your-own cigarettes, retracted so deeply between their grasshopper thighs that their bottoms rested on the gravel. They seemed never to speak, or perhaps they did so by signs. Their eyes, as they watched us up to the house, were veiled as with the smoke of bushfires, secret and – to me, anyway – frightening.

I was always glad to make the security of the side verandah, crowding my father's heels as we went up the steps to where old de Blore sat in the afternoons. Even then I sensed there were many who had trouble not spitting whenever the old man's name was mentioned, and I had heard him described variously as a tight-fisted old bugger and a damned black-birder and a bloody old gin-jockey, all without being meant to overhear, and without really understanding what I heard. To me, then, he was just another adult phenomenon. I was far more impressed by the six little ponies he used to ride behind, in his landau, on his way to what my father called "shivoos" in Perth, than by the possibility that he might in some curious way be married to one or more of his black gins – which was the way I understood it from talk suddenly curtailed whenever I came within range of it at home. *Old de Blore.* Whale-fat, turkey-red, bull-voiced, perclum-blue eyes swimming in pits of raw meat. I didn't learn until years later that he had suffered with the sandy-blight early on, up north. I just thought he was mad as a meat-axe, and he frightened the stuffing out of me sometimes, even when he laughed.

A fat, red-headed, jug-eared, freckled composite of memory and old snapshots stares back at me from the bathroom mirror in which little Dinny Walsh so assiduously slicks down his mop with Sunshine soap for his appearance on the de Blore's side verandah. I must have been a smarmy little brute. I could "take-off" people, and I was always the King or the Ogre or the Child Jesus, or whatever it might be, in the school concert every year. Although my dad was Irish, and hadn't come out to Australia until he was a grown man, he went wild for Banjo Paterson and Will Ogilvie and all that push of horse-and-stirrup singers. I, of course, was the minstrel boy. I think I must have been the only youngster extant who could say the whole of "The Man From Snowy River" by heart – with actions, and what the nuns called "expression". I wonder that people didn't just throw up at me.

My father had a horse and cart which he made use of to combine a delivery-round with his piano-tuning, taking things in to town, bringing things out, dropping things here and there about the suburb. It used to nark my mother, and I could never understand why he kept on with it. I know now, of course. Making ends meet. In those days fathers did all sorts of curious things to eke out the "sustenance" from the government. The father of one of my schoolmates had a clearing contract on a bit of land destined to become a football-field. He blew off nearly every finger of both hands, one or two at a time, and in comparison with many other families, his breezed through the Depression on the insurance money. In his own way my father blew off *his* fingers rattling around the suburb behind his gentle old Ginger. I know now that it hurt him like hell. His past was of a piece with the names of Lake Way and Nannine and Peak Hill, which were the first words I recall hearing, in casual conversation between my father and my mother, and in long afternoons of old-times talk between them and Sunday visitors in blue-serge and massive gold-nugget brooches. The aluminium nose-peg of a camel was one of my first playthings, yet it was not until I had grown up that I connected it with a time when he too, had been a sort of legend around the Murchison goldfields, a camel-master at the same time as old de Blore, and chasing the same kind of business.

What with one thing and another, we would be up at the de Blore place every few weeks. When my father had done what he had to do – he was also handy with clocks – old de Blore would settle himself on a big cane chair on the verandah, overlooking the river, and would roar, "Come on, now, Dinny Walsh! What are you going to say today?" I always had something ready, because he would give me a sixpence and an apple or an orange to go with it. Apples and oranges came in halves at our place, and sixpence was my Bijou money, Saturday nights, or fish and chips when I went to the beach, swimming, Sunday afternoons. I had got to know that his favourite was that one, "The Bush Christening". "On the outer Barcoo where the churches are few and men of religion are scanty . . . " I think I could say it right through now, if I put my mind to it. I would stand about four feet away from him, but still in the range of the blast of his breath – rum or whiskey, to this day I don't know which. He would always begin roaring with laughter even before I had begun. Then, I didn't know why, except to think that I was a gun entertainer. Now I do know. What a poor, pompous little shit I must have looked. Heels together and toes out, as the nuns had drummed into me. Bow, with my right hand flat on my paunch, my left clenched in the small of my back – the nuns' training again. And off I'd go. Now, fifty years after, the scene has become formalized in my memory as some sort of Byzantine composition of brittle, coloured glass, in a way not unlike the "tableau" the nuns crammed into every break-up concert, willy-nilly. The smallest and fairest (*non Anglei sunt, sed angeli*) in crepe-paper wings and white angels' shifts, scared witless on borrowed pedestals, staring down in adoration at somebody's sleepy-doll in somebody else's wicker washing-basket. Old de Blore in *his* huge wicker basket. My father and me. The

ferns in bailer shells about the polished floor of the verandah, the
sleeping river, the low, mauve skyline of the city. I can even
remember vividly the white centres to the heavenly-blue flowers
of a plant called "wandering Jew" that spilled over the sides of the
hanging baskets. I never think of it now without burning for the
way I exulted in my degradation, the way I so willingly sat up and
balanced the biscuit on my nose for that brutal old bastard.

Sometimes I used to see Miss Honour. Miss Honour de Blore.
Even now, just to say the name makes my heart turn over. I loved
her with the hopeless love of ten for seventeen. I don't think I
even knew it was love. All I realized was that what I felt for her
was different from what I felt for the Virgin Mary. Honour de
Blore was all but inaccessible, whereas the Mother of God was
there every day, on the shelf above the black-board, in the blue-
and-gold mantle whose protection we sought in the gabbled Oh-
Mary-my-mother-and-my-hope-I-place-myself-under-thy-mantle
last prayer of the day. Before we set out to rob the Chinamen's fig
trees on the way home from school. And Honour de Blore almost
always wore white, but soft, and so that you could see right
through it to the pink or blue underdress she wore, with embroidery on it. She was dark, with deep blue eyes. She had long hair,
and she did it pulled back loosely, red-brown and wavy, into a
huge black ribbon bow, stiff as cardboard, that sat there as if an
outsize butterfly had alighted on the nape of her neck. Sometimes
when we arrived, she would be standing in the doorway leading
into their entrance hall, with the stained glass glowing blue and
red and green and gold all around her. Further down the hall there
was a white plaster arch with carving on it and crimson velvet
curtains held back in the loops of gold cords with tassels, and on
either side huge Chinese vases full of pampas grasses from their
garden. Sometimes, when we had made our way past the black
gardeners down the side path to the steps leading up onto the
verandah, she would come out and would lean her back against
the rail to watch us, the blue of the river behind her. Usually,
with her white dress she wore a narrow black patent-leather belt,
and almost always she had stuck a red rose or a red geranium in it.
Right below her, it seemed, you could see the dark green swathe
of rushes beside the river, on the far side of the Chinamen's
gardens. *Come down the rushes,* we would say, when we were little
nippers, and we would play explorer or pirate, or would fish for
gilgies in the springs. *Come down the rushes,* we'd say later on,
when we were in the district football team, and picking up girls at
the edges of the dances in the Mechanics Institute Hall, with my

own father, like as not, pounding out the "Pride of Erin" or the "Jazz Waltz" inside. *Come down the rushes.*

The only time I ever saw Miss Honour away from old de Blore's was down there. It was a grey-satin evening the colour of a mullet's belly, when the electric signs in the city across the water bled blue and green and red and gold in wavering lines almost to where we stood on the southern bank. Three of us had been down crabbing in the shallows. We were walking home along a raised mud dyke between two of the Chinamen's irrigation ditches, in the cool, swamp-smelling last light of shrilling frogs and night-herons booming in the she-oaks which used to fringe the river on our side. We were cold in our sodden shirts and shorts, and were laden down with our catch and our nets. In single file, like the Chinamen, we were lurching down along the path when the Jim or the Jack or the Joe in front said, in a breathless and surprised sort of way, "Uh . . . good evening, Miss de Blore." I was last in line, and for a moment I thought he was having us on. We used to talk about her, and about meeting her, and getting fresh with her, in the way of boys just beginning to feel their oats. In the way, maybe, boys living around Windsor Castle might talk about the unattainable occupants whom they only see but never get to speak to. But as we drew level, I could see it was she, all right, in one of those luminous white dresses and a scarf around her shoulders. She said, "Helly, Dinny!" even though it was two or three years since I had been up there to recite for them. But she didn't pause for so much as a second. Almost immediately she was out of sight in the brown shadows, and when we had gone some distance in the other direction, the one in the lead said what we had all been thinking, I guess. "I wonder what the hell she's doing down here, this time of night?" The one in the middle said, with a giggle, "I never saw any bloke lurking around!" Being last in line, I had the privilege of the last comment, and I know they would have accepted it without question. "Don't be bloody silly about blokes!" I said. "Miss Honour!"

Time passes, and usually it demonstrates just how wrong you can be.

That was the summer I got my Junior, which was the big deal in those days. Rather miraculously for the times, I got a job also. In the Post Office, for which I suspect I had to thank the influence of old de Blore — at my father's request, of course. Within a year I was sent to a country centre in the south of the state. The "post office Johnny" I replaced had doubled as sports reporter for the local paper, and I was offered the job. I found I had a flair for it, and before long I was submitting pars about all sorts of things, and having them accepted. Then I got an offer to string for one of the Perth dailies, and finished up drifting into journalism. The war lifted the lid of the oyster for me, and when it was over I began working my way around, looking for the pearl. The trail led me half-a-dozen times in and out of Hong Kong, so that before I knew it had happened, that bright jewel had sunk its proboscis into my veins like a true anopheles, and had infected me for life. Only less a disease with me was Macau, and on my last visit, about five years ago, I settled for living there and commuting to and from Hong Kong by hydrofoil. I had a small suite at the old Hotel Belvedere, a Charles Addams pile of flaking stucco and blocked drains crowning a rocky bluff that does sentry over a wide, junk-haunted expanse of the Pearl River estuary. There, of all the places in the world, I met Honour de Blore for the first time since she had walked away from me that summer evening in the Chinamen's garden in South Perth, the luminous white of her dress drifting like a moth towards the river bank and the rushes.

I met her one Sunday morning in the flush of spring, when every foot of the hillside below the hotel seemed covered with greenery, and every spray of greenery seemed covered with blossom, and every blossom seemed covered with butterflies, in the Chinese manner: for don't forget it, in Macau you are in China, for all that several centuries of Portuguese rule have scattered the mouldering facades of beautifully-iced churches and convents all across that high ridge overlooking the Baia do Praia Grande. I had been sitting out on that little bit of the terrace where the busy coconut-fibre brooms of the *farwongs* still manag-ed, somehow, to keep at bay the encroaching tide of rubbish. The spring was still morning-cool, so I had my back to the warming rock wall. At the other end of the terrace, perhaps forty feet from me, a very well-put-together woman was leaning her elbows on the balustrade, her chin in her hands, staring out to where the misty Ladrone Islands sailed, unseen, like the ghosts of robber junks on the amethyst water. Is it because of what I now know that I can say that from the moment I walked out onto the terrace and saw her there, I suspected it might be Honour de Blore? In any case, I had been willing her to turn around and put me out of my doubt — when she did, eventually, and stared straight back at me, her eyes narrowed in the bright sunlight. Then she walked over to me. There was no hesitation, no coyness.

"Dinny Walsh," she said. "You're a long way from South Perth."
"Honour de Blore," I said, standing up. "So are you."
We stared at each other for — I don't know. Maybe five seconds.
I have no idea what she saw. Like most people, I believe, I hold
some sort of appreciation of what I look like. It probably flatters
me to myself. It hasn't changed for years, anyway. What I saw
was a woman still beautiful, her brown hair heavily streaked with
grey but suiting her, her face lined, but gently. Eyes calm among
their crow's-feet. Or resigned? Again, I don't know. Whether
naturally or by some artful dodge, her figure seemed hardly
changed at all, although perhaps a little heavier. She was dressed
with that deceptively simple elegance which cripples bank
accounts, in a long-sleeved blouse of some sheer white stuff tucked into a full-bottomed skirt, knee-high, of some sheer black stuff.
At collar, wrists, waist and hem, deep bands of Chinese brocade
on which the design had been picked-out with seed-pearls and
semi-precious stones. After two marriages to extravagant women,
I have a pretty lively appreciation of the look and the cost of good
clothes. It occurred to me at the time that it was costing someone
plenty to dress Honour de Blore. It was I who broke the silence.
"Then — what are you doing here?" I said. Maybe, in the twilight of my male chauvinism, I thought she couldn't possibly have
as much right as I to be rolling around the world, or as much
competence to keep herself while she was doing it. She must have
read me correctly, for she said simply, "I am Li Po. In Hong Kong,
of course. Not here."
As she spoke the words "Li Po", the name Hetty Chia flashed
through my mind, like the kingfisher's wing that glitters in so
much Chinese poetry. I could not even pause to wonder why.
I lost it immediately, in my surprise at what she had just said.
There are only two Li Pos worth talking about. She couldn't be the
Tang Dynasty poet who drowned himself first in wine, and then
in a lake, trying to embrace the reflected moon. So she must have
meant the high fashion house — not the biggest in Hong Kong, but
certainly the most exclusive, with half the world's jetset clothes-
horses on its waiting-list. It was above any banal preoccupation
with the right moment to reveal or conceal the knee, or liberate or
confine the bust. It meant simply supreme elegance. Its signature
was the opulent embroidery I had been staring at, and to which
my attention returned as Honour de Blore said the name. She
caught the direction of my glance, and shook one of the glittering
cuffs.
"I'm my own best advertisement," she said, smiling. "As a matter

of fact, it's why I'm over here this weekend." She waved to the
tangle of pink-tile roofs below us, the teeming cock-lofts crowding
crooked lanes from which hundreds of years of European commerce had not been able to remove the ingrained obstinacy of
their Chineseness. "There must be three or four score women
going blind down there, embroidering this kind of thing for me. I
used to get it done in Hong Kong, but . . . you know. Trade
unions. They're not so particular here in Macau." She smiled, and
shrugged. "Still the oppressors of the workers, us de Blores. Once
it was the blacks we diddled. Now it's the . . . the Chows." She
emphasized the word, long discarded I imagine, except among
Australians, in a way which whisked me straight back to my boyhood in South Perth, and my mother saying: *Go down the Chows
and get me* . . .

At the same moment, I recalled why the name Hetty Chia had
jumped into my mind a moment ago: from a conversation half-
heard, during a previous visit to Hong Kong, at a sunset cocktail
party in one of those crazy towers of splintered glass that rear like
jewelled chopsticks on the perilous dark slopes of the Peak.
During the sort of sudden silence when one surreptitiously looks
at the clock to see if it is quarter-to anything, someone close
behind me had said, "Hetty Chia was to have come tonight. She
owns Li Po." Someone else, very English, had said, "Remarkable
flair. Different from most Australians." And somebody else, very
Australian, very ocker, said, "I'll say, different! She married a
Chow. What price the White Australia Policy now?"

I stared at Honour de Blore. "But, if you own Li Po . . . "

She looked back at me with an amused smile. I think she must
have read me again, or perhaps she was just used to it. She said,
"I really can't be Honour de Blore, eh?"

"You are Hetty Chia?"

"For business purposes. Hetty was my mother's name, so I
borrowed it. Honour Chia is a bit awkward — and in any case, the
Hetty sort of name is in, in the rag trade. I prefer plain Mrs Chia,
but of course nobody will use it." She gestured toward the bench.
"But please sit down, Dinny. And I will, too." She sat, as gracefully
as I should have expected, and tucked her high-heeled shoes
becomingly beneath the bench. As I lowered myself beside her
she said, again with that amused smile, "You most likely would
have known my husband."

"Chia?" I spent a moment or two thinking back to Chinese I had
met at her level, in Hong Kong and elsewhere. "Maybe," I said, at
length. "But I'm afraid I can't recall."

"It was a long time ago," Honour de Blore said. She was no longer smiling. "Chia Kuan Yu. You would have called him Charlie." One of those enormous black, blue-splashed Macau butterflies landed on the warm rock above her head, and hung there, voluptuously pulsing its wings to the rhythms of that shimmering spring morning. I saw instead a black ribbon bow on a girl's neck, and her leaning against the lacy-iron balcony on the side verandah at old de Blore's place. Behind her and below her, blue-clad figures of Chinamen weeding, tying, hoeing, watering among the vegetables they cultivated in exquisite order to the very edge of the dark swathe of rushes by the river. And any of them would have glanced up at a call of *Hey, Charlie!* They had names – Sun Kwong Wah, Sook Lee, Yeang Lo Chee. Chia Kuan Yu. But we had called them all, indiscriminately, Charlie.

"Jesus Christ!" I said.

Honour de Blore ignored my exclamation. "My father used to do all their business for them," she said. "They were always up at the house about something or other – leases, bad debts, letters they couldn't understand. You know the sort of thing. He had always done the same things for our station blacks, so I guess it was second nature to him. I used to meet them all, on and off. It is how I met Chia. It was the only way I *could* have met him. He hadn't been in the country for very long. It was something about his indenture that he came up about. One of the older men brought him. He was young, and beautifully built. A slight sort of build, but very strong. Good-looking. And exquisitely courteous. And about my age." She laughed, unaffectedly. "As a matter of fact, he was the sort of bloke, if he had been a pale-face my father would have made good and certain that he didn't get within spitting distance of me. As it was, I think he believed I couldn't actually see a Chinese market-gardener as a man, let alone as a man I might fall in love with. I'm sure he would have had just as much expectation of my falling for one of our Abo stockmen." She paused for a moment, and stared at her hands, lying serenely in her lap. "Isn't it strange? Everything against it except that it *would* happen. Class, colour, religion, language, money. Even probability. Most of all, that. It was so *improbable*." She looked up at me. It was her damned uncompromising honesty and lack of side that got me. "The very next evening I went for a walk down to the river, on that raised path through the garden. The night you met me. The first time I had ever done it. And I met him down there, of course. I knew he would be there. And I suppose he knew that I knew."

"And friendship ripened into love, and love into marriage?" I couldn't keep a touch of — what? — disbelief? — out of my tone. She ignored it, and immediately set me right back on my butt.

"Something like that — although we had no time for first steps," she said. She even smiled. "It might be more accurate to say love ripened into intimacy, and intimacy into conception. Because that's how it happened."

Now, of course, something like that would be a breeze. Things were different, then. While she had been speaking, half my mind had been remembering about an Australian woman, a friend of my parents, who had married a Chinese much older than herself, a respectable, moderately wealthy sort of bloke who otherwise would have been considered a fabulous catch for this particular suburban belle. In Perth, particularly. At my local-football-team level, the comment was all about the legendary sexual prowess of the Chinese, and how she must have heard about it. The only adult comment I ever heard was my mother's tight-lipped observation to my father, when she thought I wasn't around. *They might at least have spared a thought for the unfortunate children!* I don't know what that woman's life was like behind her own door, but it must have been sheer hell outside. She was immediately completely ostracized, of course, but she was hounded as well, with the kind of Christian brutality you encounter only, still, in Australian middle-class xenophobes. I felt a sort of horror that Honour de Blore might have been subjected to anything like it. I also could not credit that old de Blore could have let it happen.

"But what about your father?" I said, following up the thought. "Surely to God he didn't . . . well, didn't go along with the deal?"

"There was no orange-blossom festival at the old homestead, if that's what you mean." She gave me a wry smile. "When I knew I was pregnant, I told him. He nearly shed his skin. *Him* — with a tribe of half-caste kids on every one of his stations. And still sleeping two or three nights a week with one or another of the Abo housemaids. Then I told him who the father was. He didn't even answer me. He never spoke to me again."

"You mean, literally?" My mind was full of that mad, red face, those eyes that had glittered at me from their pits of suffering flesh. "Never again, not one word?"

"Literally, never again, not one word. And he disinherited me, into the bargain."

"So what did you do?"

"Chia and I got married. I bought him out of his indenture, and we came back here to live."

"But all of that must have cost you plenty?" I couldn't see the apprentice market-gardener having the kind of money implied, so she must have footed the bill. "How did you manage if your father had cut you off?"

"My mother left me a packet when she died," Honour de Blore said. "And the house – it was hers. So was all the money, for that matter. It was she gave him his start." She glanced at me, quizzically. "You know she was drowned, don't you? In a willy-willy, up at Broome?"

"We used to hear it talked about, when we were kids."

"You heard wrong. She committed suicide. She just followed the tide out, one morning. And didn't turn back when it did."

"What do you mean – followed the tide out?" I said.

"You've been in Broome?"

"Lots of times."

"Then you know how far the tide goes out on that coast. Miles, in some places – and you've got to be damn careful when it turns. But she knew. She was born there. She didn't get back because she didn't mean to."

"Who told you? Who told you it wasn't in a willy-willy at all?"

"He did. My father. When I was fifteen."

"Then – why didn't you put him in?"

"My word against his." She shrugged. "He said that if I passed it on to anyone, he'd have me committed. And he would have. I can hear him now. *You'll be in a strait-jacket before your next period's due.*"

"Jesus," I said. "And I always thought you had it made. I used to look into your hallway, and the stained glass, and the velvet curtains. And the gardeners, and the ponies in the stables. And you, with a red rose in your belt. Jesus Christ."

"I think, now, he was mad," Honour de Blore said. "When you get older, you piece things together out of what you heard and saw when you were a child. And didn't understand. For instance . . . do you know why he used to pay you to recite?"

I had been listening to her but looking down to the roadway, where a skinny little woman was calling the tiny Chinese pineapples she carried in two baskets, one at either end of a pole across her shoulder. If Honour de Blore hadn't been there, I would have run down the steps and bought a couple. They were the sweetest things I've ever eaten. The word "recite" brought me back. For a split second I was on that side verandah bowing and smarming my way through some bit of ballad, with actions and expression. Old de Blore roaring in his huge wickerwork chair, my father never

saying a word at the top of the steps leading down to the garden.
I swear, I could smell the huge creamy trumpet lily that overhung
the end of the verandah. "Well – why?" I said. And knew as I
spoke that what she would tell me would kill me. "I thought it was
because I amused him, or something."

"He hated your father for some reason. They were running
camel-teams in opposition, once. Lake Way to Sandstone, with
mining machinery. Did you know?"

"I didn't then, but I do now." I felt again in my hand the cool,
sharp edges of the aluminium nose-peg I had played with as a
child. With it, my father had directed a camel across that blood-
red never-never long before the days of walkie-talkies and surfac-
ed roads – on the great, high-wheeled, lumbering waggon behind
his team, perhaps, a choice load he had snatched from under old
de Blore's nose. Young de Blore then, of course. "Did they have a
run-in?" I said.

"Probably. Whatever it was, he knew it crucified your father to
have to watch you being a good dog for *him*. Wagging your tail for
the sixpence, or the apple, or whatever it pleased him to throw at
you."

I managed a laugh, but I don't think I had ever felt my heart
closer to breaking. Not for me. For that poor, funny, pompous
little bugger old de Blore paid to make a goat of himself in front of
his father. I said lightly, "I suppose you used to have a good laugh,
too, when I'd gone?"

"I thought you were so good." Honour de Blore spoke so gently
that I knew she was well aware of how I felt. "I really did look
forward to your coming up with your father. You believe me?"

A very proper amah in black satin trousers and a white linen
jacket led two little Chinese girls out onto the terrace. There was
one of those vermilion-painted shrines against the balustrade, and
they made a beeline for it. The amah lit the joss-sticks, and with
immense solemnity and self-importance the little girls stuck them
in the tray of sand at the base of the shrine. They stood back, their
hands closed together in front of their noses, as we do. The one
who was facing me went cross-eyed, trying to peer around the
church-roof of her fingers. "What was your kid?" I asked Honour
de Blore. "A boy, or a girl?"

"A girl," she said.

"I suppose she'd be married, now?" I said. "Does she live here, in
Hong Kong?"

She didn't answer me immediately. The little girls had finished
their devotions and were now, just as solemnly, playing stone-

scissors-paper. She watched them for a moment and then looked out over the estuary, her face away from mine. Fairly obviously, she was commanding her composure, so I waited for her to speak. When she did, it was quite matter-of-factly, as if she were discussing some acquaintance. She looked straight at me.

"When I first came here, with Chia, I bought a place out in the New Territories − out beyond Sha Tin," she said. "You could, then. Dirt cheap. And so beautiful. I still live there."

She seemed to want to steer clear from talk of her child, so I said the first thing that came into my mind. "And your husband, too?"

"The Japs killed him, when they took over," she said. "We stayed in the house and when they came, he went to the door. They must have thought he was a house-boy, or something. They bayonetted him, there in the hall. I saw them do it. They shunted me off to the compound, out at Repulse Bay. I stayed there for the duration. When I got out, after the war, I couldn't trace my little girl. You see − she looked quite Chinese. She would just have got caught up with the mob. I know the amah took her and hid her. And then the amah was killed." She glanced away, briefly, to the tumbling rooftops of the slums, crowding the Belvedere's high stone wall. "For all I know, she could be down there. She could be one of the women going blind, doing embroidery for me." There was nothing I could say, and it seemed she had said all she wanted to say, because she turned again to me and closed the past up, like a book finished. "So I became Li Po."

"Just like that."

"You go so far, and it's all against you. Then . . . it's as though they'd had their fun. You can't put a foot wrong." She shrugged. "When it really doesn't matter, any more."

"Why Li Po?" I asked. For no reason other than that it would push our conversation further along in the direction she seemed to want it to take, away from her husband and her child. To say nothing of all she had been through before she had ever got so far. "Was he such a hot dressmaker?"

I think she knew what I was up to, because she followed my lead without missing a beat. "Why not?" she said. "When he writes things like: *The dragon roars, stopping the thunder, and bamboo rustles, breeze-driven, in the courtyard?*"

I gave her the two lines leading into her quotation: *The fierce sun scorches, blazing, then black clouds come, pouring rain from above.* I had done a lot of reading in ancient Chinese poetry, mainly because some of it is among the most beautiful ever written. As the best of everything Chinese is among the best of all time. She glanced at me, in real surprise.

"We're a long way from 'The Bush Christening'," she said, smiling.

"We're a long way from where I used to say it."

"Indeed. I guess South Perth has changed a lot?"

"There's a twenty-storey block of dinky little flats where your old home was," I said. It seemed to say as much as could be said about what had happened to that dreamy riverbank where, in my memory, it is always summer.

"I know," Honour de Blore said. "I own them."

I was incredulous. "You mean, it was *you* had that beautiful old place bulldozed?"

"He wouldn't die, until I did it," she said, simply. She stood up and walked over to the balustrade, and leaned against it, as she had been when I had first seen her that morning. Looking out across the estuary. I felt in my bones that she was leaning against another verandah rail, looking across another stretch of water. When she spoke, I knew I was right. "I wonder who walks who down the rushes, these days?"

"There's no rushes," I said, and felt some satisfaction, to pay her back for the house. "They bulldozed them, too. For a carpark."

She glanced briefly at her watch, then walked back to me. "I've got an appointment, Dinny. It's been good to see you again." She was above all that banal nonsense about let's lunch one day, soon, or don't forget next time you're up this way. I was thankful for it.

"Are you ever coming home?" I asked.

"You can't." She held out her hand, palm upward. A curious gesture, as if she could see in it what they had put in pickle for her in the years ahead. Or in syrup. "You'll find out one of these days, maybe. It's like the gins used to say up on the station when I'd tell them it was time they stopped going walkabout. *No more, Missus.*"

She took my hand, shook it and let it go. She smiled at me once more, and walked away towards the steps leading down to the roadway. She did pause there for a moment, though, and glanced back at me, a big *mok-min-fah* tree spreading the first of its mushy, crimson blossoms just above her head. They were a famous Macau cure for tummy-trouble. By the time I was back in Australia, they would be a blood-red carpet on the terrace, and the locals would be coming from far and near to gather them.

Running Nicely

Morris Lurie

See them go! Clock their speed! Nightly at ten, the Bornstein boys
run together along the quiet streets of suburban Melbourne, a mile
and a quarter under the full-leaved summer trees. Here comes
Moses, down the stairs from the flat. He's twenty-two, five five
and a half, brown hair, dressed tonight in jungle-green shorts
(deep pockets, balloon seat) and horizontally-striped (maroon and
cream) light-weight Italian mohair shirt, the collar stylishly flared.
Brown shoes, blue socks. On his heels comes Ben, twelve, blond-
ish, five eight, crisp and correct in sporting white, save for the
soles of his tennis shoes, which pop up brick-red. They jog to the
front gate, and from here the run may be said properly to begin.
Go?

"You lock the door?" Moses asks.

"Yes," says Ben.

"Turn off the lights?"

"Yes."

"All of them?"

"You told me to leave one on."

"Where's the key? I don't trust your pockets."

Moses buries the front-door key in a pocket of his shorts under
five ancient Kleenexes, tamping them down for extra security, and
then, without further word, is suddenly off, assuming an instant
five-yard lead. Ben narrows it at once to two, and, keeping this
formation, they head down the road.

They're off!

Not too fast, thinks Moses, pacing himself carefully, introducing
the night air slowly into his lungs. Nice and easy, he thinks.
There's a long way to go. A lifetime sufferer from flat feet, he
concentrates on the proper placement of his toes, affecting a slight
springy bounce. He wiggles his arms loosely by his sides. He
throws back his head and takes some deep sniffs. Ah! Ah! Ben is a

silent white blur in the corner of Moses' eye. Good, thinks Moses, pleased at the running order. A little respect.

Cars zoom. A heavy truck rumbles and roars. Next comes a bus, lit up like a travelling house. Overhead the trees are a sickly yellow from the fluorescent lights on the main road, their leaves like old paper stuck up in the branches and twigs. Moses doesn't like this stretch of the run. He feels exposed. Anyone could go shooting past in a car and see them, running like lunatics in the night. Oh, it's the poor Bornstein boys! What a tragedy! To be orphaned so young! What are they doing, running at this hour? Look how thin they are! Anyone could see them here — Mr Pincus, Mr Sharp, Mrs Goldberg and her three chins, an uncle, an aunt, an old family friend, all those sad faces at the funeral. Moses feels they're all watching, horrified, as he runs with his brother, and he is relieved when he and Ben turn the corner, off the main road, and true suburban night descends.

Now it's nice. The trees are leafier, the street is darker, private, and the roar of the traffic, like the sea, has dropped away; now the only sounds are the fall of their feet and the regular puffing of breath. Ben closes the gap and they run together, side by side.

There is a smell of water in the air here, a smell of flowers and moist earth, but the gardens, as they pass, are dark. Grass is dark. Flowers are dark. The trees are dark, except where at regular intervals the street lights shine through, a row of moons down the length of the street. They run from light to light, breathing easily, and the only other light is the weird flickering blue of television screens, one without fail in every house they pass.

Fools, thinks Moses, and feels a certain pride at how he has weaned his brother, a former three-hours-a-night man, off that awful habit. Not by any stern command — the set's there, and he can turn it on any time he likes — but by getting him interested in other things, widening his horizons. They watch reruns of *Naked City* and on Friday nights an old movie, if there's a good one, but the best evenings are when Ben has finished his homework and they turn on the hi-fi and listen to early Coleman Hawkins, Django and Bird. "Listen to this," says Moses, popping on Art Tatum. "Just listen to that left hand!" And one afternoon, Moses remembers, he came home early from work, and there was the flat filled with his brother's friends, Lester Young soaring, and Ben delivering to his contemporaries an authoritative history of jazz.

There's another corner coming up. Moses feels Ben speeding up a fraction, and paces himself accordingly. They turn the corner in unison, running in step.

There's a cluster of shops here, five stores serving the neighbourhood – there used to be six, but the grocer went self-service and swallowed up the lending library next door – and, as they go past, Moses sneaks a look at himself and Ben, mirrored in the dark windows. Ben, he sees, has his mouth open, but not too wide, breathing easily. He notes the steely concentration in his brother's eyes. A champion! He rejoices, and then almost lets out a small laugh as he sees himself, a crazy hotchpotch of patterns and colours, the collar of his Italian mohair poking up at the back like a foolish bird hanging on for the ride. Then his brother surges ahead five or six yards, and he lets him go. I can catch him in a second, Moses thinks. Let him run a bit.

Look at him, Moses thinks, as Ben flashes past the last shop – a chemist's – his reflection riding over bottles and jars and the faces of beautiful women. Where'd he get that style? Where'd he learn to run so nicely like that? Not from me, that's for sure. The thing is, he hasn't got my flat feet. Thank God.

Running behind his brother, but keeping the distance between them steady, Moses thinks of many things, quickly, one after the other. How his brother is adept at tossing green salads, his French dressing a joy to behold. How his brother dresses neatly, the right tie with the right jacket, the right socks. How he comes home to find his brother has cleaned the flat, straightened the rugs, made the beds. How his brother can tell Charlie Parker from Sonny Stitt with his eyes closed. How his brother is halfway through *Catch 22*. "You skipping?" Moses asked him. "Of course not," said Ben. "I'm reading every word."

"You know what you're doing to him," said Moses' girl, eating dinner at the flat one night. "You're taking away his youth."

"What?" said Moses. "What a load of rubbish. He's an intelligent kid, that's all."

And he could have said more, but he didn't feel, just then, like getting dragged into it.

A car goes past. For a second, Moses is annoyed. What's this intrusion? But the car is quickly gone, all trace of it, all sound, and once again they run through immaculate suburban night, past the houses with their weird blue lights, past the neat gardens, too dark to admire, under the canopy of black trees and the regular moons of the street lights shining through. And suddenly Moses has a vision. The whole world has been constructed for him and his brother to run through, the trees planted, the houses built, the television sets turned on, the smell of water in the air, even the stars in the sky – everything arranged and set into place, thous-

ands of years of preparation for this moment in time, the whole
world dark, at peace, with no sound allowed but his and Ben's
breathing and the fall of their feet in the night.

Nice, thinks Moses, running easily.

They're almost at the end of the street now, Ben still ahead.
Well, thinks Moses, I'd better catch him up, and he quickens his
pace, coming up to his brother in a rush just as they get to Brown
Street, where there's another corner to turn. Ben, on the inside,
gets around nimbly, not losing an inch, but Moses overshoots,
runs with a clump into the gutter and onto the road, and, by the
time he has sorted himself out and is running straight again, Ben is
fifteen yards ahead, maybe more.

Hey, what's he doing? thinks Moses. It's not a race. We're
supposed to be running together. And he speeds up, flat feet thudding the ground, his hands balled into tight fists up by his heaving
chest. Here I come, boy! he announces. Watch my speed.

Brown Street is famous in the neighbourhood. Halfway along its
length it takes a sudden plummet, a totally unexpected plunge.
The incline is fantastic. Children love it. They roar down on their
bikes, screams like streamers flying from their mouths. Wheee!
Brown's Hill! Race ya to the bottom! The postman hates it,
mothers with prams curse it, old people have to pause three times,
gasping, as they slowly ascend, and here comes Moses, his flat feet
making an unholy racket as he streaks after his sporting brother,
all proper toe placement forgotten, his hair standing up wildly in
the self-generated wind.

The gap whittles down. From fifteen, it goes to ten, six, two, and
− flash! − he's passed him, roaring like an engine, but what's this?
He's forgotten the hill, aaarrrhhh, and down he goes, picking up
speed by the second, his feet out of control, a terrible mistake.
Tree trunks whip past, fences, windows, one street light after
another. Moses is a train. Moses is the stagecoach racing driver-
less to the cliff. How to slow down? How to stop? Impossible.
Can't be done. God, thinks Moses, I'm going to break a leg.

Ben is forgotten as Moses charges down the famous hill, insane
thoughts of grabbing a tree or suddenly sitting down flying
through his head. He's two-thirds of the way to the bottom, and by
some manner unknown even to himself has managed to keep
upright, when who should pop out from her gate but a little old
lady from No. 26, her night of television viewing at an end, time to
take the dog for a stroll. Her dog is the size of a handbag or muff,
and is attached to the woman by a length of fine chain, and as
Moses approaches, puffing like a furnace, the dog whips around

and lets out a terrified squeaky bark, like one pump on an old pair of bellows. Reeee! The little lady turns, looks up, and sees, advancing in the night, a wild-eyed maniac streaked with sweat. A rapist! A fiend! Her small mouth falls open. Her rimless spectacles catch a street light and turn dead white. "Good evening and don't worry," Moses wants to say. "I intend you no harm." But of course he can't. It's all he can do not to crash into her, not to go flying over the thin chain connecting her to her petrified dog, but somehow, miraculously, he veers around, panting madly.

But who is this streaking up behind him? Why, it's Ben, coming up with Olympic prowess, and for a moment, as Brown's Hill flattens, they're together, running side by side. For ten yards, they're neck and neck, but Ben is in fine control and Moses is not, and, almost before he knows what's happening, an assortment of wind escapes Moses' body, five fine blasts, thundering in the jungle green.

"Hee hee," laughs Moses, and sees on the face of his brother the beginnings of an answering laugh, and, as though to encourage him, Moses laughs again. "Hee hee, ha ha," he laughs, and is about to do a "ho ho" when he sees a look of annoyance flick across his brother's face; then a mask of severe determination descends, and Ben is off, streaking free into the night.

Hold it a second, Moses wants to say, but can't. Something is happening to his lungs. His breath is all over the place. His running rhythm is upside down. "Ooooh!" he cries, feeling a sharp pain in his side, and then there flashes into his brain the rimless spectacles of the old lady from No. 26, and he begins once more to laugh. "Ha ha," he laughs, "hee hee," but between each laugh there is a stab of pain, and when he tries not to laugh it's worse. "Ow!" cries Moses. "Oooh!" Still running, blood pumping in his head.

He stops. His breath is a hot wind through parched lips. Black spots jump in front of his eyes. He stands, hands on hips, bent forward, shot through with pains. When at last he has calmed down enough to look up, Ben is a hundred yards away, running nicely, a crisp white figure diminishing in the night.

"Rat!" Moses calls, mopping his brow with a mohair sleeve. He's wet through. He's hot. His ankles are agony, his thighs throb with aches. "I'm not running with you again," he says, and pushing up his sleeves (Italian mohair for running? thinks Moses. Fool! Fool!) he starts again.

It's no good. He can't do it. Something's gone inside. He drops down to a jog, but even that's too much. He wants to sit down. He wants to lie down. He wants to close his eyes. Moses has run this course with his brother two dozen times at least, but it's never been like this before. Even the first time, completely out of training, he managed to jog home. And woke up the next morning full of aches and pains – but during the course of the day they lessened, and that night they ran again, a little faster if anything.

Brown's Hill, thinks Moses. Never lose control on Brown's Hill.

It is all he can do to walk, past the quiet gardens, the flickering blue windows, under the dark trees, but it's not the same anymore, it's no longer that special world made for brothers to run in, it's not peaceful and quiet, it's all changed. He looks up and sees that Ben has gone. A champion, he thinks, but doesn't feel happy. He's alone. Stumbling home, he feels, all at once, a fool.

He sees himself – hypocrite! – lecturing his brother on fair play and sporting style. I never made the football team, he thinks. I was always the last one they picked for cricket. Pop goes the bat and out of the sky drops the shiny red ball, right to him with slow-motion ease and – oh – he drops it. The crowd moans. Moses feels his face lighting up with shame, and is thankful for the dark.

He stumbles on, the sweat on his face cooling down. Ahead, through the trees, he sees the main road again, cars and trucks rolling past, their bodies flashing with neon. He takes a breath, then another, and somehow gets running again for this last stretch, where everyone can see.

It's awful. He feels a thousand years old, half jogging, half limping, a ruined, broken man. He is about to give up and walk the rest of the way – what the hell, who cares about the Pincuses and Sharps and Goldbergs of this world? – when he sees his brother waiting for him at the gate. Ben stands there, fresh and straight, in his crisp sporting whites, not a trace of the night's run on his face. Hey, I've never played him Thelonious Monk! Moses thinks. He'll love him. Ben raises both arms in the air, like a Grand Prix judge ready to bring down the winning flag, and not to disappoint him, his heart beating to burst, Moses finishes strong, the last surge of energy summoned up from God knows where carrying him all the way home.

Winter Nelis

Elizabeth Jolley

Leonora Brown, lying in a hot bath in the middle of the day for gynaecological reasons, relaxed into the drifting thoughts which accompany hot water and steam at an unaccustomed time.

All night old Smith's rooster had crowed with a mechanical regularity, as though the old man had wound up the bird before going to bed himself. Two cars crashed somewhere quite near and through the noise of the car bodies indescribably wounded, dragging their tormented wreckage, she heard someone crying and crying.

"I think there's been a crash," she said to her husband, but he said he'd been awake all night and had heard nothing.

"It's only your imagination," he said. And she lay beside him, separated by a knowledge, which he did not share, of something sinister; of wounding, of unhappiness and of pain.

At breakfast she asked him, "How much water does the bath hold?"

He was hidden behind the newspaper.

"Water? The bath? Absolutely no idea, but there's no shortage just now is there?"

So Leonora guessed the quantities of vinegar and bicarbonate of soda for her remedial bath. A person couldn't dissolve in a mixture of this sort. In any case, the vinegar in the hot steam was sharp and medicinal, very reassuring.

She sang. The bathroom encouraged her.

"I had not," she said to herself in a rich deep contralto, "I had not known Ludwig many months before he decided to make me the heroine of his opera. . . . " She laughed and then stopped laughing. There was nothing, nothing in that, especially her singing, nothing at all that was laughable.

"I've had some bad times. Oh but these bad times!"

"That's no way to speak to a guest!" Leonora remembered it clearly, her own voice sharp and unpleasant in the foyer of the unfashionable hotel she had misguidedly chosen.

"That's no way to speak to a guest!" And the young receptionist looked up from the counter and at once she saw her mistake. An unbearable mistake. She remembered his pale eyes bulging as he looked in disbelief, and the little veins and capillaries misplaced on his crooked boyish face slowly reddened. The painful blush was to her a greater pain, she had not imagined she could, and had, stripped him of covering and dignity. It was as if she peeled off his unhealthy skin leaving him raw. Later that evening the memory of it was so close she couldn't bear it. Miss Butterick, sitting with her third brandy, couldn't possibly have understood so why try and tell her. But she did tell, concluding with, "I can't imagine why I was so rude and impatient."

Miss Butterick's speech was somewhat slurred, and her voice deepened with alcoholic compassion.

"It's awful when you know you've hurt someone." She didn't care really, Leonora knew, she just said the safe thing. For the moment Butterick was warm, and she'd had her brandy, and she might even have something else later on if Leonora felt sorry enough for the whole world to feel she could satisfy Miss Butterick's repetitious physical need.

All too vividly Leonora recalled the bandy goblin legs clambering up into the Paris Express, and the stuffy warmth which came from that region under the tweed skirt where those concave thighs met with so little magic. She followed Miss Butterick with misgivings which told all too plainly at the outset that she had made a mistake. . . .

The bath water was cooling off. Leonora turned on the hot tap with one foot and the warmth surrounded her reluctantly.

"I hardly knew Ludwig when he insisted on making me the heroine. . . . "

What did Miss Butterick know of Beethoven, so how could one make that sort of joke? At dinner, she remembered, the Butterick pretended a preference of wines. For sophistication, she scooped a tiny fragment of melting camembert and ate it hastily, without relish, as if it was a medicine. She ate furtively wiping suspected crumbs from the corners of her boring mouth.

Leonora remembering, shuddered. The rhythm of the railway wheels seemed to send the knowledge of the mistake straight into her, just as the rhythm sent another experience into Miss Butterick sitting opposite. Leonora couldn't fail to notice the furtive moment of feeling so quickly achieved and so quickly brushed aside like a mistake in a typed letter, as it was followed by the all too familiar, "Oh! Naughty me!"

The bitter drops of the after dinner coffee had to come to an end and there was nothing to do but shepherd Miss Butterick, pathetically proud of having had more than enough to drink, upstairs to the cold dingy room.

"But Butters, you can't possibly sleep with me without washing!" Leonora came from the unexpectedly pleasant comfort of a hot bath to where Miss Butterick sat like an imp in the bed.

"Try me!" She twisted her mouth in a smile and Leonora opened the tall window. She wanted to call out her unhappiness to someone, she wanted to call it across the clean moonlit roofs and chimneys of a strange city.

"If Ludwig had only known me a few months he would have made me the heroine. . . . " There are times when the imagination is not enough. . . .

Tears trembled on Miss Butterick's eye lashes and her hands were cold and Leonora knew, and went on knowing, how wrong it was to explore, to unmask, to get complete revelation and then to leave off, to discard; no, it was not discarding, it was more a moving away because of being too frail to continue. She never meant to be guilty of discarding. Never.

Leonora added more hot water, it brought poetry. Horace? Campion T.? *The man of life upright / whose guiltless heart is free / from all dishonest thoughts / and deeds of vanity: that man needs neither towers / to shield him from the sky / nor armoured vaults to fly / from thunder's tyranny.*

The water slapped the bath in lukewarm idleness.

"Whose are these?" With a terrible voice the Night Superintendent held up the scattered shabby underclothes indecently inadequate, ragged with black lace and, with them, more than a hint of leather and feathers. Peacocks are supposed to be unlucky but Haddon said that was rubbish. With her had come things which had never existed for Leonora before, the Beethoven and the poetry. The feathers were crushed and broken as if from some kind of indescribable wounding.

Leonora never owned up to the clothes but kept her eyes turned away and let Sister Haddon, in her well bred voice say in front of the assembled staff,

"I'd like to explain in private please, if I may, to Matron."

Haddon, who off duty, was well tailored and wore shirts with
collars and ties left that night and Leonora stayed.

In the school of nursing she was not allowed to have curled hair
showing, or to wear lipstick, bracelets or rings, and she had to
have the gold studs removed from her shoes. There was something indefinable about her. The Home Sister and the Tutor Sister
felt this intangible quality which they did not quite understand or
like. She seemed in some way shop soiled, but they were never
able to openly accuse her of anything to do with that odd collection of clothing and accessories. Only in their secret imagination
could they reconstruct what might have been confessed in Sister
Haddon's explanation. It was agreed that Leonora was a conscript,
and that she would probably fail her examinations. So many only
chose nursing to avoid the forces or the munition factory.

The Buyer for Fancy's Fashions straight away liked Leonora's way
with the customers, only fresh from school and she could do it!
Fancy herself approved.

"Take Lady Moneybags to the fitting room," Fancy whispered
from the side of her soft red mouth. "Take the sequins, the gold
leaf and the ermine, take the lot in with you." The hoarse whisper
intended for Leonora alone came through the racks of dresses and
furs. Even in her youthfulness she was able to match customers
and clothing and the expensive vulgarity of certain kinds of
jewellery.

Big Fancy, trying on in advance the summer beach wear, stood
partly naked surveying her creamy folds, pressing her pale flesh
with her palms. There was a smell of fresh new cotton.

"Leonora! Zip me up!" she whispered. "Try harder! Do it harder!"

If Leonora at times seemed to stay too long in the fitting room,
Big Fancy, with a flurry of the beaded curtain, would pull out the
bent-wood chair from under her, violently, and a few minutes
later, with equal violence, would send the chair screeching over
the inlaid linoleum back through the frantic leaping beads.

"Thanks Fancy," calmly Leonora reseating herself would continue her contemplation which often became a kind of simultan-
eous act of praise and betrayal.

Leonora, lying in the indifferent water, walked with her mother
who said, "No one can earn a living singing. When I was your age I
already had four children."

She remembered the smell of the promise of summer between deep hedges, darker at the tops where they had not been cut. There were delphiniums in her mother's garden, blue and white, thrusting right up into the apple tree as if feeling for the little hard nipples of the ungrown fruit hidden in the safety of the leaves.

Telling a lie about her age, she married Desmond. He was ten years younger and this showed quite quickly. Horribly. It really was unimportant, but she did worry. There was the constant watchfulness over the persisting truth in the parting of her hair, and that exhausting search for dresses with high necks. She had pills to take but they made her sleepy and, even worse, she was sure they made her fat.

In the mid-day silence, the next door car came home. The car door opened and slammed shut and the new little next-door woman ran quickly, gack gook gack gook up the concrete path.

Leonora heard the neighbour woman give a moan, a subdued cry suggesting a burst of tears and the front door opened and slammed shut and across the silence came the muffled sound of crying.

Leonora wondered whatever could have happened to make her come rushing home like that, hardly able to wait till she could reach the seclusion of the house before crying, and then to go on crying as if there was something unbearable for her, as if something terrible had happened, or was going to happen. Whatever could there be in the lives of the newly married young people to wound and torment, to make her weep in such a broken hearted way.

The Browns did not know the Banks at all yet. They had only moved in a few days before. Mr Banks looked fresh faced and quiet, he went to the bus in the mornings with a brief case. So many people had a brief case now it was impossible to draw any kind of conclusion. Mrs Banks was small and neat, and pink like a hygienic doll. She usually had the car.

Leonora had not liked to intrude, she and Desmond were so much older. Leonora, lately resented people, even disliked them. Often the only conversation she and Desmond had was to talk about people they knew, and find fault.

The noise of the sobbing went on and on. Leonora dressed herself quickly and went round to the other house. She wished she had a little jar of something home-made to take, but she had given up long ago shredding orange peel and removing plum stones. It was so much easier just to buy a tin of marmalade somewhere, it was too sweet, but she did not bother about flavours enough now to mind.

When she thought about it, what did any of it really matter.
There was always this feeling of being only temporary. Thinking
back about Miss Butterick, of Haddon, of Big Fancy and of her
mother, life seemed endless and yet one's turn of being was so
limited, so brief, it really was a waste to care. Sometimes Leonora
cried, not out loud like young Mrs Banks, but quietly inside
herself. On these days she did not dress and she did not even
comb her hair. It seemed to Desmond then that women in their
wanting wanted something indefinable and, when he could, he
persuaded Leonora to go into a nursing home for a rest.

The little hospital was high up overlooking a place where some
old houses were being pulled down to make way for a new shopping centre.

"Why don't you go for a little walk," the Sister said. "It'll do you
good." So Leonora went out.

The road went below the escarpment; two men were working,
as if chained to the steep dusty slope, with their hand drills and
shovels, trying to build up the crumbling side. It seemed so hopeless, and a sunburnt young man went to and fro on a bulldozer,
like a clockwork toy wound up and rewound, destined to go on in
the noise and the dust for ever.

"Take me home!" Leonora sobbed when Desmond came to see
her. "I can't stand being here." So she went home somewhat worse
than before.

Mrs Banks had dropped some of her shopping. Little russet
pears lay scattered all over the red path and on the grass and on
the doorstep and on the new door mat.

Leonora knocked on the door too softly. The sobbing could be
heard quite plainly. She knocked again. She waited but no one
came to the door. The garden was untidy with the little pears.
They had a look of autumn about them. They were shining and
healthy and nut brown. Leonora wondered what they were like,
so often appearances were deceptive.

She tried again knocking at the door, but no one came. She felt a
curiosity mixed with concern and she was irritated too because
Mrs Banks did not come.

In the end she went home.

The afternoon was peaceful with the soft voices of the doves.
Leonora sat on the edge of her verandah. She seemed to notice,
as if for the first time, the warm fragrance of the earth. Leaves,
like approaching footsteps, rustled and fell from the flame trees,

a few scarlet flowers were already splashed on the blue sky and the monotonous climbing notes of the rain bird sounded from somewhere quite near. It really was the autumn.

Across the road, two women were talking together. Expensively dressed and well groomed they were sitting on a lawn. Their high pitched voices pierced the tranquillity, they sounded conceited and false and then serious in their own self importance as they asked questions and did not listen to answers. Every now and then one sighed but the other paid no attention and, occasionally, one of them, or both of them together burst out with little cries of insincere mirth.

Leonora never went to her hairdresser these days. Most of the time she just sat doing nothing. And if she did force herself to do things, perhaps to weed the flower beds, it always seemed afterwards that the tall feathery grasses and the wilderness of nasturtiums really looked better than the bare fences and the edges of the garden where her restless hands had torn up everything in order to neaten. The sight, on these occasions, of the ragged and bruised flowers was so appalling that she often did not go out of the house until the memory of them had faded a little.

The women across the road went indoors. Leonora, on this day, did not mind them. She was listening to the house next door, but all was quiet there. She did not pause to be surprised at herself as she went into her kitchen where she cut bread and butter on a clean white cloth. While she worked she sang in her deep rich voice, she had forgotten how much she enjoyed singing. She said to a saucepan,

"I had not known Ludwig many months when he decided to make me the heroine of his opera ... ", she was laughing at herself when Desmond came home. Quickly she told him about Mrs Banks and they both wondered what dreadful thing could have happened.

"I'll go out and have a yarn with young Banks," Desmond said. "He's just out there in his yard now."

"Hullo there! How're you making out?" he called across the low fence to Mr Banks.

"Good thanks!" Mr Banks called back as he went into his own house.

The Browns were disappointed and after their meal Leonora said, "Go round and ask them in for the evening." She seemed quite eager. Desmond was surprised and pleased. This was an improvement in Leonora beyond any hopes he might have dared to have. He noticed the golden sponge fingers on the table. Leonora hadn't baked anything for a long time.

"They were pleased to be asked," he said when he came back. "But they want us to go round there to sort of warm the house, you know, their first real visitors," he added. He was afraid Leonora would lack courage at the last moment. But he need not have been afraid.

"I'll change my dress then," she said. "I'll not be long."

Perhaps the Banks needed to talk to someone about what had happened. She and Desmond were older and would be able to help in some way. Leonora had never heard a woman weep like that.

When Miss Butterick cried all those years ago, her tears, in an attempted silent restraint, hung as if held back shining on the lashes above the bluish puffed cheeks. With those furtive tears it had come to Leonora that it was wrong to give the appearance of loving when there was no love. How bitter is understanding when it comes through someone else's pain. It was something she would never be able to forget.

But this weeping was different. Leonora could not think of anything sinister, painful, frightening or sad ever happening to little Mrs Banks. She always looked so well and so happy, and so competent too.

She changed hurriedly and combed her neglected hair. Somehow, for the first time, it did not worry her that she no longer looked young. Soon they would know what had upset Mrs Banks so much.

And the Browns went quietly together to visit the Banks.

"Come in! Come in please." Young Mr Banks led them into the sitting room which gave the impression of being lovingly arranged. They sat in matching chairs drawn up to the hearth, lively with a small fire which had just been lit. The new warm flames ran laughing all round the dry crackling sticks. The russet pears were arranged with other fruits in a pyramid on a polished silver tray.

"What nice little pears!" Leonora said as Mrs Banks came in. Perhaps the pears would lead them straight to the necessary conversation. She smiled as kindly as she knew how at Mrs Banks whose serene face and dress were as if embroidered with matching pink and white silk.

"Yes," Mrs Banks said, and her voice suited her; it was clear and full of confidence. "Aren't they exquisite! They're called Winter Nelis. You must try one," she said. And then she said, laughing, "D'you know, I think I've forgotten the pepper!" With a pink finger-tip she lifted the corners of one or two of her tiny sandwiches.

"Fetch the pepper please Honey," she smiled prettily at Mr Banks.

Leonora chose a little pear, one of the Winter Nelis. She wondered if it had any flavour. So often things which looked attractive were not.

And she took a polite little bite nervously.

Sex in Australia from the Man's Point of View

Michael Wilding

We were lying on the beach when we first saw sex in Australia from a man's point of view, coming low over the horizon, just clipping the tops of the waves; doing that limping in on a wing and a prayer routine, two wings, it was a biplane, one of those old canvas and struts amphibious biplanes that had been continually in the wars, ripped again without a doubt.

"Lily," I said, "there's sex in Australia from a man's point of view just clipping the tops of the waves."

"What a strange sound," said Lily, "is that a jet?"

"I've never seen a jet biplane. Biplanes generally just cruise around at a pretty gentle speed, they can land on a pocket handkerchief and drop in for a cup of tea and a smoke."

"We should have brought some tissues," said Lily. "Then we could get it to land."

"I think that's what it's going to do anyway," I said. It was flying very low. The wheels were spinning round as they touched the crests of the waves. They were those old blocked in wheels, not even spokes, unless the spokes were behind the blocked in part. We lay on our backs and shaded our eyes against the sun as it came in closer, our legs and arms spread out like a double X to mark a landing spot.

XX

Touching. We touched fingers and toes of one hand and one foot each. We couldn't tell whether it was going to come in on the sea or the land, being amphibious. We lay there together, leaving the choice up to it. I guess one of us could have stayed on the sand and Lily could have floated on sea and marked a single X for each possibility, but we preferred to be together.

"It's not a jet, it's a pusher prop," I said as it banked round. "They're pretty rare now, I hope it lands, I'd really like to take a good look at it."

I pointed out to Lily how the propellor was pushing from behind, not drawing the plane along like a conventional prop job, not sucking and blowing like a jet.

It banked over us and then flew along the line of the beach, dropping all this shit out of the back. It had what they call a hopper, they often fit them into old biplanes for crop dusting. Well, it had all that sort of gear and what it was doing laying its own grass on us to make a landing strip. The sand was covered with this fine layer of grass. It wasn't pure grass, there were a lot of stalks and seeds in it, tea leaves and oregano and all that sort of shit, so that the surface was kind of bumpy. And then having laid all this trail of grass, it banked round again and came into land.

We watched entranced as its wheels came closer to the ground, waiting for that moment of pure excitement as they would touch, bounce up, touch again, bounce up. The old Tiger Moths were apparently terribly difficult to land, every time you touched down you'd bounce up again and get this lift beneath the wings, so sometimes they just never came down. The sky is full of these old trainee pilots, circling round and round in the upper ether, never coming down. They just take deeper and deeper breaths, upper lip stiff, and stay there. Occasionally they set their joy sticks at automatic and undo their safety harnesses and walk out along the wings and leap across to each other's planes, to have a friendly talk; or sometimes they wrestle with each other's pistols there in duels of life and death, Biggles and the Red Baron, tugging away at each other's guns for hours up above the clouds.

So we waited for sex in Australia from the man's point of view to touch down on our beach. And there it was, that beautiful ship of the sky, dropping down with its beautiful young pilot all over now baby blue, speeding along the improvised landing strip, the wind whistling harmonica melodies through the struts and wires, and wow, oh no, its wheels have caught on one of those stalks in the grass and it's lurched forward, its tail's coming up, the pilot is suddenly shot forward before he knows it, he tries to hold on, he grasps the windshield with both hands, we can see his muscles tensing, his helmet flies free from his head and hangs strapped round his neck choking him, his hair flies up like a piano player's, can he hold it, no, no, he catapults forward and sex in Australia from the man's point of view noses into the wet sand and the tail kicks up in the air and the fertilizer hopper door beneath the tail springs open and lets out the remainder of the grass.

But it's an arrival.

We get up off the sand and walk towards the boy in blue.

We lift him from his crumpled position on the sand.

"Don't worry," we say, "you did great."

We unbuckle his leather helmet, we undo his leather tunic, we unstrap his leather gaiters, take off his flying boots, and massage the wings at his ankles gently. Then we carry him between us.

"Would you like to stay at our place for the night?" Lily asks him. "Just while you get oriented."

His mouth breaks open into a truly happy smile.

"You're sure?" he says.

"Sure we're sure," we say.

"Oh thank you," he said, "thank you for a lovely evening in advance."

He was that sort of person.

The Rages of Mrs Torrens

Olga Masters

The rages of Mrs Torrens kept the town of Tantello constantly in gossip.

Or more accurately in constant entertainment.

It was a town with a sawmill, some clusters of grey unpainted weatherboard cottages, a hall and the required number of shops for a population of two hundred.

Even while Mrs Torrens was having a temporary lull from one of her rages the subject was not similarly affected.

"How's the wife these days?" a mill worker would say to Harold while they shovelled a path through the sawdust for a lorry.

The man's eyes would not meet Harold's but slide away.

Remarks like this would be made when life was more than usually dull in Tantello, for example during the long spell between the sports' day in midwinter and the Christmas tree in December.

A mill wife having seen Mrs Torrens behaving like other mill wives in Tantello that day would suggest while chopping up her meat for stew or melon for jam that Kathleen may never have another of her rages.

It was not said hopefully though just dutifully.

It took some time for Tantello to settle down after the rage that sent Mrs Torrens and the five little Torrenses flying over the partly-built bridge across Tantello Creek.

The barrier at the finished end was down so Mrs Torrens one of the few women in Tantello who drove a car ripped across towards the gaping workmen standing with crowbars and other tools.

"Whee-eee-eee!" they called as they flung themselves out of her way clinging to the rails while she flung the old Ford across sending the temporary wooden planks on the gaping floor sliding dangerously and landing the car on the gravel bridge approach.

It paused a second with the workmen expecting it to dive backwards into the creek, then with a groan negotiated the little ridge with the back wheels spitting stones and dust.

A little Torrens screamed in ecstasy (or relief) and standing behind her mother scooped up handfuls of Kathleen's magnificent red hair and laid her face in it.

"Stop that!" cried another little Torrens beside her. "Mumma can't drive the car properly if you do that!"

The little Torrenses told their father this and Harold although not often moved to do so repeated the remark to the mill hands and for weeks afterwards Tantello feasted on it.

"Mumma can't drive the car properly if you do that!" they chuckled over and over above the screams of the machinery cutting timber, not always seeing each other clearly through the smoke from the smouldering sawdust.

"How many stories have you got Dad, on Raging Torrens?" asked a little Cleary one night from the floor where he was doing his homework.

He was Thomas Cleary, aged eleven, and Thomas senior, when there were no fresh stories on the rages of Mrs Torrens to relate or repeat, boasted to the mill hands on the cleverness of his son and his promising future.

"Head stuck in a book all day long," Thomas senior would say disregarding the predictions of other workers that he would end up in the mill like most other youth of Tantello.

Seated by the stove fire now Thomas senior burst into proud laughter at this fresh evidence of his son's calculating mind and whispered the sentence to have it right to tell at the mill next day.

"How many stories have you got on Raging Torrens?" he whispered into the fire averting his face so that his wife would not see.

Thomas and Evelyn Cleary no longer shared anything. She was a stout plain woman with a lot of hair on her face who pulled her mouth down at most things Thomas said. The day before Thomas had brought home a gift of turnips from a fellow mill hand but Mrs Cleary threw them to the fowls declaring they gave her wind.

"Now the eggs'll give you wind," said Thomas but the little Clearys did not laugh with him because they sided with the stronger of their parents in the uncanny way children have of defining where their fortunes lie.

As far as the stories on Raging Torrens or Roaring Kathleen went there were too many to list here.

There was the time when she charged out at midnight and flung Harold's pay in the creek.

It was an icy July night with a brilliant moon and when the catastrophe was discovered all the Torrenses went to the creek to try and recover the two pounds in two shilling pieces.

"Oh, Harold I must be mad," moaned Mrs Torrens thigh deep in water groping around a rock and coming up mostly with flat stones.

(Harold did not tell the mill hands this.)

"My little ones'll die of pneumonia!" she cried, "Oh my little Dollikins, forgive your wicked Mumma!"

Harold had to rise at four o'clock next morning for an early shift so it was he who said they should go home.

"What will we eat now?" murmured a little Torrens old enough to understand the simple economics of life, like passing money across the counter of Bert Herbert's store before goods were passed back.

"Oh, Harold," moaned Mrs Torrens. "We can't even make a pot of tea. There'll be none for tomorrow if we do!"

"O, my poor mannikin! You can't go to work with your innards as dry as the scales on a goanna's back!"

She stood in the glow of the stove fire which Harold had got going among the little Torrenses all crouched over it. Her nightgown slipped from her shoulders showing her white neck threaded with blue veins. Her red hair wet from her wet hands was strewn about and her blue eyes welled with tears. Harold stood staring long at her and the little Torrenses looked from him to their mother and back into the heart of the glowing stove. In a little while without anyone speaking they scurried off to bed.

Kathleen rubbed one icy foot upon the other clutching a threadbare towel about her waist under her nightie to rub dry her icy thighs and buttocks.

"Lie down on the floor close to the fire," whispered Harold. "And afterwards I'll rub you warm again."

"Of course," she whispered back and sinking down reached up both arms to him.

When the pain of the loss of Harold's pay had eased it actually became a subject for discussion. Gathered around the meal table the Torrenses talked about what the two pounds would have bought.

"Pounds and pounds of butter!" cried a little Torrens whose teeth marks were embedded in a slice of bread spread with grey dripping.

"How many pounds then?" asked Harold. "How much is butter? One and threepence? How many pounds in two pounds? Come on, work it out! Thomas Cleary could!"

"What else would it have bought Mumma and Dadda?" cried the seven year old Torrens.

"Tinned peaches, jelly, fried sausages!" screeched her sister.

"Blankets! One for each of our beds!" cried Mrs Torrens unable to contain herself.

Then she dropped her face on her hand and shook her hair down to cover her lowered eyes and dripping tears.

"A new coat with fur on it for Mumma!" said an observing little Torrens.

Kathleen lifted her head and shook back her hair.

"I like my old coat best!" she said.

"See," said Harold clasping his wife's hand. "Mumma doesn't want a new coat. So the money was no use to us after all!"

Although this deduction puzzled some of the little Torrenses they were happy to see their mother smiling and ecstatic when she flung her head towards Harold and fitted it into the curve of his neck and shoulder.

They trooped outside to play soon after.

The creek figured in many of the rages of Mrs Torrens particularly her milder ones.

When in one of these she took the children to picnic below the bridge on a Sunday afternoon.

The normal Tantello people considered this the height of eccentricity, the place for Sunday picnics being the beach twenty-five miles away available to those with reliable cars, and for the others there was the annual outing with the townspeople packed into three timber trucks.

Tantello Creek was a wide bed of sand with only a trickle of water in most parts, but there was a sandbank a few yards upstream from the bridge with a miniature waterfall and a chain of water holes most of them small and shallow petering out as they moved towards the main stream.

This is where Mrs Torrens took the children for a picnic in full view of Tantello taking Sunday afternoon walks across the bridge.

Mrs Torrens spread out the bread and jam and watercress gathered by the children and they ate on the green slope below the road with an occasional car passing in line with their heads and the walking Tantello staring from the bridge.

"Go home you little parlingtons and stop staring!" cried Mrs Torrens waving a thick wedge of bread towards the bridge.

"Are you swearing at us, Mrs Torrens?" said one of the starers.

"You know swearing when you hear it! Or do you plug your ears after closing times on Saturday when your Pa comes home?"

"Oh, Mumma," breathed an agonized Torrens named Aileen, the eldest of the family.

She shared a seat at school with the group on the bridge.

Aileen left the picnic then and moved with head down towards the water.

"Only mad people make up words," called a daring voice from the bridge.

Aileen lowered her head further in the silence following.

Mrs Torrens jumped to her feet to herd the little Torrenses to the water to join their sister.

"We'll gather our stones and hold them under the water!" she cried and the little Torrenses with the exception of Aileen dispersed to hunt for flat round stones that changed colour on contact with the running water.

The little Torrenses watched spellbound when the stones emerged wet and glistening and streaked with ochre red, rich browns, soft blues and greys and sometimes pale gold.

"Oh don't go dull!" screamed the little Torrenses hoping for a miracle to save the colours from merging into a dull stone colour when the water dried.

Aileen some distance away dug her toes into the sand and stared down at them. Her lashes lay soft as broken bracken fern on her apricot cheeks.

"Come on Snobbie Dobbie!" called Mrs Torrens.

"Come and wash the beautiful stones and see the colours!

"They're brown and beautiful as your eyes, Snobbie Dobbie!"

"Come on, come on!" called the other little Torrenses.

In the end Aileen came and the high voices and peals of laughter from the creek bed had the effect of sending the walking Tantello mooching home across the bridge.

Then came the rage that ended all the rages of Mrs Torrens in Tantello and drove the family from the town.

Harold lost the fingers of his right hand in a mill accident.

Holding a length of timber against a screaming saw, a drift of smoke blew across his eyes and the saw made a raw and ugly stump of his hand and the blood rushed over the saw teeth and down the arm of his old striped shirt and the yelling of the mill hands brought the work to a halt and for a moment all was still except the damaging drift of smoke from a sawdust fire.

A foreman with a knowledge of first aid (for many fingers were lost at the mill although Harold was the first to lose all four) stopped the flow of blood and drove Harold twenty miles to the nearest hospital.

When the mill was silenced an hour before the midday break the townspeople sensed something was wrong and Mrs Torrens came running too.

A chain of faces turned and passed the word along that it was Harold. Mrs Torrens stood still and erect strangely dressed in a black dress with a scarf-like trimming from one shoulder trailing to her waist. On the end she had pinned clusters of red geraniums and on her head she wore a large brimmed black hat with more geraniums tucked into the band of faded ribbon. On her feet she wore old sandshoes with the laces gone.

All the eyes of the watching Tantello were fixed on Mrs Torrens who stood a little apart. She stared back with a tilted chin and wide and cold blue eyes until they turned away and one by one left the scene. When the last had gone she walked into the mill to the cluster of men around the door of the small detached office.

"We're sorry, Mrs Torrens," said one of them.

Behind the men was a table with cups on it for the bosses' dinner and a kettle set on a primus stove. Mrs Torrens looked from the cups to the men's hands and back to the cups and a strange, small smile lit on her face.

Then she stalked to the timber stacked against the fence and climbed with amazing lightness and agility for a big woman onto it stepping up until her waist was level with the top of the fence. The men watched in fascination while she hauled herself onto the fence top and stood there balancing like a great black bird.

Her old sandshoes clinging to the fence top were like scruffy grey birds.

"Come down! We don't want no more accidents," called the mill owner.

But Mrs Torrens walked one panel with her arms out to balance herself. Then satisfied she was at home she straightened up and walked back coming to a halt at the fence post and standing there looking down on the men whose faces were tipped up like eggs towards her.

She stared long at them.

"What have you done to my mannikin?" she said.

They were silent.

"My beautiful, beautiful mannikin?" she said slightly shaking her head.

"Accidents happen," said a foreman a small and shrivelled man who wet his lips and looked at the boss for approval in making this statement.

Mrs Torrens walked like a trapeze artist along the fence top to reach the other post.

She swooped once or twice to the left and the right and when she settled herself on the post she lifted her chin and adjusted her hat.

The foreman encouraged by the success of his earlier remark wet his lips again.

"Go home to your kiddies, Mrs Torrens," he said. "They need you at home."

He considered this well worth repeating in the hotel after work.

Mrs Torrens stared dreamily down on the men giving her head another little shake.

"My beautiful, beautiful mannikin," she said.

Then she put out both arms and almost ran to the other post laughing a little when she reached there safely.

Someone had lit the primus stove and the shrill whistle of the boiling kettle broke the silence causing everyone except Mrs Torrens to start.

She merely lowered herself and jumped lightly onto the timber picking her way down until she reached the ground. She shook the sawdust from her old sandshoes as if they were expensive and elegant footwear.

Then she looked about her moving pieces of timber with her foot until she found a shortish piece she could easily grip.

She then walked into the office and swung it back and forth among the things on the table sending the primus like a flaming ball bowling across the floor and pieces of china flying everywhere.

The men were galvanized into action beating at the blaze with bags jumping out of the way of the steam of boiling water and trying vainly to save the cups and avoid contact with the timber wielded by Mrs Torrens.

After a while she threw her weapon among the debris and stalked off walking lightly casually through the mill gate and up the hill to where the Torrens house was. The little Torrenses home from school for midday dinner stood about with tragic expressions. Mrs Torrens broke into a brilliant smile.

"All of us will be Dadda's right hand now!" she called. "Dadda will have six right hands!"

She went ahead of them into the house.

"My beautiful, beautiful mannikin," she said.

It may seem strange but that, the most violent of all the rages of Mrs Torrens, was not generally discussed in Tantello.

Mill wives standing on verandahs and at windows saw her walk the fence and saw she spoke but the husbands evaded the questions on what was said.

Some repeated her words but kept them inside their throats in the darkness of their bedrooms and seizing their wives for love-

making held onto the vision of Mrs Torrens with her still face
under her black hat and her strong thighs moving under her black
dress as she walked the fence.

Even Thomas Cleary couldn't be persuaded to repeat what Mrs
Torrens said.

Young Thomas tried from the kitchen floor where he was doing
his homework.

"What did Rager say, Dad?" said young Thomas. "What was she
saying when she walked the fence top?"

"Don't you get ideas about walking the fence top," said Mrs
Cleary from the table where she was sullenly making Thomas
senior's lunch for the morrow. "Don't you go copying that crazy
woman!"

Thomas senior jerked his head up and opened his mouth but
closed it before a denial escaped his lips.

"Go on Dad! You musta heard Rager!" said young Thomas.

But Thomas senior staring into the scarlet stove fire saw only
the flaming red of Mrs Torrens's hair and when a coal broke it
seemed like the petals of red geraniums scattering into the ashes.
He opened and closed his two good hands on his knees but even
that did not ease the hunger inside him.

The Torrenses left Tantello soon after the accident. The towns-
people let the family go without ceremony fearful that an appearance of support might jeopardize others' jobs at the mill.

The Torrenses left their furniture to sell for the rent they owed
(for they never caught up from the week Kathleen threw Harold's
pay into the creek) and took their clothing and what else could be
stowed in the car besides the five children.

Mrs Torrens drove with Harold's useless heavily bandaged hand
beside her.

She did in effect become his right hand.

The work they ultimately found in the city was cleaning a
factory in two shifts a day, early morning and late afternoon.

Harold learned to wield a broom holding the handle in the crook
of his right arm and Kathleen worked beside him picking up the
rubbish he missed.

After some practice he was proficient and she could work
independently so that they sometimes had time to sit on an upturned box and eat their sandwiches together Harold laying his on
his knee between bites and holding his mug of tea with his left
hand.

The rages of Mrs Torrens subsided with the help of medication
from a public hospital not far from where they lived.

During these times Mrs Torrens's blue eyes dulled and her beautiful red hair straightened and she moved slowly and heavily with no life in her step or on her face.

She looked like a lot of the women in Tantello.

The little Torrenses did very well which would have amazed the people of Tantello if they had followed their fortunes in professions and trades.

Mrs Torrens was in her fifties when she died from a heart attack and Harold made his home with the second daughter Rachel who was a nurse educator in a big hospital with a flat of her own.

It was Aileen who won some modest fame in the rag trade.

She started sweeping floors and picking up pins and scraps of cloth then graduated to more important things.

When she was a beautiful young woman nearing thirty she was designing her own materials and having them made up into styles she created.

Long pursued by a colleague who designed and cut clothes for men she eventually married him and he agreed to her whim to drive through Tantello while on their honeymoon.

"Did you live here?" he said standing with her near the little grey house with the small square verandah now with all the railings missing and the roof on one side dipping dangerously over a tank tilted dangerously too from the half rotted tank stand.

She stood near a clump of red geraniums cold and proud and still as Kathleen stood outside the mill the day Harold lost his fingers.

"I lived here," she said and looked down on Tantello with the mill shut down now and only a few of the houses occupied mostly by Aboriginal families.

"Is that bridge safe to cross?" her husband asked looking at her profile with her lashes lying soft as brown bracken fern on her apricot cheeks.

She stretched her mouth in a smile he didn't understand and began to walk with Kathleen's walk light and casual towards the car.

He was a little ahead and his heart leapt when he heard her speak.

"My beautiful, beautiful mannikin," she said low and passionate.

He turned swiftly to take her hand.

Then he saw her face and felt he shouldn't.

Ismini

Beverley Farmer

Behind its hooded verandah the house was deep in evening shadow. Ismini unlocked the front door, trudged through the green gloom to the kitchen and dumped her schoolbag on the plastic table cloth among long slabs of late sun. A fly nodded, stroking its hinged legs.

With a wince she unwrapped the two slimy speckled translucent squids and rinsed them under the tap. Their beaks and torn eyes had to be prised out, then the fretted glassy backbones, the inksacs. She cut up the ornate tentacles and the sheaths of their bodies. She made a salad glowing green and red, put it with the *retsina* and the blubbery squid in the refrigerator, poured a glass of milk and sat down to her homework.

One morning on a hot wooden jetty her father had hauled a squid out of the flashing sea. Dripping, its bright mantle fading, it had shuddered and wheezed at her feet, blind in the white sun, as it died.

Oh, what is it, Baba?

Kalamari.

Mummy, Baba's caught a kamalari!

Oh yes, look. A squid.

In English it was a different creature.

Write a pen-portrait of a person you know well. The subject's appearance, attitudes, way of life, character, should be covered. 250–500 words.

She scribbled notes. My Grk grandmother. Yiayia Sophia. Will Mrs Brown object if the subject is dead? She won't know. Red eggs for Easter, the lamb on the iron spit, the awful offal soup. The brain broiled in the charred skull. Mother cat, kittens buried alive. Bad luck to kill a cat. Perpetual mourning.

A hard marker, Mrs Brown had said that Ismini was clever and should have no trouble getting a studentship to Teachers' College, if that was what she wanted. Mrs Brown had said after class that she might need Ismini to baby-sit on Saturday if her live-in girl was still ill. Oh yes, I'd love to, Mrs Brown.

The deep sun was making Ismini's face burn like a brass gong in the window pane, like the mask of Agamemnon, long-eyed, long-lipped. Her breasts lay round and heavy under her uniform. She fingered her warm hair.

Doan be hard on your Yiayia, Ismini *mou*. She give up everythink to come out here, look after us.

We didn't need her, Baba, did we?

We need her, you know that. She been like a mother to you.

She's always picking on me.

She just frighten. She tell your Theia she see your mother in you.

Oh does she? Good!

Baba once said Ismini could cook squid better than Mummy could, even better than Yiayia. These squids were fresh ones from the market especially for his birthday. Out of her pocket money she had bought real Greek *feta* cheese and the *retsina* and a carton of the Greek cigarettes he loved, Assos Filtro, supplied by Poppy's sister, an air hostess. In Greece, Baba said, they didn't celebrate birthdays. Mummy loved birthdays. If Mummy had been Greek and not Australian, who knew if she would have left home like that? Theia Frosso said no Greek woman would. Today there was no letter, no birthday card, in the box. Yet they had been one flesh.

She had run into Mummy the other day by chance in the Mall. She had stopped to chat, her own mother, grinning and tapping her foot on the hot tramlines, lighting a quick cigarette and blowing out smoke. She was really sorry to have to rush off like this.

I saw Mummy in town today, Baba.

Doan talk to me about that bitch.

"Ismini?" Theia Frosso was shrilling from outside. Ismini sighed. Theia Frosso, not her real aunt but Baba's second cousin, lived next door and felt responsible. The doors slammed. She strutted in, kissed Ismini and sank on to her usual chair.

"Ach! All alone, you poor gel, why you doan come an watch television with the kids, eh?"

"I haven't even started my homework, Theia."

Ismini poured her the daily, the ritual dose of sweet vermouth; caught a coil of her orange-peel preserve glowing and porous in the jar of heavy syrup and set it still in the spoon on a glass dish; poured iced water; mixed coffee for two in the red *briki*. It frothed and sputtered in the gas flame. She bit her lip.

"It boil out? Is nothing. *Yeia mas*." Theia Frosso ate and drank and licked her lips. "I tell you, your Baba, he a very lucky, he hev a daughter like you look after him. A good little Greek housewive."

"I'm not really Greek."

"What you tokkink about? You Greek."

Theia Frosso lit a cigarette and turned the coffee cups upside-down to read the future in the grounds. Yet Theia Frosso was *moderna*: she encased her flab in pantsuits, she dyed her hair red, she smoked cigarettes.

The telephone rang.

"Hullo?"

Theia Frosso was intent.

"Ismini? Hullo, love, it's me. Look, somethink's come up, I be home late. Sorry, eh? You doan mind, do you, love?"

"Well, how late will you be?"

"Dunno for sure. Doan wait up."

"You won't be home for dinner?"

"Doan worry, I grab a *souvlaki*."

"Baba, I got *kalamaria!*"

"Tomorrow. We hev them tomorrow. Sorry, love, I gotta go, I double-parked. Make sure you lock up, all right?"

"All right. *Yeia sou*."

"*Yeia*."

She slammed the phone down. Happy birthday, Baba.

"He hev gel fren." Theia Frosso giggled, inspecting the brown ripples in Ismini's cup. "You hev to expect. A taxi-driver metink lotsa people. He still a quite yunk men, you know thet."

"So what if he has?"

"He never tell you, *kale*, he be shame."

"Why should he be?"

"Mama? Eh, Mama?" Theia Frosso's scrawny youngest was shrilling out over the grey fence. She rose sighing, her duty done at least, stubbed out her cigarette, planted more rubber kisses.

"Without me they carn do nothink. Sorry, I betta go. You come an hev dinner, eh? Why you wanna stay here all alone? No good for you."

"Too much to do, Theia."

Ismini rinsed the dishes. The sun had left the window in a bronze haze. She switched the sallow bulb on and sat down under it to write.

MY GREEK GRANDMOTHER

My Greek grandmother, Yiayia Sophia, was swathed in her widow's mourning clothes and headscarf until she died. Her mouth was folded over her toothless gums, her skin yellow and creased, her grey hair worn in two long pigtails even in bed. A wick floating in oil on water kept a flame sputtering all night in front of the ikon in her room.

She knew all the prayers. All through Lent she fasted until she could hardly stand, her candle shaking, outside the church at the Easter midnight service. There were fireworks hanging and flaring, and we all cracked our red eggs and ate them and nursed our candle flames all the way home for luck. Then we had to eat her magieritsa.

I remember her hoarding our hens' eggs for days beforehand and hard-boiling them on Holy Thursday in red dye. We polished them, still warm, with cloths dipped in oil. She baked plaited tsoureki *loaves. She made the* magieritsa, *the traditional soup of lamb offal, flushing out the lungs and entrails with the garden hose, screeching at the avid hens, stirring it all in the pot with onions and herbs like a witch at her cauldron.*

The lamb itself my father had skinned and impaled on an iron rod. Its red eye-sockets, its grinning teeth with the spit thrust out like an iron tongue. All Easter Sunday morning it was twisted and basted over the trench of coals, speckled with charred herbs, while it turned dark brown and neighbours and relatives danced to the record player on the back lawn. When they split the skull for my grandmother, she offered me a forkful of the brains.

"Eat it, silly," she cackled. "God gave it to us."

"Ugh, no! I don't want it."

She shrugged, mumbling the grey jelly.

Our cat had kittens once. A lovely pure black cat, a witch-cat, she lay purring, slit-eyed, as they butted and squeaked at her pink teats. Our cat was necessary, as the hens attracted mice. Kittens weren't. One day the cat was crying and clawing at a damp patch of ground under the tomatoes. I dug up the corpses, their fur and tiny mouths and moonstone eyes all clogged with earth. I accused Yiayia.

"Don't be silly," was all she said.

She is dead and buried herself now, in foreign earth. I saw her dying, her old mouth agape fighting for breath; and dead in her coffin at last, a yellow mask and folded lizard-claws. She was always too old to love me. I'm too old to hate her any more.

(430 words)

At the funeral Baba had sobbed on Theia Fosso's shoulder. Mummy hadn't been there. Ismini shuddered. In her old sepia wedding picture nailed up beside the ikon, Yiayia had Ismini's face: everyone said so. Ismini had wanted to burn all the photos, but Baba made her put them back up in the hollow room. There was one of Mummy in Greece, on a plump donkey with her legs sticking stiffly out; Baba was there, and Yiayia, swathed even then, and a crowd of solemn children with shaved heads. Mummy looked happy.

The phone rang. Ismini's lip curled. So he was sorry, was he? Well, better late than never.

"Yes."

"Hullo? That's you, Ismini, is it? Good."

"Oh! Mrs Brown!"

When she had just finished the essay!

"I was hoping you'll still be free to baby-sit for us this Saturday. Have I left it too late?"

"Oh yes, I'd love to!"

"Oh good. The thing is, though, we'll be very late home. Will your parents let you stay the night?"

The wood-fire whispering, Ismini thought, flaring over the crammed bookshelves and the sofa bed in the bow window.

"Oh, yes!"

If Baba says no this time, then I'll leave home.

"You're sure? Oh good. I'll pick you up at seven on Saturday, then. Can you hear the bub bawling his head off? I'd better go. 'Bye, Ismini."

The first time she stood for ten minutes on their front verandah, too nervous to knock. When she asked Mrs Brown what to do if the baby cried, the eight-year-old scoffed, but the two-year-old patted her knee: I'll help you, Minnie, he said. He always stops for me.

They sat round the fire while she read them Little Golden Books; calling her Minnie Mouse, exploding with giggles, chanting Meany, Meany, when she said lights out at nine.

I'm eight. I don't have to go to sleep yet.

You do so. Mummy said. He does so have to, Minnie.

Shut up you.

It was a funny name though, a fancy classical name, a whim of her pompous old godfather's, when she should have been called Sophia after Yiayia. His wife had lapped Ismini in rosy withering flesh, pressing lips soft as a cocoon on her wincing cheeks. Once her parents split up, her godparents stopped visiting. Only her name was left of them.

If Baba said no, she couldn't stay the night, then she'd ring Mummy. No, don't be silly. The last time, a man had picked up the phone. Lyn, it's for you, he'd called.

Mummy, it's me. Can you come over just for a while? Baba's gone out. Can you, please?

Darling, no, sweet, you know I can't, I have to get up at five to go to work –

I want to talk to you!

Well go ahead, sweet, what's the matter?

Baba says I can't go to Poppy's birthday party.

Oh, lovey, I'm sorry. What a shame.

I'm sixteen! I'm not a child! The whole form's going. He won't let me go anywhere. Please, will you just ring and talk to him?

He wouldn't listen to me. You know that. God, I'm the last person –

I'm sorry. You're otherwise engaged, aren't you?

Ah, Ismini –

She'd cut Mummy off. Mummy hadn't tried to ring back. Baba had been right all along, of course: forget about your Mummy, Ismini *mou*, she doan want you. Sixteen, Ismini said aloud, is old enough to leave home legally. She wondered if Poppy would like to share a flat.

It was getting late. She trailed down the dark passage to her father's room. Its velvet curtains were the same, like sleek brown fur, and the painted-over fireplace in the wall, and in the wardrobe doors those long hazed mirrors that she and Mummy had always polished together. She had dressed up and posed in the dim mirrors. Baba slept alone now. When nightmares had woken her he had come and carried her in to sleep between their big warm bodies.

Mummy's old forgotten red nightdress lay hidden under sheets in the bottom drawer. Ismini undressed to slip it on: it fitted now. She stroked Red Ruby on her lips and cheeks, and rimmed her long eyes with kohl. She brushed out her hair. In the blurred gold of the mirror a dusty ghost looked back.

Once, black and faceless against a half-light from the passage, Mummy had stooped over her, dragged down her pants and crammed a suppository like an iron spit up her bottom. She had had to rush out to the toilet, her bowels surging and snorting. Poppy said sex hurt like that. Poppy was raped.

Room by room Ismini snapped on the lights and checked that all the doors and windows were locked. Yiayia's room of dead faces, the kitchen, laundry, bathroom, the musty sitting room, and her own room last.

She had been lying awake, trying to make sense of their jumbled shouts in the kitchen, when Mummy had come bursting in, sobbing and shuddering, and slammed the door. They clung together in the dark until at last Baba's yells and crashes petered out, daring only to whisper.

I'm leaving. This time I'm leaving.

What's happened?

He's insane. He's capable of anything. God, I hate that man!

But what about me?

I'll have to go into hiding. I'll find somewhere to live where he won't find me. Ring you at school.

I'm coming with you!

No, sweet, you can't. He won't let you go. He'd stop at nothing if I took you. He said so.

Mummy, don't go. Don't, please.

In the chill of daybreak they found him asleep with his head in his bloodstained arms on the kitchen table glittering with smashed glass. Mummy crept past with her suitcase. Ismini draped his jacket over his wet shoulders, switched off the light, and crawled back into bed.

Now Mummy got up before daybreak and stood waiting among furled glittering lamps and skeletons of trees for the first golden tram to trundle up wrapped in fog like a caterpillar in a cocoon.

If I fail HSC, Ismini had remarked the other day, you can get me a job at the hotel with you.

Oh, you'll pass. Still want to be a teacher?

I don't know what I want.

In the kitchen Ismini lit the stump of her Easter candle and switched off the light to watch the little flame flap and tower. She thought of opening the *retsina*. No. Well, why not? She prised the cap off and filled a glass with the acrid wine. Happy birthday, Baba. She drank it in gulps, and ate all the salad, since it wouldn't keep, dipping chunks of bread in the juice, sucking the olive pits. Lovely ripe plums for later.

By candlelight her arms shone, and her breasts too, only half hidden in crimson silk.

You're so beautiful, he would say, sitting opposite, and she would smile mockingly over the rim of her glass at this dark tall grave man, a man who had lived, who had known sorrow. His name? What did it matter? He would bend to heap hot kisses on her hands.

Ah! But you're too innocent, my darling.

I'm so tired of innocence. Slowly, significantly.

God! Don't tempt me! And overcome by a wave of passion, crushing her fiercely in his arms, he would carry her limp and golden to her bed.

Ismini took a long swig and held her glass against the swelling candleflame. Light swung rocking all over her, the kitchen walls, the window panes. The luminous crimson plums sat glowing there. She bit one through its skin and its juice spurted.

Darling, she murmured out loud across the table. Oh, my darling.

The Courts of the Lord

Fay Zwicky

Growing older they have decided to separate. He thinks that he loves her but is tired of waiting for something to happen. He is not sure that happiness is what he should be wanting but this does not stop him from wanting it. She knows that anything would be better than the way they live together and has taken up yoga. They both fear that the children know them better than they know themselves.

Stumbling from what has been their bed in the early morning chill, he catches his foot in a pile of books on her side. Lillian Hellman's *An Unfinished Woman*, the diaries of Anais Nin, something about the crisis in sex hormones, and a couple of books about anxiety and depression. She reads a lot. Especially in bed. This morning she is already on the floor, helpless in the pose of the Locust, chin resting on the rug, hands by her sides in tight baby-like fists, left leg barely an inch off the ground. She is breathing heavily and fairly steadily. Breathing is important. He listens to the rhythm as he looks around for his underwear.

The spectacle of this self-help saddens and irritates him. His heart is wrung by the little roll of white flesh bulging over the elasticized waist of her green pyjamas. In what way is a humanist education relevant to this? He thinks he loves her and would like to touch her. He has wanted to touch her for years, but they have been too formal with each other.

Does she love him? She is not sure and keeps him at bay with the steady rhythm of her breathing. Her fists clench hard by her sides as he steps past her on his way to the bathroom.

"You will discover remarkable new strength and energy", said her yoga instructor, elegant yesterday in a striped black and white leotard. "Your mind and your body will experience the joy that is life at its best." And, lying on the floor of the local Baptist church hall, along with twenty or so other women, in that hour she look-

ed for an answer. Lying down, stretching out, giving herself over
to the slow rhythmical movements, she imagined herself briefly
as graceful and sensuous and in pursuit of happiness.

Another colder voice was less sentimental about her chances.
It reminded her that the body had a name. It also spoke of death.

Still helpless in the Locust position she turns her head in his
direction and smiles apologetically for yesterday. She smiles at the
way she must look today. He does not see the smile but watches,
in the bathroom mirror, the little white roll of flesh lap over the
green of her pyjamas.

"This exercise will strengthen muscles in the lower abdomen,
groin and buttocks", said the instructor.

Groin. Buttocks. Buttocks. Groin. The parts that sound sexy in
the books, but which she has never related to herself. The
buttocks are for sitting on and she has never been sure where the
groin is.

She obediently tenses, remembering the instructor's commands
to clench her fists under her thighs. He would like to touch her
but, as so often has happened, he has to get ready to leave for
work. Through the open doorway he hears the sawings of a
baroque fiddle on the radio yield to a deep female voice. It is
strong and steady and the enunciation is crisp and unaffected. Her
old friend, Jenny Byrne, is reading psalms.

"My soul longeth for the courts of the Lord . . .", and she is back
in the school hall listening to Jenny reading the morning lesson.
Even as a child she had a deep voice. The sensuous images of the
psalm wash over her soothingly. The courts of the Lord are full of
green vines. Curling tendrils of the passion vine and the sweet
starflowers of the stephanotis. And there is water in the courts of
the Lord. In the trees are singing birds.

She wonders what happens to those who were once happy. "Did
you know I went to school with her?" "What did you say?" His
voice sounds impatient in the bathroom. "I went to school with
the woman who is reading." "Oh? Have you seen my other sock?"
"She always knew what she was going to do." "Yea, the sparrow
hath found a house, and the swallow a nest for herself." The voice
was balanced and purposeful. "She knew exactly what she
wanted, and did it. She sounds very happy. She never married."
"Sensible of her."

It is all talk and gesture now. Both know that sensible isn't the
word. Both know that words are running out. He finds the pathos
of the sparrow and the swallow unendurable. She, who once had
a home, can handle the idea of having none. He has had to build

one from scratch and does not want to put words to the loss. Her
old friend finishes the psalm and starts on a passage from Isaiah.

"Have a look in the top left-hand drawer." Her voice is tense.
Her body is now contorted in another position. Still on her
stomach, she bends her knees, reaches behind her and attempts to
grasp her feet. They are broad and white. There is a bunion on the
right foot. The effort is too much and she is forced to let her feet
go. Stretching her legs behind her, she rests helplessly on her
chin. He has found his sock and stands looking down at her. Her
defeated posture moves him strangely and he defends himself
against her. "Hello! What's it like down there." She winces and, as
if challenged to fight, bends her knees and again tries to grasp her
feet. Her breathing comes fast and awkwardly. She looks
resolutely ahead, grasping her feet in both hands. He walks across
to the window and flings it open wider. "You'd be better off if you
didn't smoke so much," he says. "Thanks. Thanks a million." She is
trembling, but still holding on to her feet, looking straight ahead.

"The wilderness and the solitary place shall be glad for them . . . "
Her friend's voice gives her courage of a sort. " . . . and the tongue
of the dumb shall sing." She loses her balance and slowly hunches
back into a sitting position. She is fighting silently with herself.
To get up as she has done many times, or to stay on the floor. She
finds it difficult to go near him and yet she has once promised to
grow old alongside this man. They scarcely hear each other now.
She is still listening to the radio.

"Jenny never left her parents' house. I think she still lives with
them." Was that the secret of that confident purposeful voice?
"You know you can't go back," he says, putting on his shoes on his
side of the bed. She laughs and says "Perhaps not." "There's no
perhaps about it." He knows. He has never wanted to go back.
There is nothing for him to go back to. There is nothing for her
either but she doesn't know it. Yet. They are both in need of
instruction. They are both growing older.

"I'm sorry I said anything but her voice brings so much with it.
She had the most comforting mother when we were nine."

He shifts on the bed, away from her bowed body. She suddenly
looks years older and yet seems younger and more helpless than
their youngest child. She shrugs, pushes back her hair from her
forehead and begins to cry. His heart contracts but he moves
further away. "No lion shall be there nor any ravenous beast . . . "

"I wish I weren't so childish. I want to die every morning but I
don't because of the children."

"What about you? Don't you care about yourself?"

" . . . and sorrow and sighing shall flee away . . . "

He doesn't have any more conviction about this new utopia than she, but he is trying to stop the avalanche.

To live for yourself? What does this mean to either of them who years ago promised to live for each other? Who have given each other the rich unhappy hoard of their patience? How can one such say to the other "You don't know what it means." Nevertheless, she says "You don't know what it means." And, because he believes in agreeing to anything that will put a merciful end to this guttering life they share, he agrees that he doesn't know what it means. What he does know, however, is that when he looks at her bowed head and the little lines round her eyes and mouth, he, too, wants to die. But right now he has to go.

"I'm late already. Please don't be too depressed today. I don't know what it all means any more than you do. We'll have to talk about it later."

He looks at his watch and gets up, hoping she hasn't seen him looking. It always makes her furious. No, she hasn't seen the gesture. She is looking straight ahead, the tears streaking the front of her green pyjamas. He bends down and puts an arm around her bent shoulders as she shrinks into herself. "Perhaps you should go and see the doctor." One of their well-worn formulas. He uses it when his head aches and he hasn't had any breakfast. The children are making noises out in the kitchen and there probably won't be any bread left because it's Monday.

"It's just that − " She stops short.

"What? What is it? What can I do?"

"I just want you to feel what it's like."

"That wouldn't help either of us."

"It might if you tried."

"If I had ever known what you felt like, we wouldn't be talking about leaving each other right now." She is obliged to agree, always proud of her capacities to summon control at critical moments. She gets up and goes to the kitchen.

He is surprised to discover how well he feels as he gets into his car to drive off to work. He will buy her a present this afternoon. Something beautiful. A statue for the garden maybe. A stone angel or a bird-bath. Something that no younger man would ever have thought of and certainly couldn't afford.

Lizards

Barry Hill

They were easy enough to find. You only had to lift a rock in the stone wall and there they were: or there was one at least – flat as a tack, an eye watching, legs in that dancing position, like a frog about to leap, except that lizards seldom leap, they dart, sliding off and out and under. You have to be really quick; I had no trouble catching half a dozen in a Saturday afternoon.

Most of the kids chucked them away before we got home; or they let them go on the spot, since catching lizards wasn't much compared to catching snakes, which we were also after, moving around the stone walls as far as the coal dump, then out behind it onto the swampy part of the flats. Our house, in those days, was on the edge of the flats. I kept lizards because I liked them; I was not that keen on the big ones that reminded you of goannas, their pale bellies pulsing and swollen as if they'd been drinking too much beer as they lay in the sun, but the slim quick ones as long as your finger, I tucked into my pocket, or carried home in a brown paper bag. They seemed quite happy travelling there, in the folds of things, and when I showed them to mum and dad I had that nice feeling which comes from being proprietorial and kind.

I especially liked taking them into our front room when people were there. On Saturdays dad was usually talking with his union mates and members of the party. They were big blokes mostly (or they seemed to be at the time) – boilermakers, blacksmiths, welders, filling up our armchairs. They could talk those men, and to listen to some of them there you might have thought they were standing on boxes in the back yard: but when I came in with the lizards they went quiet, and grinned, and asked if they could have a look.

I held up my favourite. The best way to hold a lizard is just below the skull, towards the back of its head rather than low down near the throat. When you're not squeezing its gizzard it can look at its audience quite comfortably.

Give it a run, someone said, as if he was unhappy with the idea of anything being held in captivity.

No, I'd say, it's not ready yet. What I meant was that it would run under his chair and try to get into the fringe of the mat. It would be hard to get out again, and mum would go crook.

Let's have a go, he said, reaching towards the lizard.

I backed off a bit. I don't want it to drop a tail, I explained.

Fair enough, mate.

They were all pretty pleased with this and went on talking. I could hear mum in the kitchen, coughing, and moving about getting the cups and saucers. I sat down on the floor, slipping the lizard up under my collar. I felt it wriggle to the back of my neck, and settle down to doze, apparently soothed by the growling tones of the conversation.

There was a war on, I knew that much. The newsagent was selling a beaut new comic called "Marines", and one copy my dad had held up to his mates, saying, "propaganda". They had shaken their heads and the comic was passed back to me. I remember reading it in a fresh light then; I could see that the Yanks couldn't be as good as all that, even though the drawings were the best I'd seen. Yet each week the comic seemed to have more rather than less pages for the same price.

I listened to them talk about the war, and I heard them speculate on the possibilities of the General getting permission to drop the bomb. There were no comics, as yet, about the bomb; or, if it came to that, about the banning of the party. As I understood it, the Government wanted to lock up people like my dad and his mates, and if they didn't watch out it would happen soon, while no one else gave a damn.

Most people don't care, one way or the other, someone said. Capitalism has it in the bag.

Oh yes they do, it's a matter of people being brought into the picture, becoming part of the struggle.

Let's hope so, I heard my father say, as the tea was served.

As much as a boy of that age could, I worried too. A disciple, I entered into their disgruntlements, and the tension and determination that went into their conversation made me feel satisfied rather than unhappy; it gave me a sense of self-assurance, as if an important part of me could afford to stretch out and be comfortable against the body of their opinion. Even today, I think that I owe a good deal of myself to the strength and warmth that inhabit-

ed the room, though the odd thing was that there was an under-
current to their conversation which made me think of crabs rather
than lizards.

The crabs we used to hunt at the back beach. We tied cat's meat
to a length of string and when the tide was out fished the crabs out
from beneath the rock ledges. As soon as a claw took hold of the
meat you pulled it up, flicking the crab onto the dry rock. Then
with the knife you stabbed the crab through the back; there was
an explosion of sea water and flesh, and the crab was grounded.
Some of us had spears – bamboo with scrap metal as tips, which
we used as well, crushing through the shells as near to dead centre
as possible, swearing and screaming at the crab as we did.

It was interesting the way we carried on like that. I remember
using words that I was not going to use freely again until I'd grown
up, but somehow, leaping and dancing about the broken shells, it
seemed the right thing to do, a way of making up for the creatures
being so well defended, and otherwise so inaccessible. Since
so much that worried my dad and his mates was invisible and
intractable, I suppose I felt that some purpose might be served by
yelling a lot, and tearing into things, though at the time, I was
incapable of making this connection clear to myself, or to anybody
else.

In any case I had come to prefer lizards. I liked their silkiness,
their liquid movements and their apparent adaptability, and I had
been pleased to leave the crabs rotting in the sun, despite the fact
that if I'd brought them home alive dad would have cooked them
in a pot and eaten them as a treat – as chicken was then a treat,
and pork. Lamb was not a treat as we had it hot every Sunday and
for the following two nights ate it cold with plenty of pickles. The
point is, I didn't care for delicacies so much as keeping things that
seemed to invite a secure alternative to what they had known, and
which seemed able to survive in the conditions I was able to
provide myself.

The box I built for the lizards was about three feet long with
wire netting on top. Beneath the wire were rocks, weeds, sand,
clay soil – an attractive and varied landscape, with a lake as its
centre. This was the top of a jam jar filled with water from the
gully trap. From the army of ants at the base of the gully trap it
was a simple matter to ambush provisions for the lizards; flies
were harder to get, but you could raid the cobwebs in the back of
the tool shed. All food was placed into the nooks and crannies of
the lizard's garden, and for ages it puzzled me as to why they
seemed to have very little appetite.

At school, my lizard for the day was transferred from pocket to collar to another box: the pencil case which sat on the edge of my desk. It seemed happy enough in there. Occasionally, when we were not flat out putting our hands up to answer questions, I gave it a run on top. It would make a dart for the aisle and was checked with a ruler when it dipped its tongue into the inkwell, I would, for its own good pull it back then before it got too frisky, I put it back in the case – though never, never, before showing it to Mary, the girl who sat right in front of me.

Mary had long blonde hair that hung down her back as far as my pencil case, and when I chose to fiddle about in that area the tips of her hair touched my knuckes.

Look, I'd say. She was the first girl I ever wanted to show anything to.

I can see, she replied. She was not frightened. I was not trying to scare her as some kids would.

Does it have a name?

Nup.

It looks sick, she said.

It did too, now that she came to mention it. At recess time I let it run along the wet bottom of the tap troughs. Afterwards I gave her another look.

You're torturing it, she said. The comment hurt me deeply, and made me realize, much later, how much I'd been in love with her. She had given me my first experience of hopes dashed. At the time it struck me that the word torture was vicious and unjust, entirely unsuited to my best intentions, and I had as much trouble getting to grips with it as my dad and his mates were having with terms like purge, and slave labour camp. It was a word that I found impossible to accept, until, one by one, my lizards began to die. I'd open the garden box, lift a stone, and there another would be – dead, and wizened looking. I imported new batches but they went as well. Then Stalin died too, and I could see that my dad was having to do a lot of thinking about that. My box had become pungent and rank, as if disappointment, or folly, had developed a special smell of its own. Mum helped me clean the box out: in the end I gave lizards away, and threw myself into that enterprising schoolground sport of marbles.

We give up one thing, we take up another, something is cleared away, something else takes its place: life seems to be like that. In the years I was going through school, from primary school into high school, moving past the Merit Certificate that had been the stopping post for my father and his mates, the stone walls out on the flats were being taken down, thistles cleared away, the swamps drained and cranes and wild duck driven off. Lizards and snakes moved west as the great paddocks were bought up and sold for factory allotments. One day a leaflet appeared in our letter box saying that the sky at night would take on an orange glow: we were not to be alarmed at this, the leaflet said, as the new cloud was harmless. A refinery was to be built, and a refinery had to burn off its waste.

The construction of the refinery was followed by a plant to produce carbon black: then another which turned out polyethylene and styrene; and another which extracted chemicals from the by-products of its neighbours. A petrochemical complex as big as any in the world had grown up, the affairs of which were directed from boardrooms as far as Kansas City and London, places I had read about in books. There was something remote and grand about the gleaming assembly of pipes and tanks that roared and hissed all day and all night, ejecting their flames, invisible heat, and unnameable gases into the sky.

The landscape was becoming, now I think of it, more political, but the strange thing was that in so many other ways our life was not. Over many weekends dad spent his time building a garage to house and protect our first car. We already had a refrigerator, and mum had enough money left out of housekeeping to layby a washing machine. In the old days, when I left my towel at the beach, I got into trouble: there were now plenty of towels to go round which meant that, my anxiety lowered, I seldom left a towel or anything else behind. In fact in most respects this was an orderly, forward-looking period, where talk about the days when people had to battle for a decent living, while it was interesting in a way (and was written up in some of our history books), was not the sort of information you needed to base a decision on. We were eating chicken once a week, I was getting on well at school and mum and dad were going to keep me there until I had gone as far as I could go — so while none of these things were planned, they kept happening, they evolved, enemy or no enemy.

Oh, there *was* an enemy all right, I still felt that. At school I spent a lot of time defending, or being seen to defend, moves to oust the agents provocateurs in Hungary, the liberation of Tibet from feudalism, and the assaults from all fronts upon our unions, the unions which some of dad's mates were now working for full time, having responded to suggestions that organization at levels other than the shop floor was necessary. The enemy was the misrepresenter of the truths I had carried within me for so long, and I saw no reason why people should get away with mutilating them. I was an energetic protagonist, sometimes lying low and making quick, attacking runs on an argument; sometimes using crab hunting strategies. These habits I carried from school to university, through election campaigns and into the movement against the next war in Asia, the war that never ceased to remind me of the one dad and his mates had worried about when I was a boy. Now we – two or three generations – were in a united opposition, we had revived the old warmth and strength and there was no questioning the worth of any of us. The war carried on, as did we, opposing it, and the battle, from my point of view, was desperate and exhilarating. At the same time the experience was profoundly and unexpectedly tedious, as if I had found myself marching backwards, wearing someone else's heavy trousers.

Social being determines consciousness. But consciousness, I had also come to feel, is made by one's willingness to shed one's social being. I had become a teacher. I was already paid to stand and talk. Now I would go off to London, to live. There I found that I enjoyed the sound of people talking differently. I must say that at the time I thought much of this talk, in its fluency and ease, in its poise and assurance, in its gracious assumption that if an enemy was to be identified it was hardly worth mentioning, was in many ways preferable to my own, and that it was worth emulating. The feeling I had then was akin to one I'd had in the school playground, soon after becoming adept at marbles. Most of us remember the feeling surely? The kids have suggested that you join a team, play as a group, the better to knock the dickens out of the big kids. But you decline; you hold out – no you'll keep playing alone. You squat at the end of the ring with your taw at the ready. It's a hot day and the northerly scorches the back of your neck. You take a shot – a good one: you take another, which earns you the next. On you go, and before you know it you've cleaned up the ring, your pockets are full of glass eyes and though the other are watching, you can't help strutting: you just have to walk off and sit down in the shade and count the proceeds.

From London I wrote regularly to my parents. They were proud of my achievements: a post-graduate degree and then a research job with the BBC. Had I gone over to the other side? Hardly: my letters conveyed a radical critique of the circles I was moving in, mixed with acerbic remarks about the defensiveness of dad's union, and the lame political inheritance at home. Communiqués are neat cocktails, and I was becoming a pretty smooth operation. In the absence of – what, an alternative? – I was going as far as I could go. And the journey was unquestionably an achievement, a mark of my freedom, which in turn, was as concrete a measure of accomplishment as marbles filling your hip pocket, marbles that one could not help but take out one at a time to hold up against the light, inspecting each for flaws. For brief periods it is sometimes possible to fully possess things without being troubled by the hollowness of winning.

St Augustine refers somewhere to a *ventosa professio*, a puffed-up profession, and to *ventosa tempora*, a puffed-up existence, which indicates that Communism is not the only faith which is intolerant of egoisms. My melancholia was probably in search of a religious house to inhabit, but I had little time for a credo that made a sin of disobedience and knowing. Nor did I like the idea that all worldliness was empty, as if the devil, or the self as the devil in thin disguise, had put a straw up my bum and blown me up like a frog. When I saw kids do that at school I ripped their straws into pieces, and pushed them about. Besides, I knew, deep down, that I had not really changed and was, for better or worse, the same person I'd been years before. I knew this most clearly late in the evenings at London dinner tables, when conversation turned to questions of class (which I liked to pronounce as in "mass") and power. Then out of the dark, drunken vacuity of self, out of the rage that lusts for its own form, there was no more pretending, and the buggers had to sit back and listen. I made them suffer, they copped it, they were left sitting there, and hours later when I returned to my place, I discovered that I was in myself positively happy.

We come home in order to be real again, and when I decided to come back, after five years away, my mother was ill, and the nation on the eve of an election. For the first time in the history of my generation there might be a change of Government. There was: a Labor Government took office; there was a bubble of optimism and reform and then it burst – pricked by the tip of an enemy weapon. We caught a glimpse of the steel, then it had gone again. There were protests, but life gradually slipped back to normal. People drove about in their station wagons, pulling their trailers and boats; they pushed lawnmowers, hedge clippers, car washers: they buzzed at the end of hair dryers, fruit mixers, electric tooth brushes and dish washers, while his union, my father told me, was worrying the issue as to whether the order for their next fleet of cars should go to the established American firm or to the Japanese company about to open a new plant near our petro-chemical complex. I should have known from this perhaps, that my seeing his mates again was going to be as painful as anything I had known.

I met them one at a time, mostly, through the period my mother was convalescing from one of her lung infections. They had dropped in to see dad, and I was sometimes sitting on the end of mum's bed. Hi, hello Jack. Ah, they'd say, how are you going? Terrific thanks. We shook hands, letting go after the standard indications of strength. I asked about the union, the latest campaign. They inquired about my job, and whether I had further plans to travel. We swapped comment on recent Government bastardries. Then, that was it.

We had nothing more to say to each other. They went back into the front room to talk with dad, leaving me with mum. While trying to talk with her my mind ran back through the conversation: maybe I had been a bit sharp, a bit glib, rather brittle; there was still the overlay, perhaps, of the old London — "his master's" — voice. It occurred to me that it might serve a reconciling purpose to pick myself up and join them in the front room, claiming one of the chairs that they had occupied for so long. But I dismissed the idea as I did not wish to leave my mother alone, and in any case I realized that my presence would cramp their style: I'd read too many books, done too much, in going as far as I could, had gone too far. It would be stupid to say that they disliked me personally. But to most of them I was the lizard that had dropped its tail.

The idea of telling them about complex feelings at dinner tables was too silly for words: saying what brought me back would have been exhibitionist. Then of course there was an obvious fact; they were remembering me most clearly as a small boy, with my future before me, a future they would not have presumed, in our era of opportunity, to confine. In many ways then my need for some comradely recognition must surely be an expression of egoism. This is one truth I am trying to face, just as I'm trying to live with the steady decline of my mother.

She has been going down for a number of years. Her lungs, her heart, the circulation of her blood, are cracking up. Most of all her lungs are failing her, and it is all she can do, some days to prepare a meal. The most ego-less person I know, self-denying to a fault, has difficulty walking from the oven to the kitchen table, and when she gets as far as the garden she inhales, as best she can, the air of our neighbourhood: with what she has working of the wretched sacks in her chest, she takes in the output from our petrochemical complex.

Her throat and neck have become swollen from the exertion of breathing. Her face is ruddy, blotched and puffy, and even describing her like this makes me wince on her behalf, for her

despair at the disintegration of her looks. She would prefer to have
no face at all. Already she has known degrees of self-loathing that
would send most men to their graves in a month. Yet there is
nothing direct, is there, that the men, my dad and his mates, I –
can do? We live where we live. It must be conceded that the
drugs which have helped wreck my mother's appearance have
also given her great relief, and that no doubt many of them have
their origins in some of the plants nearby. You have to retain a
degree of rationality about such matters.

Going away, then coming back, makes any steady change, or no
change, much more conspicuous, and the other thing I struggle to
be rational about is the fact that I have seldom, as an adult, found
it easy to talk with my mother. She remembers my lizards all
right, but I have spent so much time, over the years, in a spoken or
silent dialogue with my dad and his mates, a dialogue that she has
removed herself from or was in other ways discouraged from joining, that I find it difficult to get a bearing on her being.

There are long silences between us: one of us seems always to
be waiting for my father to come in. I fear that I lack generosity.
As I sit with her I often think of Brecht's song about his mother.
*Oh, why do we not say the important things, it would be so easy, and
we are damned because we do not,* and at night when I leave to go
home, I drive out and around the complex, circling and circling.

Land Deal

Gerald Murnane

> After a full explanation of what my object was, I purchased two large tracts of land from them — about 600,000 acres, more or less — and delivered over to them blankets, knives, looking-glasses, tomahawks, beads, scissors, flour, etc., as payment for the land, and also agreed to give them a tribute, or rent, yearly.
>
> John Batman, 1835

We certainly had no cause for complaint at the time. The men from overseas politely explained all the details of the contract before we signed it. Of course there were minor matters that we should have queried. But even our most experienced negotiators were distracted by the sight of the payment offered us.

The strangers no doubt supposed that their goods were quite unfamiliar to us. They watched tolerantly while we dipped our hands into the bags of flour, draped ourselves in blankets, and tested the blades of knives against the nearest branches. And when they left we were still toying with our new possessions. But what we marvelled at most was worth their novelty. We had recognised an almost miraculous correspondence between the strangers' steel and glass and wool and flour and those metals and mirrors and cloths and foodstuffs that we so often postulated, speculated about, or dreamed of.

Is it surprising that a people who could use against stubborn wood and pliant grass and bloody flesh nothing more serviceable than stone — is it surprising that such a people have become so familiar with the idea of metal? Each one of us, in his dreams, had felled tall trees with blades that lodged deep in the pale pulp beneath the bark. Any of us could have enacted the sweeping of honed metal through a stand of seeded grass or described the precise parting of fat or muscle beneath a tapered knife. We knew the strength and sheen of steel and the trueness of its edge from having so often called it into possible existence.

It was the same with glass and wool and flour. How could we not have inferred the perfection of mirrors — we who peered so often into rippled puddles after wavering images of ourselves? There was no quality of wool that we had not conjectured as we huddled under stiff pelts of possum on rainy winter evenings. And every day the laborious pounding of the women at their dusty mills recalled for us the richness of the wheaten flour that we had never tasted.

But we had always clearly distinguished between the possible and the actual. Almost anything was possible. Any god might reside behind the thundercloud or the waterfall, any faery race inhabit the land below the ocean's edge; any new day might bring us such a miracle as an axe of steel or a blanket of wool. The almost boundless scope of the possible was limited only by the occurrence of the actual. And it went without saying that what existed in the one sense could never exist in the other. Almost anything was possible except, of course, the actual.

It might be asked whether our individual or collective histories furnished any example of a possibility becoming actual. Had no man ever dreamed of possessing a certain weapon or woman and, a day or a year later, laid hold of his desire? This can be simply answered by the assurance that no one among us was ever heard to claim that anything in his possession resembled, even remotely, some possible thing he had once hoped to possess.

That same evening, with the blankets warm against our backs and the blades still gleaming beside us, we were forced to confront an unpalatable proposition. The goods that had appeared among us so suddenly belonged only in a possible world. We were therefore dreaming. The dream may have been the most vivid and enduring that any of us had known. But however long it lasted it was still a dream.

We admired the subtlety of the dream. The dreamer (or dreamers — we had already admitted the likelihood of our collective responsibility) had invented a race of men among whom possible objects passed as actual. And these men had been moved to offer us the ownership of their prizes in return for something that was itself not real.

We found further evidence to support this account of things. The pallor of the men we had met that day, the lack of purpose in much of their behaviour, the vagueness of their explanations — these may well have been the flaws of men dreamed of in haste.

And, perhaps paradoxically, the nearly perfect properties of the stuffs offered to us seemed the work of a dreamer, someone who lavished on the central items of his dream all those desirable qualities that are never found in actual objects.

It was this point that led us to alter part of our explanation for the events of that day. We were still agreed that what had happened was part of some dream. And yet it was characteristic of most dreams that the substance of them seemed, at the time, actual to the dreamer. How, if we were dreaming of the strangers and their goods, were we able to argue against our taking them for actual men and objects?

We decided that none of us was the dreamer. Who, then, was? One of our gods, perhaps? But no god could have had such an acquaintance with the actual that he succeeded in creating an illusion of it that had almost deceived us.

There was only one reasonable explanation. The pale strangers, the men we had first seen that day, were dreaming of us and our confusion. Or, rather, the true strangers were dreaming of a meeting between ourselves and their dreamed-of-selves.

At once, several puzzles seemed resolved. The strangers had not observed us as men observe one another. There were moments when they might have been looking through our hazy outlines towards sights they recognised more easily. They spoke to us with oddly raised voices and claimed our attention with exaggerated gestures as though we were separated from them by a considerable distance, or as though they feared we might fade altogether from their sight before we had served the purpose for which they had allowed us into their dream.

When had this dream begun? Only, we hoped, on that same day when we first met the strangers. But we could not deny that our entire lives and the sum of our history might have been dreamed by these people of whom we knew almost nothing. This did not dismay us utterly. As characters in a dream, we might have been much less at liberty than we had always supposed. But the authors of the dream encompassing us had apparently granted us at least the freedom to recognise, after all these years, the simple truth behind what we had taken for a complex world.

Why had things happened thus? We could only assume that these other men dreamed for the same purpose that we (dreamers within a dream) often gave ourselves up to dreaming. They wanted for a time to mistake the possible for the actual. At that moment, as we deliberated under familiar stars (already subtly different now that we knew their true origin), the dreaming men were in an actual land far away, arranging our very deliberations so that their dreamed-of-selves could enjoy for a little while the illusion that they had acquired something actual.

And what was this unreal object of their dreams? The document we had signed explained everything. If we had not been distracted by their glass and steel that afternoon we would have recognised even then the absurdity of the day's events. The strangers wanted to possess the land.

Of course it was the wildest folly to suppose that the land, which was by definition indivisible, could be measured or parcelled out by a mere agreement among men. In any case, we had been fairly sure that the foreigners failed to see our land. From their awkwardness and unease as they stood on the soil, we judged that they did not recognise the support it provided or the respect it demanded. When they moved even a short distance across it, stepping aside from places that invited passage and treading on places that were plainly not to be intruded on, we knew that they would lose themselves before they found the real land.

Still, they had seen a land of some sort. That land was, in their own words, a place for farms and even, perhaps, a village. It would have been more in keeping with the scope of the dream surrounding them had they talked of founding an unheard-of city where they stood. But all their schemes were alike from our point of view. Villages or cities were all in the realm of possibility and could never have a real existence. The land would remain the land, designed for us yet, at the same time, providing the scenery for the dreams of a people who would never see either our land or any land they dreamed of.

What could we do, knowing what we then knew? We seemed as helpless as those characters we remembered from private dreams who tried to run with legs strangely nerveless. Yet if we had no choice but to complete the events of the dream, we could still admire the marvellous inventiveness of it. And we could wonder endlessly what sort of people they were in their far country, dreaming of a possible land they could never inhabit, dreaming further of a people such as ourselves with our one weakness, and then dreaming of acquiring from us the land which could never exist.

We decided, of course, to abide by the transaction that had been so neatly contrived. And although we knew we could never truly awake from a dream that did not belong to us, still we trusted that one day we might seem, to ourselves at least, to awake.

Some of us, remembering how after dreams of loss they had

awakened with real tears in their eyes, hoped that we would somehow wake to be convinced of the genuineness of the steel in our
hands and the wool round our shoulders. Others insisted that for
as long as we handled such things we could be no more than characters in the vast dream that had settled over us — the dream that
would never end until a race of men in a land unknown to us
learned how much of their history was a dream that must one day
end.

Pension Day

Archie Weller

All day the old black man sits, away from everyone else. He wears the same old black coat every day. Once it had silver buttons and a silk collar and was worn in the best society — with speeches, silver and champagne.

Now it has no buttons and sits upon the hunched back of the leader of the redback people. The people who hug the dark corners and scuttle hideously from rusted hiding place to rusted hiding place. Away from the pale blue eyes that are like the sun, burning everything away so all is stark and straight and true, and there are no cool secrets left.

No one wants to know any of the secrets, anyway.

He sits in the park, the old man, like one of the war cannons that guard the perimeter and stick their long green noses out threateningly at the cars that swish by, not even knowing they are there. Today's children leap and laugh over silent steel to further demolish yesterday's pride.

There is no room for yesterday's people.

He is a Wongi from out near Laverton, and he can hardly speak English. When he first came to Perth many years ago, he huddled in the back of the police Land Rover and moaned in terror as the ground swept away before him and trees and rocks and mountains and towns and his whole universe disappeared in a blur. Had it not been for the handcuffs around his great wrists, he would have leaped out the door and ended it all then.

The white men had torn him away from his red land's breast for a crime he could not understand.

A life for a life. That was how the law had worked since before everything. The law was the law.

Yet the Land Rover lurched out to the camp and the three

policemen had sprung upon him, taking him by surprise as he sat, singing softly, by his campfire.

The dogs had barked, the children screamed, his young girl-woman, already full with a child-spirit, cried, and he had fought with all his strength.

The old men had watched with silent, all-knowing eyes as he was overpowered and two policemen held him while the sergeant clipped on the handcuffs triumphantly.

He took one last look at his night-blackened land and the black shut faces in the red firelight. Rubbed red dust over his horny feet before being pushed gently into the hard, hot Land Rover. A tear slid out of his frightened, puzzled eyes before he closed his mind and hunched into himself.

He was only about eighteen then and although he wore a pair of scruffed grubby moleskins (and an army slouch hat he kept for special occasions) he had only seen white men six times in his whole life.

So that was that.

When he came out of jail seven years later, he was still strong and proud. No one had been able to touch him in there. He had worked all day and at night he had willed himself out over the walls back to his country.

Red dust and thin mulga bushes and glittering seas of broken glass from the miners' camps. Yellow-sided holes many metres deep. Black open mouths gulping in the hot air and holding white man secrets and dreams.

Just the place to hide a body snapped in two by powerful hands.

He could never go home again. He would have been killed out at the gabbling, dusty camp, if not by the relatives of his victim, certainly by the new husband to whom the elders would long ago have given his woman.

So he had no country. He had no home. He decided to learn more about the white man's ways that had so awed him.

But what could *he* do? A young man with big muscles, a quick temper, not much knowledge of English — and a black skin? After a few fights in a few country towns, he settled down, working for a produce store deep down south and doing some shearing on the side.

He loved that town. His boss was a good man who protected the angry giant from the taunts that sometimes whipped through the air. It was his boss, too, who found him a good half-caste girl from the nearby mission.

They called him "Jackie Snow" and the name stuck: Snowy

Jackson, the straight-shouldered, black colossus among his brown, sharper brethren. There was no love lost between the full-blood and the half-castes. They jeered at the way he worked so hard and refused to share his money around. But they were afraid of his physical and spiritual powers. For wasn't he one from the shimmering emptiness of the desert, a man who came with laws and secrets the brown staggering people had lost or only half-remembered?

He did not tell them that he had lost those, too.

At the produce store he was always cheerful and he kept out of trouble. His educated half-caste wife taught him a little more English, but he never learned how to read or write.

They got their citizenship rights and a little house, just off the track to the town's reserve. Every evening, especially in winter, his wife read the Bible and he stared into the searing heart of the fire with thoughtful, quiet eyes, and tried to remember before.

But this was his life now.

At shearing time they put him on the yard work. He loved to stride through the greasy, grey sea, shouting in his own language and clapping his huge hands so they sounded like the echoes from the thunder in the sky above. He would fling his head back and flare his nostrils like a wild black horse, and the sheep would pour into the darkened tin woolshed with a furious clicketty-clatter on the wooden grating floor. He felt like a king then, a leader of the people.

The other shearers respected Snowy Jackson for his size and strength. Who else could lift a bleating struggling sheep up above his head and still flash the huge white grin he wore (like his slouch hat for special occasions).

But he used to grow angry sometimes, and picking the stupid sheep up by their shaggy necks he would hurl them into the yard, sometimes killing them.

Then they put him on the shearing team alongside all the white men. He was at last one of them, and he took great pride in his new position. After he got over his first hesitation at the whining shears, he became quite skilled at peeling off the curly wool so it lay, wrinkled and ready, around his feet. Each bald, skinny, white sheep that he pushed down the chute was a new piece of juicy fruit for him to chew up, until his belly was full of white man respect.

Every night when he went home, he would try to explain his joyful day to his little wife, just as once, as a successful hunter, he had recounted his stories to his young woman way away up in the red, swirling Dreaming. But he could not tell the half-caste anything and, after a while, he would stop his broken, happy mumbling and stare into his fire. He would smile softly at things that had happened that day, while the stories came out of his eyes and nestled amongst the coals so he could see them again the next night.

Dreams, dreams.

One year, his young wife died giving birth to her fourth child.

All her relatives came down for the funeral. They sat around talking and remembering, and catching up on the news. Then they all got back in their old cars and trucks and left.

He just has the rain now, turning the sky grey and the world cold. He used to love the rain. He could stand for hours in the soft drizzle and let all the secrets from the heavy black clouds soak into his soul. But he hated the rain, that day, for it was there and his little quiet wife was dead.

He just has the rain — and his tears. All his secrets and the love the half-caste girl had taught him, dripping from his puzzled eyes.

When he was alone, he became roaring drunk and smashed up his house that he and the girl had been so proud of then went and started a brawl amongst the Nyoongah people.

He might have been getting older, but his huge angry fists put three of the men in hospital. He was put in jail.

The next morning the boss came and got him out. As he walked down the muddy street in the sultry sun, everyone stared at him, shocked or disgusted at the damage he had done. He followed his boss's footsteps like a huge dog.

So he lost even his pride and gave up.

He worked at the store for a few more years. Every time he thought of his woman he went out and got drunk. He lived in a little humpy in the bush, where no one could find him.

The Community Welfare took away his children one day whilst he was out hunting. All except the baby, whom Mrs Haynes the boss's wife was looking after.

He never saw his children again.

He did not shear any more, as he was getting too old. Beer fat lay over him, like bird dung greening a famous statue.

Just as he had been shearing beside the white men and had gained a type of pride, now he could drink beside white men with another sort of pride. They were all brothers now — getting drunk together.

He left to wander.

He has memories of countless tin-and-asbestos towns with cold white people and whining brown people. He has memories of

crowded hotels and fights, and falling asleep, drunk in the slimy
gutter or under a tree. He tried his hand at boxing on a
showground troupe. But soon he fell down, forever. His body was
left to moulder where it lay, while the laughter bored into him like
busy constant ants.

Boys drag lazily past, going nowhere. Cigarettes hang from their
thin lips, phallus-like, to prove they are men.

The old man would like to beg for a smoke, but the wine he has
drunk today thickens his tongue. All that comes out of his mouth is
a thin dribble of saliva that hangs off his scraggly grey beard.

Devils dance out of the boys' black eyes. They swagger, shout
and laugh loudly. The words and laughter are caught by the fingers
of the Moreton Bay fig trees. Later, they will be dropped to rot
away with the stinking, sticky fruit. But the boys don't know that.

Two peel away from the sly dark group and squat down beside
him.

"G'day, ya silly ole black bastard. Gettin' stuck into th' gabba at
this time a day? Hey, ya wanna tell us 'ow ya was the state boxer,
ole man?"

"Look at the metho e's got 'ere, Jimmy."

"Unna? 'E got no sense."

"Look out, Snowman! Featherfoot comin' your way, ya ole
murderer."

"Jesus, don't 'e stink, but?"

They laugh.

He smiles, uncomprehending, and nods his head. He knows
they are laughing at him. Once he would have leaped to his feet
and pulverised the whole group. That was a long time ago, though.
He cannot remember.

They steal $20 from him with quick black fingers. They always
do, every pension day. Where they had been afraid of his powers
before, now they laugh and steal from him. He has no people to
look after him. Only himself.

He sits under the tree, surrounded by empty wine bottles. He
staggers over to the tap and bumps into two young girls, who
shriek and squeal with mirth at him.

"The Snowman's drunk!" they shriek.

Once, they would have had to respect and admire him, as he
told them about the ways and laws of their tribe.

Once.

Now they have no tribe, and he has no ways.

He half-fills a bottle with water and pours the last of his methylated spirits into it. He sits and drinks, lonely.

He watches as the groups gather in circles. People wander from one group to another or stagger across to the hotel, waiting on the corner. The tribe goes walkabout. They stumble over to the brick toilets, as lonely as he is. They clutch onto the tight circles and pass the drink and words around.

Drink gets hot, words get hot in the cold wind.

The boys strip off their shirts and fight out their quarrels, while the women join them or egg them on.

The people play jackpot or two-up or poker. Some grow rich, some grow poor; almost everyone grows drunk.

Everyone goes home, to wherever home is.

He stays.

The sky gets darker and more oppressive. Then it rains.

First there are the whipcracks rattling across the sky, rolling and growling like puppies playing in the fleeciness of the clouds. The lightning leaps and bounces like children; here, there and gone. The rain starts off fat and slow but becomes faster and leaner.

He just sits there, finishing off his metho and wishing he had a smoke. He suddenly vomits up all his pension day money. All over his coat and face and trousers.

Time to sleep.

The old Aboriginal lies underneath his tree that cannot help him, for it, too, is old and sparse of gentle green leaf. The tree and the man get wet; neither cares, though.

So cold. That rain runs in streaks down his face and body. It washes the vomit off him, with soft hands. The pattering of the rain is interrupted only occasionally by short harsh coughs.

In the early hours of the morning, the cruising police van that, like the gardener, is searching for a few weeds to pull up by the roots and throw in the bin, finds him.

His rain has taken him away from his useless, used-up life. Perhaps back to the Dreamtime he understood.

No one knew the old Wongi was dead until the next pension day.

Heart is Where the Home is

Thea Astley

The morning the men came, policemen, someone from the government, to take the children away from the black camp up along the river, first there was the wordless terror of heart-jump, then the wailing, the women scattering and trying to run dragging their kids, the men sullen, powerless before this new white law they'd never heard of. Even the coppers felt lousy seeing all those yowling gins. They'd have liked the boongs to show a bit of fight, really, then they could have laid about feeling justified.

But no. The buggers just took it. Took it and took it.

The passivity finally stuck in their guts.

Bidgi Mumbler's daughter-in-law grabbed her little boy and fled through the scrub patch towards the river. Her skinny legs didn't seem to move fast enough across that world of the policeman's eye. She knew what was going to happen. It had happened just the week before at a camp near Tobaccotown. Her cousin Ruthie lost a kid that way.

"We'll bring her up real good," they'd told Ruthie. "Take her away to big school and teach her proper, eh? You like your kid to grow up proper and know about Jesus?"

Ruthie had been slammed into speechlessness.

Who were they?

She didn't understand. She knew only this was her little girl. There was all them words, too many of them, and then the hands.

There had been a fearful tug-o'-war; the mother clinging to the little girl, the little girl clutching her mother's dress, and the welfare officer with the police, all pulling, the kid howling, the other mothers egg-eyed, gripping their own kids, petrified, no men around, the men tricked out of camp.

Ruthie could only whimper, but then, as the policeman started to drag her child away to the buggy, she began a screeching that opened up the sky and pulled it down on her.

She bin chase that buggy two miles till one of the police he ride back on his horse an shout at her an when she wouldn take no notice she bin run run run an he gallop after her an hit her one two, cracka cracka, with his big whip right across the face so the pain get all muddle with the cryin and she run into the trees beside the track where he couldn follow. She kep goin after that buggy, fightin her way through scrub but it wasn't no good. They too fast. An then the train it come down the line from Tobaccotown an that was the last she see her little girl, two black legs an arms, strugglin as the big white man he lift her into carriage from the sidin.

"You'll have other baby," Nelly Mumbler comforted her. "You'll have other baby." But Ruthie kept sittin, wouldn do nothin. Jus sit an rock an cry an none of the other women they couldn help, their kids gone too and the men so angry they jus drank when they could get it an their rage burn like scrub fire.

Everything gone. Land. Hunting grounds. River. Fish. Gone. New god come. Old talk still about killings. The old ones remembering the killings.

"Now they take our kids," Jackie Mumbler said to his father, Bidgi. "We make kids for whites now. Can't they make their own kids, eh? Take everythin. Land. Kids. Don't give nothin, only take."

So Nelly had known the minute she saw them whites comin down the track. The other women got scared, fixed to the spot like they grow there, all shakin and whimperin. Stuck. "You'll be trouble," they warned. "You'll be trouble."

"Don't care," she said. "They not takin my kid."

She wormed her way into the thickest part of the rain forest, following the river, well away from the track up near the packers' road. Her baby held tightly against her chest, she stumbled through vine and over root, slashed by leaves and thorns, her eyes wide with fright, the baby crying in little gulps, nuzzling in at her straining body.

There'd bin other time year before she still hear talk about. All them livin up near Tinwon. The govmin said for them all to come long train. Big surprise, eh, an they all gone thinkin tobacco, tucker, blankets. An the men, they got all the men out early that day help work haulin trees up that loggin camp and the women they all excited waitin long that train, all the kids playin, and then them two policemen they come an start grabbin, grabbin all the kids, every kid, and the kids they screamin an the women they all cryin an tuggin an some, they hittin themselves with little sticks. One of

the police, he got real angry and start shovin the women back hard.
He push an push an then the train pulls out while they pushin an
they can see the kids clutchin at the windows and some big white
woman inside that train, she pull them back.

Nelly dodged through wait-a-while, stinging-bush, still hearing
the yells of the women back at the camp. Panting and gasping, she
came down to the water where a sand strip ran half way across the
river. If she crossed she would only leave tracks. There was no
time to scrape away telltale footprints. She crept back into the rain
forest and stood trembling, squeezing her baby tightly, trying to
smother his howls, but the baby wouldn't hush, so she huddled
under a bush and comforted him with her nipples for a while, his
round eyes staring up at her as he sucked while she regained her
breath.

Shouts wound through the forest like vines.

Wailing filtered through the canopy.

Suddenly a dog yelped, too close. She pulled herself to her feet,
the baby still suckling, and went staggering along the sandy track
by the riverbank, pushing her bony body hard, thrusting between
claws of branch and thorn, a half mile, a mile, until she knew that
soon the forest cover would finish and she'd be out on the fence-
line of George Laffey's place, the farm old Bidgi Mumbler had
come up and worked for. She'd been there, too, now and then, help
washin, cleanin, when young Missus Laffey makin all them pickles an things.

For a moment she stood uncertain by the fence, then on impulse she thrust her baby under the wire and wriggled through
after him, smelling the grass, smelling ants, dirt, all those living
things, and then she grabbed him up and stumbled through the
cow paddock down to the mango trees, down past the hen yard,
the vegetable garden, down over a lawn with flower-blaze and the
felty shadows of tulip trees, past Mister Laffey spading away, not
stopping when he looked up at her, startled, but gasping past him
round the side of the house to the back steps and the door that was
always open.

Mag Laffey came to the doorway and the two young women
watched each other in a racket of insect noise. A baby was crying
in a back room and a small girl kept tugging at her mother's skirts.

The missus was talkin, soft and fast. Nelly couldn't hear nothin
and then hands, they pull her in, gently, gently, but she too frightened hanging onto Charley, not lettin go till the white missus she
put them hands on her shoulders and press her down onto one

them kitchen chairs an hold her. "Still, now," her voice keep sayin. "Still."

So she keep real still and the pretty white missus say, "Tell me, Nelly. You tell me what's the matter."

It took a while, the telling, between the snuffles and the coaxing and the gulps and swallowed horrors.

"I see," Mag Laffey said at last. "I see," she said again, her lips tightening. "Oh I see."

She eased the baby from Nelly's arms and put him down on the floor with her own little girl, watching with a smile as the children stared then reached out to touch each other. She went over to the stove and filled the teapot and handed the black girl a cup, saying, "You drink that right up now and then we'll think of something. George will think of something."

It was half an hour before the policemen came.

They rode down the track from the railway line at an aggressive trot, coming to halt beside George as he rested on his spade.

Confronted with their questions he went blank. "Only the housegirl." And added, "And Mag and the kids."

The police kicked their horses on through his words and George slammed his spade hard into the turned soil and followed them down to where they were tethering their horses at the stair rails. He could see them boot-thumping up the steps. The house lay open as a palm.

Mag forestalled them, coming out onto the veranda. Her whole body was a challenge.

"Well," she asked, "what is it?"

The big men fidgeted. They'd had brushes with George Laffey's wife before, so deceptively young and pliable, a woman who never knew her place, always airing an idea of some sort. Not knowing George's delight with her, they felt sorry for that poor bastard of a husband who'd come rollicking home a few years back from a trip down south with a town girl with town notions.

"Government orders, missus," one said. "We have to pick up all the abo kids. All abo kids have got to be taken to special training schools. It's orders."

Mag Laffey inspected their over-earnest faces. She could't help smiling.

"Are you asking me, sergeant, if I have any half-caste children, or do I misunderstand?" She could hardly wait for their reaction.

The sergeant bit his lower lip and appeared to chew something before he could answer. "Not you personally, missus." *Disgusting,*

he thought, *disgusting piece of goods, making suggestions like that.*
"We just want to know if you have any round the place? Any belonging to that lot up at the camp?"

"Why would I do that?"

"I don't know, missus." He went stolid. "You've got a
housegirl, haven't you? Your husband said."

"Yes, I do."

"Well then, has she got any kids?"

"Not that I'm aware of," Mag Laffey lied vigorously. Her eyes
met theirs was amused candour.

"Maybe so. But we'd like to speak to her. You know it's breaking the law to conceal this."

"Certainly I know." George was standing behind the men at the
foot of the steps, his face nodding her on. "You're wasting your
time here, let me tell you. You're wasting mine as well. But that's
what government's for, isn't it?"

"I don't know what you mean, missus." His persistence moved
him forward a step. "Can we see that girl or not?"

Mag called over her shoulder down the hall but stood her
ground at the doorway, listening to Nelly shuffle, unwilling, along
the lino. When she came up to the men, she still had a dishcloth in
her hands that dripped suds onto the floor. Her eyes would not
meet those of the big men blocking the light.

"Where's your kid, Mary?" the sergeant asked, bullying and
jocular. "You hiding your kid?"

Nelly dropped her head and shook it dumbly.

"Cat got your tongue?" the other man said. "You not wantem
talk, eh? You lying?"

"She has no children," Mag Laffey interrupted coldly. "I told
you that. Perhaps the cat has your ears as well. If you shout and
nag and humiliate her, you'll never get an answer. Can't you understand something as basic as that? You're frightening her."

She looked past the two of them at her husband who was smiling his support.

"Listen, lady," the sergeant said, his face congested with the
suppressed need to punch this cheeky sheilah right down her own
hallway, "that's not what they tell me at the camp."

"What's not what they tell you?"

"She's got a kid all right. She's hiding it some place."

George's eyes, she saw, were strained with affection and concern. *Come up,* her own eyes begged him. *Come up.* "Sergeant,"
she said, "I have known Nelly since she was a young girl. She's
helped out here for the last four years. Do you think I wouldn't

know if she had a child? Do you? But you're free to search the house, if you want, and the grounds. You're thirsting for it, aren't you, warrant or not?"

The men shoved roughly past her at that, flattening Nelly Mumbler against the wall, and creaked down the hallway, into bedrooms and parlor and out into the kitchen. Cupboard doors crashed open. There was a banging of washhouse door.

George came up the steps and took his wife's arm, steering her and Nelly to the back of the house and putting them behind him as he watched the police come in from the yard.

"Satisfied?"

"No, we're not, mate," the sergeant replied nastily. "Not one bloody bit."

Their powerful bodies crowded the kitchen out. They watched contemptuously as Nelly crept back to the sink, her body tensed with fright.

"We don't believe you, missus," the sergeant said. "Not you or your hubby. There'll be real trouble for both of you when we catch you out."

Mag held herself braced against infant squawls that might expose them at any minute. She made herself busy stoking the stove.

"Righto," George said, pressing her arm and looking sharp and hard at the other men. "You've had your look. Now would you mind leaving. We've all got work to get on with."

The sergeant was sulky. He scraped his boots about and kept glancing around the kitchen and out the door into the back garden. The Laffeys' small girl was getting under his feet and pulling at his trouser legs, driving him crazy.

"All right," he agreed reluctantly. "All right." He gave one last stare at Nelly's back. "Fuckin' boongs," he said, deliberately trying to offend that stuck-up Mrs Laffey. "More trouble than they're worth. And that's bloody nothing."

The two women remained rooted in the kitchen while George went back up the track to his spadework. The sound of the horses died away.

At the sink Nelly kept washing and washing, her eyes never leaving the suds, the dishmop, the plate she endlessly scoured. Even after the thud of hoof faded beyond the ridge, even after that. And even after Mag Laffey took a cloth and began wiping the dishes and stacking them in the cupboard, even after that.

Mag saw her husband come round the side of the house, toss his hat on an outside peg and sit on the top step to ease his earth-stuck clobbers of boots off. Nelly's stiffly curved back asked question

upon question. Her long brown fingers asked. Her turned-away
face asked. When her baby toddled back into the kitchen, taken
down from the bedroom ceiling manhole where George had hidden him with a lolly to suck, Nelly stayed glued to that sink washing that one plate.

"Come on, Nelly," Mag said softly. "What's the matter? We've
beaten them, haven't we?"

George had picked up the small black boy and his daughter and
was bouncing a child on each knee, waggling his head lovingly between them both while small hands pawed his face.

Infinitely slowly, Nelly turned from the sink, her fingers dripping soap and water. She looked at George Laffey cuddling a white
baby and a black but she couldn't smile. "Come nex time," she
said, hopeless. "Come nex time."

George and his wife looked at her with terrible pity. They knew
this as well. They knew.

"And we'll do the same next time," Mag Laffey stated. "You
don't have to worry."

Then George Laffey said, "You come live here, Nelly. You come
all time, eh?" His wife nodded at each word. Nodded and smiled
and cried a bit. "You and Charley, eh?"

Nelly opened her mouth and wailed. *What is it?* they kept asking. *What's the matter? Wouldn't you like that?* They told her she
could have the old store shed down by the river. They'd put a stove
in and make it proper. Nelly kept crying, her dark eyes an unend-
ing fountain, and at last George became exasperated.

"You've got no choice, Nelly," he said, dropping the baby pid-
gin he had never liked anyway. "You've got no choice. If you come
here we can keep an eye on Charley. If you don't, the government
men will take him away. You don't want that, do you? Why don't
you want to come?"

"Don't want to leave my family," she sobbed. "Don't want."

"God love us," George cried from the depths of his non-
understanding, "God love us, they're only a mile up the river." He
could feel his wife's fingers warning on his arm. "You can see
them whenever you want."

"It's not same," Nelly insisted and sobbed. "Not same."

George thought he understood. He said, "You want Jackie,
then. You want your husband to come along too, work in the garden maybe? Is that it?"

He put the baby into her arms and the two of them rocked som-
berly before him. He still hadn't understood.

The old men old women uncles aunts cousins brothers sisters

tin humpies bottles dogs dirty blankets tobacco handouts fights
river trees all the tribe's remnants and wretchedness, destruction
and misery.

Her second skin now.

"Not same," she whispered. And she cried them centuries of
tribal dream in those two words. "Not same."

What We Say

Helen Garner

I was kneeling at the open door, with the cloth in my right hand and the glass shelf balanced on the palm of my left. She came past at a fast clip, wearing my black shoes and pretending I wasn't there. I spoke sharply to her, from my supplicant's posture.

"Death to mother. Death," she replied, and clapped the gate to behind her.

It had once been a kind of family joke, but I lost the knack of the shelf for a moment and though it didn't break there was quite a bit of blood. After I had cleaned up and put the apron in a bucket to soak, I went to the phone and began to make arrangements.

In Sydney my friend, the old-fashioned sort of friend who works on your visit and wants you to be happy, gave me two tickets to the morning dress rehearsal of *Rigoletto*. I went with Natalie. She knew how to get there and which door to go in. "At your age, you've never been inside the Opera House?" Great things and small forged through the blinding water. We hurried, we ran.

At the first interval we went outside. A man I knew said, "I like your shirt. What would you call that colour — hyacinth?" At the second interval we stayed in our seats so we could keep up our conversation which is no more I suppose than exalted gossip but which seems, because of her oblique perceptions, a most delicate, hilarious and ephemeral tissue of mind.

At lunchtime we dashed, puffy-eyed and red-cheeked, into the kitchen of my thoughtful friend. He was standing at the stove, looking up at us over his shoulder and smiling: he likes to teach me things, he likes to see me learning.

"How was it?"

"Fabulous! We cried *buckets*!"

Another man was leaning against the window frame with his

arms crossed and his hair standing on end. His skin was pale, as if he had crept out from some burrow where he had lain for a long time in a cramped and twisted position.

"You cried?" he said. "You mean you actually shed tears?"

Look out, I thought; one of these. I was still having to blow my nose, and was ready to ride rough-shod. My friend put the spaghetti on the table and we all sat down.

"I'm starving," said Natalie.

"What a plot," I raved. "So tight you couldn't stick a pin in it."

"What was your worst moment?" said Natalie.

"Oh, when he bends over the sack to gloat, and then from off-stage comes the Duke's voice, singing his song. The way he freezes, in that bent-over posture, over the sack."

The sack, in a sack. I had a best friend once, my intellectual companion of ten years, on paper from land to land and then in person: she was the one who first told me the story of *Rigoletto* and I will never forget the way her voice sank to a thread of horror: "and the murderer gives him his daughter's body on the riverbank, in *a sack*." A river flows: that is its nature. Its sluggish water can work any discarded object loose from the bank and carry it further, lump it lengthwise, nudge it and roll it and shift it, bear it away and along and out of sight.

"Yes, that was bad all right," said Natalie, "but mine was when he realised that his daughter was in the bedchamber with Duke."

We picked up our forks and began to eat. The back door opened on to a narrow concrete yard, but light was bouncing down the grey walls and the air was warm, and as I ate I thought, Why don't I live here? In the sun?

"Also," I said, "I *love* what it's about. About the impossibility of shielding your children from the evil of the world."

There was a pause.

"Well, yes, it is about that," said my tactful friend, "but it's also about the greatest fear men have. Which is the fear of losing their daughters. Of losing them to younger men. Into the world of sex."

We sat at the table quietly eating. Words which people use and pretend to understand floated in silence and bumped among our heads: virgin; treasure; perfect; clean; my darling; anima; soul.

Natalie spoke in her light, courteous voice. "If that's what it's about," she said, "what do you think the women in the audience were responding to?" — for in our bags were two sodden handkerchiefs.

The salad went round.

"I don't know," said my friend. "You tell me."

We said nothing. We looked into our plates.

"That fear men have," said my friend. "Literature and art are full of it."

My skin gave a mutinous prickle. *Your* literature.

"*Do* women have a fundamental fear?" said my friend.

Natalie and I glanced at each other and back to the tabletop.

"A fear of violation, maybe?" he said. He got up and filled the kettle. The silence was not a silence but a quietness of thinking. I knew what Natalie was thinking. She was wishing the conversation had not taken this particular turn. I was wishing the same thing. Stumped, struck dumb; failed again, failed to think and talk in that pattern they use. I had nothing to say. Nothing came to my mind that had any bearing on the matter.

Should I say "But violation is our destiny?" Or should I say *"Nothing can be sole or whole/That has not been rent"*? But before I could open my mouth, a worst moment came to me: the letter arrives from my best friend on the road in a far country: "He was wearing mirror sunglasses which he did not take off, I tried to plead but I could not speak his language, he tore out handfuls of my hair, he kicked me and pushed me out of the car, I crawled to the river, I could smell the water, it was dirty but I washed myself, a farm girl found me, her family is looking after me, I think I will be all right, please answer, above all don't tell my father, love." I got down on my elbows in the yard and put my face into the dirt, I went. I groaned. That night I went as usual to the lesson. *All I can do is try to make something perfect for you, for your poor body, with my clumsy and ignorant one:* I breathed and moved as the teacher showed us, and she came past me in the class and touched me on the head and said, "This must mean a lot to you — you are doing it so beautifully."

"Violation," said Natalie, as if to gain time.

"It would be necessary," I said, " to examine all of women's writing, to see if the fear of violation is the major theme of it."

"Some feminist theoretician somewhere has probably already done it," said the stranger who had been surprised that *Rigoletto* could draw tears.

"Barbara Baynton, for instance," said my friend. "Have you read that story of hers called 'The Chosen Vessel'? The woman knows the man is outside waiting for dark. She puts the brooch on the table. It's the only valuable thing she owns. She puts it there as an offering — to appease him. She wants to buy him off."

The brooch. The mirror sunglasses. The feeble lock. The

weakened wall that gives. What stops these conversations is shame, and grief.

"We don't have a tradition in the way you blokes do," I said.

Everybody laughed, with relief.

"There must be a line of women's writing," said Natalie, "running from the beginning till now."

"It's a shadow tradition," I said. "It's there, but nobody knows what it is."

"We've been trained in *your* tradition," said Natalie. "We're honorary men."

She was not looking at me, nor I at her.

The coffee was ready, and we drank it. Natalie went to pick up her children from school. My friend put in the plug and began to wash the dishes. The stranger tilted his chair back against the wall, and I leaned on the bench.

"What happened to your hand?" he said.

"I cut it on the glass shelf yesterday," I said, "when I was defrosting the fridge."

"There's a packet of bandaids in the fruit bowl," said my friend from the sink.

I stripped off the old plaster and took a fresh one from the dish. But before I could yank its little ripcord and pull it out of its wrapper, the stranger got up from his chair, walked all the way round the table and across the room, and stopped in front of me. He took the bandaid and said.

"Do you want me to put it on for you?"

I drew a breath to say *what we say*: "Oh, it's all right, thanks — I can do it myself."

But instead, I don't know why, I let out my independent breath, and took another. I gave him my hand.

"Do you like dressing wounds?" I said, in a smart tone to cover my surprise.

He did not answer this, but spread out my palm and had a good look at the cut. It was deep and precise, like a freshly dug trench, bloody still at the bottom but with nasty white soggy edges where the plaster had prevented the skin from drying."

"You've made a mess of yourself, haven't you," he said.

"Oh, it's nothing much," I said airily. "It only hurt while it was actually happening."

He was not listening. He was concentrating on the thing. His fingers were pale, square and clean. He peeled off the two protective flaps and laid the sticky bandage across the cut. He pressed

one side of it, and then the other, against my skin, smoothed them
flat with his thumbs, and let go.

What Do You Know About Friends?

Lily Brett

In Renia Bensky's world, people were pigs. "Don't be a greedy pig," she would say when Lola reached for another potato. Renia's neighbour, Mrs Spratt, was "a dirty pig". Her favourite grandchild was "a little piggy", her cousin Adek "a big pig".

Josl chauffeured his two daughters around every Saturday morning. To the city, to the dressmaker, to the hairdresser. On the way home he liked to stop and buy himself a double chocolate gelato. "What a pig!" Renia said when they arrived home.

When Renia talked about Josl's father, who had died in the ghetto, she said, "such a pig". Sometimes she would say a bit more, although the past, their lives before they came to Australia, was definitely out of bounds, their own private territory. Sometimes a small sliver of detail would slip out. "Such a pig he was. In the ghetto he cried because he was so hungry. Children were dead in the streets and he was crying because he was hungry."

Until she was twenty Lola had never seen a pig. When she saw her first pigs, she was fascinated by how unself-conscious they were. They snorted their way through their food, big and pink and bulky. They weren't holding their stomachs flat or sucking in their cheeks. They weren't expecting judgments. They seemed quite happy to be pigs.

If people weren't pigs, then they were idiots. Even when she was quite small Lola knew that Mrs Bensky was an authority on pigs and idiots. "Such an idiot!" Mrs Bensky would shout. "Such an idiot is that Mrs Berman. An idiot, an i-d-i-o-t. She thinks she speaks a perfect English. In the butcher I heard her say 'Cut me in half please'. Such a perfect English!"

Mrs Berman had been Mrs Bensky's friend. Until Mrs Berman left Mr Berman and Mrs Bensky could no longer be friends with

her, the two women had baked cakes in Mrs Bensky's kitchen on
Saturday afternoons. Mrs Berman made her honeycake and
rugelachs and Mrs Bensky baked her lakech. Working in the
kitchen together, they looked like good friends.

"Friends," Mrs Bensky said to Lola. "What do you know about
friends? Friends, pheh! You can trust only your family."

And what did Lola know? She had watched the Benskys and
their friends, their "company", as they called themselves. The
company went to the pictures together every Saturday night and
then to supper afterwards. On Sunday evenings they played cards.
If there was a good show on, sometimes they went out during the
week. They celebrated each other's birthdays, anniversaries, bar-
mitzvahs, engagements and weddings, and were present at the
operations, illnesses and funerals.

Lola thought that the company were family. She called them
Uncle and Aunty and believed that they would always care about
her. What did Lola know?

Mrs Bensky hated Mrs Ganz. She was irritated by the way that
Mrs Ganz kept inviting her to fashion parades, card afternoons
and charity luncheons. Couldn't Mrs Ganz see that she was very
busy? Every day Mrs Bensky had to wash six sheets, four pillow
cases, three eiderdown covers and seven towels. She had to scrub
and polish the floors, and vacuum the carpets. And on top of this
she had to cook and to wash up. She was not the kind of woman
who had time to go to a fashion parade. Why couldn't Mrs Ganz
understand this?

Mrs Bensky thought that Mrs Ganz had always been spoilt. In
the ghetto Mrs Ganz's father had been a Jewish "policeman".
Their family had rarely been hungry. In 1943 they were smuggled
out of the ghetto and spent the rest of the war hiding in a cellar.
Mrs Bensky often chatted to Mrs Pekelman on the phone. She felt
that Genia Pekelman had her problems, but above all she had a
good heart. Mrs Bensky advised Mrs Pekelman about which
clothes suited her best, how to cook a good gulah, where to buy the
freshest Murray Perch. She also shared some beauty tips with her,
including the fact that if you rinsed your hair with a bit of beer
after washing it the waves stayed in much longer. Renia Bensky
and Genia Pekelman, both non-drinkers, often trailed an alcoholic
air around with them.

Lola learnt about friendship from listening to the two women
on the phone. Last week Mrs Bensky had said in an affectionate
tone, "Genia darling, I bumped into Yetta Kauffman in the city.

Such an ugly face that woman has got. You think you are ugly, Genia darling? Next to Yetta Kauffman you are a big beauty."

This may have seemed harsh to an outsider, but Lola knew that it was affectionate and well-intentioned. In this company one of the friendliest and most enthusiastic responses to anything was: "What, what, you are crazy or something?"

Things cooled off between Renia Bensky and Genia Pekelman when Genia took up dancing lessons. She was forty-seven. At thirteen, Genia had been a promising young dancer. She had won a ballet scholarship to study in Paris. She was counting the days to her fourteenth birthday, waiting to leave for Paris, when the Germans arrived in Warsaw.

Now, Mrs Pekelman was learning Indian dance. She went to dancing classes twice a week. She was taught by Madame Sanrit. Mrs Pekelman wore leotards under her sari and practised at home every afternoon. She loved to dance and danced at every opportunity.

If a group of women were having a charity luncheon, Mrs Pekelman asked if she could dance at the lunch. When Mrs Pekelman learnt that Mrs Small was taking a group of voluntary Jewish Welfare kitchen helpers on a tour of the Victorian National Gallery, she begged her to bring the group to her home, where she would dance for them.

Some of the company were embarrassed by Genia Pekelman and her dancing. Mrs Small was furious. She said to Mrs Bensky, "Look at her! She is so big and fat and ugly, and she wants to dance for everybody. When she moves her big tuches around the room it is shocking."

"She can't help it," Mrs Bensky replied. "She doesn't know how she looks. She is not so intelligent."

As well as pigs and idiots, Mrs Bensky knew about intelligence. She dismissed most people as "not intelligent". One year Mrs Small, who spoke Russian, Polish, Yiddish, French and English, interpreted for the members of the Moscow Circus when they came to Melbourne. Mrs Bensky was clenched with anger for the entire season.

"She thinks she is such a big intelligence," Mrs Bensky railed. "What does she read, this big intelligence, this Mrs Intelligentsia? Maybe a *Women's Weekly* under the hair dryer once a week? I remember her mother delivered our milk in Lodz. Two big cans across her shoulders, she walked from house to house in bare feet.

And both daughters finished school at twelve. Now, suddenly, Ada Small is a genius. She tells everybody that she matriculated in Poland. Soon she will say she was almost a doctor. Everybody who came here after the war was almost a doctor. Mrs Ada Intelligentsia thinks she is important because she is translating for an acrobat."

Mrs Bensky did know about intelligence. She was the only one of the group who had been at university. She still kept her student card in her handbag. In 1972, Mrs Bensky enrolled at Melbourne University. She did one semester of "Physics In The Firing Line". Lola had suggested that Mrs Bensky study Russian or German, languages she was fluent in. Lola thought that this would have been a gentler introduction to university life, but Mrs Bensky insisted on "Physics In The Firing Line". Science had been Mrs Bensky's great love in Lodz. When she spoke about Copernicus and the planets, Mrs Bensky was at her most tender. It was science that Mrs Bensky wanted to go back to.

In Lodz, Mrs Bensky came top of her class every year. She was every teacher's favourite student. Her curiosity was as immense as her ambition. Other people in the neighbourhood laughed at her father for wasting his money on a daughter. "You'll make her too clever for a husband," one neighbour repeated regularly.

At the University of Melbourne, Renia Bensky was so tense she could hardly hear the lecturer. His words flew around the auditorium. Mrs Bensky had to grab each word and put it in its correct place. Sometimes she lost a few words and the sentence didn't make sense. She sat in a sweat through most of the professor's speeches. Later she learnt that this heat was menopausal.

Renia worked feverishly on her first assignment, "Molecules and The Future". At last it was finished. Fifteen pages on bright yellow notepaper. Lina corrected the English, and they hired a professional typist to type the essay.

Mrs Bensky got a "C" for "Molecules and The Future". She wept and wept.

Mr Bensky tried to comfort her. "This assignment, Renia darling, is out of this world. Something special. There is no question about it. It is perfect, believe me." But Mrs Bensky went on weeping.

Mrs Small gave Mrs Bensky her sympathy and support. "I think it is anti-Semitism," she said. "For what other reason would he give such a beautiful piece of work only a 'C'? He is an anti-Semite, for sure."

Most of the company called around to offer their condolences.

They knew it wasn't Mrs Bensky's fault. A "C" for Renia Bensky, whoever heard of such a thing? Everybody knew she was too intelligent. But Mrs Bensky was inconsolable.

She rang her tutor, a young, pale-faced boy of twenty-five, to ask if maybe it was her English that wasn't perfect. Maybe that was why she had got a "C".

"Excuse me, tutor," she began. "I want to know if you have made a mistake with my essay. I think the English was very good. My young daughter who is a lawyer with an honours degree did correct my writing, so it couldn't be my bad English. And my English is very good. She didn't find many mistakes at all. I understand you did give young John Matheson an 'A'. Well, he told me himself that I did understand the molecules much better than him. In fact, I explained some of the facts to him. So, he got an 'A' and I got a 'C'? Maybe I shouldn't have hired a typist? Maybe you think I have got money to burn or to throw away that I hired a typist? My husband worked very hard for fifteen years in factories so I could afford a typist. Maybe you were prejudiced against my typing? Did Mr Matheson type his essay? I'm sure not. As a matter of fact I know his mother, Mrs Matheson. She told me he was talking about how much I know about molecules. You know, I, myself, don't think you are an anti-Semite. My friend Mrs Small does, but she is not intelligent. She doesn't see we are in a modern world and this is not Poland.

"So, do you have an answer, Mr Tutor? Do you know how many years I dreamed of going to university? Do you know this? I dreamed of studying at university when I was a small girl. And I kept dreaming. Even in Auschwitz, when I didn't dream any more, sometimes when I was standing in roll-call for six hours, barefoot in the snow, I would try to think about what subjects I could study one day."

Now Mrs Bensky was crying. "Do you have an answer, Mr Tutor? When I came to Australia my sister-in-law said to me that all women work in Australia. She said to me I should have considered if I could afford to have a baby before I got pregnant. So I took my baby every day to Mrs Polonsky, a woman in Carlton. I had never been apart from my baby. Sometimes I vomited on the tram on the way to the factory. I felt so frightened. Josl told me that Mrs Polonsky was a good woman and nothing would happen to little Lola, but I couldn't stop being frightened. When I finished work I picked Lola up. Mrs Polonsky lived just next to the university, and when I stopped vomiting, I made myself a promise that one day I would go there. Did you hear me, Mr Tutor?"

Mrs Bensky left "Physics In The Firing Line" six weeks after she had begun. She left the University of Melbourne a wiser person. The rest of the company acknowledged this and accorded her new respect. "She studied at Melbourne University", they now said when they spoke of her.

Wedding Cake

Susan Hampton

It is the year dot. A young woman and a slightly older man are living together. The four parents who come to visit are whispering and wearing special sunglasses through which they see a potential bride and a potential groom.

The day of the wedding arrives almost before the bride has time to arrange a gown. She has never worn a gown before. The whole notion of the word "gown" is somehow legendary.

Her father says at breakfast, "Well, I hope this Peter's all right in his motel?"

"He'll be OK," said the woman.

"He'll just be nervous." Her father shook salt into his porridge.

Her mother reached for the milk. "Your father fainted at our wedding," she said, "and at Uncle Jack's."

"Oh please, Dad."

"I can only try," he smiled pleasantly. "Well, today's the big day." He laid down his spoon. "You'll be a princess."

"I have to go to the station, Dad, so I'll need to borrow the car. The gown should be there by now."

He sat back and motioned her mother to pick up the keys from a doily on the china cabinet.

The young woman felt uncomfortable. She'd been put in the wrong movie. Wasn't she an amazon? Couldn't she read and think and swim a lap in thirty-eight seconds?

The stationmaster was apologetic with crooked teeth. The box wasn't there. She could use his phone to ring Sydney. The man at the hire shop was apologetic too. "You know how the dress you chose wasn't really a wedding gown?" he said. "Well, it was hired out to a woman who went to the Black and White Ball, and she was in a car accident on the way home, so there's blood on the dress. I'm sorry about this. Can I send you another one of the size tens?"

"No," she said, "don't worry now. Thanks anyway."

Later that day a relative came in with a dress that more or less fitted. Now it was time for the hairdresser. When the woman walked home the wind whistled through the cylinders on her head, and in the bathroom mirror she didn't recognise herself. She dunked her head under the tap and washed out the spray. Then she cut her hair short, down to an inch all over. Now it was time to get dressed.

"You look beautiful," her aunties exchanged looks, "your hair really suits you like that!" They were hovering over the tupperware and the vertical grill that had been put on her bed. The phone rang. It was the best man, calling from the motel. "Peter's been sick," he said, "he's a bit white but OK. He's all right now."

The woman's younger sisters stood in a row. Their dresses were yellow. They had pink flowers pinned on them. Their shoes were all the same. A car horn sounded outside, there was a brief gliding motion and then they were inside the giant wooden doors. She felt her father beginning to sink. "I am not a princess," she whispered, "straighten your legs." "I am an amazon," she said to herself, and she hitched her father onto her hip and dragged him down the aisle.

He regained his legs and stood stiffly. The bride saw this from the corner of her eye, in the area past the blue make-up. She'd worried about putting blue make-up on green eyes; but when she tried the green it made her look like someone from *Twilight of the Zombies*.

She smiled cheerily at the minister who was worried about her father. At her side her husband was like a ghost or a shop dummy, his hair neat, his suit pressed, a carnation he'd grown himself in his lapel. Everything was going according to plan, except there was no action. What happens next, she thought. "Pardon?" said the minister, tilting forward with his shiny shoes and the King James Bible.

"Let's start," she said, nodding.

When the minister opened his mouth it went white and huge and the whiteness was a wedding cake expanding till it filled his mouth and then the air around him. He had been swallowed in the cake.

Someone handed her a large silver knife with a ribbon tied on the handle. The same person picked up her husband's hand and clamped it on her own. Lights flashed. Outside it had started to

rain. The guests were silent. "You may cut the cake," said someone slightly to her left. "Just a minute," she said to her husband.
Could she risk slicing the minister in half? Had he dug his way
through, eating a currant here and a candied ginger there and
come out drunk from underneath?

She leaned over and peered at the cake. There was a mousehole
in the side. Good. Now she noticed a small plastic bride and groom
on the top layer. There was a piece of glass in the corner of the
bride's eye — a tear of happiness, which matched the glass dia-
monds in her veil. You couldn't see the expression on her face.

The boy doll had a manly chin and a red bow tie. His hair was
just like her husband's.

The woman felt strange. The girl doll was some sort of siren
under that veil — why hide it if it's not forbidden, a secret? The
siren called her, and called and called, and the bride felt herself
being sucked away serenely, like an acrobat, into the plastic
mouth.

Notes to the Introduction

1. Nadine Gordimer, "The Flash of Fireflies", in *Short Story Theories,* ed. Charles E. May (Athens, Ohio: Ohio University Press, 1976), 179.
2. Ibid., 178.
3. Elizabeth Bowen, "The Faber Book of Modern Short Stories", in May, *Short Story Theories,* 152-54.
4. Beatrice Davis, ed., *Short Stories of Australia: The Moderns* (Sydney: Angus & Robertson, 1947), viii.
5. Frank Moorhouse, ed., *The State of the Art* (Ringwood: Penguin Books, 1983), 1.
6. A selection of Clarke's stories has recently been reprinted in Michael Wilding, ed., *Marcus Clarke: Stories* (Sydney: Hale & Iremonger, 1983).
7. For example, see Douglas Jarvis, "The Development of Egalitarian Poetics in the *Bulletin,* 1880–1890", *Australian Literary Studies* 10 (May 1981): 22-34; Richard White, *Inventing Australia* (Sydney: George Allen & Unwin, 1981), chap. 6.
8. See, for example, statements by authors in "The Contemporary Australian Short Story – Special Issue", *Australian Literary Studies* 10 (October 1981).
9. Stephen Torre, "The Australian Short Story 1940 to 1980: A Critical Survey and Bibliography", 2 vols., University of Queensland, 1982.
10. Ibid., 6.
11. Frank O'Connor, *The Lonely Voice: A Study of the Short Story,* cited in Elizabeth Webby, "Australian Short Fiction from *While the Billy Boils* to *The Everlasting Secret Family*", *Australian Literary Studies* 10 (October 1981): 151.
12. Webby, ibid., 148.
13. Chris Wallace Crabbe, "Lawson's *Joe Wilson*: A Skeleton Novel", *Australian Literary Studies* 1 (June 1964): 147; rptd. in Wallace Crabbe, ed., *The Australian Nationalists* (Melbourne: Oxford University Press, 1971).
14. See John Barnes, "Lawson and the Short Story in Australia", *Westerly,* no. 2 (1968): 442.
15. For example, in Brian Matthews, *The Receding Wave* (Melbourne: Oxford University Press, 1972).

16. Nettie Palmer, *Fourteen Years* (Melbourne: Meanjin Press, 1948), 22-23.

17. For example, Kay Iseman, "Barbara Baynton: Woman as the Chosen Vessel", *Australian Literary Studies* 11 (May 1983): 25-37.

18. Torre, 25.

19. Ibid.

20. Vance Palmer, ed., *Coast to Coast* (Sydney: Angus & Robertson, 1945), vii-ix.

21. For Chekhov's influence see Barnes, "Lawson and the Short Story", 444.

22. Peter Cowan in "The Contemporary Australian Short Story – Special Issue", *Australian Literary Studies* 10 (October 1981): 197.

23. Marjorie Barnard, ibid., 188.

24. Judah Waten, ibid., 234.

25. Webby, "Australian Short Fiction", 155.

26. Ibid.

27. Michael Wilding, "A Survey", in "New Writing in Australia – Special Issue", *Australian Literary Studies* 8 (October 1977): 115-26. Wilding's comments are adapted and extended in Wilding, ed., *The Tabloid Short Story Pocket Book* (Sydney: Wild & Woolley, 1978), 295-316.

28. For example, see comments by editors Clem Christesen and Peter Cowan in "The Contemporary Australian Short Story"; and also comments by Wilding in "A Survey".

29. For example, see Webby, "Australian Short Fiction".

30. Douglas Steward, ed., *Short Stories of Australia: The Lawson Tradition* (Sydney: Angus & Robertson, 1967), xiv.

31. Hal Porter, "Beyond Whipped Cream and Blood", *Bulletin*, 28 April 1962, 166.

32. Hal Porter, ed., *It Could Be You* (Adelaide: Rigby, 1972), 1-2.

33. For example, see Anthony Burgess, *Ninety-Nine Novels: A Personal Choice* (London: Allison & Busby, 1984), reviewed by J.D. Pringle, *Sydney Morning Herald*, 9 January 1984, p. 43. Porter is not commented on in Walter Allen, *The Short Story in English* (Oxford: Clarendon, 1981).

34. Wilding, "A Survey", 125.

35. Richard Kostelanetz, "Notes on the American Short Story Today", in May, *Short Story Theories*, 220-21.

36. Randall Jarrall, "Stories", in May, *Short Story Theories*, 35.

37. Murray Bail, in "New Writing in Australia – Special Issue", *Australian Literary Studies* 8 (October 1977): 188.

38. Frank Moorhouse, *The State of the Art*, 5.

Textual Note

Efforts have been made to ensure that the texts are reliable without striving for a definitiveness which would be inappropriate for the occasion. Where later texts are known to be unreliable, as in the case of Henry Handel Richardson, an earlier text, which the author would have proofread, has been drawn upon. Book publication has been preferred to magazine publication. The following is a list, in order of appearance, of the sources against which the anthologized texts have been checked. Where necessary other texts have been referred to:

Henry Lawson, "The Union Buries Its Dead", *The Country I Came From* (Edinburgh: Blackwood, 1901); "Water Them Geraniums", *Joe Wilson's Mates* (Sydney: Angus & Robertson, 1904); both Lawson texts have also been checked against *Henry Lawson: Short Stories & Sketches 1888-1922*, ed. Colin Roderick (Sydney: Angus & Robertson, 1922); Henry Handel Richardson, "And Women Must Weep", *The End of a Childhood and Other Stories* (London: Heinemann, 1934); Katharine Susannah Prichard, "Happiness", *A Kiss on the Lips* (London: Cape, 1932); Christina Stead, "The Triskelion", *The Salzburg Tales* (London: Peter Davies, 1934); Gavin Casey, "Short-Shift Saturday", *It's Harder for Girls* (Sydney: Angus & Robertson, 1942); Vance Palmer, "Josie", *Let the Birds Fly* (Sydney: Angus & Robertson, 1955); Alan Marshall, "Trees Can Speak", *How's Andy Going?* (Melbourne: Cheshire, 1956); Marjorie Barnard, "The Persimmon Tree", *The Persimmon Tree and Other Stories* (Sydney: Clarendon Press, n.d.); Judah Waten, "Mother", *Alien Son* (Sydney: Angus & Robertson, 1952); John Morrison, "The Incense Burner", *North Wind* (Ringwood, Vic.: Penguin, 1982); Peter Cowan, "Shadow", *The Unploughed Land* (Sydney: Angus & Robertson, 1958); Hal Porter, "A Double Because It's Snowing" and "At Aunt Sophia's", *Selected Stories*, ed. Leonie

Kramer (Sydney: Angus & Robertson, 1958); Patrick White, "Down at the Dump", *The Burnt Ones* (London: Eyre & Spottiswoode, 1964); Thelma Forshaw, "The Mateship Syndrome", *An Affair of Clowns* (Sydney: Angus & Robertson, 1967); Dal Stivens, "The Unicorn", *The Unicorn & Other Tales* (Sydney: Wild & Woolley, 1976); Peter Carey, "Crabs", *The Fat Man in History* (St Lucia: University of Queensland Press, 1974); Thea Astley, "Seeing Mrs Landers", *Festival & Other Stories*, ed. Brian Buckley and Jim Hamilton (Melbourne: Wren Publishing Company, 1974); Murray Bail, "Ore", *Contemporary Portraits*, (St Lucia: University of Queensland Press, 1975); Frank Moorhouse, "The Airport, The Pizzeria, The Motel, The Rented Car and The Mysteries of Life", *Tales of Mystery and Romance* (Sydney: Angus & Robertson, 1977); T.A.G. Hungerford, "Green Grow the Rushes", *Wong Chu and the Queen's Letter Box* (Fremantle: Fremantle Arts Centre Press, 1977); Morris Lurie, "Running Nicely", *Running Nicely & Other Stories* (Melbourne: Nelson, 1979); Elizabeth Jolley, "Winter Nelis", *The Travelling Entertainer* (Fremantle: Fremantle Arts Centre Press, 1979); Michael Wilding, "Sex in Australia from the Man's Point of View", from *Pacific Highway* (Sydney: Hale & Iremonger, 1982), previously published separately and with minor alterations in *Tabloid Story*, no. 25 (1978); Olga Masters, "The Rages of Mrs Torrens", *The Home Girls* (St Lucia: University of Queensland Press, 1982); Beverley Farmer, "Ismini", *Milk* (Melbourne: McPhee Gribble/ Penguin, 1983); Fay Zwicky, "The Courts of the Lord", *Hostages* (Fremantle: Fremantle Arts Centre Press, 1983); Barry Hill, "Lizards", *Headlocks & Other Stories* (Melbourne: McPhee Gribble, 1983).

Biographical Notes

Thea Astley

Novelist, short story writer; born in Brisbane in 1925, educated All Hallows Convent School, and University of Queensland 1943-47; taught English in Queensland schools 1944-48 and New South Wales 1948-67, married in 1948; taught English at Macquarie University, Sydney, 1968-79; now lives near Cairns in North Queensland; winner of three Miles Franklin Novel Awards. Story collection: *Hunting the Wild Pineapple* (1979); *It's Raining in Mango* (1987). Novels include: *A Descant for Gossips* (1960); *The Slow Natives* (1965); *The Acolyte* (1972); *A Kindness Cup* (1974); *An Item from the Late News* (1982); *Beachmasters* (1985); *Reaching Tin River* (1990).

Murray Bail

Born in Adelaide in 1941; published some stories before going abroad to Bombay (for two years) and London (1970-74), where he wrote for *Times Literary Supplement* and other periodicals. Although publishing stories since 1960s, his first collection was *Contemporary Portraits* (1975) republished as *The Drover's Wife and Other Stories* (1986); it showed him to be the most experimental and theoretically aware of the Australian new fiction writers; stood against what he saw as the deadening influence of the so-called Lawson tradition of bush realism (e.g. see his story "The Drover's Wife"); his sympathies are with speculative, experimental writing, such as that of Marquez and Calvino. Bail agrees that the "artist should not hesitate to exceed the norm' . . . I find it natural to dwell more on situatins, propositions, speculations than traditional character analysis"; deeply interested in the graphic arts. Novels: *Homesickness* (1980); *Holden's Performance* (1987).

Marjorie Barnard

Short story writer and novelist (1897-1987); did not go to school until ten years old; educated the Cambridge School, Hunters Hill, which included the creative arts in its curriculum, then Sydney Girls' High from which she won a scholarship to the University of Sydney; at the latter won the first medal given in History; parents would not allow her to take up a scholarship abroad; became a librarian. Collaborated with friend from university days, Flora Eldershaw, to write well known novels, including *A House is Built* (1929); *Tomorrow and Tomorrow and Tomorrow* (1947, 1983) was largely written by Barnard; "as well as reading my interests have been music and theatre, not politics"; wrote a number of historical works. Stories: *The Persimmon Tree and Other Stories* (1943); *But Not for Love: Stories of Marjorie Barnard and M. Barnard Eldershaw*, introduced by R. Darby (1988).

Barbara Baynton

Short story writer and novelist (1857-1929). Born at Scone, New South Wales, the daughter of a carpenter who later moved to Murrurundi. Baynton became a governess and thereby met and in 1880 married the first of her three husbands, Alexander Frater, a selector; she had three children and moved to Sydney when her husband left her. In 1890 she married a wealthy doctor, Thomas Baynton, and her life at last became financially secure. Her first story was published in the *Bulletin* 1896; she had difficulty in finding a publisher in Australia and England for her collection of stories, *Bush Studies* (1902), a fierce indictment of women's lives in the bush, but was helped by Edward Garnett who had earlier helped Henry Lawson. After her husband's death in 1904, Baynton lived much of her time in London and busied herself with antique collecting. In 1911 she married Lord Headley; they separated in 1924. Baynton divided her time between London and Melbourne (Toorak), built up outstanding collections of china and furniture, and was known for her independence and outspokenness. Novel: *Human Toll* (1907).

Lily Brett

Born 1946 in Germany. Came to Australia with her parents in 1948. Lives in New York. Married to artist David Rankin; three children. In 1986 her sequence of poems "Poland" won the Mattara Poetry Prize. Her poems and stories have appeared in various journals such as *Overland, Meanjin, Island Magazine*. Stories: *Things Could Be Worse* (1990); *What God Wants* (1991). Poetry: *The Auschwitz Poems* (1986); *Poland and Other Poems* (1987); *After the War: Poems* (1990).

Peter Carey

Copywriter, short story writer, novelist, born at Bacchus Marsh, near Melbourne in 1943. Carey is one of the "new" fiction writers of the 1970s who challenges the limits of realism and of limited conceptions of "reality", and for this purpose makes individual use of fantasy, sometimes futuristic, elements: "my stories are the result of day-dreaming questions. What would happen if . . ."; stories usually involve some form of social criticism: "my stories often involve a form of political questioning: do people want to, or have to, live the way they do now? What will happen to us if we keep on living like we do now?" Stories: *The Fat Man in History* (1974); *War Crimes* (1979). Novels: *Bliss* (1981); *Illywhacker* (1985); *Oscar and Lucinda* (1988); *The Tax Inspector* (1991).

Gavin Casey

Short story writer, novelist, journalist (1907-64). Born in Kalgoorlie, Western Australia, and attended School of Mines; Kalgoorlie gold mines are a frequent setting for his stories. Contributed stories to the *Bulletin* and other journals; for a period on staff of Perth *Daily News*; 1943-44 publicity censor for Western Australia; 1944-45 Director of the Australian News and Information Bureau in New York, and afterwards became Chief Publicity Officer in the Department of Information, Canberra. Stories: *It's Harder for Girls* (1942), republished as *Short-Shift Saturday* (1973); *Birds of a Feather* (1943).

Peter Cowan

Short story writer and novelist; born in 1914 in Perth, Western Australia, where he has spent most of his life; educated at University of Western Australia; 1943-45 with Royal Australian Airforce; tutor in English Department at the university and currently honorary research fellow; coeditor of *Westerly*; currently working on some fiction, a biography and research on Western Australian writing. Stories: *Drift* (1944); *The Unploughed Land* (1958); *The Empty Street* (1965); *The Tins and Other Stories* (1973); *Mobiles*

(1979); *A Window at Mrs X's Place: Selected Stories*, ed. Bruce Bennett (1986).

Beverley Farmer

Short story writer novelist; born in Melbourne in 1941; educated MacRobertson Girls' High School and Melbourne University; various jobs, mainly teaching and waitressing; was married to a Greek migrant from Thessalonika for thirteen years and has a twelve-year-old-son who is bilingual; lived in Greece three years, mainly in village of husband's family; most of stories are centred "on moments of — truth? — anyway, of intense awareness of the tenuousness of the self and the bonds it sustains — or fails to . . . The experience of being foreign is rich in such moments and so is a favourite subject of mine". Stories: *Milk* (1983); *Home Time* (1985). Other: *A Body of Water: A Year's Notebook* (1990).

Thelma Forshaw

Short story writer and journalist; born at Glebe Point, Sydney in 1923; random schooling to age of fiteen, thereafter self-education at Sydney Public Library; particular interests were biographies of great artists, anthropology, psychology, science and classical literature. After wide publication in journals published a collection, *An Affair of Clowns* (1967), at encouragement of Hal Porter; published in many anthologies and is well known as reviewer for main newspapers and journals.

Helen Garner

Born 1942 in Geelong, Vic.; educated there and at Melbourne University. Taught in Melbourne secondary schools. She then worked as a freelance journalist. In 1974, living on a supporting mother's benefit, she began writing fiction. She has also written rock lyrics and has acted on stage and film. Garner received several fellowships from the Literature Board of the Australia Council; with her first grant she went to live in Paris (1978-79). Was writer-in-residence in Tokyo, at Griffith University and the University of Western Australia. Now lives in Melbourne. Stories: *Postcards from Surfers* (1985). Novels: *Monkey Grip* (1977). Won National Book Council Award in 1978, was filmed in 1981. *Honour and Other People's Children* (1980); *The Children's Bach* (1984).

Susan Hampton

Born 1949 in Inverell, NSW. Graduate of Newcastle and Macquarie Universities. Taught primary school for 4 years; worked as a public servant; taught writing and theory in Sydney and Newcastle. Hampton is a single parent and has one son. Her poems and short stories have been published in literary journals, poetry magazines and anthologies since 1975. She received writing grants from the Literature Board in 1979, 1983 and 1984. Joint winner of the Patricia Hackett Award in 1977; Dame Mary Gilmore Prize for Poetry in 1979; Steele Rudd Award for Short Stories, 1990. Edited (with Kate Llewellyn) *The Penguin Book of Australian Women Poets* (1986). Stories: *Surly Girls* (1989). Poetry: *Costumes: poems and prose* (1981); *White Dog Sonnets* (1987).

Barry Hill

Born in Melbourne in 1943; has worked as a teacher, psychologist and journalist. Since the publication of *The Schools* (1977) has been writing fiction; lives at Queenscliff, Victoria. Stories: *A Rim of Blue* (1978); *Headlocks and Other Stories* (1983). Novel: *Near the Refinery* (1980).

T.A.G. Hungerford

Novelist, short story writer, journalist; born in Perth in 1915, educated Perth Boys' School, Perth Senior Technical College; worked *Daily News*, Perth, 1932-42; active service in the Army in New Guinea; 2/8 Australian Cavalry Command squadron; with British Commonwealth Occupation forces in Japan, 1945-47; various jobs after war as journalist (Sydney and Canberra) and kitchenhand; work with Australian News and Information Bureau included jobs in Canberra and every Australian capital; four years in New York; six years as Press Officer in Perth; then freelance writer, apart from period in Premier's Department, Perth. Stories: *Wong Chu and the Queen's Letterbox* (1976); *Stories from Suburban Road* (1983); *A Knockabout with a Slouch Hat* (1985); *Red Rover All Over* (1987); *Hungerford: Short Fiction*, ed. Peter Cowan (1989). Well known for award-winning war novels *The Ridge and the River* (1951); *Sowers of the Wind* (1954).

Elizabeth Jolley

Novelist, short story writer; born into English-Viennese household in the English midlands in 1923; educated at home and at a Quaker boarding school; came to Australia in 1959 with her husband and three children; has worked as a nurse, in real estate, as domestic and door to door salesperson; cultivates a small orchard and goose-farm, and teaches part-time in the School of English at the Western Australian Institute of Technology and at the Fremantle Arts Centre. Stories: *Five Acre Virgin and Other Stories* (1976); *The Travelling Entertainer* (1979); both foregoing collected as *Stories* (1984); *Woman in a Lampshade* (1983). Novels include *Palomino* (1980, 1984); *Mr Scobie's Riddle* (1983); *Miss Peabody's Inheritance* (1983); *Milk and Honey* (1984); *Foxybaby* (1985); *The Well* (1986); *The Sugar Mother* (1988); *My Father's Moon* (1989); *Cabin Fever* (1990).

Henry Lawson

Poet, journalist and Australia's most famous short story writer (1867-1922); born on Grenfell goldfields, son of Norwegian seaman; family lived on poor selection, Mudgee district; deafness from early age; apprentice in Sydney; parents separated 1883; carried swag to Bourke 1892; worked in New Zealand 1893; mother Louise devoted to women's rights movement and started magazine *Dawn* 1888; her press published Lawson's first book of stories, 1894; from 1889 Henry worked for the *Bulletin, Worker, Republican* and other Sydney papers; married Bertha Bredt, 1896; worked in London 1900-1902; separated from wife 1903; struggled for many years with problems of drinking and poverty; spent time in gaol for non-payment of maintenance; died in Sydney. Stories include: *Short Stories in Prose and Verse* (1894); *While the Billy Boils* (1896); *Over the Sliprails* (1900); *Joe Wilson and His Mates* (1901).

Morris Lurie

Short story writer, novelist; born in Melbourne in 1938; studied architecture and worked in advertising; in the mid 1960s travelled to Europe, and became a full-time writer; his stories have appeared in leading magazines around the world, including Britain and the United States of America and he has been widely translated and anthologized; it has been said that he was the first of his generation "to hit an 'international' note"; his five novels to date began with *Rappaport* (1966); his fourth, *Flying Home* (1978) cited by National Book Council as one of ten best books of 1970s. Stories: *Happy*

Times (1969); *Inside the Wardrobe* (1975); *Running Nicely* (1979); *Dirty Friends* (1981); *Outrageous Behaviour* (1984) offers a selection from four earlier volumes.

Alan Marshall

Short story and travel writer (1902-84); born in Noorat, Victoria, a country region which he used as setting for many stories; severe infantile paralysis when six and spent rest of his life on crutches; nevertheless led an independent, much-travelled life; father was a horse-breaker and drover, and the family moved to Melbourne in 1918 for Alan's education at a business college; married in 1941; worked as journalist; popular in Australia and abroad as a prolific writer of stories, often about children and about the bush, and for his autobiographies, including *I Can Jump Puddles* (1955). Stories *Tell Us About the Turkey, Jo* (1946); *How's Andy Going?* (1956); *Short Stories* (1973); *Wild Red Horses* (1973); *Hammers over the Anvil* (1975); *Complete Stories* (1977).

Olga Masters

Born in Pambula, New South Wales in 1919; first job as a journalist on country newspaper; moved to Sydney and married at twenty-one; with teacher husband moved around the country towns and returned to work as a journalist in Lismore; last move to Sydney and last job on *Manly Daily*, "writing mainly human interest stories"; radio play won award 1977, as did a number of stories; all seven children are in films and writing. Stories: *The Home Girls* (1982). Novels: *Loving Daughters* (1984), *A Long Time Dying* (1985); *Amy's Children* (1987); *The Rose Fancier* (1988). Other: *Olga Masters: Reporting Home. Her Writings as a Journalist*, ed. Deirdre Coleman (1990).

Frank Moorhouse

Short story writer, journalist; born in 1938, south coast of New South Wales; educated Nowra High School and Wollongong Technical College; has worked as journalist in city and country; was editor *Australian Worker*; has written social and political commentary for *National Times* and the *Bulletin*, and has scripted films, including *Between Wars*; one of the early editors of *Tabloid Story*; has travelled widely in Australia and abroad including the USA, Europe and India; "my preferences are for stories that present an open-ended aesthetic experience which the sensibility can take for its own use". Stories: *Futility and Other Animals* (1969); *The Americans, Baby* (1976); *The Electrical Experience* (1974); *The Everlasting Secret Family and Other Secrets* (1980); *Selected Stories* (1983). Social commentary: ed. *Days of Wine and Rage* (1980). Anthology: ed. *The State of the Art: The Mood of Contemporary Australia in Short Stories* (1983); *The Coca Cola Kid and Other Stories* (1985); *Room Service* (1985); *Forty-Seventeen* (1988). Other prose: *Late Shows* (1990).

John Morrison

Short story writer and novelist; born in Sunderland, England in 1904; left primary school at fourteen to go to work; first job in Sunderland Museum, then "learner-gardener" on a local private estate; began writing during this period, then migrated to Australia; in 1928 married Irish Frances Jones, and settled in Melbourne, making a living as a casual gardener until 1963; recipient of Commonwealth Literary Fund pension. Stories: *Sailors Belong Ships* (1947); *Black Cargo* (1955); *Twenty Three* (1962); *Selected Stories* (1972); *Australian by Choice* (1973); *North Wind* (1982); *Stories of the Waterfront* (1984); *The Best of John Morrison*, introduced by S. Murray-Smith (1988); *The Happy Wrrior* (1987). Essays: *This Freedom* (1985).

Gerald Murnane

Born 1939 in Melbourne. Spent part of his childhood in country districts of Victoria. Moved back to the suburbs of Melbourne in 1949 and has lived there continuously since then. Married; three adult sons. Since 1980 full-time position of lecturer in fiction writing in the Faculty of Arts at Victoria College. Fiction consultant for *Meanjin* since 1988. Stories: *Velvet Waters* (1990). Novels: *Tamarisk Row* (1974); *A Lifetime on Clouds* (1976); *The Plains* (1982); *Landscape with Landscape* (1985); *Inland* (1988).

Vance Palmer

Novelist, short story writer, critic (1885-1959); born in Bundaberg, Queensland; educated Ipswich Grammar; clerk and journalist in Brisbane, then freelance writer in London 1905-8; tutor and bookkeeper on Queensland stations, then in 1910 returned to England for five years and found a mentor in A.R. Orage, editor of the *New Age*: travelled in Russia, and North and South America; in 1914 married writer Janet Gertrude Higgins (Nettie Palmer); in World

War I he served with AIF; lived for some time in Spain; then set-
tled in Melbourne. Stories: *The World of Men* (1915); *Separate
Lives* (1931); *Sea and Spinifex* (1934); *Let the Birds Fly* (1955). Prose:
The Legend of the Nineties (1954); *National Portraits* (1940).

Hal Porter

Poet, novelist (1911-1984), but best known for his short stories and
his series of autobiographies; born in Melbourne; grew up mainly
in Bairnsdale (Victoria); educated and became librarian there;
worked as teacher and librarian in Victoria, South Australia, Tas-
mania and New South Wales; from 1949-50 taught children of Australian occupation forces in Japan and senior Japanese pupils;
extensive traveller in Europe and Japan, in both of which he has
set many stories; spent latter part of life living in the country, near
Garvoc, and at Ballarat, Victoria. Stories: *A Bachelor's Children*
(1962); *The Cats of Venice* (1965); *Mr Butterfry and Other Tales of
New Japan* (1970); *Fredo Fuss Love Life* (1974); *The Clairvoyant
Goat* (1981); *Selected Stories*, ed. Leonie Kramer (1971); *Hal Porter*
(1980), Portable Australian Authors series, ed. Mary Lord. Autobiography: *The Watcher on the Cast-Iron Balcony* (1963); *The Paper
Chase* (1966); *The Extra* (1975).

Katharine Susannah Prichard

Novelist and short story writer (1883-1969); born in Fiji of Australian parents and came to Australia in her infancy; educated in Melbourne; journalist in Melbourne then freelance writer in London;
in 1919 married Captain Hugo Throssell VC, son of Western Australian premier; then lived at Greenmount, Western Australia,
near Perth; travelled extensively overseas; committed as writer to
the political left and had an active political life. Stories: *Kiss on the
Lips and Other Stories* (1932); *Potch and Colour* (1944); *N'goola and
Other Stories* (1959); *Happiness: Selected Short Stories* (1967);
Tribute: Selected Stories of Katharine Susannah Prichard ed. R.
Throssell (1988). Novels include *Coonardoo* (1929), first important
novel about the Aborigines. Essays: *Straight Left: Articles and Addresses on Politics, Literature and Women's Affairs . . . 1910 to
1986*. Sydney: Wild & Woolley (1982).

Henry Handel Richardson (Ethel Lindesay Robertson)

Known chiefly as novelist (1870-1946); born in Melbourne; daughter of Irish migrant doctor who became mentally and physically in-

capacitated; his widow became postmistress after he died; Richardson attended Presbyterian Ladies College, Melbourne; at seventeen went abroad to study as pianist at Leipzig; here she met Scottish student (J.G. Robertson, later professor German literature at London University) and married him in 1895; spent rest of life in Germany and England (London mainly); returned to Australia for one short visit. Stories: *The End of a Childhood and Other Stories* (1934); *The Adventures of Cuffy Mahony and Other Stories* (1979); Novels: *Maurice Guest* (1908); *The Fortunes of Richard Mahony* (a trilogy published in three parts 1917-30; Omnibus edition 1930).

Christina Stead

Novelist (1902-83); born in Rockdale, Sydney; briefly a schoolteacher then demonstrator in Psychology, University of Sydney; 1928 went to London and later lived in Paris and elsewhere in Europe, travelling extensively; married to William J. Blech ("William Blake", novelist and businessman); went to live in USA in 1937; later lived mainly in England, returning to Australia in 1974; winner of Patrick White Award. Stories: *The Salzburg Tales* (1934); *Ocean of Story: The Uncollected Stories of Christina Stead*, ed. R.G. Geering (1985). Novellas: *The Puzzleheaded Girl* (1967). Novels include: *For Love Alone* (1944) and *The Man Who Loved Children* (1940).

Dal Stivens

Novelist, short story writer; born at Blayney, New South Wales in 1911; educated Barker College, Hornsby; journalist on *Daily Telegraph* 1939-42; Army Education Service 1943-44; several years with Commonwealth Department of Information; married in 1945; wrote stories for *Bulletin* and other Australian journals in 1930s; a collection from these, *The Tramp and Other Stories* (1936), was published in London where it was highly praised; then wrote for book collections rather than magazine publication; winner of Patrick White Award and Miles Franklin Award; his stories show a range of styles including social realism, fantasy, fable, "tall" stories: "I want the reader to use his imagination . . . a good story should tease the mind". Stories iclude: *The Tramp* (1936); *The Courtship of Uncle Henry* (1946); *The Gambling Ghost* (1953); *The Scholarly Mouse* (1958); *Selected Stories, 1936-1968* (1969), ed. H.P. Heseltine; *The Unicorn and Other Tales* (1976); *The Demon Bowler and Other Cricket Stories* (1979). Novels include: *Jimmy Brockett* (1951); *A Horse of Air* (1970).

Judah Waten

Novelist and short story writer (1911-1985); born in Odessa, Russia in 1911; migrated with parents, who were Russian Jews, to Western Australia in 1914; educated at Christian Brothers College, Perth and University High School in Melbourne; married Hyrell McKinnon Ross in 1945; began to write in 1928, subjects including the unemployed of the 1920s; in 1930s and 1940s wrote for left-wing press and remained politically committed; resumed writing fiction in the 1940s. Stories: *Alien Son* (1952), his first book and one of the first of important modern Australian works to deal with migrants from the inside; *Love and Rebellion* (1978). Autobiography: *Scenes of Revolutionary Life* (1982).

Archie Weller

Born 1957 in Perth; partly Aboriginal (Nyoongah people). Grew up on isolated farm, eight years in boarding school. Parents divorced, lived with mother in East Perth. Was jailed at one stage, allegedly in connection with his Aboriginal background. Went overseas. Worked as dishwasher, wharfie, printer, hospital orderly, lecturer, scriptwriter, broadcaster. Published several short stories under the pseudonym Raymond Chee in *Identity* (1977 and 1979), a periodical edited by Jack Davis. Runner-up for *Australian*/Vogel Award 1980; won WA Fiction Week Award 1982; joint winner ABC Bicentennary Prize; Literature Board Fellowship 1983; numerous short story and poetry awards. Novel: *The Day of the Dog* (1981). Stories: *Going Home* (1986).

Patrick White

Novelist, short story writer, playwright (1912-1990); born in London in 1912 of Australian parents; brought up in Sydney; educated private school in Moss Vale, New South Wales, and Cheltenham College, England; after period as a jackeroo at Walgett and the Monaro, New South Wales, graduated in Modern Languages at King's College, Cambridge, 1935; remained abroad about fourteen years; travelled in Europe and America; war service with Intelligence Section of RAF in Greece and Middle East, where he met Manoly Lascaris, a Greek with whom he formed a lasting partnership; they returned to Sydney after White's demobilization and settled on a small farm outside Sydney, and later in the suburb of Centennial Park; Nobel Prize 1975; Companion of the Order of Australia, 1975. Stories: *The Burnt Ones* (1964); *The Cockatoos* (1974). Autobiography: *Flaws in the Glass* (1981). Novels include: *The Aunt's Story* (1948); *The Tree of Man* (1955); *Voss* (1957); *The Eye of the Storm* (1973); *A Fringe of Leaves* (1976); *The Twyborn Affair* (1979). Speeches: *Patrick White Speaks* (1989).

Michael Wilding

Short story writer, novelist, critic; born (1942) and educated in Worcester in the English Midlands; graduated from Oxford 1963; lecturer in English at University of Sydney 1963-66, then University of Birmingham 1967-68; senior lecturer University of Sydney, 1969-72, then reader 1972- ; one of the main influences on the Australian "new" writing of the later 1960s and the 1970s as a writer, critic, publisher (Wild and Woolley), editor (e.g. of *Tabloid Story*); high reputation as a critic of English as well as Australian literature; in his creative work he is committed aesthetically and socially to constant change. Stories: *Aspects of the Dying Process* (1972); *The West Midland Underground* (1975); *The Phallic Forest* (1978); *Reading the Signs* (1984); *The Man of Slow Feeling: Selected Short Stories* (1985). Novels include: *The Short Story Embassy* (1975) which relates to the "new" short fiction scene in Sydney; *Living Together* (1974). Criticism includes: *Political Fictions* (1980); *Under Saturn: Four Stories* (1988); *The Paraguayan Experiment* (1984).

Fay Zwicky

Poet, short story writer, critic; born in Melbourne in 1933; educated at the University of Melbourne; has since divided her time between a career as a concert pianist and as a teacher of literature; has lived and worked in Indonesia, America and Europe; now lives permanently in Western Australia and is currently senior lecturer in English at the University of Western Australia. Stories: *Hostages* (1983). Poetry: *Isaac Babel's Fiddle* (1975); *Kaddish and Other Poems* (1982); *Ask Me* (1990).

Select Bibliography

The following listing draws on two main sources: first, Stephen Torre's bibliography in his Ph.D. thesis (see under Torre in the General Section); secondly, on the bibliographical services and index of the Fryer Library, University of Queensland. Thanks as well as acknowledgment is due to both, and also to Mr Andrew Wallace, English Department, University of Queensland, who helped with the compilation of this bibliography.

The following abbreviations are used:

ABR	*Australian Book Review*
ALS	*Australian Literary Studies*
A & R	Angus & Robertson
MUP	Melbourne University Press
OUP	Oxford University Press
SMH	*Sydney Morning Herald*
UQP	University of Queensland Press
WLWE	*World Literature Written in English* (University of Texas at Arlington)

General

Anderson, Don. "Contemporary American and Australian Short Fiction". *Westerly* 25, no. 1 (1980): 83-90.

——. *Transgressions: Australian Writing Now*. Ringwood, Vic: Penguin, 1986.

Bail, Murray (ed.). *The Faber Book of Contemporary Australian Short Stories*. London, Boston: Faber and Faber, 1988.

Barnes, John. "Lawson and the Short Story in Australia". *Westerly* no. 2 (1968): 442.

——. "The Stories of White, Porter and Cowan". *Meanjin* 25, no. 2 (1966): 154-70.

Beasley, Jack. *Red Letter Days: Notes from Inside an Era*. Sydney: Australasian Book Society, 1979.

Bennett, Bruce. "Australian Experiments in Short Fiction".
  WLWE 15 (1976): 359-66.

____ . "The Short Story". In *The Literature of Western Australia*, edited by Bruce Bennett. Nedlands: University of Western Australia Press, 1979.

Burns, Connie (ed.). *Feeling Restless: Australian Women's Short
  Stories 1940-1969*. Sydney: Collins, 1989.

Burns, D.R. *The Directions of Australian Fiction: 1920-1974*. Melbourne: Cassell, 1975.

Clancy, Laurie. "The Short Story is Alive and Well". *ABR* (November 1980): 3-5.

Clunies Ross, Bruce. "Laszlo's Testament or Structuring the Past
  and Sketching the Present in Contemporary Short Fiction,
  Mainly Australian". *Kunapipi* 1, no. 2 (1979): 110-23.

____ . "Some Developments in Short Fiction, 1969-1980". *ALS* 9
  (1981): 165-80.

"The Contemporary Australian Short Story". Special issue of *ALS*
  10 (October 1981). Contains writers' statements, critical commentary, bibliography.

Daniel, Helen (ed.). *Expressway*. Ringwood, Vic.: Penguin, 1989.

Davis, Beatrice, ed. *Short Stories of Australia: The Moderns*. Sydney: A & R, 1967.

Day, A. Grove. *Modern Australian Prose, 1901-1975: A Guide to Information Sources*. Detroit: Gale Research Co., 1980.

Disher, Garry (ed.). *Personal Best: Thirty Australian Authors
  Choose Their Best Stories*. Sydney: Collins, 1989.

____ . *Personal Best 2: Stories and Statements by Writers*. Sydney:
  Angus & Robertson, 1991.

Drake-Brockman, Henrietta. "The International Symposium on
  the Short Story, Part One: Australia". *Kenyon Review* 30, no. 4
  (1968): 478-85.

Dutton, Geoffrey (ed.). *The Illustrated Treasury of Australian Stories*. Melbourne: Nelson, 1986.

____ . *The Literature of Australia*. Rev. ed. Harmondsworth: Penguin, 1976.

Falkiner, Suzanne (ed.). *Room to Move: The Redress Anthology of
  Australian Women's Short Stories*. Sydney, London, Boston:
  Allen & Unwin, 1985.

Gelder, Ken. "Character and Environment in Some Recent Australian Fiction: With or Without Reference Points". *Waves* (Tor-
  onto) 7, no. 4 (1979): 98-104.

____ . "Uncertainty and Subversion in the Australian Novel:

Recent Fiction in a Framework". *Pacific Moana Quarterly*, 4, no. 4 (1979): 437-44.

Goldsworthy, Kerryn (ed.). *Australian Short Stories*. Melbourne: Dent, 1983.

Green, H.M. *A History of Australian Literature: Pure and Applied*. 2 vols. Sydney: A & R, 1966.

Harrison-Ford, Carl. "Fiction". *ALS* 8 (1977): 172-78.

Harrower, Elizabeth. "The International Symposium on the Short Story, Part Three: Australia". *Kenyon Review* 31, no. 4 (1969): 479-85

Harwood, Lyn, Pascoe, Bruce and White, Paula (eds). *The Babe Is Wise: Contemporary Stories by Australian Women*. Fairfield, Vic.: Pascoe Publishing, 1987.

Healy, J.J. *Literature and the Aborigine in Australia: 1770–1975*. St Lucia: UQP, 1978.

Heseltine, H.P. "Thirty Years of the Australian Short Story". *Rajasthan University Studies in English* (Jaipur, India) 15 (1982/83): 33-40.

Hickey, Bernard. *Lines of Implication: Australian Short Fiction from Lawson to Palmer*. Venice: Cafoscarini, 1984.

Jarvis, Douglas. "The Development of Egalitarian Poetics in the *Bulletin*, 1880-1890". *ALS* 10 (1981): 22-34.

Kiernan, Brian. *Criticism*. Australian Writers and Their Work Series. Melbourne: OUP, 1974.

——. ed. *The Most Beautiful Lies*. Sydney: A & R, 1977.

——. "Recent Developments in Australian Writing, with Particular Reference to Short Fiction". *Caliban* (Toulouse) 14 (1977): 123-24.

Kramer, Leonie, ed. *The Oxford History of Australian Literature*. Melbourne: OUP, 1981.

Matthews, Brian. *Romantics and Mavericks: The Australian Short Story*. Townsville Foundation for Australian Literary Studies, no. 14, 1986.

May, Charles Edward, ed. *Short Story Theories*. Athens: Ohio University Press, 1976.

Miller, E. Morris, and Frederick T. Macartney. *Australian Literature: A Bibliography*. Sydney: A & R, 1956.

Moorhouse, Frank. "Regionalism, Provincialism and Australian Anxieties". *Westerly* 23, no. 4 (1978): 61-66.

——. "What Happened to the Short Story?" *ALS* 8 (1977): 179-82.

——. (ed.). *The Mood of Contemporary Australia in Short Stories: The State of the Art*. Ringwood, Vic.: Penguin, 1984.

"New Writing in Australia". Special issue of *ALS* 8 (October 1977).

O'Connor, Frank. *The Lonely Voice: A Study of the Short Story.* London: Macmillan, 1963.

Palmer, Vance. Introduction to *Coast to Coast.* Sydney: A & R, 1945.

Phillips, A.A. "Three Short Story Writers [Hal Porter; John Morrison; Van Palmer]". In his *Responses: Selected Writings.* Melbourne: Australia International Press and Publications, 1978.

Reid, Ian. *The Short Story.* The Critical Idiom, no. 37. London: Methuen, 1977.

Semmler, Clement. *The Art of Brian James and Other Essays on Australian Literature.* St Lucia: UQP, 1972.

Smith, Graeme Kinross. *Australia's Writers.* Melbourne: Nelson (Australia), 1980.

Stead, Christina. "Ocean of Story". *ALS* 10 (1981): 181-85.

Stewart, Douglas. "The Moment of Vision". In *The Flesh and the Spirit: An Outlook on Literature.* Sydney: A & R, 1946.

——. ed. *Short Stories of Australia: The Lawson Tradition.* Sydney: A & R, 1967.

Torre, Stephen. "The Australian Short Story 1940 to 1980: A Critical Survey and a Bibliography". Ph.D. thesis in two volumes, University of Queensland, 1982.

——. "Selective Bibliography of the Contemporary Australian Short Story". *ALS* 10 (1981): 275-86.

Webby, Elizabeth. "Australian Short Fiction from *While The Billy Boils* to *The Everlasting Secret Family*". *ALS* 10 (1981): 147-64.

——. "The Long March of Short Fiction: A Seventies Retrospective". *Meanjin* 39, no. 1 (1980): 127-33.

——. and Weavers, Lydia. *Goodbye to Romance: Stories by Australian and New Zealand Women, 1930s to 1980s.* Wellington: Allen & Unwin, 1989.

Whitlock, Gillian (ed.). *Eight Voices of the Eighties: Stories, Journalism and Criticism by Australian Women Writers.* St Lucia: UQP, 1989.

Wilding, Michael. "A Survey [of Australian 'new' writing]". *ALS* 8 (1977): 115-26.

——. "The *Tabloid Story* Story". In *The Tabloid Story Pocket Book*, edited by Michael Wilding, 295-316. Sydney: Wild & Woolley, 1978.

Individual Authors

Thea Astley
Astley, Thea. "Authorial Statement". *ALS* 10 (1981): 186-87.

_____. "Being a Queenslander: A Form of Literary and Geographical Conceit". *Southerly* 36, no. 3 (1976): 252-64.

_____. "The Idiot Question". *Southerly* 30, no. 1 (1970): 3-8.

Clancy, Laurie. "The Fiction of Thea Astley". *Meridian* 5 (1986): 43-52.

Goldsworthy, Kerryn. "Thea Astley's Writing: Magnetic North". *Meanjin* 42 (1983): 478-85.

Matthews, Brian. "Life in the Eye of the Hurricane: The Novels of Thea Astley". *Southern Review* (Adelaide) 11 (1973): 148-73.

_____. "Thea Astley: Before Feminism . . . After Feminism" in *Romantics and Mavericks: The Australian Short Story*. Townsville Foundation for Australian Literary Studies, no. 14, 1986.

Smith, Ross, and Cheryl Frost. "Thea Astley: A Bibliography". *LiNQ* 10, no. 4 (1982-83): 87-105.

Murray Bail

Ahearne, Kate, Myron Lysenko, and Kevin Brophy. "An Interview with Murray Bail". *Aspect*, no. 21 (1981): 55-59.

Anderson, Don. "Contemporary American and Australian Short Fiction". *Westerly* 25, no. 1 (1980): 83-90.

Bail, Murray. "Authorial Statement". *ALS* 8 (1977): 188.

_____. "Authorial Statement". *ALS* 10 (1981): 187.

Davidson, Jim. "Interview — Murray Bail". *Meanjin* 41 (1982): 264-76. Reprinted in *Sideways from the Page*, edited by Jim Davidson. Melbourne: Fontana, 1983.

Kiernan, Brian. Review of *Contemporary Portraits*. *National Times*, 2-7 August 1976, 36-37.

Legasse, Jim. "The Voice of the Form and the Form of the Voice". *Westerly* 25, no. 1 (1980): 97-101.

Lippard, Lucy R. Review of *Contemporary Portaits*. *Quadrant* 20, no. 1 (1976): 62-63.

Marjorie Barnard

Barnard, Marjorie. "Authorial Statement". *ALS* 10 (1981): 188.

"Marjorie Barnard's Stories". *Bulletin*, 26 January 1944, 2.

Giuffre, Giulia. Interview in *A Writing Life: Interviews with Australian Women Writers*. Sydney: Allen & Unwin, 1990. 131-49.

Rorabacher, Louise E. *Marjorie Barnard and M. Barnard Eldershaw*. Twayne's World Authors Series, no. 257. New York: Twayne 1973.

Williamson, Kristin. "The Remarkable Marjorie Barnard". *National Times*, 19-25 August 1983, 32.

Barbara Baynton

Baynton, Barbara. *Barbara Baynton*, edited by Sally Krimmer and Alan Lawson. Portable Australian Authors. St Lucia: UQP, 1980.

Frost, Lucy. "Barbara Baynton: An Affinity with Pain" in Shirley Walker (ed.) *Who Is She?* St Lucia: UQP, 1983.

Hackforth-Jones, Penne. *Barbara Baynton: Between Two Worlds* (biography). Ringwood, Vic: Penguin, 1989.

Iseman, Kay. "Barbara Baynton: Woman as 'The Chosen Vessel' ". *ALS* 11 (1983): 25-37.

Kirkby, Joan. "Barbara Baynton: *An Australian Jocasta*". *Westerly* 34 (1989): 114-24.

Lindsay, Jack. "Barbara Baynton: A Master of Naturalism". In his *Decay and Renewal: Critical Essays on Twentieth Century Writing*. Sydney: Wild & Woolley, 1977.

Moore, Rosemary. "Squeaker's Mate: A Bushwoman's Tale". *Australian Feminist Studies* 3 (1986): 26-44.

Schaffer, Kay. *Women and the Bush*. Melbourne: CUP, 1989.

Lily Brett

Reviews of *Auschwitz Poems*: Harris, R. *Overland* 105 (1986): 80-81; Roridguez, J. *Sydney Morning Herald* 18 October 1986: 49; Strauss, J. *Fremantle Arts Review* 2.3 (1987): 14-15.

Reviews of *Poland*: Coleman, S. *Australian Jewish News* 4 March 1988: 24; Doyle, J. *Canberra Times* 20 February 1988: B2; Zwicky, F. *Age Saturday Extra* 13 February 1988: 11.

Review of *After the War* and *Things Could Be Worse*: Coleman, S. *Australian Jewish News* 56.32 (1990): 21; Hanrahan, John, *Overland* 119 (1990): 87-91; Jurgensen, M. *Sydney Review* 119 (1990): 9-10; Salusinszky, I. *Weekend Australian* 5-6 May 1990: Review 6; Sorensen, R. *Sydney Morning Herald* 17 March 1990: 79.

Peter Carey

"An Interview with Peter Carey". *Going Down Swinging*, no. 1 (1980): 43-55.

Carey, Peter. "Authorial Statement". *ALS* 8 (1977): 182-87.

——. "Authorial Statement". *ALS* 10 (1981): 191-93.

Dovey, Teresa. "An Infinite Onion: Narrative Structure in Peter Carey's Fiction". *ALS* 11 (1983): 195-204.

Green, W. Review of *The Fat Man in History*. *Westerly* (December 1974): 73-76.

Ikin, Van. "Answers to Seventeen Questions: An Interview with

Peter Carey". *Science Fiction: A Review of Speculative Literature* 1, no. 1 (1977): 30-39.

Munro, Craig. "Building Fabulist Extensions". *Makar* 12, no. 1 (1976): 3-12. Interview.

Ross, Robert. "'It Cannot Be Thee': Borges and Australia's Peter Carey" in Edna Aizenberg (ed.) *Borges and His Successors*. Columbia, Miss.: U of Missouri, 1989. 44-58.

Turner, Graeme. "American Dreaming: The Fictions of Peter Carey". *ALS* 12 (1986), 431-41.

Webby, Elizabeth. Review of *War Crimes*. *Meanjin* 39, no. 1 (1980): 127-33.

Gavin Casey

Barnes, John. "Gavin Casey: The View from Kalgoorlie". *Meanjin* 23, no. 4 (1964): 341-47.

Casey, Gavin. "The Writing of Novels and Short Stories". *Commonwealth Literary Fund Lectures, 1962*. Canberra: Australian National University, 1964.

Hewett, Dorothy. "Literary Obituary". *The Critic*, no. 7 (1964): 62-63.

Waldock, A.J.A. Review of *It's Harder for Girls*. *Southerly* 3, no. 3 (1942): 30-31.

Peter Cowan

Barnes, John. "New Tracks to Travel: The Stories of White, Porter and Cowan". *Meanjin* 25 (1966): 154-70.

Bennett, Bruce. "Regionalism in Peter Cowan's Short Fiction". *WLWE* 18 (1979): 366-44.

Cowan, Peter. "Authorial Statement". *ALS* 10 (1981): 196-98, 239-41.

Jolley, Elizabeth. "Silence and Spaces". *Overland* 108 (1987): 59-64.

Beverley Farmer

Farmer, Beverley. "Preoccupations". *ALS* 14 (1990): 390-92.

Jacobs, Lyn. "The Fiction of Beverley Farmer". *ALS* 14 (1990): 325-35.

Ommundsen, Wenche. "An Interview with Beverley Farmer". *Mattoid* 31 (1988): 110-21.

Reviews of *Milk*: Baranay, Inez, *SMH*, 10 December 1983, 38; Bedford, Jean, *National Times*, 2-8 December 1983, 24; Dutton, Geoffrey, *Bulletin*, 17 January 1984, 60; Forshaw, Thelma, *Quadrant* 28 (September 1984): 83-84; Frost, Lucy, *ABR*

(December 1983-January 1984); 15-16; Keesing, Nancy, *Weekend Australian Magazine*, 14-15 January 1984, 12; Webb, John, *Westerly* (July 1984): 107-8.

Thelma Forshaw
Forshaw, Thelma. "Authorial Statement". *ALS* 10 (1981): 199-201.
Reviews of *An Affair of Clowns*: Keesing, Nancy, *Bulletin*, 2 December 1967, 80; Vinter, M., *SMH*, 2 December 1967, 21.

Helen Garner
Ashcroft, W.D. "The Language of Music: Helen Garner's *The Children's Bach*". *ALS* 14. 4 (1990): 489-98.
Burns, D.R. "The Active Passive Inversion: Sex Roles in Garner, Stead and Harrower". *Meanjin* 45 (1986): 346-53.
Craven, Peter. "Of War and Needlework: The Fiction of Helen Garner". *Meanjin* 44. 2 (1985): 209-18.
Hope, Deborah. "Helen Garner: Reflections on Life as Writer and Artist". *Bulletin* 5 November 1985: 82-84.
Taylor, Andrew. "Desire and Repetition in the Novels of Helen Garner". *Aspects of Australian Fiction*. Ed. Alan Brissenden. Nedlands, WA: U of Western Australia Press, 1990. 113-26.

Susan Hampton
Interviews: By Mansell, Chris. *Scarp* 13 (1988): 6-18. By Varnish, N. *Campaign* 165 (1989): 60-64.
Reviews of *Surly Girls*: Capp, F. *Australian Women's Book Review* 2.1 (1990): 11; Eldridge, M. *Canberra Times* 17 February 1990: B4; Elliott, H. *Weekend Australian* 3-4 February 1990: Weekend 8; Maclean, M. *ABR* 116 (1989): 17.

Barry Hill
Hill, Barry. "Authorial Statement". *ALS* 10 (1981): 208-9.
Reviews of *Headlocks and Other Stories*: Kellaway, Frank, *Overland* (December 1983): 65-66; Hildyard, Annette, *Island Magazine* (Autumn-Winter 1984): 40-44; Matthews, Brian, *Age*, 30 July 1983, 13; McInherney, Frances, *ABR* (December 1983-January 1984): 16-17.
Reviews of *A Rim of Blue*: McDonald, Roger, *ABR*, no. 7 (1978): 27-28; O'Hearn, D.J., *Overland*, no. 74 (1979), 52-54; Webby, Elizabeth, *Meanjin* 39, no. 1 (1980): 127-33.

T.A.G. Hungerford
Bolton, G.C. "A Local Identity: Paul Hasluck and Western Australian Self Concept". *Westerly* (December 1977): 71-77.
Hungerford, T.A.G. "Authorial Statement". *ALS* 10 (1981): 208-13.

Ikin, Van. Review of *Wong Chu and the Queen's Letterbox*. *Quadrant* 21, no. 10 (1977): 79-80.

Smith, Graeme Kinross. "T.A.G. Hungerford". *Westerly* (June 1976): 35-41.

"I Write Basically Because . . .". *ALS* 12 (1985): 263-64.

Elizabeth Jolley

Bennett, Bruce. "Versions of Ageing: Olga Masters and Elizabeth Jolley", in *Olga Masters*, Proceedings of the Olga Masters Memorial Conference. Ed. W. McGaw and P. Sharrad. Wollongong: U. of Wollongong, New Literatures Research Centre, 1990, 84-96.

Clancy, Laurie. "Love, Longing and Loneliness: The Fiction of Elizabeth Jolley". *ABR*, no. 56 (1983): 8-12.

Daniel, Helen. "Elizabeth Jolley: Variations on a Theme". *Westerly* 31. 2 (1986): 50-63.

Jolley, Elizabeth. "Authorial Statement". *ALS* 10 (1981): 213-15.

____ . "A Child Went Forth". *ABR* no. 56 (1983): 5-8. Self Portraits 5.

____ . "On Being an Australian Author — 'Living on One Leg Like a Bird' ". *Island Magazine* No. 30 (1987): 25-31.

Riemer, A.P. "Between Two Worlds — An Approach to Elizabeth Jolley's Fiction". *Southerly* 43 (1983): 239-52.

Henry Lawson

Clark, Manning. *In Search of Henry Lawson*. Melbourne: Macmillan, 1978.

Heseltine, H.P. "Saint Henry, Our Apostle of Mateship". *Quadrant* 5, no. 1 (1960-61): 5-11.

Matthews, Brian. *The Receding Wave: Henry Lawson's Prose*. Carlton, Vic.: MUP, 1972.

____ . "Eve Exonerated: Henry Lawson's Unfinished Love Stories" in Shirley Walker (ed.) *Who is She?* St Lucia: UQP, 1983.

Pons, Xavier. *Out of Eden: Henry Lawson's Life and Works*. Sydney: Angus & Robertson, 1984.

Phillips, A.A. *Henry Lawson*. Twayne's World Authors Series. New York: Twayne, 1970.

____ . "Henry Lawson as Craftsman". *Meanjin* 7 (1948). Reprinted in his *The Australian Tradition*. Rev. ed. Melbourne: Cheshire, 1966.

____ . "Henry Lawson Revisited". *Meanjin* 24 (1965): 5-17. Reprinted in *The Australian Nationalists* edited by Chris Wallace-Crabbe. Melbourne: OUP, 1971.

Prout, Denton. *Henry Lawson: The Grey Dreamer*. Adelaide: Rigby, 1963.

Roderick, Colin, ed. *Henry Lawson Criticism 1894-1971*. Sydney: A & R, 1972.

Wallace-Crabbe, Chris. "Lawson's *Joe Wilson*: A Skeleton Novel". *ALS* 1 (1964): 147-54. Reprinted in his *Melbourne or the Bush*. Sydney: A & R, 1974.

Zinkhan, E.J. "Louisa Lawson's 'The Australian Bush-Woman' — A Source for 'The Drover's Wife' and 'Water Them Geraniums?'" *ALS* 10 (1982): 495-99.

Morris Lurie

Lurie, Morris. "Authorial Statement". *ALS* 10 (1981): 216-18.

O'Hearn, D.J. "Morris Lurie: The Humour of Survival". *Overland*, no. 89 (1982): 24-28.

Reviews of *Running Nicely*: Grant, B., *ABR*, no. 14 (1979): 12-13; Hall, R., *SMH*, 7 July 1979, 18; O'Hearn, D.J., *Age*, 16 June 1979, 23; Perkins, E., *Quadrant* 23, no. 12 (1979): 68-69.

Alan Marshall

Beasley, Jack. "Gurrawilla the Song Maker: Alan Marshall: Writer versus Cult Figure". In his *Red Letter Days: Notes from Inside an Era*, 1-52. Sydney: Australasian Book Society, 1979.

Clancy, Laurie. Review of *The Complete Stories*. *Overland*, no. 69 (1978): 68-71.

Lindsay, Jack. "A Triumph over Adversity: Comments on Alan Marshall's Writing". In *Meanjin* 28, no. 4 (1969): 437-45. Reprinted in *Decay and Renewal: Critical Essays on Twentieth Century Writing*, 335-48. Sydney: Wild & Woolley, 1976.

Marks, Harry. *I Can Jump Oceans, the World of Alan Marshall*. Melbourne: Nelson (Australia), 1976.

Marshall, Alan. "Some Aspects of the Writer's Craft: A Talk". *Opinion* 10, no. 2 (1966): 20-30.

Olga Masters

Jones, Dorothy. "Digging Deep: Olga Masters, Storyteller". *Kunapipi* 8. 3 (1986): 28-35.

——. "Drama's Vitallest Expression: The Fiction of Olga Masters". *ALS* 13 (1987): 3-14.

McGaw, W. and Sharrad, Paul (ed.) *Olga Masters*. Proceedings of the Olga Masters Memorial Conference. Wollongong: U of Wollongong, New Literature Research Centre, 1990.

Reviews of *The Home Girls*: Dutton, Geoffrey, *Bulletin*, 7 December 1982, 82, 85; Forshaw, Thelma, *Quadrant* 27 (December 1983): 89-90; Halloran, Delia, *Luna*, no. 15 (1982): 34; Lord, Mary, *ABR* (April 1983): 14; McKernan, Susan, *Canberra Times*, 21 January 1984, 18; Potter, L., *Ash Magazine* (Autumn 1983): 30-31; Stretton, Andrea, *SMH*, 9 October 1982, 38; *SMH*, 24 September 1983, 39; Webby, Elizabeth, *Meanjin* 42 (March 1983): 34-41.

Frank Moorhouse

Anderson, Don. "Contemporary American and Australian Short Fiction". *Westerly* 25, no. 1 (1980): 83-90.

——. "Frank Moorhouse's Discontinuities". *Southerly* 36, no. 1 (1976): 26-38.

Bennett, Bruce. "Frank Moorhouse and the New Journalism". *Overland*, no. 70 (1978): 6-10.

Harrison-Ford, Carl. "The Short Stories of Wilding and Moorhouse". *Southerly* 33 (1973): 167-68.

Kiernan, Brian. "Frank Moorhouse: A Retrospective". *Modern Fiction Studies* 27, no. 1 (1981): 73-94.

——. "Notes on Frank Moorhouse". *Overland* (Spring 1973): 9-11.

Kirby, Stephen. "Homosocial Desire and Homosexual Panic in the Fiction of David Malouf and Frank Moorhouse". *Meanjin* 46 (1987): 385-93.

Moorhouse, Frank. "Authorial Statement". *ALS* 8 (1977): 189-91.

——. "Authorial Statement". *ALS* 10 (1981): 222-23.

Pope, William. "Frank Moorhouse's *Tales of Mystery and Romance*: A Study in Narrative Method". *Southerly* 42 (1982): 412-23.

Raines, Gay. "The Short Story Cycles of Frank Moorhouse". *ALS* 14 (1990): 425-35.

Reid, Ian. "Writing from the Third Position: Frank Moorhouse's Recent Fiction". *Meanjin* 37, no. 2 (1978): 165-70.

Smith, Graeme Kinross. "Liberating Acts — Frank Moorhouse, His Life, His Narratives". *Southerly* 46 (1986): 391-423.

Wilding, Michael. Review of *Futility and Other Animals*. *Southerly* 29, no. 3 (1969): 231-36.

John Morrison

Indyk, Ivor. "The Economics of Realism: John Morrison". *Meanjin* 46 (1987): 385-93.

Loh, Morag. "John Morrison: Writers at Work". *Meanjin* 46 (1987): 496-501.

Martin, David. "Three Realists in Search of Reality". *Meanjin* 18, no. 3 (1959): 305-22.

Morrison, John. "Authorial Statement". *ALS* 10 (1981): 223-26.

——. "The Books that Drove me on". *Educational Magazine* 35, no. 2 (1978): 22-24.

——. "English Is Good Enough". In *Australian by Choice*, 167-75. Melbourne: Rigby, 1973.

O'Brien, Patrick. "Zhdanov in Australia". *Quadrant* 18, no. 5 (1975): 37-55.

Phillips, A.A. "The Short Stories of John Morrison". *Overland* (Winter 1974): 31-35.

Reid Ian. Introduction to *Selected Stories*. Adelaide: Rigby, 1972.

Gerald Murnane

Daniel, Helen. "The Landscape of the Lie: Gerald Murnane". In *Liars: Australian New Novelists*. Ringwood, Vic.: Penguin, 1988. 307-41.

Gillett, Sue. "Inland with Gerald Murnane: An Interview". *Meridian* 7 (1988): 163-74.

Murnane, Gerald. "Why I Write What I Write". *Meanjin* 45 (1986): 514-17.

Salusinszky, Imre. "Murnane, Husserl, Derrida: The Scene of Writing". *ALS* 14 (1989): 188-98.

——. "On Gerald Murnane". *Meanjin* 45 (1986): 518-29.

Vance Palmer

Burns, D.R. "Vance Palmer and the Unguarded Awareness". In *The Directions of Australian Fiction 1920-1974*, 32-42. Melbourne: Cassell, 1975.

Heseltine, Harry. *Vance Palmer*. St Lucia: UQP, 1970.

Indyk, Ivor. "Vance Palmer and the Social Function of Literature". *Southerly* 50 (1990): 346-58.

Matthews, Brian. "Vance Palmer's Long Journey" in *Romantics and Mavericks: The Australian Short Story*, Townsville: Foundation for Australian Literary Studies, 1986: 23-33.

Palmer, Vance and Nettie. *Letters, 1915-63*. Selected and edited by Vivian Smith. Canberra: National Library of Australia, 1977.

Phillips, A.A. "The Short Stories". *Meanjin* 18 (1959): 173-81.

Smith, Vivian. *Vance Palmer*. Australian Writers and Their Work Series. Melbourne: OUP, 1971.

——. *Vance and Nettie Palmer*. Twayne's World Authors Series. Boston: Twayne, 1975.

Torre, Stephen. "Psyche as Text: The Short Stories of Vance Palmer". *LINQ* 15. 1 (1987): 64-78.

Walker, David. *Dream and Disillusion: A Search for Australian Cultural Identity*. Canberra: Australian National University Press, 1976.

Hal Porter

Burns, D.R. "A Sort of Triumph Over Time: Hal Porter's Prose Narratives". *Meanjin* 28, no. 1 (1969): 19-28.

Capone, Giovanna. *Incandescent Verities: The Fiction of Hal Porter*. Rome: Bulzoni, 1990.

Duncan, R.A. "Hal Porter's Writing and the Impact of the Absurd". *Meanjin* 29, no. 4 (1970): 468-73.

Forshaw, Thelma. Review of *Selected Stories*. *Age*, 15 May 1971, 15.

Hawley-Crowcroft, Jean. "Hal Porter's Asian Stories". *Quadrant* 28 (1983): 41-45.

Lord, Mary. *Hal Porter*. Australian Writers and Their Work Series. Melbourne: OUP, 1974. With select bibliography.

____. "Hal Porter's Comic Mode". *ALS* 4 (1970): 371-82.

____. "Interview with Hal Porter". *ALS* 8 (1978): 269-79.

Matthews, Brian. "Ruminating Among the Ruins" in *Romantics and Mavericks: The Australian Short Story*. Townsville: Foundation for Australian Literary Studies, 1986: 23-33.

Moorhouse, Frank. Review of *Mr Butterfry*. *Bulletin*, 12 December 1970, 54-55.

Porter, Hal. "Answers to the Funny Kind Man". *Southerly* 29 (1969): 3-14. Reprinted in *Hal Porter*, edited by Mary Lord, 379-91. Portable Australian Authors Series. St Lucia: UQP, 1980.

____. "That Certain Book: Beyond Whipped Cream and Blood". *Bulletin*, 28 April 1962.

____. Introduction to *It Could Be You*. Adelaide: Rigby, 1972.

____. "Reputation's Blowflies or, Read Any Good Books Lately?" *Bulletin*, 6 January 1962, 21-22.

Wilding, M. Review of *The Cats of Venice*. *Southerly* 26, no. 3 (1966): 208-12.

Katharine Susannah Prichard

Beasley, Jack. *The Rage for Life: the Work of Katharine Susannah Prichard*. Sydney: Current Book Distributors, 1964.

Buckridge, Pat. "Katharine Susannah Prichard and the Dynamics of Political Commitment" in Carole Ferrier (ed.) *Gender, Politics and Fiction*. St Lucia: UQP, 1985, 85-100.

Drake-Brockman, Henrietta. *Katharine Susannah Prichard*. Australian Writers and Their Work Series. Melbourne: OUP, 1967.

Hay, J.A. "Betrayed Romantics and Compromised Stoics: K.S. Prichard's Women". In *Who is She?*, edited by Shirley Walker, 98-117. St Lucia: UQP, 1983.

Lindsay, Jack. "The Novels of Katharine Susannah Prichard". *Meanjin* 20, no. 4 (1961): 366-87. Reprinted in his *Decay and Renewal*. Sydney: Wild & Woolley, 1976.

Prichard, Katharine Susannah. "The Art and Craft of the Short Story". In *Straight Left: Articles and Addresses on Politics, Literature and Women's Affairs Over Almost 60 Years from 1910 to 1968*, collected and introduced by Ric Throssell, 122-30. Sydney: Wild & Woolley, 1982.

Henry Handel Richardson

Button, Kim. "Henry Handel Richardson: 'Growing Pains' ". *Meridian* 1 (1982): 49-57.

Clark, Axel. *Henry Handel Richardson's Fiction in the Making*. Brookvale, NSW: Simon & Schuster, New Endeavour Press, 1990. (Biography).

Franklin, Carol. "Mansfield and Richardson: A Short Story Dialectic". *ALS* 11 (1983): 227-33.

Green, Dorothy. *Ulysses Bound: Henry Handel Richardson and Her Fiction*. Canberra: Australian National University Press, 1973.

Howells, Gay. *Henry Handel Richardson 1870-1946: A Bibliography*. Canberra: National Library of Australia, 1970.

McLeod, Karen. *Henry Handel Richardson*. Melbourne: CUP, 1985.

Christina Stead

Brydon, Diana. *Christina Stead*. London and New York: Macmillan/Barnes & Noble, 1987.

"Christina Stead: A Celebration". *Stand* 23, no. 4 (1982).

Ehrhardt, Marianne. "Christina Stead: A Checklist". *ALS* 9 (1980): 508-35.

Geering, R.G. *Christina Stead*. Australian Writers and Their Work Series. Melbourne: OUP, 1969.

——. *Christina Stead*. Twayne's World Authors Series, no. 95. New York: Twayne, 1969. Rev. ed. Sydney: A & R, 1979.

Lidoff, Joan. *Christina Stead*. New York: Ungar, 1982.

Raskin, Jonah. "Christina Stead in Washington Square". *London Magazine* n.s. 9, no. 11 (1970): 70-77. Interview.

Sheridan, Susan. *Christina Stead*. Hemel Hempstead: Harvester Wheatsheaf, 1988.

Stead, Christina. "Authorial Statement". *ALS* 10 (1981): 228-29.

_____ . "Ocean of Story". *ALS* 10 (1981): 181-85.

_____ . "A Writer's Friends". *Southerly* 28 (1968): 163-68.

_____ . Interview in Giuffre, Giulia. *A Writing Life: Interviews with Australian Women Writers*. Sydney: Allen & Unwin, 1990. 73-87.

Thomas, Tony. "Christina Stead: *The Salzburg Tales, Seven Poor Men of Sydney*". *Westerly*, no. 4 (1970): 46-53.

Tracy, Lorna. "The Virtue of the Story: *The Salzburg Tales*". *Stand* 23, no. 4 (1982): 48-53.

Wetherell, Rodney. "Interview with Christina Stead". *ALS* 9 (1980): 431-48.

Whitehead, Ann. "Christina Stead: An Interview". *ALS* 6 (1974): 230-48.

Wilding, Michael. Review of *The Puzzleheaded Girl*. *Meanjin* 30 (1971): 263.

Williams, Chris. *Christina Stead: A Life of Letters*. Melbourne: McPhee Gribble, 1989. (Biography)

Dal Stivens

Levis, K. Review of *The Courtship of Uncle Henry*. *Meanjin* 5, no. 4 (1976): 328-30.

McLaren, J. Review of *Selected Stories*. *Overland*, no. 44 (1970): 52-53.

Semmler, C. Review of *Selected Stories*. *ABR* (October 1969): 268-69.

Stivens, Dal. "Authorial Statement". *ALS* 10 (1981): 229-33.

_____ . "A *Bulletin* Short Story". *Southerly* 40, no. 2 (1980): 211-21.

Wilding, Michael. Review of *Selected Stories*. *Meanjin* 30 (1971): 261-63.

Judah Waten

Beasley, Jack. "Echoes of Ancestral Footsteps: Judah Waten: A Conflict in the Mind". In his *Red Letter Days: Notes from Inside an Era*, 97-128. Sydney: Australasian Book Society, 1979.

Kiernan, Brian. "Memoirs of an Australian Alien Son". *Australian*, 1 April 1972, 14. Interview.

Martin, David. "Three Realists in Search of Reality". *Meanjin* 18, no. 3 (1959): 305-22.

Morrison, John. "Judah Waten". *Overland* (January 1958): 13-14.

Waten, Judah. "Authorial Statement". *ALS* 10 (1981): 234-36.

_____. "Books that Influenced me Deeply". *Educational Magazine* 36, no. 3 (1979): 30-32.
_____. "A Child of Wars and Revolution: An Autobiographical Sketch". *Southerly* 33, no. 4 (1973): 411-19.
_____. "Marxism and Literature". *Issue* (May 1971): 8-10.
_____. "My Literary Education". *Bulletin Literary Supplement*, 21 April 1981, 24-28.
_____. "My Two Literary Careers". *Southerly* 31, no. 2 (1971): 83-92.

Archie Weller
Muecke, Stephen. "On Not Comparing". *Age Monthly Review* 5/7 (1985): 8-10.
Shoemaker, Adam. "Fiction or Assumed Fiction: The Short Stories of Colin Johnson, Jack Davis and Archie Weller". *Connections: Essays on Black Literatures*. Ed. Emmanuel Nelson. Canberra: Aboriginal Studies Press, 1988. 53-59.
Tiffin, Chris. "Relentless Realism: Archie Weller's *Going Home*". *Kunapipi* 10. 1 & 2 (1988): 222-35.

Patrick White
Barnes, John. "New Tracks to Travel: The Stories of White, Porter and Cowan". *Meanjin* 25, no. 2 (1966): 154-70.
Beatson, Peter. *The Eye in the Mandala: Patrick White: A Vision of Man and God*. London: Elek; New York: Barnes & Noble, 1976.
Bjorksten, Ingmar. *Patrick White: A General Introduction*. St Lucia: UQP, 1976.
Bliss, Caroline. *Patrick White's Fiction*. London: Macmillan, 1986.
Brady, Veronica. " 'Down at the Dump' and Lacan's Mirror Stage". *ALS* 11 (1983): 233-37.
Burrows, J.F. "The Short Stories of Patrick White". *Southerly* 24, no. 2 (1964): 116-25.
Colmer, John. *Patrick White*. London, New York: Methuen, 1984.
Hassall, A. "Patrick White's *The Cockatoos*". *Southerly* 35, no. 1 (1975): 3-13.
Heseltine, Harry. "Show Me the Way to Go Home': *The Burnt Ones*". In his *Acquainted with the Night*. Townsville: Foundation for Australian Literary Studies, 1979.
Kiernan, Brian. *Patrick White*. Macmillan Commonwealth Writers Series. London: Macmillan; New York: St Martin's Press, 1980.
Lawson, Alan. *Patrick White*. Australian Bibliographies. Melbourne: OUP, 1974.

Lindsay, Jack. "The Stories of Patrick White". *Meanjin* 22, no. 4 (1964): 372-76.

Myers, David. *The Peacocks and the Bourgeoisie: Ironic Vision in Patrick White's Shorter Prose Fiction*. Adelaide: Adelaide University Union Press, 1978.

Riemer, A.P. "Landscape with Figures — Images of Australia in Patrick White's Fiction". *Southerly* 42 (1982): 20-38.

Tacey, David. *Patrick White: Fiction and the Unconscious*. Melbourne: OUP, 1988.

White, Patrick. "The Prodigal Son". *Australian Letters* 1, no. 3 (1958): 37-40.

Wilson, R.B.J. "The Rhetoric of Patrick White's 'Down at the Dump' ". In *Bards, Bohemians, and Bookmen: Essays in Australian Literature*, edited by Leon Cantrell, 281-88. St Lucia: UQP, 1976.

Wolfe, Peter, ed. Critical Essays on Patrick White. Boston, Mass: G.K. Hall, 1990.

Michael Wilding

Albahari, David. "Michael Wilding". *ALS* 9 (1980): 321-27. Interview.

Brophy, Kevin and Myron Lysenko. "Talking Together — an Interview with Michael Wilding". *Going Down Swinging*, no. 3 (1981): 50-62.

Clunies Ross, Bruce. "A New Version of Pastoral: Developments in Michael Wilding's Fiction". *ALS* 11 (1983): 182-94.

——. "Paradise, Politics and Fiction: The Writing of Michael Wilding". *Meanjin* 45 (1986): 19-27.

Giuffre, Giulia. "An Interview with Michael Wilding". *Southerly* 46 (1986): 313-21.

Harrison-Ford, Carl. "The Short Stories of Wilding and Moorhouse". *Southerly* 33, no. 2 (1973): 167-78.

Hutchinson, G. Review of *The West Midland Underground*. *Makar* 11, no. 3 (1975): 42-51.

Kiernan, Brian. Review of *Aspects of the Dying Process*. *Meanjin* 34, no. 1 (1975): 34-35.

——. Review of *The West Midland Underground*. *National Times*, 2-7 August 1976, 36-37.

Krausmann, Rudi. "A Reluctant Moralist". *Aspect* (Spring 1975): 21-24. Interview.

Wilding, Michael. "Authorial Statement". *ALS* 10 (1981): 238.

——. "A Survey [of Australian 'new' writing]". *ALS* 8 (1977): 115-26.

_____ . ed. *The Tabloid Story Pocket Book*. Sydney: Wild & Woolley, 1978.

Fay Zwicky

Reviews of *Hostages:* Causley, Charles, *Westerly* 29 (March 1984): 90-91; Hildyard, Annette, *Island Magazine* (Autumn-Winter 1984): 40-44; Kellaway, Frank, *Overland* (December 1983): 65-66; Kerr, David, *ABR* (October 1983): 22-23; Stead, C.K., *SMH*, 2 July 1983, 37; Webby, Elizabeth, *Meanjin* 42 (September 1983): 399-400.

UQP AUSTRALIAN AUTHORS

Writings of the 1890s
edited by Leon Cantrell
A retrospective collection, bringing together the work of thirty-two
Australian poets, storytellers and essayists. The anthology challenges
previous assumptions about this romantic period of galloping ballads
and bush yarns, bohemianism and creative giants.

Catherine Helen Spence
edited by Helen Thomson
An important early feminist writer, Catherine Helen Spence was one
of the first women in Australia to break through the constraints of
gender and class and enter public life. This selection contains her
most highly regarded novel, *Clara Morison*, her triumphant autobiography, and much of her political and social reformist writing.

Henry Lawson
edited by Brian Kiernan
A complete profile of Henry Lawson, the finest and most original writer in the bush yarn tradition. This selection includes sketches, letters,
autobiography and verse, with outspoken journalism and the best of
his comic and tragic stories.

Christopher Brennan
edited by Terry Sturm
Christopher Brennan was a legend in his own time, and his art was an
unusual amalgam of Victorian, symbolist and modernist tendencies.
This selection draws on the whole range of Brennan's work: poetry,
literary criticism and theory, autobiographical writing, and letters.

Robert D. FitzGerald
edited by Julian Croft
FitzGerald's long and distinguished literary career is reflected in this
selection of his poetry and prose. There is poetry from the 1920s to the
1980s, samples from his lectures on poetics and essays on family origins and philosophical preoccupations, a short story, and his views
on Australian poetry.

Australian Science Fiction
edited by Van Ikin

An exotic blend of exciting recent works with a selection from Australia's long science fiction tradition. Classics by Erle Cox, M. Barnard Eldershaw and others are followed by stories from major contemporary writers Damien Broderick, Frank Bryning, Peter Carey, A. Bertram Chandler, Lee Harding, David J. Lake, Philippa C. Maddern, Dal Stivens, George Turner, Wynne N. Whiteford, Michael Wilding and Jack Wodhams.

Barbara Baynton
edited by Sally Krimmer and Alan Lawson

Bush writing of the 1890s, but very different from Henry Lawson. Baynton's stories are often macabre and horrific, and her bush women express a sense of outrage. The revised text of the brilliant *Bush Studies*, the novel *Human Toll*, poems, articles and an interview, all reveal Baynton's disconcertingly independent viewpoint.

Joseph Furphy
edited by John Barnes

Such is Life is an Australian classic. Written by an ex-bullock driver, half-bushman and half-bookworm, it is an extraordinary achievement. The accompanying selection of novel extracts, stories, verse, *Bulletin* articles and letters illustrates the astounding range of Furphy's talent, and John Barnes's notes reveal the intellectual and linguistic richness of his prose.

James McAuley
edited by Leonie Kramer

James McAuley was a poet, intellectual, and leading critic of his time. This volume represents the whole range of his poetry and prose, including the Ern Malley hoax that caused such a sensation in the 1940s, and some new prose pieces published for the first time. Leonie Kramer's introduction offers new critical perspectives on his work.

Rolf Boldrewood
edited by Alan Brissenden

Australia's most famous bushranging novel, *Robbery Under Arms*, together with extracts from the original serial version. The best of Boldrewood's essays and short stories are also included; some are autobiographical, most deal with life in the bush.

Marcus Clarke
edited by Michael Wilding

The convict classic *For the Term of His Natural Life*, and a varied selection of short stories, critical essays and journalism. Autobiographical stories provide vivid insights into the life of this prolific and provocative man of letters.

Nettie Palmer
edited by Vivian Smith

Nettie Palmer was a distinguished poet, biographer, literary critic, diarist, letter-writer, editor and translator, who played a vital role in the development and appreciation of Australian literature. Her warm and informative diary, *Fourteen Years*, is reproduced as a facsimile of the original illustrated edition, along with a rich selection of her poems, reviews and literary journalism.

Colonial Voices
edited by Elizabeth Webby

The first anthology to draw on the fascinating variety of letters, diaries, journalism and other prose accounts of nineteenth-century Australia. These colonial voices belong to adults and children, some famous or infamous, others unknown, whose accounts reveal unusual aspects of Australia's colourful past.

Eight Voices of the Eighties
edited by Gillian Whitlock

These eight voices represent the crest of the wave of women's writing that has characterised the 1980s. Short fiction by Kate Grenville, Barbara Hanrahan, Beverley Farmer, Thea Astley, Elizabeth Jolley, Jessica Anderson, Olga Masters, and Helen Garner is supported by a selection of their criticism, reviews, interviews and commentary, to give an unusual perspective on the phenomenon of women's writing in Australia today.

Randolph Stow
edited by Anthony J. Hassall

Stow's most powerful novel, *Visitants*, is reproduced in full, together with episodes from *To the Islands*, *Tourmaline*, the semi-autobiographical *The Merry-go-Round in the Sea*, the satiric comedy *Midnite* and *The Girl Green as Elderflower*, as well as a generous selection of his poems, many not previously collected.

David Malouf
edited by James Tulip

A well-balanced, compact selection of David Malouf's intricately connected work. Short stories, poems, essays, interviews and the classic novel *Johnno*, reproduced in full, show the range of his remarkable achievement.

John Shaw Neilson
edited by Cliff Hanna
John Shaw Neilson was the most original poet of his time, able to imbue the Australian landscape with a universal significance. This volume gathers together Neilson's poetry, arranged chronologically from his earliest work to the confidence and maturity of his last poems, his "Autobiography", and correspondence. It also includes an interview with members of his family.

Kenneth Slessor
edited by Dennis Haskell
This collection of Kenneth Slessor's writing — poetry, essays, journalism, war despatches and diaries, personal notes and letters — allows a fuller, more rounded view of his work than has previously been possible. Slessor emerges as a sensitive, complex and sophisticated person and writer — in any medium.